"Thick with mystery, buried secrets, and magic, nothing is safe in *The Disappearances*. Be careful, or you might lose yourself in this strange and wondrous world, where stars go missing, reflections don't exist, and the question, how much would you sacrifice for love? is given entirely new meaning. I adored this book!"

Stephanie Garber, author of *Caraval*

"Sumptuous worldbuilding, richly developed characters, and a swoon-worthy romance elevate this delightful, fantasy-tinged mystery"

Publishers Weekly (starred review)

"Full of twists and surprises. Murphy's novel is delightfully whimsical and unsettling… a story bursting with color and originality"

Kirkus

"The riddle behind the town's curse is an intricate and surprising one, and readers will happily join the clever and witty Aila on her hunt for clues"

Bulletin

*   *   *

Emily Bain Murphy grew up in Indiana, Hong Kong, and Tokyo. She loves books, macarons, Japanese karaoke and exploring new cities, and is a long-time volunteer with Love146, a non-profit that fights child trafficking. Murphy currently lives in San Francisco with her family, where you can find her working on her second YA novel – somewhere between the bakery and the beach.

THE
DISAPPEARANCES

Emily Bain Murphy

PUSHKIN PRESS

Pushkin Press
71–75 Shelton Street
London, WC2H 9JQ

Copyright © 2017 by Emily Bain Murphy

Published by special arrangement with Houghton Mifflin
Harcourt Publishing Company and Rights People, London

First published by Pushkin Press in 2017

1 3 5 7 9 8 6 4 2

ISBN 978 1 782691 49 5

Offset by Tetragon, London
Printed and bound by CPI Group (UK) Ltd, Croydon CR0 4YY

www.pushkinpress.com

For Greg, James, and Cecilia.
You are the hearts drawn on my arm.

It is an abomination to put a price on the few things in life that are the free right of every human being.

—MYTHS, LEGENDS, AND LORE: A HISTORY OF STERLING

Our revels now are ended. These our actors,
As I foretold you, were all spirits and
Are melted into air, into thin air:
And, like the baseless fabric of this vision,
The cloud-capp'd towers, the gorgeous palaces,
The solemn temples, the great globe itself,
Yea, all which it inherit, shall dissolve
And, like this insubstantial pageant faded,
Leave not a rack behind.

— *William Shakespeare*, THE TEMPEST

CHAPTER ONE

Gardner, Connecticut
September 27, 1942

want something of hers.

There's a teacup downstairs, the last one she used before she died. She didn't finish her chicory coffee that morning, and what she left stained the porcelain in a faint ring. Her lipstick remains smudged in Red Letter Red along the rim. It's been three weeks, and I still haven't been able to wash it away.

But I shouldn't choose the teacup. Nothing fragile is going to survive today.

"Aila?" Cass opens my bedroom door, her white blond hair pinned up in a plait, her wide eyes darker than normal. "Your father says I can come with you to the train station, but we have to leave in five minutes."

"I'll be ready," I say softly. "I would be more worried about Miles."

She nods and disappears back into the hallway. Her footsteps fall on creaking boards, and then the house returns to its solemn hush, so quiet you can almost hear the dust settle. As if we have all already left it.

Five minutes.

I go to my parents' room.

It's been tidied since the last time I was here, the day of my mother's memorial. Now the bed is made. All the flowers have been cleared away. Her vanity is free of her compacts and even the precious glass vial of Joy perfume she always displayed but hardly ever wore. I open her drawers, run my fingertips over her jewelry, but it's all tangled and gaudy, and I want to leave it there, just as she left it. As if she could come in at any moment and clip on her big ugly earrings, as bright and jagged as suns.

I turn to the bookshelf. It, too, has been sorted, but I prefer the way it used to look, when the books were all jumbled and wedged in at odd angles, threatening to fall onto my feet.

My eye catches a large leather volume, its spine dwarfing all the others. I've never seen it before. I kneel down in front of it, my knees finding the threadbare place where the rug has worn almost through to the floor.

I pull out the book and flip through the pages. They whisper against my fingers, thin and delicate, like moth wings. It is Shakespeare, a collection of his plays and poems, and my mother's handwriting is everywhere in it, littering the margins and cluttering the white gaps between sentences in different-colored ink. The pages are yellowing, as if Mother has had this book for a long time. I wonder where it's been hiding until now.

An envelope is taped to the back cover. It is blank, and unsealed, and there is a note inside.

"Aila! Miles!" Father's voice rings out from the kitchen.

"Coming!" I call back.

The note was written recently; I can tell by the way her handwriting shakes, like it did when she was nearing the end. It says:

Stefen: You will find what you asked for within this. I will always love you.
    Your Viola

My attention snags on the two names. Because the first one does not belong to my father. And the second, though it is definitely my mother's handwriting, was not her name. My mother was the *other* well-known Shakespeare heroine. The one who also died young.

Juliet.

"Aila!" my father calls again. This time it's more of a warning.

Leave it, I think. *You don't even like Shakespeare.*

And maybe I don't want to know who this Stefen is.

I put the book back on the shelf and decide that I want the teacup. It is my mother just as I remember her, safe and familiar, and it is still marked by her touch. I'll bring it even if I have to hold it on my lap, cupped in my hands like a butterfly for the entire journey.

I hurry down the narrow stairs, which seem to slope more and more to the right each year. I've never lived anywhere but this house —which we fondly call "the Tilt"—and I know just where to place my hand on the banister to keep my balance and where to step so the stairs don't creak. When I reach the landing, I hear my next-door neighbor, Mrs. Reid. She's in the kitchen with Father, taking final instructions for watching over the Tilt while we're gone. She's opening drawers and closing them, and I'm sure she's the one who organized my mother's books. Maybe out of guilt.

"I'm sorry, again, Harold, that we aren't able to take the children," she says. I pause on the staircase, in the shadows. All I can see are her stockinged calves and the worn leather of her pumps, but I

picture her lips pursing down, her white hair wispy and always looking as though it's being swept heavenward by the wind. "With Earl's
health," she continues, "I just didn't feel that we could manage them
both."

She means that she would have taken me, but not Miles. She
doesn't want to be responsible when he inevitably steals something or
sets a fire. The creases in Mrs. Reid's pumps deepen as she shifts her
weight. "I thought someone else in town would surely be able to help,
but . . ."

"Well, thankfully, we've found other arrangements," Father says
stiffly. Then he turns away to yell again, but I appear in front of him
before he can say my name.

"I'm here," I say. My eyes fall from Mrs. Reid's overly rouged
cheeks to her hands, where she's been anxiously fiddling with something. A tea towel embroidered with green leaves — and my mother's
teacup, scrubbed shiny clean.

I swallow. "I forgot one thing," I say, turning and running back
up the stairs. I touch my mother's dresses one more time, hanging in
neat, still lines in the closet, knowing they will be packed in storage
or given away by the time I return. Then I grab the book of plays,
stuffing it into my knapsack without another thought.

Father drives us to the train station in our mud-streaked Studebaker
— he and Miles in the front and Cass and me in the back seat, my
knapsack with the book in it lying heavy on the seat between us.
"Think Mrs. Reid can handle the Tilt while we're away?" Father
asks. He smiles at me in the mirror and reaches over to ruffle Miles's
hair, but Miles just stares straight ahead. As we pull away, I don't let
myself look at the browning dahlias in Mother's flower boxes.

Everything is in motion when we arrive at the station, as if the air itself were anxious. Posters flutter on the walls, pigeons flap and peck, tow-white strands of Cass's hair whip loose from her braid. She helped me set my wave this morning because I've always liked the way she does it best, but I can already feel it starting to fall. My dress clings to my legs, and my ankles are sweating inside my bobby socks. It's unseasonably hot for late September. Cass and I step into the shadows of the eaves while Miles and my father purchase our tickets. I lean against a war poster that warns, "Telling a friend may mean telling THE ENEMY." An advertisement over Cass's head promises an "ALL-AMERICAN sugar with energy crystallized by the sun!"

Overhead, the clouds swirl like soup.

"You'll come back soon," Cass says.

"You'll write," I answer.

"I wish you could stay with me," she says, tears brightening her eyes. She is my oldest friend, the one who climbed into bed behind me on the day my mother died and braided my hair until I fell asleep. The next morning, I found that she'd woven in her favorite ribbon, the cerulean one embroidered with flowers. The one she'd always planned to wear to our first school dance.

"I wish I could, too," I say. Being stuffed in a room with Cass and her three older sisters sounds better than the unknown ahead, even though I've always been a little frightened of Cass's mother.

Cass stares at the suitcase at our feet. "You're not going to fall in love with some swoony out there and never come back, are you?"

I squeeze her hand. "Maybe now Dixon Fairweather will finally realize what a dish I am."

She starts to cry-laugh as my father joins us on the platform, looking down at the newly purchased tickets in one hand and clutching my brother's suitcase in the other. "Where's Miles?" I ask, and my father glances up with the pained look of someone who has spent too long staring at the sun.

"He was just here," he says.

Our train is coming down the tracks, its white smoke pillowing up into the sky. The brassy clang of the bell grows louder.

"I'll check the entrance," I say, snatching up my bag.

"Lavatory," my father says.

"I'll take the staircase," Cass volunteers.

There are people everywhere in the depot, mostly women and children now that so many of the men have been plucked away to fight. I walk through the snaking line and peer out into the street, the heat and train bell in my ears, my heart quick and light. He is not there.

I'm searching for the burnt copper of his hair, but on the way back to the platform I glimpse the tweed of his cap instead. Miles is sitting on the floor of the station, eating a half-melted Peppermint Pattie he must have hidden in the pocket of his shorts.

I want to jerk his arm or at least rip the candy from his hand. Instead I stand and let my shadow fall over him.

"Golly gee," he says flatly. "You found me."

"Miles," I hiss. "We were looking for you. Why did you run off?" I ask, although part of me wishes that he had actually gone far enough to make us miss the train.

"Use your eyes," he mumbles. "I was hungry."

"Use your head. You wreak havoc wherever you go." *You're the very reason no one here was willing to take us,* I want to say, but instead

I offer him a hand up. He follows me, dragging his feet, back out to the platform, to my father and Cass.

"Found him," I say unnecessarily.

I can tell that my father doesn't want to yell at Miles in these last moments. He squints at us and picks up our suitcases, his broad, tall frame sharp against the sagging leather. He won't leave until tomorrow, heading in the opposite direction. A plane to San Francisco. Then out to the endless Pacific.

"It's time," he says.

I embrace Cass first and try to think of the perfect words to say, but Father's foot is tapping, his eyes never leaving the nearest conductor, and somehow Miles has managed to ruin even this. "Well," I say, suddenly shy, "goodbye." I take out one of my own ribbons and push it into Cass's hand.

Then I turn to my father. He's shaved for the first time in weeks, and his cheek is so smooth I want to stay there for just a moment longer, to breathe in that smell of star anise and lather. I used to lie awake at night, fearing that he'd be called up in the draft. But now that it has happened, I know he will not die in the war — because my mother just died, and that will serve as some sort of protection around him, like a halo. This makes perfect sense to me. So I press my cheek against his one last time and then let him go.

"It won't be long before I'll see you again," Father says. Miles sets his chin but then drops his bag and throws his arms around our father in a hard hug. "It's only temporary," Father says. He swallows, his voice catching. He lets go of Miles and leans down to whisper in my ear, "My little elf."

Miles and I board the train, and Cass stands just below the

window, tears streaming down her face. She's tied my ribbon into her hair. As the porter loads my suitcase, its tag turns over like a browned leaf and I catch the swirl of my mother's handwriting.

I wave to my father, but he has already turned away. Now there is not a doubt left that I will see him again. This can't be my final memory of him, his shoulders weighted under a sky the color of graphite, my reflection flickering and fading as I wait for him to turn back one last time and watch us go.

The train ride north to Sterling is four hours. I don't mean to fall asleep, but halfway there I do. My neck has a crick in it when I jerk awake. Every dream is the same: the bright puffs of flowers around Mother's bed; how still she is, her hands like marble when I reach up to touch them; and then the chill that echoes through to my bones until I gasp awake.

For a moment I think we've missed our stop, but Miles is sitting across from me, sketching, and there's nothing out the window but fields and sky.

I reach for the hidden tip of my knobby right ear, a habit of childish comfort I've been trying to give up. I can tell that Miles notices by the way he smirks down at the notepad in his lap. His fingers guide various pencils over the page until the familiar curve of our mother's headstone appears, wreathed with a rainbow of flowers.

It's all he draws lately, the same picture repeating, just like my dream. I wonder which one of us will stop first.

"Are you hungry?" I ask, unwrapping the peanut butter sand-wiches Mrs. Reid packed and handing a half-smashed one to Miles. The train car is almost empty now. We eat without talking, and when I tire of staring out the window, I pull out the Shakespeare book.

The cover is thick, bound with burgundy leather. I flip through the pages, wondering where to start. There are pen markings under certain lines, and she's written nonsensical notes in the margins, circling words like *nose-herb* and scribbling *Sounds like Var's . . .*

The play *Twelfth Night* seems to have the most markings. Some of the pages are bent, and the ink is smeared. I flip to the end again, but this time I ignore the envelope. The back cover is lined with velvet, and my fingertips leave patterns on it the way they would on a frosted window.

And then I notice the smallest tear fraying at the corner.

I glance at Miles. He is absorbed with drawing the yellow burst of a sunflower, so I pull on the cover's thread. It comes away, and I realize it's been sewn on in faint stitches. My curiosity catches like a white flame, and I work out the stitches with my nail, staring out the window so that I won't draw Miles's attention. When the flap is loosened enough, I slide the book back into my knapsack to hide it. Then I sweep my fingers into the opening.

Even before my fingertips feel glass, I know it.

There's something hidden inside.

CHAPTER TWO

· · ● ● ● ● · ·

tear the opening a little more to give my fingers space to work. Whatever is hidden there feels cold and smooth. I draw it out and examine it in the palm of my hand.

It is a colorless jewel, as clear as water, with a teardrop suspended inside, set in a gold band. The familiar chill from my dream suddenly seeps through my fingertips. It's my mother's ring. I never saw her right hand without it, and I assumed it had been buried with her. Her rings were usually caked with dirt from her garden, but this one looks as though it's been thoroughly cleaned. It stings a little to see it now. This is what I would have wanted to take with me if she had given me the choice. Why would she hide it in a book and plan to send it off to some stranger named Stefen?

I slip the stone onto my finger, but it's too big, so I hold it in my palm. It takes not half a minute for Miles to notice.

"What's that?" He looks up from his drawing, his eyebrows knitting.

"It's Mother's ring. She gave it to me," I lie, and hurriedly unclasp my necklace, exchanging my small heart pendant for the stone. It clinks against the buttons lining my dress.

"Next stop is yours," says a gruff voice behind me, so near that I jump. The conductor's breath is stale with coffee, staining the air around us. I haven't seen any signs of a town since I jerked awake from my dream, and fields stretch out endlessly from beyond the window, only occasionally split by a farmhouse or barn. Gardner had been a small town to grow up in, but this feels like being dropped in the middle of an ocean. An ocean of cornstalks burnt gold by the sun.

"The finishing word," Miles says, putting his boots up on the seat next to me and closing his notepad. *"Go."*

I play with the clasp of my tortoiseshell barrette. The finishing word was Mother's game, and I'm not sure I ever want to play it again. Every mile on this train, every minute that passes is taking me farther away from my old life. The life I still want to be living.

A thought comes to me gently, and it is in my mother's voice: *That ship has sailed, honey. Now you can either drown or hitch a ride on the next one.*

Will anyone put flowers on her grave while we are all away?

Even though I'm only half thinking, I have a stroke of genius. "My finishing word is *palimpsest,*" I say. I snap the hair clip triumphantly.

Miles slumps back in his seat. "I've never heard of that word. You probably made it up."

"No, I didn't. You know *tabula rasa?*"

He gives me a vacant stare.

"We're starting over with a blank slate, but we haven't completely left our past."

He chews on his cheek as if he's trying to decide whether to believe me.

"What's yours, then?" I ask over the train's shrieking brakes. A patchwork of fields is rolling into the paved streets of a small town center.

"My finishing word is *forsaken,*" Miles says.

"How dramatic."

"Fine. Then I'll make it *emprise.* A fancy word for adventure."

"That's a good one," I admit. "You win." It's a strong finishing word, especially for an eight-year-old—even if I hadn't already decided that I would let him win. "Grab your bag."

Miles's eyebrows arch together, and then his green eyes narrow.

"What will you do if I don't get off?" he asks.

"You will," I say, picking up his bag along with mine. I pretend they aren't as heavy as they are.

"No one would blame me, you know," he says, but he shimmies down the aisle toward the exit. "My mother just died."

"Right, because I have no idea what that feels like," I say, and when Miles pauses on the train step, I give him a shove. Then I take a deep breath of my own and step down onto the platform.

There are only two people waiting in the shade of the station's overhang: a middle-aged woman and someone I assume is her son. I remember Mrs. Cliffton from my mother's funeral. She was the only person not from Gardner, so she stuck out in the blurred line of mourners who went through the receiving line that day. She had been formal and reserved when she took my hand. "Matilda Cliffton. I was your mother's best friend from childhood," she explained, and I recognized her name. "My mother was always so pleased to get a letter from you," I told her, and I had already moved on to greet the next person when she suddenly hugged me, as if she couldn't leave until she had done it.

I overheard her offer to help my father however she could. I'm guessing she probably hadn't envisioned Miles and me stepping off this train three weeks later.

"Hello!" Mrs. Cliffton calls, stepping toward us. Her black crepe funeral dress has been replaced with a day suit the color of plums and a matching hat. Her red hair is pulled up in a smart bun. She is more handsome than I remembered. But maybe it's because this time she's smiling. "Welcome!" she says. "Aila, seeing you here is like stepping back in time. You look just like Juliet did when we were young."

"Thank you," I say. I am grateful that she can say my mother's name. That we can still talk of her. "You remember my brother, Miles."

Miles sticks out his hand. "Miles Quinn," he repeats solemnly as Mrs. Cliffton takes it. Our father's pomade has evaporated, and Miles's cowlick now stands up like a missed clump of grass.

"Welcome, Miles. And this is my son, William. He'll get your bags," Mrs. Cliffton says.

"Will," the boy says, extending his hand. He looks to be about my own age, with dark hair that is slightly overgrown, and I can't help but notice it covers the tips of his ears. His teeth are slightly crowded in his mouth, and his eyes are a blue I've never seen before.

He's sort of handsome, in a way that falls between scruffy and striking.

"So this is Sterling," I say quickly, glancing around.

"Actually, no," Mrs. Cliffton says. "Sterling's still a good drive from here, but this is our nearest station." She glances up at the darkening sky. "We'll want to try to beat the rain." Will takes our bags from the porter, and Mrs. Cliffton leads us to a Ford station wagon with wood paneling so smooth it looks glazed.

Miles nudges me. "Just so you know," he whispers, "your ear is showing."

My hand flies to the tip of my right ear, but it is still hidden under the carefully arranged layers of my hair. Miles's face breaks into a grin wide enough to reveal the small space between his two front teeth.

"The finishing word just became *insufferable*," I hiss. I ignore his wiggling eyebrows and climb into the car.

Mrs. Cliffton opens the driver's door and takes her place behind the steering wheel. She starts the engine and pulls out onto the road, hunched forward, her gloved fingers wrapped around the wheel. She doesn't make much conversation, and when the car heaves and jerks, the corners of her mouth tighten. It takes her a moment to find the windshield wipers once the raindrops begin to splatter like paint against the window glass.

"Thank you for bearing with me," Mrs. Cliffton says, her foot easing and catching on the clutch. "We recently lost our driver. I suppose we're all doing our best to adapt." She colors, as if she realizes how this must sound to us. I nod rather than answer. "We are all so hopeful that the war will be over quickly," she adds.

This is just temporary, my father's voice echoes in my head.

My mother's ring hangs weighted around my neck.

The Clifftons' car sends up thick plumes of dust behind us on the road, and we don't pass any other drivers or dwellings for miles. "We're largely farm country," Mrs. Cliffton explains.

"What does Dr. Cliffton do?" I ask politely.

My question provokes the slightest moment of hesitation. "He's a scientist," Mrs. Cliffton says. "He had polio as a child, so he isn't much use for farming or fighting." She glances at William. "Now he . . . looks for ways to improve our quality of life. Look ahead, dears —here is Sterling."

I peer out the window as we come into town. The main street is lined with American flags. There are a handful of stores, all crowned with tan awnings. Letters are painted across the glass windows of a tiny diner.

"That's Fitz's," Will says, nodding toward the rust-red bricks of a general store. We pass a bank, a hardware store, a milliner, a bakery, an empty Texaco station, all drab and gray through the rain. It looks like any other sleepy farm town, but this is the one where my mother grew up. Maybe something of her is still here for me to find, like sunlight catching a handprint on glass.

"Home's just a bit farther," Mrs. Cliffton says, humming, and turns onto a smaller road. Houses and farms are scattered along it like jacks between fields and a thick patch of forest. The sky is wide and laden with heavy clouds. Mrs. Cliffton turns off the road, and Will jumps out to open a large cast-iron gate. When he returns, the rain has speckled his white shirt with gray. Then the car climbs the curving drive, and the Clifftons' house comes into view.

The house falls somewhere between the cramped and cozy nooks of the Tilt and the sprawling mansions my father once took us to see on the cliffs of Rhode Island. Lights blaze from a first-floor window through the shimmer of rain. Four chimneys rise from a slate roof, and rooms spread from the central house in two glass-covered wings. The red bricks glow as if they would be warm to the touch. I suddenly notice a faint stain blotting the hem of my dress and move my hand to cover it.

"I'm sorry, we seem to have forgotten the umbrellas," Mrs. Cliffton says, pulling around the circled drive to the front of the house. "We'll have to make a run for it. The three of you go on in, and I'll be right behind you."

Will opens the door to a crack of thunder, and even though Miles and I sprint up the stone steps behind him, the rain soaks my dress until it clings to me. The careful wave Cass set in my hair this morning is now slicked to the side of my cheek.

Will pulls open the heavy front door to a bright yellow foyer, and I hurry inside. The rainwater runs down my legs into a puddle on the checkered marble floor. A chandelier hangs two stories above our heads, twinkling like the sun.

"Wow," Miles says, gaping at the raised ceiling, his boots squeaking against the polished floor. At least the rain has masked the stain on my hem.

Raindrops bead on Will's forehead and drip down his lashes. He reaches a hand to brush them away. "I'll get us some towels," he says, and by the time he returns with them, Mrs. Cliffton is coming in through the front door. She starts when she sees us still standing there and heavily sets down our luggage.

I look again at the water that has pooled at my feet, and I narrow my eyes.

The wind has taken on a shrieking tone. The rain continues to beat against the windows. Yet Mrs. Cliffton and our leather suitcases are perfectly dry.

We towel off and meet the Clifftons' only remaining staff: a live-in cook and housekeeper named Genevieve. She is tall and rail thin and has hair the color of smoke. The tea she offers us is scentless but strong. It feels like embers going down my throat, heating me from the inside as we follow Mrs. Cliffton on a tour of the house. I try not to compare it to the Tilt, but I can't help noticing that the door handles are made of curved brass rather than our rounded glass knobs. There's no beautiful grandfather clock that clicks and bongs throughout the night, no collection of frog knickknacks with little pieces of paper wedged beneath them so they don't slide down the slope of the shelves. Instead there are decorative books and patterned curtains and tiny painted porcelain boxes that sit in perfectly level display cases. The hallways bear paintings of vases and bowls spilling over with fruit rather than Father's nautical maps and sketched prints of archipelagos. *At least he'll get to see more of the ocean while he's away,* I think. Some of the furniture looks as though it's never even been used. But Mrs. Cliffton is enthusiastic when we round a corner and she points out a wooden chair.

"Will built this for me when he was thirteen," she says proudly.

"It's really more functional than beautiful," Will says.

"I adore it," Mrs. Cliffton says.

"You're my mother," Will says, smiling at me with a hint of embarrassment and running his hands along the scruffy hair at the back of his neck. He trails behind as we tour the sunroom and formal dining room and Dr. Cliffton's library, where books cover the walls, their spines as ordered as piano keys. I'm examining an old Victrola and a tidy line of wooden canes when Miles reaches out to twirl the large midnight orb of a celestial globe. I grab his wrist. He still has peanut butter smudged on his hand.

I shoot him a look before turning to Mrs. Cliffton. "Your home is lovely," I say.

"Yes," Miles echoes. He wipes his palms on the tail of his shirt. "Thank you for having us."

Mrs. Cliffton waves this off. "Your mother was like my sister," she says. She blinks rapidly, and for a moment I worry that she's going to cry. Miles stiffens like a rod next to me. "So you and Miles are family," she finishes, and smiles instead, and Miles's shoulders relax again.

"Shall we head upstairs? You can get settled in." Mrs. Cliffton leads us back to the foyer, where I grab my knapsack from the floor and Will collects our suitcases. "Aila," Mrs. Cliffton says brightly, leading us up the stairs, "do you remember the time I came to Gardner? Not for the funeral, but years back? You were still very young then. Actually, William was with me as well. Do you recall meeting as children?"

"No," I say after a beat. The pins in my hair are starting to tug, and I want to find my room and take them out.

"Juliet and I turned our backs for one minute," Mrs. Cliffton says, reaching the second floor, "and the next thing we knew, you were both down in the field, covered head to toe in dirt." She stops in front of the first door beyond the balcony. "We promptly threw you both in the tub."

When I realize that this means Will and I have seen each other in our unmentionables, and possibly even less than that, I do everything I can to avoid his face. Miles makes it worse with a muffled snicker.

"That's right," Will says quickly, juggling our suitcases for a better grip. "We were burying something we'd found in the field, some treasure. I can't remember what it was. Maybe with some Mind's Eye we could . . ."

The way he cuts off makes me look up to catch the most peculiar expression cross his face. His mother's hand jerks back from the doorknob, and the air strains and crackles with a sudden tension, as if they are waiting for some sort of reaction from us.

"What is Mind's Eye?" Miles asks, and Mrs. Cliffton gives Will an almost imperceptible shake of the head.

"Oh, just something we can talk about later," Mrs. Cliffton says to Miles, pushing open the door to the first guest bedroom. "Aila, that's a lovely necklace," she continues, changing the subject as she ushers us inside. "I remember that ring. Wasn't it your mother's?"

"Yes," I say.

"Did she really give it to you?" Miles asks quietly as Will places my suitcase on the floor. I nod, uncomfortable with how intently both he and Mrs. Cliffton are looking at my neck.

"She didn't give me anything," Miles says, and I wait until their backs are turned and then hide the ring behind the collar of my dress.

My bedroom is simple and cheerful, with yellow walls that are cozy even with the storm beating against the window. There is a white four-poster bed with an embroidered quilt, and a window seat that looks out on the branch of a large oak. Mrs. Cliffton has placed tight puffs of cabbage roses and a picture in a silver frame on the bureau. The image holds younger versions of her and my mother. Juliet and Matilda wear matching school uniforms, their arms slung around each other, their faces caught in open-mouthed laughs.

I've never seen a picture of Mother at my age. Her hair was a lighter auburn than mine, but she has my gray eyes that are a bit too wide, a small nose, and a sharp chin. It's startling how much I look like her.

I unpack my dresses and line my toiletries on top of the milk-white sink, then shelve the poetry volumes I've taken from the cast-away pile at the Gardner library over the years. Stevenson, Frost, Dickinson, Yeats, and Wilde, each missing its cover or spidered with stains the color of light tea. I can't bring myself to unpack my winter clothes just yet. Maybe we'll be home by then. Instead I arrange my father's dulled throwing dart, Mother's Shakespeare volume, and

Cass's ribbon on my nightstand. Then I run a bath in the porcelain claw tub and dress for dinner. There are no mirrors in the bathroom —odd for a house that has just about everything else. I wonder if it would be too forward to ask Mrs. Cliffton for one.

I do the best I can with my hair, feeling only by touch, and head downstairs for dinner.

Dr. Cliffton stands from where he is seated at the mahogany dinner table to greet me when I enter the dining room. He is an older, softer version of Will, with blue eyes that aren't quite as striking and are framed by wire-rimmed glasses. I make polite, stilted conversation—"I've never been this far north before"; "The rain sure is coming down"—over a dinner of watercress and grilled peach salad, roast chicken, and some sort of squash tart, all served by Genevieve. We did not eat like this even before the war and the rationing started. "One of the benefits of living in farm country," Dr. Cliffton says as he notices me eyeing the small pat of freshly churned butter. I want to smear it, salty and smooth and creamy, all along my slice of bread, but I pretend that I don't care for it and pass the plate on. Miles takes my cue and declines as well. We are impinging on the Clifftons enough without eating their precious butter.

Dr. Cliffton clears his throat. "Did your mother speak often of Sterling?" he asks me. He pauses in cutting the tart. His knife and fork hover over his plate.

"Only a little," I say. In truth, she'd barely spoken of it at all. There is a long beat, as if this wasn't the correct answer. For a moment all I can hear is cutlery scraping and the sound of my own chewing.

"She told me once she didn't much like it," Miles offers, followed by a yelp as my heel catches his ankle.

Dr. Cliffton laughs graciously, but there is something else in it as well. He pushes his chair back in concert with a loud crack of thunder and says, "You know, I believe I've just the thing for this occasion." His right foot drags as he leaves the room, and I recall the collection of canes I'd seen during my tour of the house.

Dr. Cliffton reappears a moment later, trailing bright strains of Glenn Miller from down the hall. It helps to drown out the steady patter of the rain. "Shall we move into the library?" Mrs. Cliffton suggests. "Genevieve could bring us some coffee, maybe even some ice cream?"

Miles jumps up with a nod.

They are all trying so hard, I realize. But I don't have the energy to keep up. "Actually, I think I'll turn in," I say.

"Long day," Mrs. Cliffton says, nodding. The lights flicker.

The four of them move on to Dr. Cliffton's library, and I climb the stairs to my room. "Good night, Miles," I call from the balcony, and he gives a short wave without really looking.

I change into my nightgown and brush my teeth, staring at the blank wall in front of me. Tomorrow I'm going to ask about the mirror.

I climb into bed, rolling my father's dart between my hands. I hear Will challenge Miles to a game of checkers, followed by an amused "Hot dog!" barely five minutes later. Miles rarely loses games. He never loses at checkers.

Someone changes the record to Billie Holiday, her voice drowsy and warm. She was Mother's favorite. I return my dart to the night-stand and use my pillow to block out the music and the sound of the rain.

It's the first night in three weeks that I do not dream of her.

CHAPTER THREE

The summer I was thirteen, there was a storm that swept through during the night. The thunder was loud enough to wake us all, and Miles cried out until Mother went to him. I don't know if she ever went back to sleep, but at dawn she knelt to wake me.

"Come with me," she said, pulling me from the warmth of my bed. I was grumpy until she handed me a mug of hot chocolate. "The sunrise is always best after a big storm," she said. We pulled on coats over our nightgowns and shoved our feet into rubber boots, and she led me out to the garden.

Mother toweled dry one of the rusty wrought-iron chaises so I could sit and keep her company while she cleared out the debris cast by the storm. She hadn't lied about the sunrise. It started out a soft pink and then heated into a searing orange.

"I was reading the other day about it raining frogs and fish," she said. She wore gloves, picking through the splintered branches and tucking dirt back into divots. "It's been documented as really happening. Can you imagine what it would be like if you were just walking along, minding your own business, and you got thumped in the head by a falling fish?"

She'd been laughing about it until she abruptly stopped. She bent down to nudge a nest that had been battered. I could see the white shards of egg by her boots. "Poor birds," she said, her mood suddenly darkening.

Sometimes she was like that. A paper crane, folding in on herself without warning. I didn't say anything else, and neither did she. I hated her moods. I could never tell when they would strike or how long they would last. I just watched her step around the puddles as I sipped my hot chocolate until it grew cold.

"I'm sorry about the birds," I said when we were taking off our boots in the front hallway. "I'm sorry it made you sad."

"Not the birds, honey," she said. She tucked my hair behind the ear she never wanted me to hide. "Just reminded me of someone I used to know."

"Tell me more about the frogs raining down, then," I said, and just as quickly as it had come, her mood passed. After that morning we'd never say it was raining cats and dogs outside. We'd say our version instead.

Frogs and fish, I'm thinking when I wake, and for a moment I'm disoriented. I'm not in my own bed. The quilt on top of me is stiffer than the one I'm used to and it isn't thrown to the floor, the sheets tangled around my legs. I must have slept peacefully.

Because I didn't have the dream.

My heart isn't racing and freshly torn apart, and that makes me feel lighter than I have in weeks. I push free of the covers, throw on a white cotton dress, and comb my fingers through my hair. But a thought nags: Shouldn't I want to have the dream—even one that tortures me—if it's the only way I can still see her?

When I reach the kitchen, Genevieve hands me a steaming cup of coffee, which I take even though I wouldn't normally drink it. "Morning," she says briskly. "He's out there," and she points me to the garden.

Miles is sitting alone at a table, surrounded by a spread of popovers, jam, cream, and berries. It's more food than the two of us could ever eat, and I can't help but think of the rations back home. Miles barely stops shoving food into his mouth to acknowledge me.

"Good morning to you, too," I say. The air feels clear and new after the storm. I bet this morning's sunrise would have been worth waking to see.

I set my coffee down, fill my plate, and point to a pitcher of orange juice. "Does that have any feathers in it?"

Miles rolls his eyes. "I haven't called pulp 'feathers' since I was five."

I grin obnoxiously at him and pour myself a glass. The juice is tart and thick, the freshest I've ever had. "Where is everybody?" I ask.

Miles shrugs. "Will's at school. Dr. Cliffton's working. Mrs. Cliffton is running errands but said she'd be back soon. Look." He nods behind him. "They have hens."

While I'm looking, he slips two extra pastries into a napkin and tucks it into his pocket.

"Don't do that, Miles," I say. "It's tacky."

"Do what?" he asks. Now it is his turn to smile—his widest gap-toothed smile. Sometimes that smile is worse than a flick straight to the forehead.

I sigh. "Never mind."

"Mrs. Cliffton gave me some new pencils. I'm going to draw," he says. He waves his notebook and saunters away through the garden paths lined with jewel-toned monkshood and patches of hyssop. I take a sip of coffee, surprised at how much I like its bitterness. And how sleep, a little sun, and a real breakfast can make everything seem infinitely better than it was yesterday.

As I reach for a pecan bun, Miles's head bobs between sprays of orange Oriental lilies and a cluster of snowy hydrangeas, then back again. He is so close to the flowers, they are all but up his nose.

For the love of everything holy — why can't he ever just act like a normal person?

"Aila," he calls. "It's wild. None of these smell."

"Okay," I say. I don't move. This is another one of his tricks, just to make me get up when I'm enjoying a nice breakfast.

"I'm not ragging!" he calls. "I haven't smelled a single flower in this entire garden. See for yourself."

"Okay," I repeat. I start grinning again as a thought comes to me. "So does that mean your finishing word is *non-scents?*"

"Har har," he says. He puts a hand on his jutting hip. "But bully for you. You remembered how to make a joke."

I saunter toward him and lean down to where he points, expecting to breathe in the sweet fragrance of fading summer. But — for once, anyway — he isn't exaggerating. There isn't even the hint of a scent. It is as if the lily petals are cut from scraps of colored paper. I take them in my fingers. They feel like velvet; they feel alive.

"Huh," I say, thinking again of Mrs. Cliffton coming in from the rainstorm, of the words Will had started to say. Each strange little thing seems like a puzzle piece, or like the riddles Mother always loved. Riddles: the use of maddening clues, subtle wordplays, and obscure patterns to point to an answer no sensible person would ever think of.

I hate riddles.

Miles rests his notebook and pencils on the table, then strikes out on a mission to personally smell every flower in the garden. I watch him as I fill a plate with blueberries and a second sticky bun. "I'm taking paper," I call to Miles. "To write Cass." I flip through his endless pages of colorful drawings and tear out a blank sheet near the back.

But instead of a letter, I start a list.

Flowers without scents, I write, in very small letters.

Something called Mind's Eye?

Dry suitcases . . .

I look out at Miles's head, bobbing copper in the sun, and with a prick of unease I fold the secret list into my pocket.

"I thought we could take a trip into town tomorrow," Mrs. Cliffton says to Miles and me over dinner that night. "Get you the things you'll need for school?"

I accept a basket of rolls from Dr. Cliffton and clear my throat. "School, right," I say. "When will we start?"

"I've arranged for you both to begin the day after tomorrow."

Mm. Sooner than I was expecting.

"I picked up the list of books you'll need, Aila," Will says. He spears a steamed carrot with his fork. "Most of them are the same as last year, so you can have mine."

"Thanks," I say. His dark hair is unkempt, and the ends are starting to curl. He pushes it off his forehead with a rough hand and smiles at me. I glimpse his crooked eyetooth and smile back.

After dinner, I linger behind to help clear the table.

"How are you doing, Aila?" Mrs. Cliffton asks when Genevieve has taken a tray of dirty dishes into the kitchen and we are alone. "Is there anything you need?"

I hesitate, fingering the ring hidden behind my dress, wanting to ask her to make sense of the strange things I've seen. But what, exactly, can I say?

"I didn't see a mirror upstairs?" I start tentatively. "Maybe I could pick one up when we're in town tomorrow?"

She blinks at me a few times. "Of course. And, dear, there's something I wanted to talk with you—"

"We're playing gin rummy tonight," Miles announces, waltzing into the room, oblivious that he's interrupting. "We took a vote— Dr. Cliffton, Will, and me. Aila, are you going to play this time?"

"Not tonight," I say sharply. "What were you saying, Mrs. Cliffton?"

I turn back to her, but with Miles still standing there, it's clear the moment has passed.

"Let's talk more tomorrow," she says. "We'll get an early start. Sleep well, Aila."

I climb the stairs, my annoyance at Miles mounting with each step. I close the door to my room, fall into the downy pillows of my bed, and unfold the list I started earlier.

"No mirrors?" I add. I pick up my father's old dart and roll it between my fingers.

The dart's pointed edge is bent and dull. For years I used it to carve lines in my bedroom floor, which I then hid under the corner of my rug. The lines recorded things like girlhood fights at school—many with Cass over things now forgotten—and one long, jagged line on account of Dixon Fairweather, the boy I had liked since fourth grade. But most were there because of Miles: Miles being annoying or wretched and somehow still ending up as Mother's favorite. Miles stealing things and breaking things and bringing us embarrassment rather than sympathy when Mother first took ill.

When I hear him cheering over gin rummy downstairs, his voice raised in victory, I stiffen.

Bully for you, I echo him cruelly. *You remembered how to be part of a family. Even if it's not your own.*

Everything here is the opposite of what I was expecting: somehow I am the one who is distant and sulking, he the one adjusting without a hitch. I push my thumb into the dulled point of the dart and wish for my room, for the feel of the carved lines under my fingertips, the tree rings marking the seasons of my life.

Thankfully, the Clifftons have chosen to listen to the radio tonight instead of Billie Holiday. I open my mother's book to a new play and start to skim *Love's Labour's Lost.* I examine one of the passages she's circled.

⤳

Biron: Your mistresses dare
never come in rain,
For fear their colours
should be wash'd away.

⤳

I look up at a sudden outburst of Will's laughter followed by a good-natured groan by Mrs. Cliffton. Then I hear Miles's cackle, high and easy to recognize. I smile in spite of myself. *He's allowed to laugh,* I think. *And right now, he's the only family you have.*

I close the book and roll the dart between my fingers, wondering if it's too late to join them. If I should swallow my pride and ask to be dealt in, instead of hearing everything filtered through the slats of the Clifftons' pure, unmarked floorboards.

But by the time I reach the bottom of the stairs, they are emerging from the library. I pretend that I was coming down for another reason and give a small wave, then keep walking. "I hope we weren't too loud," Mrs. Cliffton says.

"I barely heard a thing," I lie. "Good night."

I wait until their footsteps fade on the stairs, and then I crack open the side door to walk in the garden. The air is cooler than I thought it would be. I look up, expecting to see stars spread out overhead like a dewy web, but instead the sky is black and endless, punctured only by the stark white moon.

I circle the garden pathway and lie down on one of the benches, watching the moon until the iron laths dig into my back. I sit up, sneak a look to make sure no one is watching, and stoop to smell the flowers. Nothing, just like before.

When I straighten, voices are murmuring from the second floor.

"I tried to talk to Aila earlier, but I didn't get very far," Mrs. Cliffton says. My ears prick.

Dr. and Mrs. Cliffton's bedroom window is cracked just enough to carry out their drifting conversation. I move out of sight beneath the window and perch on the fountain ledge, waiting. I pretend to examine the fountain's statue. It's of a stone girl, frozen in a skip across the water's surface.

"We're working on borrowed time at this point," Dr. Cliffton says. "I can't believe they haven't noticed something by now."

"I can tell Aila is suspicious," Mrs. Cliffton says. "Maybe I should have told them first thing. I just didn't want to scare them, after they've already been through so much. I thought they could settle in a bit first. But you're right. It can't wait any longer."

"Do you really think they know nothing about it? If Juliet hid all of this from them, it complicates things even more." Dr. Cliffton sighs. "Maybe this was a mistake . . ."

"Malcolm," Mrs. Cliffton says, her voice sharpening. "These are Juliet's children. I could never live with myself if I turned them away when they had nowhere else to go. We said we would try it, and if it doesn't work out, then we've at least bought Harold some time to find another arrangement."

She pauses. I slide along the wall and crouch under the window, holding my breath until Dr. Cliffton's low voice begins again.

"All right, Matilda. I agreed to try it, and we will. But their being here is going to stir things up again at the worst possible time. And I just don't want them to walk into a hornets' nest."

There's a long pause, and I wonder if the conversation is over. But then Mrs. Cliffton asks softly, "Do you really think we made a mistake?"

"No," Dr. Cliffton says. "Well, I don't know," he clarifies. "Let's just hope Sterling treats them better than it treated Juliet at the end."

The hair on the back of my neck prickles. I lean forward, pretending to look at my reflection in the fountain, waiting for him to elaborate.

But I don't see anything. The water is cool and clear and dark. No stars or moon reflect above me. I wave my hand above the water, but it is opaque. Blank. As though I have disappeared.

I stumble backwards into the steadying bricks of the house.

What is this place?

"Juliet must not have wanted them to know, if she never told them," Dr. Cliffton says. I gulp at the night air, barely able to hear his voice over the thundering of my own heart. "But now that they're here, Sterling isn't going to hold on to her secrets for long before it starts giving them up."

CHAPTER FOUR

Date: 8/29/1940

Sketching of bay-breasted warbler

Bird: Warblers. Type of songbird (oscine).

Songbirds aren't born knowing how to sing.

They learn by listening to their fathers.

The night I met Phineas, I'd been planning to jump in front of a train.

But I was thirty-three years old, and something made me want to see him first. So I took the train an hour's ride to his house.

I'd actually tracked down his address the month before. Even went so far as to visit his street. But I'd ended up sitting on a bench that time, sketching song sparrows. Watching them as they flew up in sprays from the ground to land in branches. Like falling leaves, in reverse.

It's possible that the very first seed of my idea was planted then, in those moments when I'd sat watching the birds, wishing for a hit of courage. Wanting to shoot it into my own veins like an inoculation.

But the night Phineas and I did finally meet, I didn't need courage quite as badly. I had already decided to jump. There really wasn't much left to lose.

So I went to the door and knocked.

I remember those endless moments waiting for him to answer. His house perched on the knife's edge of a cliff, and I'd watched the ocean hurl itself onto the rocks below. Some hideous gulls had been pecking, flapping, cawing overhead. Gulls, *I'd thought, remembering my encyclopedia.* Flight patterns sometimes called a "dread."

My nerves had jolted at the first creaking sound of his footsteps. I knew then that I cared more about his reaction than I wanted to admit.

And of course — in that split second before the door opened — I thought of Juliet.

He'd cracked open the door and squinted out at me. He was older than I had always pictured. His hair was gray, his eyes deep set and suspicious. I realize now that he probably thought I was a cop that night. Or a bruiser from the underground circuit, coming to collect on a debt. After all, who else would have been knocking at his door? Paying an unexpected visit, just as night fell, to the home of a convicted ex–grave robber?

"Hello?" I had cleared my throat to steady my voice. "Are you Phineas Shaw?"

His hand tightened on the edge of the door, ready to close it in my face at any moment. His skin was leathered, and his knuckles were notched with the type of tattoos you acquire in prison. "What do you need?"

"May I come in?" I asked.

"Not until you tell me who you are," he said, but as soon as the words were out of his mouth, I saw the strike of recognition. He knew.

"My name is Stefen," I said, tasting ocean salt on my tongue. "I'm your son."

When he hesitated, I thought he was going to turn me away. I remember hearing a train horn in the distance. Thinking that sound always means the beginning of a journey, or an end to one. And the longer Phineas waited, the more I was sure which it was going to be.

But then he surprised me.

He stepped aside and let me in.

don't dream of Mother again that night. But that's because, as the hours pass into morning, I hardly sleep at all.

Miles and I have to get out of here.

I'm out of bed as the sun rises. There's no way I can take my suitcase without raising suspicion, but I grab my knapsack and stuff it as full as I can. I hum under my breath to calm myself. My toothbrush goes in, along with an extra pair of clothes. My dulled dart. The Robert Louis Stevenson poems. All the money Father left with us, more than enough to get us back to Gardner. We can stay with Cass until we figure out what to do next.

I want to take the Shakespeare book, but it is too heavy and impractical, and at the last minute I rest my hand on it in goodbye, then shove it under the bed.

I'm still not sure what I'm going to tell Miles. I knock on his door.

"Eat a big breakfast," I say to him. When he heads for the bathroom, I slip some of his clothes into my knapsack. "And it's okay with me if you put an extra pastry in your pocket this time."

"Shall we take that trip into town now?" Mrs. Cliffton asks when I appear at the bottom of the stairs, trying to keep my overstuffed knapsack behind me. I am too nervous to eat and can barely look at her, smiling in her navy day suit and white crepe blouse as if nothing at all is wrong. She pulls on her driving gloves. "Come along," she says, and motions for Miles and me to follow her.

Miles is oblivious. He ignores me completely, blooming under Mrs. Cliffton's stream of questions about his breakfast and how he slept, if his bed was comfortable, what school subjects he likes, and I realize how much he has missed the careful attention of a mother. The distance between us has never felt greater than it has in these past few months, when I have understood so much and he so enviably little.

Without the rain, Mrs. Cliffton has better control of the car and I can look out at Sterling with a critical eye. It seems unremarkable. Forest and farms, houses that are neat and well maintained, but I notice this time that the front doors are all a variation on the same color: a taupe so bland and drab it is almost gray.

Mother had always insisted that our front door be the brightest in town: a cherry red, which my father would repaint at the very first signs of fading—and at the thought of this I can't stop myself anymore. The accusation comes bursting out.

"Mrs. Cliffton," I say, interrupting her in mid-sentence. "Something's very wrong here."

Her back straightens, but she doesn't attempt to look at me in the reflection of the rearview mirror. In fact, it seems to be there solely for decoration. I had realized, at the moment I leaned forward at the fountain ledge and failed to see my own face echoing back at me, why there are no mirrors to be found in my bathroom—or any other room in the Clifftons' house.

Because they would have been utterly useless.

I fight to keep panic from creeping into my voice. "Tell us about the mirrors."

"All right, Aila," Mrs. Cliffton says soothingly, but she grips the steering wheel, and when Miles looks back and forth between us, I regret being so impulsive. Maybe whatever she's hiding is so terrible that Miles shouldn't know of it. My panic rises a notch further.

"And tell us why your flowers don't smell," Miles chimes in, leaning forward.

Color is flooding into the skin peeking out at the nape of Mrs. Cliffton's neck, matching the maroon of her hat. "I'm sorry. It was a mistake not to say anything yet," she stammers. "I was planning to tell you today. I just wanted you to settle in, and we didn't know if—being Juliet's children," she hesitates. "If you would even be affected." She glances back at us with a look of apology. "What happens here isn't something we ever speak of to outsiders."

"What?" Miles asks. "What happens here?"

"We call them the Disappearances."

A car passes, and the woman driving it lifts her hand in a cheerful wave to Mrs. Cliffton. But the woman's smile falters when she sees me, and her brow knits.

Mrs. Cliffton says, "Your mother truly never spoke of this?"

Miles and I stay silent.

Mrs. Cliffton sighs. "I don't blame her, exactly. Just leave and forget the whole mess." She bobs her head at the road, considering. "We never knew what life was like before them. They started in 1907, the year we were born."

She isn't gripping the steering wheel quite as tightly, as if she's relieved that the secret is now out. "The first things we lost were the scents. I was there that day, at the Harvest Fair—of course, nearly everyone was—but I was just a baby at the time."

The steering wheel rolls under her hands. "It started innocently enough. We've always held a friendly competition among the townspeople to see who can come up with the best recipe for Sterling apples each year — tarts and pies, ciders, jellies. You get the idea. Everyone brings dishes to a gathering called the Harvest Fair. It's silly, of course, but people by nature can become quite competitive, especially in a town as small as this one. Everyone was so focused on who would be declared the winner, that at first, no one noticed that things weren't quite right. Not until the judge uncovered the dishes and leaned down to smell them."

The edges of town are coming into view, starting with the Texaco station. "Initially, no one was overly alarmed," she continues. "Of course, we didn't realize what it meant at the time, when the judge announced that the scents of every entry seemed to have vanished. The award was forgotten as people came forward to see for themselves."

Her voice takes on the slightest tremor. "Perhaps they thought it was only temporary. Certainly no one guessed that it would be so far-reaching, that scents had disappeared entirely from Sterling. The Disappearance affected everyone, young and old, and every *thing:* fruits and flowers, perfumes and shampoos — even those things that make people sentimental, like the smell of a child's hair, or scents linked to important memories."

I think of the scents that made up my childhood: eggs frying, cookies puffed up with sugar crystals, Mother's chicory coffee every morning, the painted bowl of lemons on the coffee table, Father's fading after-shave when he leaned down to kiss me good night — even the smells I hated. Like boiled spinach. The compost pile. The burnt whitefish that coated the Tilt's walls for days until Mother swore she'd never cook it again.

"Anosmia experts came from around the country to investigate," Mrs. Cliffton continues. "But even after Sterling began to understand the extent of what happened, no one knew what had caused it—or how to go about its reversal. No one regained their sense of scent, even when they tried to leave town. From there on after, Sterling's children were all born with it. And as the years went on, people became more resigned to the fact that this was something permanent."

"Is this—" I ask, hesitating. I swallow. "Will it be permanent for me and Miles?"

"Not for you, dear," Mrs. Cliffton says quickly. "You should step out of its hold as soon as you leave our borders."

I exhale with a swell of relief so immense that it makes me feel both guilty and selfish. I peer out at the men and women of Sterling. They all look so normal and unconcerned, walking through the center of town with packages tucked under their arms, ducking into Fitzpatrick's General Store. A woman in a large brimmed hat points out the curb to her pudgy-armed son.

"What happened next?" Miles asks.

"True panic didn't set in until later," Mrs. Cliffton says. She parks the car. "When, on the exact same date, seven years after the original Disappearance, it happened again." She turns off the engine and faces us. "Your mother and I woke one morning to find we no longer had reflections. I was only a little girl, but it was the strangest thing—to go looking for myself only to find that I had disappeared. And then, the year we turned fourteen, it was as though all the colors had been drained from our paints and pens. Anything new that we tried to paint or draw with them—it all came out gray."

I think of my mother as a girl, of the confusion and grief she must have felt when she woke up to find that something she loved was gone.

"Bit by bit, these pieces of our lives that we always took for granted have been slipping away," Mrs. Cliffton says. "Every seven years, like clockwork, something else is lost. Scents, reflections, colors—"

Miles interrupts. "But why?"

"I wish I knew, dear. No one does."

"But my mother could smell," I protest, remembering her garden, the awful coating of the whitefish.

"Yes . . ." Mrs. Cliffton says, her voice tightening. "Which is a story for later." She glances toward the town. "Not here."

I can hardly believe anything she's said, even though I've seen it with my own eyes. I'm lightheaded and sweating, trying to grasp at an unspooling thread. Trying to remember every last thing my mother ever said about growing up here, to do the math in my mind.

"If something disappears every seven years . . ." I say slowly, "how long has it been since the last one?"

Mrs. Cliffton waves at someone across the street, fixing a smile on her face. "Well, I'm afraid you've come just in time." She adjusts her hat without the use of the mirror and pushes open the door with a spark of defiance. "There's a month left before we find out what disappears next."

I stand numbly as Finch the tailor takes my measurements for school uniforms, and then Miles and I follow Mrs. Cliffton to the general store. We weave past bright splashes of oranges, aisles of glass bottles, and scentless bars of soap, and my thoughts are churning so much that at first I don't even realize we're being watched. A woman in white gloves and a dress the color of spring grass is peering out from behind the stacked cans of Spam as we pick out sketching paper for Miles and a bag of new potatoes for Genevieve. When I catch her staring, she abruptly straightens and waves to Mrs. Cliffton. A crocodile purse hangs from the crook of her elbow, bouncing exuberantly.

"Yoo-hoo!" she calls. "Matilda! What brings you here?" Dazed, I clutch my school supplies tighter, still considering whether Miles and I should find the next train and flee.

"Oh, these must be the *children!*" The woman charges toward us, and I take a step back. "Bless it, she's the spitting image of Juliet, isn't she? *So* charitable of you to take them in, Matilda. I simply wouldn't have had the gumption after the Council voted against it —"

Mrs. Cliffton glances at me and says sharply, "Aila, Miles, this is Agatha Mackelroy. She was a friend of your mother's when we were young." But my thoughts have tripped and are slow to catch up. A council voted on Miles and me?

A vote we *lost?*

"Matilda, what year will that little boy be in?" Mrs. Mackelroy whispers loudly, nodding toward Miles. He shoots me a look, steps behind a display of evaporated milk, and pretends to choke himself. I stare pointedly to the right of him and pray he stops before anyone else notices, but instead he escalates with an imaginary arrow to the neck. Only Miles would react to the most earthshattering bombshell of our lives by pretending to off himself in the middle of the canned goods aisle.

"Fourth," Mrs. Cliffton answers, and I send Miles my most murderous glare. But then something makes me change my mind.

Perhaps it's because he is the only person in the world who could possibly understand how I feel today. So instead, I look him squarely in the eye, take a deep breath, and stab an imaginary dagger into my heart. I even dabble a spurt of fake blood down my dress for extra effect.

Miles gapes.

"The finishing word is *unprecedented*," I whisper.

He breaks into a grin. "You win," he whispers back.

"Matilda, you wouldn't believe the things I hear as head of the Library Preservation Society," Mrs. Mackelroy is saying now. "Mrs. Belinda Babcock was found in quite a predicament last week. Let's just say it involved her famous baked cinnamon apples and quite a bit of rum. If I were a Harvest Fair judge, I'd march right over and demand that she return every one of those tainted blue ribbons."

"Oh?" Mrs. Cliffton says wearily. As she moves to pay, I glimpse a collection of small pouches in the shadows of her pocketbook.

Mrs. Mackelroy is undeterred. "Well, if she's won all those blue ribbons for spirit-filled apples, then we just can't stand for it. Think of the *children*."

Miles's attention is now caught on the row of newspapers, and I step in front of him to block the headlines: U.S. FLIERS BAG 42 PLANES AND HIT 2 CRUISERS IN THE SOLOMONS: NAZIS ADVANCE ON RIM OF STALINGRAD.

I imagine Father, safe in a ship's hull, and am caught off-guard by a fierce swell of anger. How could he send us here without even warning us?

But somehow I know he wouldn't have.

I swallow. Could Mother have kept all this even from him?

"Oh, Agatha, I'm sure there's a perfectly reasonable explanation," Mrs. Cliffton says. "I hate to be rude, but I feel a headache coming on. Tell George hello."

"Of course. Aila, do look for my George at school," Agatha says. "Matilda, I hope the headache passes soon."

I nod at Mrs. Mackelroy and paste a smile on my face, certain that Mrs. Cliffton's headache will go away as soon as she does.

The bell above us clangs as we step back out into the sunlight with our shopping bags. "Though it was my intention for you to know the town a bit better today," Mrs. Cliffton says, rubbing her temples, "I'm not sure I wanted you to know it quite that well."

"But Mrs. Cliffton," Miles says impatiently, as if his question's been building. "The rolls we had at dinner last night — I could smell them."

"Yes, you could. And that, dear," she says, "is where this story takes a more pleasant turn." She rummages through the depths of her pocketbook, retrieving the small plump pouches I'd glimpsed. One is made of dark chocolate leather, the other a maroon velvet.

She holds them out to us in the palm of her hand. "Let me show you."

CHAPTER SIX

M rs. Cliffton leads us down a side street and stops in front of a large window shaded by an awning. A sign with an arrow points to BLOOM'S HARDWARE.

"You were able to smell the rolls last night because Genevieve applied a touch of these," she explains, holding the pouches out to us. "The Variants."

She dips her hand inside the chocolate-hued pouch. When she opens her palm, it is filled with thousands of tiny crystals, as fine as dust. Depending on the way the light hits, they are as dull as sand or they sparkle like diamonds.

"I'm not supposed to do this in public," she says, looking furtively around us. "It draws too much attention to have reflections appearing and disappearing for any of our occasional visitors. Otherwise, you'd be surprised how many people don't pay much attention to the world around them." She looks at our faces and smiles. "Ah well. This feels like a worthy exception."

Mrs. Cliffton gestures toward the window of Bloom's. The surface is clear, as though the glass isn't even there, as if we can reach right through it to select a coil of hose or one of the stacked rakes. Then she flicks her wrist and sprinkles a dash of the dust onto the windowpane.

"And just like that," she says, "here you are."

The Variants hit the glass like pebbles rippling the surface of water. My reflection suddenly materializes in the resulting waves.

I step forward in awe. The girl looking back at me is clearer than any image I've ever seen. I stare at the contours of my cheekbones, the flush that is appearing on my cheeks, the sharp gray of my widened eyes. I'm surprised to realize that I actually look quite pretty.

"Looking Glass Variants. They're temporary—the reflection will last for a quarter of an hour, and then it will vanish again," Mrs. Cliffton explains. She turns to go, but I pause, relishing one long, last look at my reflection, wondering when I will see myself again. "There are rules about when you can use the Variants. Most of them are permitted when you turn Of Age at seventeen and can be trusted to use them in a way that isn't obvious. I suppose I've already been a poor example of that. But Aila—you'll be seventeen soon?"

"Not until May," I say. How strange, that until then I will have to ask for permission to see my own face.

"Matilda Fine Cliffton, *I never!* What are you *thinking?*"

A woman in a hat with a small veil barges out from Bloom's Hardware. Another woman is close behind her.

I step back, trying to block the window. Our reflection hasn't faded yet. It is behind us, giving us away.

"Violet, Clara, allow me to introduce you to Juliet's children," Mrs. Cliffton says smoothly. "Aila, Miles, this is Mrs. Fogg and Mrs. Patton." She tugs on the ends of her jacket to straighten the fabric. "I'm just showing them a bit of the real Sterling."

Mrs. Fogg narrows her eyes at us. "So the Council decided to let them in after all." She moves her gaze to Mrs. Cliffton. "Matilda, this is highly disappointing from a woman of your place. People look to you to set an example. I hope you haven't forgotten that. It's bad enough you took them in—and right before the fair."

"Thank you, Violet," Mrs. Cliffton says, her voice crisp. "I'm quite aware of my responsibilities around the Variants."

The second woman, Mrs. Patton, the one with piercing jade eyes, attempts to smooth things over. Her dress suit is sharp and tailored, her cheekbones striking. "I'm sure it won't happen again." She adds pointedly, "Please do give our best to Malcolm."

Mrs. Fogg purses her lips but stays silent.

"Yoo-hoo!" Across the street, Mrs. Mackelroy steps out of the general store and is waving wildly. "Violet! Clara!"

"Oh for heaven's sake, let's pretend we didn't see her," Mrs. Patton says. They duck their heads and hurry away. Mrs. Fogg brushes into me when she passes.

"Let's head home, shall we?" Mrs. Cliffton says to us. "I *would* run into them," she adds sheepishly as she leads us away. Her mouth tightens. "I'm sure I'll be hearing about this later."

"Will Dr. Cliffton be angry?" Miles asks knowingly.

Mrs. Cliffton gives a short laugh. "No, dear. Not Dr. Cliffton. Some other people in the town are just very concerned that this should all stay a secret."

As we drive home, Mrs. Cliffton rolls down the windows so that the breeze comes in. I slump back in the seat, suddenly wanting nothing more than to sleep.

Whenever I asked Mother about her childhood, she just shrugged her shoulders and said there wasn't much to tell. She hid this. From all of us. Which means she was not the person I thought she was. Not fully, anyway.

In some ways, this is almost worse than the day she died. It feels like falling backwards in a chair and not knowing when I'm going to hit the ground.

It feels like a betrayal.

My eye catches the flap of something in the cream paper of my shopping bag. It flutters with the breeze until I pluck it out. The rough grain of the paper is folded into a sharp crease, the letters inside written hastily in large, bold print, with an intensity that almost forced the pen right through the paper.

I swallow. It's an anonymous message of five simple words:

You are not welcome here.

I steal up to my room as soon as we reach the Clifftons' and shred the note into little pieces.

If I were at home, this would have earned a nice deep line for my floor.

My eyes burn with tears, and I throw the shredded paper into the waste bin. I wish I could show it to Cass. Her mouth would form a perfect *0,* her eyes narrowing in indignation on my behalf. Instead I go in search of Mrs. Cliffton. She is in the dining room, pouring water from a decanter into glasses filled with ice. When she smiles at me, I decide I won't tell her about the note.

"Mrs. Cliffton," I say, threading my fingers together nervously, "does my father know about the Disappearances?"

Mrs. Cliffton pauses in her pouring. "I'm not sure he does," she says. She moves to the next glass. "Of course, I don't know that for sure —" She hesitates, choosing her words. "But when I hinted at how different things are here, I had the sense he didn't fully grasp what I was getting at. He was more focused on making sure you all would be cared for by someone he could trust."

She straightens a knife. "Please know that you are perfectly safe here, Aila." The ice shifts and crackles in the glasses. I think again of the Council.

I'm trying to decide which thread I want to pick up — Why do you stay here? Why did Mother hide this? What's the Council, and why don't people want us in Sterling? — when Genevieve appears, balancing a platter of ham. "Aila," Mrs. Cliffton says, picking up the silver ice tongs, "I'm sure this all must come as quite a shock and you have many questions. There will be time for them all. But for now, would you call everyone for dinner?"

Reluctantly, I leave to look for Miles and Will. I find them outside, kicking a ball back and forth. Will appears to have gotten a haircut since yesterday. The scruffy hair at the back of his neck is now a sheared, sharp line, and pomade has darkened the color to almost black. I pause at the window, letting myself really look at him — at cheekbones that I can see now are his mother's, the carved edge of his jawline, dark, long lashes. I flush when he turns and suddenly looks up at the window, and I knock on the glass to wave them inside. Then I duck my head and hurry toward the wide oak door of Dr. Cliffton's library.

"Dr. Cliffton?" The door is ajar, and I knock before pushing it open, but I can tell when I enter that I've caught him off-guard. He stands abruptly and closes the book he is reading. His glasses slide down the bridge of his nose.

"Aila?" he asks, and I could swear he almost looks guilty.

"Dinner's ready," I say. He smiles as if he is dismissing me, and I realize he's not going to follow until I've left the room.

But I catch a glimpse of the book he is reading before he can fully hide it. The silver letters along the spine say *Myths, Legends, and Lore: A History of Sterling.*

I wash up for dinner and pinch my cheeks. Things still aren't adding up. The reluctance of Mrs. Cliffton to tell us things. The way people stared at us in town. Mother's secrecy, even from Father. I'm starting to sense that if I want answers — real ones — I'm going to have to find them myself.

Although, when I'm spooning maple syrup over a plump acorn squash, I feel the first glimmer of understanding for my mother. No wonder she left all those years ago and never spoke of Sterling again. After everything I've seen so far, what could she possibly have said?

After dinner, I bump into Will when we both stand to leave the table at the same time. "Sorry," I say, drawing back. Our eyes meet.

"My fault," he says. He steps aside to give me more room than is really necessary. "Think you'll join us for a game tonight?" he asks. He shifts his weight. "No pressure. Only if you want."

I think of the book Dr. Cliffton was trying to hide. "Yes," I say to Will, pushing my chair in. "I think tonight I'll join you."

We sit in a lopsided circle around the library: Will in the oversize leather chair, Dr. Cliffton in a Hitchcock straight back, Miles on the floor. I sink onto the couch next to Mrs. Cliffton. "It will be fun to have another gal in the room," Mrs. Cliffton says, dealing me in, and I'm surprised to find that it *is* fun, even though I play horribly. I'm distracted by the fact that Dr. Cliffton's desk has been cleared and the book is gone.

When we turn in, I can hear Mrs. Cliffton's voice from the neighboring room as she tells Miles good night. "Miles," she says, "is there anything you'd like to ask me? Do you want to talk about school tomorrow, or anything else?"

I pause mid-line in my reading of Coleridge to listen, wishing I had thought to ask him that. I never would have before, but it feels like I should start, somehow.

He doesn't ask her about the Variants or the Disappearances or Mother or the war or any of the thousands of questions that I wish he would. "Does the tooth fairy come to Sterling?" he says instead. "I have a very loose tooth."

I roll my eyes. I'm fairly certain Miles knows the tooth fairy doesn't exist. I'm also fairly certain he's saving pennies for a new *Sub-Mariner* comic.

"Of course," Mrs. Cliffton says. "Sterling is one of her favorite places. But you must tell me when it comes out so I can make sure she knows where to find you."

"Oh," he says. "All right."

"Tomorrow's going to be wonderful," she continues. "There are so many nice people at your school. It's exciting, isn't it? Knowing that tomorrow you'll meet so many new friends."

Miles is quiet. And then I hear him repeat the words my mother always said to us when we were young. I haven't heard them in years. I didn't even know he remembered them.

"Mrs. Cliffton, may your dreams be filled with stars and not with shadows," he says. Now that I can't see him, his voice seems to belong to someone smaller.

"Thank you, Miles," Mrs. Cliffton says, so softly I almost don't hear it. "But I'm afraid dreams are another thing that have been gone from Sterling since long before you were born."

I close my eyes. So it wasn't a coincidence that my nightmares stopped once we got to Sterling. Dreams, even the bad ones, were the last way I could reach out and touch my mother. And even that figment of her was better than nothing at all.

That night I wait in my room for the house to quiet. My new uniform hangs in the closet. The white blouse, necktie, and dark skirt pressed into crisp pleats seem to promise *I will make you appear like you belong.* I try not to look at it.

Instead I pull my hair up into a bun, allowing my ears to breathe in the secrecy of my own room. Of all the features I don't like, it's the ugly bump of cartilage, knotted like a kernel of corn on the tip of my right ear, that I hate the most. For a few months I'd almost grown to like it when it inspired my father's nickname for me. "My little elf," he'd say, and pull me into his lap.

But that all ended one spring day in eighth grade when Dixon Fairweather, the boy I'd secretly pined over for four years, tapped me on the shoulder in class. I'd leaned toward him with the stupidest smile on my face until he suddenly jumped back. "Say, what is that?" he asked, pointing. "Is that a *wart?* That's repulsive."

Repulsive.

The finishing word. For me and my ear.

I'd waited to cry until I was at home, carving the deepest gash into my floorboard. Two weeks later Dixon busted his own nose trying to wallop poor Simon Sneed with a tetherball.

And that time, Cass and I had both shed tears — of laughter.

I shake away the memory, figuring I've waited long enough for everyone to fall asleep. Time to take another look around Dr. Cliffton's library.

When I open the door, the hallway is dark. I steal downstairs and check the kitchen just to make sure I'm alone. The lights are out, and Genevieve has long since retired for the night. I reach for the light switch.

When it clicks on, a chair scrapes against the floor and someone jumps up. I shriek, then stifle it with my hand.

It's William.

He's been sitting at the kitchen table in the dark, and there's a partially eaten sandwich on the plate in front of him. His face looks more angled than it does in the daylight. His new haircut is a little short, but it suits him.

I freeze, realizing that my own hair is still in a bun on top of my head and there is no easy way for me to cover my ear. Not to mention that I'm wearing a nightgown so thin it probably barely conceals my chest. *You utter dip,* I tell myself, *don't look down,* and I can feel my face lighting with fire. Of course I hadn't thought to put on a bathrobe.

An endless moment goes by, and finally Will clears his throat.

"Trouble sleeping?" he asks politely. He fixes his gaze on the floor next to my feet.

"I was thirsty," I lie. Then I do something awkward with my arms and end up crossing them over my chest.

"There's some milk and soda there," he says, smiling toward the refrigerator.

"Right," I say, moving toward it as quickly as I can.

Will sits back down and gestures sheepishly at the sandwich on the table. "On the days I practice, I'm usually still hungry, even after dinner. Just promise not to tell Genevieve." I can feel his eyes taking in my flushed face before he averts them back to the wall.

He takes another bite of sandwich. "Do you want to sit?" he

asks, his mouth full. I pour a glass of milk and hesitate. He is wearing a white T-shirt and blue striped pajama pants, which makes me feel the slightest bit better.

I return the milk to the refrigerator and slide into the seat opposite him. When there is silence again, I drink my milk too quickly.

"We went into town today," I finally say. "I met Mrs. Mackelroy."

Will laughs, and I can glimpse his one slightly crooked incisor. "One of Sterling's brightest gems," he says.

"And your mother showed me the Looking Glass Variants."

"Ah, the Variants." He lets out a deep breath. "So now you know."

"I guess," I say. "I feel there's still so much that I *don't* know." I hesitate. "Does Sterling have a Council?"

"Yes. They make decisions in the town's best interests. Regulate the Variants, plan town events. My father's part of it."

"And they . . . had to vote to let us in?"

Will pushes the crusts of his sandwich around on his plate and won't quite look at me.

"Listen," he says finally. His eyes are blue and clear, and something in his voice makes my breath catch. "There are some people here who . . . didn't always have the fondest feelings toward your mother," he says. "Try not to let it get to you. My mother says she was a great person."

This shouldn't shock me, not after the note from town, but somehow it still does. "Oh," I say. "Well. I know that. I know who she was."

But really — do I?

"If anyone says anything, you can let me know," he says.

"Why . . ." My voice catches and betrays me. I clear my throat. "Why didn't they like her?"

The crumbs left from his sandwich are spread out like a constellation between us. He plays with the edge of the plate.

"I heard that she was different than everyone else. You have to understand that people here do whatever they can to prove they're not tied to the Disappearances. But your mother . . . She was the only one who could leave this place and be free," he says. "She got out and never looked back. I guess that left a bad taste in some people's mouths."

I chew on my bottom lip and process this. My mother was the only one?

"And maybe . . ." He hesitates. "Maybe that made them a bit suspicious of her."

He stands clumsily and carries his plate to the sink. "I go in early for practice tomorrow," he says. "But I'll probably see you in the halls."

When he reaches the door, he turns. "Just remember that you belong here, too." He rubs his hands along the back of his neck and looks at me as if he's trying to be sure I'm not too upset. "They wouldn't have even let you in the school if you weren't Juliet's daughter — if you weren't already tied to us somehow."

I force myself to nod. "Good night."

"'Night," he says, and leaves me to stare at the deep line one of Genevieve's knives has left scarred in the kitchen table.

I loved Dr. Cliffton's library when I first saw the hundreds of books covering the walls, but now I fight the urge to scream and hurl every last one of them from the shelves. I fumble around, trying to make out the spine I'm looking for in the dark, until exhaustion sets in. I finally admit to myself that if Dr. Cliffton was so eager to hide the title in the first place, he wasn't just going to leave it sitting out somewhere.

But I will find it. I'll keep coming back to look until I do. Because as Mother always said — with something between pride and embarrassment — I inherited all my stubbornness from her.

I return to my room. Mother's Shakespeare book is lying out where I left it on the nightstand. I pull it into my lap, opening it over my legs like a blanket, and trace my finger over the curves she left on the pages. I've opened to *All's Well That Ends Well*. I read the words she circled with her pen:

Proud scornful boy, unworthy this good gift,

That dost in vile misprision shackle up

My love and her desert; that canst not dream,

We, poising us in her defective scale,

I read it again, my eyes narrowing.

Did these passages simply strike her because they reminded her of Sterling? Or are they supposed to be clues? Some sort of message? One of her beloved riddles?

I close the book and rest it on the pillow beside me so I can sleep next to the weight of it. Then I rummage through my knapsack for a pen. Seeing her marks on the page makes me realize that I almost forgot our tradition. On the night before the first day of school she always drew a small heart on the inside of my arm. Right at the curve of my elbow, where almost no one else could see it, but I could catch sight of it like a secret love letter throughout the day.

I uncap the pen. My fingers shake slightly on the outline, and the ink is gray, but when I examine the finished product, I'm satisfied. This doesn't have to be one more thing that died when she did.

I slip into Miles's room, take his soft arm in my hand, and trace a heart to mirror my own. He stirs only slightly when the ink touches his skin.

I hope when he wakes and finds it tomorrow, he will think that Mother came back to leave him one final mark, a kiss on his body to show how much he was loved. I hope it helps him remember the Juliet Cummings Quinn who lived and moved and breathed in the space of our lives.

It is a challenge and a promise I am making to him and to myself.

I am going to find out what really happened here and use it to clear our mother's name.

CHAPTER SEVEN

Date: 8/29/1940
Bird: Magnificent Black-Winged Frigate
Forked tail.
Can stay aflight for more than a week at a time.
Forces other birds to regurgitate their food,
then steals it for itself.

Phineas's house is the strangest combination of sterility and disintegration —not unlike Phineas himself. His hair is wild and his stubble is pricked with gray. His teeth are stained from tobacco and his knuckles are tattooed, so that they appear perpetually smudged with dirt. But his fingernails are picked clean and pink.

The night we meet, when he invites me in, I stay for dinner. We dance around all the important questions as he spoons red stew into two blindingly white chipped bowls.

"Smells good," I say when he sets it in front of me. I don't know why I say it—a blatant lie. I can't smell it at all. Maybe it's just habit. Maybe it's nerves.

"So you did all right?" he asks gruffly, and I fight the urge to laugh. I'd sent him a few letters in prison, until I realized they always went unanswered. Surely he remembers that I spent most of my childhood in a wheelchair.

I don't tell him about the loneliness, how badly things ended with Juliet, or how I was planning to kill myself later tonight. I skate along the edge of that line with a cool, "I'm still here."

Then I rest my spoon and watch in horror as the weight of it falls and splatters red stew on the tablecloth. Phineas jumps up, and I sit in agony as he spends several minutes scrubbing away at the stain as if it were blood.

"Sorry," I say stiffly, and he waves it away. But I notice then how clean his house is. Spare and sterile, as if he cleans it every day with bleach.

"What were you in jail for?" I ask abruptly when he returns to his seat.

He pauses. "Robbery," he says. Which is partly true.

"When did you get out?"

"Twenty-five years ago."

"You never came back." What I meant was, You never came back for me.

He grunts and scrapes the stain of stew from the inside of his bowl.

"And what of . . ." He trails off. I know whom he means. But I don't want to tell that long, awful story. Not tonight. So I shrug and shake my head, and he doesn't bring her up again.

The rest of dinner is filled with gaping, painful silences. This, I think: the culminating event, the bookend to my life. But when he walks me to the door, he gives me his telephone number on a scrap of paper. "I need some help with odd jobs," he says brusquely. "Maybe you could come back again."

Later, on the platform, when the train hurtles toward me, I stare down into the abyss of the tracks and rock on my heels. I have not written a note to leave; there is no one to leave it for. But I feel in my pocket for that one ripped scrap of paper.

Close my fingers around my father's handwriting. When the train is almost upon me, I step safely back into the clear, starless night.

CHAPTER EIGHT

The morning Miles and I start school, Mrs. Cliffton is waiting at the bottom of the stairs, a coat slung over her arm and a leather pouch in her hand. William has already left for practice. "I'm sure you're eager for a bit of this," she says. She applies the Looking Glass Variants to a hand mirror so I can examine myself. Then, before I am quite done straightening my uniform and smoothing my hair, she ushers me and Miles out to the car.

"Don't want to be late," she says.

The drive to the school is familiar until the final fork, where we bear right instead of taking the left toward town. Mrs. Cliffton is chattering on from the front seat, but I'm only vaguely aware of what she's saying. I reach into my pocket and feel for Cass's ribbon, my reminder that I am only passing through.

When I look up, we are nearing two stories of faded brick. I take in the high school's cascade of wide concrete stairs, the apples and silver swords emblazoned on flags above the arched entrance, and, finally, the students themselves, milling in clusters around the stone wall that separates the grounds from an orchard. Miles's elementary school building is barely visible just beyond it.

"I'm going to bring Miles to his new classroom," Mrs. Cliffton says. "The principal's office will be the first door on your right. He's expecting you." She reaches into the back seat to give my knee a slight squeeze. Her hand is warm. Then so are my face, my ears, my neck.

"Don't forget that William's always there if you need anything," Mrs. Cliffton says as I climb out.

"Bye, Miles," I say. "I'll see you after."

"It's going to be great," Miles says, his chin raised defiantly. I raise my hand to wave goodbye. When he waves back, I glimpse the small heart on the inside of his elbow.

Then I close the door, the car pulls away, and I am alone.

The whispers start as soon as I cross the schoolyard. I want to shake them off, but they cling to me like strands from a web as I walk up the steps and under the curved arches of the entrance. I fight to keep my gaze at eye level, but I settle on looking somewhere on the ground just ahead. It's as though I'm watching myself under a microscope, trying my best to walk and move like a normal person. As far as blending in goes, my uniform can do only so much.

I find the principal's office just as Mrs. Cliffton directed— PRINCIPAL CLEARY carved into brass on the door—and knock.

"Come in," a deep voice says.

Principal Cleary sits behind a massive oak desk, his hands clasped in front of him. He seems to start at the sight of me, then quickly recovers. He has a high forehead, thinning brown hair, and ears that seem a degree too low. His portraits hang on three walls of the office: one of him receiving a diploma, another of him staring pensively out of a window, and another of him signing some document with an ornate pen. In each he wears the same pursed look he gives me now.

"Miss Quinn." He gestures to a chair in front of his desk. "Take a seat."

I do, tilting my arm so that I can just make out the tiny heart on the inside of my elbow.

"It's very rare for us to welcome a new student to this school," Principal Cleary begins. "I take it that you're well aware of our . . . unusual circumstances in Sterling?" He leans forward.

"I am."

"Because of these special circumstances, we have a number of rules by which you will need to carefully abide," he says, rising. The pleats of his pants are sharp and exact. "These rules will be especially strict until you are Of Age." He hands me a thick booklet, *A Guide to Complete Variant Compliance at Sterling High School.*

"And your schedule." He slides a piece of paper across his desk. Biology, geometry, dressmaking, then lunch. Afternoon classes in English, alternating days of physical fitness and family life skills, and history. I notice a final portrait, this one smaller and given prime positioning on his desk. A younger version of Principal Cleary is frozen in time, grooming a small pink-tinted poodle.

I snort, then try to hide it in a cough, then almost choke.

"Are you all right, Miss Quinn?"

I nod, my eyes watering.

"The other students in your year are already weeks ahead of you. You'll need to work hard to keep pace with them. We educate dedicated, diligent students in this school. Anything less will not be tolerated. Do you have any questions, Miss Quinn?"

Without waiting for an answer, he continues.

"I've appointed one of your classmates to ensure that you find your classes without disruption. Agatha Mackelroy was here yesterday and mentioned she'd already met you in town, so she volunteered her son, George. If you have any further questions, please direct them to him." And with that, Principal Cleary shows me the door and closes it firmly in my face.

I stand for a moment in the hall, still facing the closed door, and pretend to study my schedule. I find Cass's ribbon in my pocket. Students ripple around me, staring. Some whisper, and one knocks right into me, but no one says hello or offers help.

Then I hear a burst of Will's laughter just beyond the window.

I fold my schedule into my books and follow his familiar voice out to the courtyard.

"Cliffton!"

A boy with closely shorn hair passes a soccer ball across the courtyard to Will. I lean against the metal stair railing and watch Will stop it with his foot, then shoot it back. He pulls his uniform tie from his pants pocket and loops it around his neck.

Another boy takes the ball, then passes it with too much force. The ball rolls past Will and comes to a stop at the foot of the steps, just in front of me. Will jogs toward it and does a double take. "Hey," he says.

"Hi," I say, and flush, remembering that the last time we saw each other, I was in my nightgown.

"Who's the sugar, eh, Will?" the boy with the shorn hair yells. Another teammate raises his fingers to his lips in a short, shrill whistle.

Will doesn't look at me. He calls over his shoulder, "Leave it. She's a friend." He reaches for the spot at the back of his neck. Then he bends for the ball and tosses it between his hands. "Is someone coming to get you?"

"So I'm told," I say.

The other boy continues. "Looks like Will's already marking his territory."

Will clenches his jaw. "Hey, Peterson," he shoots back. "Then why don't you *piss off?*"

He tosses the ball in front of him and runs around his teammates in smooth, fast arcs, daring one of them to try to steal it from him. It works to distract their attention from me.

A boy appears at that moment, half jogging from the orchard to the stairs where I wait. His hair is dirty blond and sticks up as though it's rarely seen a comb. The front tail of his uniform shirt is untucked, and his tie is slightly askew.

"Aila?" He stretches out his hand as he approaches, and I release my hold on the railing to take it.

"I'm George. We have first period together — Dr. Digby's biology lab — so I'm going to show you around. Shall we go?"

"That's grand of you," I say. "Thank you." I smile at Will to let him know that I'm fine, that he doesn't have to worry.

"Well, Cliffton, looks like you've got yourself a real honey of a houseguest," the boy called Peterson says loudly as I follow George up the stairs.

"Shut it," Will says, giving Peterson a swift elbow to the ribs just as the first bell sounds across the lawn.

"So you've met Principal Cleary then?" George nods at the principal's closed door as he leads me down the hall. "We're so fortunate to have him. But I'm curious — what did you think? Personally, I've always found him to be so inspiring."

This doesn't bode well for a future friendship with George. I offer him a half smile in response and leave it at that. Principal Cleary does seem like just the sort who would stick me with the leader of his own personal fan club.

"Sometimes I'm not sure which I like more: his humility or his distinguished taste in the painted form," George continues, confirming that this is going to be a very long day. He is walking at a brisk pace, and I'm almost running to match his stride. "Take those portraits hanging in his office," he says. "Some students wait their entire scholastic careers for that honor, and you saw them on your very first day. Were you able to pick a favorite?" He stops abruptly and faces me.

His eyebrows rise as he waits for my answer, and then the corners of his mouth twitch. With his faded freckles and pleased expression, he almost looks like Miles.

He bursts out laughing. "I'm kidding," he says. "He's terrible. Loves to blow his bazoo. But you should have seen your face." He takes off walking again. "Come along," he calls back over his shoulder.

I break into a smile at the retreating back of his head and hurry to catch him. We round a corner and narrowly miss colliding with a girl wearing tortoiseshell glasses. A braid wraps around her head like a snake.

The look she gives me is something beyond curiosity. She scowls and darts away, and I think again of the note from town.

"You know, I met your mother yesterday," I tell George.

"She mentioned that." He makes a face. "Please know I take more after my father."

"She was . . . perfectly nice," I say feebly. In response, George snorts.

We slow in front of a classroom filled with long wooden tables. "Biology laboratory. My favorite class." He points me inside. "Here we are."

The entire class turns when I step into the room. Out of the corner of my eye I can see that the heart I drew is already fading.

"Welcome, welcome," Dr. Digby says, stepping forward. His magnified eyes loom behind thick glasses, and a row of pens peek from his laboratory coat pocket. "Students, this is Miss Aila Quinn," he announces.

"What a felicitous day for you to join us, Miss Quinn. Today we begin to explore the wondrous world of osmosis, on none other than the *Allium cepa*." He displays a white bulb to the class. "Better known to the layman as the common onion." With his other hand he taps a ruler twice on his desk. "Goggles, everyone!"

I follow George to the farthest lab desk. There are two seats next to a girl with eyes the color of umber and a line of rounded black bangs that graze her eyebrows. She offers me a smile with some curiosity and moves her violin case to make room. Her spectator pumps make her uniform look miles more sophisticated than my bobby socks and saddle shoes.

I set my bag down, and as soon as Dr. Digby's back is turned, a flurry of notes are passed under the lab tables. It's a special kind of agony to know they all contain my initial evaluations. I'm suddenly back in eighth grade again, feeling Dixon Fairweather's hot breath in my ugly ear.

"Beas," George says, "meet Aila. She moved here from . . ."

"Gardner," I say. "Hello."

"Welcome to the madness," Beas says, handing me a pair of goggles. Her voice is low and throaty. She pulls her own goggles down and sticks a piece of hard candy in her mouth. "Candy?" she offers. I shake my head. "So what do you think of our nuts little town so far?"

"It seems all right," I say nervously. "I'm staying with the Clifftons. Do you know them?"

"Right. With William," she says. She looks amused. Then she drops her onion on the table and George catches it just before it rolls to the floor.

He points his knife at the bulb and says, "Yes, Will's a giant hunk of heartbreak. Now let's pay attention to the task at hand, shall we?"

"No, no, it's not like that." Beas laughs. "You know I only have eyes for Thom. However . . ." She trails off. "Let's just say I know some people who aren't going to be very pleased to hear that."

George gives a sort of shrug-nod, as if he knows exactly whom she means.

"Class, turn to page fifty-two, and let's get started," Dr. Digby says. George takes out a small scalpel and begins to peel off the thin translucent layers of the onion.

"So I guess this is the part where we're supposed to tell you all the different ways you can't use the Variants," Beas says. She makes no move to help George with the experiment. Instead she reaches into my half-open bag and pulls out the *Variant Compliance* booklet. She turns to one of the earliest pages and runs her fingers over the list. It reads:

ATONING VARIANTS
Tint
Fragrance
Looking Glass

ENHANCING VARIANTS
Ember
Glimmer

Mind's Eye
Night Vision
Veil

"I had no idea there were so many," I say, pulling the list toward me for a better look. "I've only seen the Looking Glass ones." I suddenly remember the rainstorm on the day we arrived, and Mrs. Cliffton's inexplicably dry clothes. "And perhaps ones for keeping dry?"

"Yes, those are the Veil Variants," Beas says, absently wrapping the dark strands of her bangs around a pencil. "They act like a water repellent. And we use the Embers to keep warm," she explains. "Dashing a bit over you is like wearing a blanket. There's nothing against using those at school, as long as you're Of Age. But if you use the Fragrance Variants in a cooking class, it's considered cheating."

"Not smelling what I cook might be to my advantage," I say. I took over the cooking once Mother got sick. Miles and Father had pushed around the first dinner I made, mumbling how good it tasted, even though I'd turned the chicken into charred rocks.

"And we should tell you about the most forbidden Variant for school purposes," Beas says. "It's called Mind's Eye. You smear it on your eyelids, and it's more or less enhanced memory, so you could be expelled if they catch you using it for an exam."

Mind's Eye, I think, remembering Will's slip.

"The teachers always come around for an eyelid check before our tests," Beas adds.

George positions the onion slide under the microscope. "Take a look," he says.

I put my eye to the lens.

"What does it mean that the Variants are separated into different categories? Atoning and Enhancing?" I ask. I fiddle with the microscope knobs until the onion cells blur and then clear. There is something reassuring about how ordered they are, all formed in a neat row.

"Atoning Variants act as substitutes for Disappearances," George says. "We have them for scents, mirrors, and some work-arounds for color. The Enhancements are a bit harder to explain."

I straighten from the microscope and push it back toward him.

"People have stumbled upon Enhancing Variants over the years when they were looking for Atoning Variants. For instance — the ability to see stars or have dreams — we don't have Variants for those yet."

Stars, I think, my stomach clenching. *Their stars have disappeared.*

"But what do the Enhancing Variants have to do with the Disappearances?" I ask.

A fleeting look crosses George's face. "We don't know," he says, frowning. "We don't know if what they enhance are things that may eventually disappear — and we've stumbled on the cure first — or if it's something else." He turns his gaze back to the microscope. "With the Enhancements, it's as though we're hitting up against something that's been unlocked. And the pieces won't make much sense until we have the whole story."

"But look at this list, George," Beas says. She stops playing with her bangs and straightens. "All the Variants aren't even on here."

She pushes the list toward George. Then she takes my elbow and angles it out to examine my heart. "Nice," she says with approval. She gathers her uniform skirt to show the skin just above her knee, hidden under the table. "Mine changes on the day, depending on my mood."

My heart rises when I recognize the line written there. It is Elizabeth Barrett Browning, scrawled in Beas's looping hand: *Like a cheerful traveler, take the road singing beside the hedge.*

Beas lets her hem fall back down. "And don't think I can't see you looking, George."

George laughs and shakes his head as he measures liquid out in a stopper. He applies a few drops to the slides. "Such a tease, Beas."

"Fathead," she says, but she's smiling, and she flips her ponytail at him before returning her attention to the list.

"And there are more Variants than this list?" I prod.

George mixes up a solution of saltwater. "A few more. Guess they're too illegal to be included."

"*Illegal* is a little strong," Beas says, tipping open the pocket on her uniform skirt to show a purple pouch inside. "Some are merely frowned upon for the potential to draw too much attention. Like the Tempests."

"Tempests?"

"They're a real gas. Picture what running would feel like if you became the wind," George says.

"These are still left from my birthday last year," Beas says, pushing the pouch back into the fold of her skirt. "I'm already Of Age," she explains. "I'm actually in William's year." She purses her lips and doodles an owl wearing a hat on my *Compliance* list. "Let's just say biology and I didn't quite work out last time."

"It's working out just fine for you this year, though, isn't it," George says under his breath, but he's smiling as he does Beas's part of the experiment.

"I get why they don't like the Tempests," Beas says thoughtfully, as if she hasn't heard George. She adds lightning strikes around her owl. "But in the end, they're mostly harmless. Not like the darker ones."

When she turns the page back to me, I see the warning written at the bottom.

Any Variants not appearing on this list are strictly forbidden on school property at all times. Use of them will result in significant disciplinary — and potentially legal — action.

Darker Variants? I think. *Are there Variants that can cause harm?*

Dr. Digby is suddenly behind us. "Working diligently, I trust?" he asks, but he keeps moving in response to George's salute.

George bends to add drops of saltwater to the slides. "There we go. Gals, take a gander."

"No need," Beas says, bored, now examining a sheet of music she's pulled from her violin case. "I remember what it looked like last year."

George moves to make room for me, and I bend to focus the lens again. It takes a moment for my eyes to adjust. The smooth, ordered lines of the cells remain. But their insides are shrunken and disfigured, sucked dry by the salt.

It's just an onion, I think, backing away. But it unsettles me all the same: how the familiar can warp into something I no longer recognize in the space between one breath and the next.

CHAPTER NINE

After school, Mrs. Cliffton is waiting for us. She's pulled the car onto a side lane by the orchard. "Good day?" she asks when we climb in.

Miles and I both murmur something noncommittal.

"Well, there's something for you at home," she says, turning the key in the ignition.

Genevieve has made little tea sandwiches cut into triangles and rich peanut butter cookies encrusted with sugar. But even better: there is mail. Letters from Cass and Father, which means they must have mailed them as soon as we left. I'm torn between whose I want to read first, but Miles snatches Father's, so I slit open the one from Cass. It is written in her large, effusive cursive, peppered with questions about Sterling and the Clifftons. I can see her, coming home from her first day ever of school without me, climbing the rickety ladder to the only place in the house that is hers: an attic nook she's stuffed with pillows and blankets. We often used to read there, especially on days when it rained. It held just enough room for both of us to stretch our legs along the length of the floor, our feet grazing the window, an endless stash of Wint O Green Lifesavers always hidden under one of the floorboards.

I read Cass's letter twice before Miles is finished with Father's. "Can I see it now?" I ask with impatience. He hands it over reluctantly. His fingerprints have already smeared some of the words.

Father's letter is more reserved, his handwriting tight and

efficient. He probably wrote it at his desk, under the light of his green glass lamp, smoking the pipe that's engraved with a schooner. After the perfunctory questions about Sterling, he writes:

Flying to San Francisco tomorrow on a Douglas DC-3. My first time on a plane. We'll be training for a week and then setting sail. I am unsure how often I can post from sea or how much detail I can provide on my whereabouts. I don't want you to worry if you don't hear from me for stretches. But know that wherever I am, it is always farther than I wish to be from you, and that you are never beyond the reach of my thoughts.

Until the day we are all together again —

And with a heart bursting with pride for you both —

Father

"Done?" Miles asks, and plucks the letter out of my hands before I can answer.

"Oh," I say as he folds it back along its creases. I had planned to keep it and add it to my growing collection of Mother's ring and Shakespeare book, Father's dart, and Cass's ribbon. How tightly I cling to the little pieces they've shed, when for now it's all of them I have left.

"How was school?" I venture.

Miles shrugs and leaves the table. He heads outdoors, tucking Father's letter into his back pocket. Mrs. Cliffton stands up from where she was pulling a few stray weeds from her garden, and I can see her talking with Miles, but I can't make out the words.

I sit there for a moment longer before it suddenly strikes me — Will stayed after school for a project, Dr. Cliffton isn't here, and everyone else is distracted. I push back from the table, my chair scraping the floor. There won't be many better opportunities than this.

The daylight makes it easier to scan the rows of books that line Dr. Cliffton's walls from floor to ceiling. The shelves even carve around the fireplace mantel and window frames. But just like last night, the book is not there.

I pause over the neat surface of Dr. Cliffton's desk. It is clear but for a silver case holding fancy pens and a paperweight made of heavy stone. I kneel to shuffle through the drawers, careful to leave everything just the way I found it.

When I reach the final drawer, I lift a neat stack of papers. The silver lettering of the cover gleams at me: *Myths, Legends and Lore of Sterling: 35th Commemorative Edition.*

"For Council Members Only" is stamped into the leather.

I cautiously lift it out.

Five minutes, I think. *Then I'll put it back.*

I scan as quickly as I can through the first pages, which hold genealogies and family trees of what must be the most prominent families in Sterling. Mother's maiden name of Cummings isn't listed.

I keep flipping. Each section holds a story marked with the family names of people from the town — Blythe, Patton, Fitzpatrick. The opening content appears to be a history of the town's founding and important occasions, such as the inaugural Harvest Fair in the 1850s, but other words pop out at me: *guilty* and *suspicious* and *probable*. There is the occasional photograph and chart peppered throughout and then a slight gap in the pages approximately two-thirds through. I run my fingertips over the sliver of exposed binding. The page numbers jump from 203 to 208.

Someone has ripped them out.

I know I'm taking too much time. My five minutes have come and gone. I glance up, thinking I hear something, then flip to the back. There's an index. Just as I come to the *C*'s, I freeze.

There are unmistakable footsteps on the front stairs, the sound of the door handle turning. I tense as the heavy front door slams. I can tell it's Will by the rhythm of even strides, as opposed to Dr. Cliffton's shuffle and knock of cane. I shove the Sterling book back into place and shut the drawer.

Then I promptly knock over the silver cup of pens, which clatter to the floor. Will's footsteps stop. I swear under my breath, grabbing the pens and placing them back on the desk just as Will pokes his head into the library.

"Hello," he says. His dark eyebrows arch upward in surprise. "What are you doing in here?"

"Hi!" I say, my voice overly bright. "I was just looking for . . . a stamp. To write my father?"

It's clear from the look on his face that I am not the most skilled liar.

"I think they're in here," he says. He finds a roll in the top drawer of his father's desk and meets my eyes when he hands them to me. "First day okay?"

"Swell," I say. "But I'm behind on everything. So I should get started." I clutch the roll of stamps and brush past him.

When I reach my room, I set the stamps on my nightstand, then flop onto my bed, my heart still beating madly. Mother's Shakespeare book is within reach, and I want to pull it open in my lap.

Instead I make myself turn to my pile of schoolbooks. I have extra assignments in every class so I can catch up with the others.

I settle into the window seat and flip to my biology chapter. But my thoughts keep returning to the Sterling book from Dr. Cliffton's library. *You're supposed to be learning about osmosis,* I tell myself, forcing my eyes back to the words in front of me. Instead, all I can see is the index entry I'd managed to glimpse just before Will walked in.

I'd found my mother in the *C* heading, listed under her maiden name. It said "Cummings, Juliet — Possible Catalyst."

But it was the entry following "Cummings" that made the hair on my arms rise, as if the Disappearances could be part of something much more sinister. It said:

"The Curse."

CHAPTER TEN

Date: 10/15/1940

Bird: Hooded Pitohui

The bird's skin and feathers are laced with a paralyzing neurotoxin gleaned from the beetles in its diet. The poison releases upon contact to kill any enemies that dare to touch it.

The bird ingests so much poison that eventually it becomes poison itself.

When I was eleven, I'd found the hooded pitohui in the pages of an encyclopedia. I'd sketched the bird over and over, filling margins with doodles. My precision sharpened until I had all the details perfect from memory. A daggerlike beak. Head of jet-black feathers that bled into a vibrant red chest. Colors so toxic and yet so bright that they begged to be touched.

I was fascinated by the bird's powerful and terrible beauty.

It reminded me of the redheaded girl I had loved. They could both stop a beating heart if they lured you close enough.

Before the months with Phineas, those had been the happiest days of my life. Those short, shimmering weeks when I thought that she might love me back.

As it turned out, she never did.

Phineas and I get to know each other while I work odd jobs around his house.

I replace the rotting boards under the porch and learn that he likes planes and the music of Chausson. I scrape lichen from the gutters as he tells *me about maps, cigars, and a good bottle of Bordeaux. He talks about soil when he poaches eggs for us in the mornings: mine extra runny, his always as dry as chalk and firm enough to bounce against the wall.*

And most of all, I notice his obsessive tidiness. Always, the tidiness.

When I slough off the old paint that curls like hangnails around the door, he joins me and hands me a lukewarm bottle of soda. "What did you want to be when you were young?" he asks.

"An inventor."

"You like school growing up?"

I blink out at the ocean, gray and churlish, but I am picturing my wheelchair. Seeing myself as a young boy, watching the seasons go by from the window. Sketching birds. I imagine that Phineas and I spent the same years looking at the outside world, dreaming of different kinds of freedom.

"I never went to school. One year, I got far enough to be fitted for a uniform, but then influenza swept through." I hesitate. "I . . . wasn't well growing up. My legs haven't always been so good."

"What's wrong with your legs?" he'd said. "They look fine to me."

"They're much stronger now. I don't even limp anymore."

"Did you have an accident?" he'd asked. "An illness?"

"Just a runt. Born too early." I'd tried to keep my voice light, but instead I went and made it uncomfortable. Bringing up the day Mother died. I took a long swig of the warm soda, and his gaze slid away from me, the way people's always do when I realize too late that I've said the wrong thing.

"But I've always been good with my hands." I quickly reach into my pocket to show him the wooden bird I carved as a teenager. He takes it and runs his thumb along the curve of its back in the exact way I always do. It is the first echo of myself I see in him. A motion I've already done so many times that the grain there is like silk.

I'd forgotten about the school uniform I never got to use. How I used to fall asleep holding on to its sleeve, scared that it would disappear in the night. Remembering how, when the influenza epidemic was done, that uniform didn't even fit me anymore.

And then I burned it.

Phineas, I almost say then. Something disappears for me every seven years. I don't know why, or how to get it to stop. But don't worry. I've learned how to live with it.

Instead I take another sip, until the swell of my courage fades away. It's too much of a risk. The Disappearances could scare Phineas off. Take away the only thing I want. To stay here and listen to him talk about unimportant things as I tune the radio to our serial programs. So many chances like this have already passed by that it's become something too big to tell.

Just like one of Juliet's favorite riddles:

"What needs darkness to grow instead of light?" she asked me one night when we were younger.

"I give up," I finally said.

"Isn't it obvious?" Her eyes flashed more silver than gray. "Secrets."

CHAPTER ELEVEN

B y Friday morning I'm starting to get the hang of things, and I am absurdly triumphant when I find Digby's laboratory by myself.

Beas moves her violin case, and I slide into the seat next to her. Today, instead of assigning an experiment, Dr. Digby lectures on mitosis. George diligently takes notes, and Beas appears to be writing music, which she then folds into her violin case. When Digby pivots toward the chalkboard, a boy with oil-slicked hair at the table in front of ours turns his head and mouths hello at me. I smile, flush, panic, and start to furiously scribble notes across my paper.

Beas nudges me. "Are you rationed?" she asks in a whisper. "Anybody special waiting for you back in Gardner?"

"Oh." I shake my head. "Um. No."

Beas smiles wryly. "Then have you taken your pick here yet?"

She nods toward the boy in front of us. He's turned back around to rest the tip of his pencil in the hole of his notebook so it looks like he's writing. Instead he lays his head down on the desk and prepares to take a nap. It all makes me miss Cass in a sudden, fierce wave. She would have guffawed at the idea of taking my pick of boys. I can almost see her, her eyes squinting shut, grabbing a pillow to her stomach, laughing her truest, gulping laugh — the one that always ended in hiccups.

Instead, there is just Beas, her eyebrows arched, unaware of just how unprecedented this situation is.

"What are you talking about?" I ask. "I've been here for three days."

"Exactly," Beas says, and closes her notebook. "You're something new," she explains matter-of-factly. "They know what the rest of us looked like in pigtails. You're . . . mysterious."

"Right," I whisper. "They missed the bloody nose era when I was nine. Ruined any crushes that might have been," I tell her. "And all my favorite dresses."

Her laugh is low and throaty. "Well. Take my advice and don't pick that gorilla." She nods to the napping boy. "He's bad business."

The bell rings, releasing us to our next class. I'm summoning my courage to ask if Beas has any plans for the weekend when she gathers her books and says, "See you next week."

"Be seeing you," I say, suddenly wishing we were in the same year so we'd have more classes together. I stuff my textbook into my bag, telling myself, *I don't need to make best friends. Soon enough I'll be back home again with Cass and Father.*

When my final class ends, I wave goodbye to George, who is at the front of the classroom, speaking to our teacher. He doesn't stop talking, but cocks his chin at me. Today his tie is only marginally wrinkled.

I've barely joined the students in the hallway streaming toward the sunshine when someone knocks into me hard enough from behind to check me into a locker.

I slam into it and look up just in time to see the back of a shaved head.

It is the boy from Will's team — Peterson — the one who earned a jab from Will's elbow. He doesn't apologize. Instead, he keeps moving in a jaunty sort of way that makes me suspect our encounter wasn't entirely an accident.

I regain my balance and glare at the back of his head. Cass's ribbon is on the floor, where it's fallen from my pocket. I quickly crouch to dust it free of dirt. When I straighten again, I see Beas farther down the hall, making her way toward me through the shifting mass of students.

I wait for her, deciding that I'll ask if she'd ever want to study together. But as I watch, another girl gracefully parts the crowd and falls into step with Beas. Her blond hair is falling in a perfect plump wave over her shoulder, and she has blazing eyes the color of jade. Her legs are so long that her uniform seems inches shorter than everyone else's. I can feel her confidence from all the way down the hall.

"That new girl, the one staying with Will —" the blonde says to Beas when they are close enough for me to hear. I turn away and flatten myself behind a pillar as they walk by. "Do you think she knows how uncomfortable it is that she's here? With the way everyone feels about her mother, and all?"

"You know, we have a class together. And she's pretty nice. I like her." Beas adjusts her violin case as they pass.

"You say that like she's a pet you're thinking of keeping," the other girl chirps. "Goodhearted Beas, always looking out for strays. Better not get too close, though. That one might be here to finish what her mother started."

"Eliza," Beas's low voice sings, "I've heard that being cruel gives you wrinkles and turns you into a hag."

"Oh, Beas," Eliza retorts, and swats her playfully on the arm. "You're lucky I find your sass charming." They reach the front doors, disappearing into the sunlight.

I stay hidden in the shadows and smooth my hair over my ear again and again. *Don't you dare cry,* I tell myself fiercely. How could someone hate me before she's even met me?

I calm myself by coming up with a list of finishing words. Several less-flattering terms come to mind before I finally settle on *vitriolic.* Even then, it's still several moments before I am able to step out from the pillar, walk down the hall, and look for the familiar outline of the Clifftons' car.

Instead, I spot Will. He's leaning against one of the apple trees in the orchard, his schoolbag slung low over his shoulder. He isn't wearing his practice uniform, and he seems to be waiting for something.

When he catches my eye, he straightens.

"Aila," he calls. "I've got an errand to run. You want to come?"

"Sure," I say, still trying to shake off what Eliza said.

And then I see her. She's perched along the courtyard wall with Beas. A look of surprise creases her face as I walk toward Will. Then, as quickly as it appeared, her expression returns to cool glass.

Oh. It makes more sense now.

But I'm caught off-guard by the way my heart suddenly lightens with each step toward Will. How conscious I am of the wind as it ruffles my skirt against the backs of my knees, and how I'm not sure what to do with my hands in the moment he looks up and smiles just wide enough for me to glimpse that single crooked tooth.

"Aila's coming with me," Will tells his mother through her open car window. "We'll be back for dinner."

We put our schoolbags in the back seat, and Miles climbs into the front. He looks back and forth between Will and me with an expression that suggests he's about to say something embarrassing.

"Bye, Miles!" I say, and hurriedly shut the door on him. He presses his mouth and cheeks against the window glass as the car pulls away, which elicits a laugh from Will.

"Don't encourage him," I mutter. "So where are we going?"

"Thought you'd want to see the Marketplace."

"Where they sell the Variants?"

He nods, and I hurry to match his long strides through the shadows cast by the orchard's tree branches, tripping through the stripes of shade and sun. I'm conscious that we are alone together again, and for some reason it's making me feel jittery and nervous.

"Can I ask you a question?"

"Sure," he says.

I haven't been able to stop thinking about the words I saw in the book about Sterling. *The Curse.* Now, in the sunlight, with William's hand only inches from my own, it doesn't seem quite as unnerving as it had in Dr. Cliffton's library.

"Why do you think the Disappearances happened here?" I ask.

A muscle flickers in Will's jaw. "You know," he says, squinting up at the sky, "it's not just Sterling."

My mouth falls open. "What do you mean?"

I notice, with the slightest twinge of dread, that he has not actually answered my question.

"Two other neighboring towns," he says. "Corrander and Sheffield. We call ourselves the Sisters. Ever heard of them?"

I shake my head. "I hadn't heard anything about any of this. How is that possible? Why does it have to be such a secret?"

"Well, first off, think about what would happen if everyone else in the world knew they could profit from selling us the simplest pleasures in life."

"But I would think that if more people knew about it, you would have a better chance of finding—"

"Watch that." He points to a root jutting up from the ground. When I've cleared it, he says, "I guess at first, word did get around about the missing scents. There were some curiosity visits. My grandmother said that some of the residents felt as though they were being observed like animals. Most people who came were nice and hoped to help. But there were the others, too. The ones who would sell us meat going bad because they knew we couldn't smell it. Or strew rotting garbage in places we couldn't see it. Fitzpatrick's General Store lost a fortune of inventory one year; by the time he found the pile someone hid away, the maggots and vermin had set in."

I blanch. "I don't know why some people seize on any opportunity to be cruel."

He shakes it off. "Anyway, as the Disappearances kept happening, it didn't take long to see that they make us vulnerable. So the towns voted to band together, form the Council, and keep it all a secret. And we take that seriously, to protect each other."

"And people won't leave?" I ask. "Or . . ." I hesitate. "Can't?"

"My reflection won't come back just because I leave Sterling. Not like yours will." His jaw twitches again. "You're a visitor. The Disappearances will only affect you for as long as you're here. But I was born into it. It's in my blood. The only relief now is temporary, and it's with the Variants."

He curves into a thick grove of white-blossomed trees. The breeze bows the branches, loosening petals until they fall around us like snow.

It suddenly makes sense why the war feels so distant here. Sterling is like a jeweled piece of fruit locked in a glass case.

I swallow. But that piece of fruit is rotting.

Will shifts uncomfortably. His voice turns slightly bitter. "So in Sterling we stay." He offers the petals to me, as soft as down. "Here. Save these for later."

He begins walking again. The trees are crowding together until there are more shadows than sun. I'm looking at the petals he gave me, at the ridges of white veins running through them, when he suddenly grabs me and pulls me behind a tree. My breath hitches in surprise, and he raises his fingers to his lips and shakes his head.

I hear the voices now. Distant and lowered.

I am close enough to Will to feel him breathe.

"That's more than it was last time, Larkin," someone protests.

"That's economics for you. Demand's gone up. Do you want it or not?"

Will's body tightens, and I try not to think about how I've never been this close to a boy who wasn't Miles or Father.

There's a hedging pause. "Fine."

"You're sure that's all you want? I can't guarantee it won't be even more next time."

"I can't afford any more at those prices," the buyer growls. I hear the jangle of coins and the rustle of paper, then footsteps retreating deeper into the forest, in opposite directions.

Even once they're gone, Will doesn't fully relax. But he listens carefully and then takes a step away from me. "We can go now," he says. "Those were black market dealings. Would have been . . . unfortunate for us to walk in on them."

I think of the warning in my Variant handbook. Of illegal and dangerous Variants.

I hurry to keep up with him again. "You can feel the tension already," Will says, loosening the knot of his tie. "Growing. Everyone will keep getting more skittish until we find out what disappears next." He turns to look at me. His eyes are the exact color of the sky. "Unfortunately, you came just in time to see the whole town at its worst."

"Some of this still doesn't seem quite real," I confess.

"And for me it's the opposite," he says. "It's sort of fascinating, to see Sterling through the eyes of someone from the outside." I notice that he's leading us in a way that threads between the trees instead of walking in a straight line, as if to avoid cutting a path someone could follow.

"Only a few people have dared to try leaving the Sisters," he says. "Eliza Patton's older sister is at an opera company in New York. She just fakes the missing senses as best she can. But with each new Disappearance, it's becoming harder to do that."

Ahead of us is a tall stone wall covered with moss and ivy. The wall seems higher as we near until it rises above my head, and I suddenly hope that Will doesn't expect me to climb it. I could do it. But I would prefer not to in my school skirt.

Instead Will steps forward and parts the ivy on the wall. There is gray graffiti scrawled next to the rusted hinges of a door, and I can hear the low murmur of voices beyond it. Will turns the handle, and we step over the threshold.

"William!" A large man is standing just inside, apparently acting as some sort of guard. He takes Will's hand and shakes it heartily.

Then, seeing me behind him, he gives Will a strange, questioning look.

"She's with me" is all Will has to say, and the man steps back to let us pass.

We enter the courtyard of an open-air market. The boughs of the trees overhead form a sort of thatched roof. Wooden booths line a path leading up to what must have once been a stately house.

"It's big," I whisper to Will.

"There's just one Market for all three Sister Cities, and it's only open a few days a week. Now stay close with me," he says.

I hurry behind him on the path, resisting the urge to reach forward and catch his hand.

The Market is in perpetual twilight under the tree branches, but the booths and pathway are lit by stakes in the ground, glittering with something bright that isn't quite fire. "Glimmer Variants," Will explains when he sees me looking at them.

There are pouches and glass bottles shimmering in rows along the booths. The Variant names are spelled out in signs made from a mosaic of tiles. We pass a table of Variant-infused bars of soap, and I catch the faintest scent of lilac. A woman bends to smell one of the bars, a crisp slice of white tied with a lavender ribbon, and I want to reach out and touch it. Bring it up to my nose to breathe in deeply. Instead I keep walking to stay close by Will.

A handful of Variants are dashed out on the next table in samples. When a breeze parts the branches, the Variants catch the sunlight. They glitter like diamonds against the rough grain of the wood.

We climb the stairs into the ruins of the house. Part of the back wall has crumbled in on itself, and the second floor looks particularly unstable. But the floors are swept, and the rows of booths and vendors bring a certain a sense of order. I have the strangest sense of being both inside and outdoors, with vines and weeds curling in to knit along the walls in patterns of lace, and Glimmer Variants lighting the room from rusted sconces. Will leads me through a narrow hallway to a large room with tattered wallpaper covered in lichen. I can feel the pricks of notice, of subtle gazes and more blatant interest that is not altogether friendly. I am the outsider who doesn't belong here. The ghost of my mother, returning to Sterling after all these years.

I stay as close to Will as I dare, noticing that *he* seems to set people at ease. Some people ignore us entirely, but many smile at him. Dip their heads at the sight of his handsome, familiar face.

"We'll come back when you're Of Age," Will says under his breath, as if that's all it is. "Technically, you shouldn't be here until then."

Light is filtering in through the tree needles and the glassless windows. The room has three polished wooden tables, one of them with a large crack along its center. The sign on the first table reads NIGHT VISION, the second MIND'S EYE, and the last VEIL.

The Night Vision Variants are dark and look cool to the touch, like black sand. They are displayed in thick velvet pouches lined with jet-black stones, while the Mind's Eye Variants are a mix of silver and pinkish gray, the same shifting color as the inside of a shell. The thick, pearly liquid is packaged in glass vials shaped like miniature globes.

Will picks up a brown suede pouch of Veil Variants, shows the merchant his Of Age card, and hands over three gold coins that are not a currency I've ever seen before. I'm still thinking of what he said. About people feeling trapped. About the walls closing in on them, a little bit closer, every seven years.

"But the Variants," I say hopefully, reaching out to nudge one of the pouches. "Those help."

"The Variants do help," Will agrees. The merchant pockets Will's coins, and we move on. "But they only work within the Sister Cities. Once we leave the borders, they become about as useful as throwing a handful of sand. As far as I know, in all three towns, there's only been one person who was ever able to really escape the Disappearances . . ." He trails off. Clears his throat.

And I understand.

Mother. She was the only exception.

Why?

I remember her standing in her garden with her eyes closed, inhaling the air perfumed by flowers long after the rest of us grew bored and went on to other things. She'd often be out there when I woke, bent over the flowers in her galoshes, one of Father's sweaters pulled over her nightgown, her hair wild and unkempt. She cut the flowers in bunches for the chipped vase on the kitchen table, for the end table next to her bed. She dried petals between the pages of heavy books to make potpourri for little china bowls and sachets for our drawers. Why hadn't I stayed there with her, gathering bouquets of wildflowers as long as she wanted? Maybe then she would have opened up, let me glimpse this part of her life.

We move into the next room, and Will stops at a booth organized with small wooden boxes. He slides one open to reveal a rainbow array of pencils.

"For Miles," he says. He leaves two silver coins on the table in exchange for the pencil box.

"Just need one final thing," Will says, and we make our way out to the back of the house. Outside, a woman with smoke-streaked hair sits next to a man glass blowing new vials in various colors and shapes. Occasionally she bends forward to stir a small vat of steaming clear liquid tinged with amber.

"Hey-o, Viv," Will says to the woman. "Aila, do you still have the petals I gave you?"

"Yes." I open my hand. They are slightly wrinkled from my palm, but intact.

"Toss them in there."

I unfold my hand so that the blooms fall into the vat. With a crackling noise they crystallize into thin disks and float to the surface.

Viv ladles the blossoms out and threads them onto a silver strand. Will slides the first petal from the necklace and pops it into his mouth, then hands it to me to do the same. It's lighter than a snowflake on my tongue. A soft sweetness spreads out onto my lips.

"Is it some sort of Variant magic?" I ask, and he throws back his head and laughs.

"No, dear," Viv says. "Not magic. Just maple sap."

Will reaches into his pocket for another coin, but Viv waves him off.

"I heard your father's looking for a stars Variant," she says to Will. "My youngest's to be married in May. Has her heart set on dusk and lanterns and a tent and all that. Think he could find it by then?"

"For Mel's wedding?" Will asks. "I'll ask him to try extra hard."

Viv winks and tosses him another flower necklace.

Will's words land like burning embers in my ears. I can hardly hide my surprise as we turn to leave the Market.

"*Your father* discovered the Variants?"

I'd known vaguely that Dr. Cliffton was some sort of scientist, and I'd never thought to ask more than that. There had been too many other unanswered questions coming first.

"Yes. Most of them," Will says. The way he reaches up to touch the shaved part at the back of his neck lets me know that this makes him proud.

"Goodbye, Will," the guard says, clapping Will on the back as he opens the wall door. The door closes, and the ivy falls back into place behind us. And now I understand why there are so many smiles and nods of acknowledgment in Will's direction. Why the ladies in town with Mrs. Cliffton hadn't pressed too hard about her Variant infringement.

Because the Clifftons are the ones who have offered Sterling the chance to regain a part of what they've lost — one shattered, glittering piece at a time.

The sun has sunk a hand's width deeper by the time we pick through the forest and reach the main road. I don't want to tell Will what I'm thinking. Where will this end? How many more tables of Variants will be added over the years of his life?

Genevieve will be preparing dinner by now, and we should be getting home. But there's one more thing I want to see.

"Will," I say, "did my mother live anywhere near here?"

"Um, yes." We cross a wooden bridge, the water running

underneath our steps. "But I think the house might have burned a long time ago."

"Can you show me anyway—" I hesitate. "I want to see it."

He weighs this for a moment and then nods. We quicken our pace, turning off the main road and walking for a few minutes more until the burned husk of a house appears. My feet ache, and strands of my hair have come loose to whip in front of my face.

As we draw nearer, I start to wish we hadn't come. Dried, burnt cornstalks have grown tall around the foundation of the house to form an endless patterned wall that is eerily still. Broken glass bottles and cigarette butts are ground into the dirt. What remains of the house are only the gutted slabs of two walls, gaping holes of blown-out windows, and the rubble of a brick chimney. The foundation fades into the dirt in a mix of debris, ash, and clumps of decaying wet leaves.

I stop, and Will stands next to me, our shoulders almost touching, as I take in a word scrawled in graffiti on the charred remains of the house and etched over and over in the dirt under our feet.

"What does it mean?" I ask softly, toeing it with my mud-speckled boot. *"Catalyst?"*

Will exhales, as if he wishes he hadn't brought me.

"The Disappearances are so ordered that something had to happen to set them off, right? Something, or . . . someone," he says. "No one knows what happened, or why. So we just call whatever triggered it the Catalyst."

I stiffen.

He takes a deep breath. "If we can figure out who or what is to blame, we'll be a step closer to figuring out how to fix it."

I rub out a drawing of an hourglass with my toe. "Do people really think it's something intentional? Like a curse?"

"Some do," he says. "But it's all wild theories and finger-pointing, and it always has been." He picks up a glass bottle at his feet, knocks it against his palm. Then he suddenly hurls it away from us, into the cornstalks. "Because if you look hard enough, you can find a reason to suspect almost anyone."

Wind rustles the cornstalks in a wave around us, and I shiver. I think again of Mother's book, of the strange markings within it.

"One more thing," I say as we turn to go. "The Disappearances—do they have anything to do with Shakespeare?"

The look he gives me is genuine bewilderment. "Shakespeare?"

"Never mind." I shrug and give him a half smile to hide my suspicions and how much it hurts to see Mother's home burned and scrawled over with slanders. I'm learning that I'm actually quite good at hiding things.

I am my mother's daughter, after all.

CHAPTER TWELVE

Date: 2/28/1941

Bird: Jackdaw

Jackdaws are unusual in that they will often share their own food with others.

Known to steal jewelry and other shiny things to collect in their nests.

Sometimes considered to be an omen of death.

Phineas doesn't have any money.

At first I just chalk it up to his moods, which wax and wane like the moon. The way Phineas barks when I spill the milk. Drags his feet to replace burnt-out light bulbs. The way the phone jangles shrilly and his smile warps. "Don't pick it up."

Then he starts to cough. It's as though the telephone calls make it worse. "You know, you think you can repay your past mistakes," he says, hacking into one of his pristine handkerchiefs. "But you never can. That debt will just keep growing. Like mold. Until you can't breathe."

"Do you owe someone something?" I ask.

He just shakes his head. "It was a long time ago."

The sharp knock comes two days later. I'm prying off the old battens of the porch screens when I hear Phineas swear, then open the door. I grab my pocketknife and walk toward the kitchen.

An unfamiliar voice. "I've come to collect, Phineas."

I stand in the shadows and hold my breath. "I paid your father back, Victor," Phineas says. "Every penny."

"Yes, of the original loan. But not the interest we lost while you were in the clink. It's nothing personal, Phineas," the voice says. "Just business."

I click open the pocketknife. Then I flick it shut and stride into the kitchen.

"I'll get it," I say to the man. He has wispy black hair, a small beard and a pointed chin that make him sort of resemble a mouse, and small, blazing eyes that seem to be almost entirely iris. "Don't bother him anymore. He's dead broke. I'm the one you should concern yourself with. Stefen Shaw." I thrust out my hand.

Phineas glares. Takes a cut of gristly meat from the icebox and unwraps it, muttering, at the counter.

"Victor Larkin," the man says, taking my grip. He keeps shaking my hand, hard, even after I try to let go.

"Don't be a damn fool, Stefen," Phineas says.

"I'll get it," I repeat to Victor Larkin. We make arrangements for the first installment, and then I firmly escort him to the door.

Phineas lights the gas stove, his back turned to me. "Where's that money going to come from, Stefen?"

"You're going to teach me your old trade." I look at his fingers, bloody from the meat. "I told you, I've always been good with my hands."

Phineas sighs and turns the flame up as high as it goes.

"I don't like it," he says, but he throws the meat on to sizzle, and the decision is made. I will follow in my father's footsteps.

Learn the art of robbing a grave.

CHAPTER THIRTEEN

On Monday morning George stands in the hallway, examining the school notice board.

He greets me by asking, "So what are you going to do for the Sisters Tournament?"

Though the sign-up sheet appeared only this morning, it is already littered with signatures. He studies the list of events, running his fingers over his dirty-blond hair. The cuffs of his pants are stuck with dried pieces of grass.

"There's a new category this year," he says. "And I'm going to win it." He picks up the pen and writes his name under "Variant Innovation." Then he tips the pen toward me.

I shift my bag to my other shoulder.

"No thanks," I say. "I think being a new student in a new school and making all new friends in an odd new town is about enough for me this year."

"Aw, don't be a wet blanket," he says. "Everyone does something. If you don't, prepare to face the wrath of Principal Cleary. Maybe he'll paint a portrait of himself lecturing you on the values of school spirit." He pushes the pen at me again.

I study the list of categories. There are close to twenty, including everything from fencing to equestrianism. "What are Stars?"

"They're Throwing Stars. Kind of like darts," George says. "Corrander usually dominates that one, so no one from Sterling ever signs up."

"Huh," I say. Will is signed up for the soccer portion of the tournament. And then I notice Eliza Patton's name on the board. It appears she's signed up for three separate events.

"Come on, the tournament's not until spring. You'll be all well-adjusted by then." George elbows my arm.

Or maybe the war will have ended, I think, *and I won't even be here anymore.*

"We should get to class," I say, setting the pen back up on the rim of the notice board. The space next to my name remains blank.

Later that day I face the wall of the girls' locker room and dutifully pull my gym uniform over my head. It is made of gauzy material the color of dust bunnies. I wince and try to pull the wrinkles to fall into a more flattering shape.

Normally, we're separated from the boys during fitness class, but today they are lined up against the painted bricks of the back wall. George stands at the front of it, his knobby knees peeking out from under his shorts. He waves me over.

"So, for that tournament—" I say. I lean against the wall next to him, folding my arms to cover myself. "Sterling competes against the other Sister Cities?"

"Yes." George cracks his knuckles in succession, fidgeting, as if he's overly aware that he doesn't quite fill out his uniform. "It takes place over three days. Your town gets points with every first place, second place, or third place in the events, and whoever has the most collective points at the end gets to host the Harvest Fair the next year."

"I guess that sounds fun."

"At first it was. Now people have started taking it real seriously. Principal Cleary always acts as though his very job hangs in the balance."

I make a face.

"I know." George grins. "He should rethink his motivation strategy."

Mrs. Percy, the girls' gym teacher, bursts through the door and claps her hands. "Hello, everyone. You're here together today because you'll need one another to learn a new skill."

"No." George's hands grow even more frenetic. "It better not be waltzing. I thought that was just a rumor."

"You're going to learn how to waltz!" Mrs. Percy beams at us, as if she's expecting us to applaud. "By the time this year's Christmas Ball rolls around, you should be able to dance Viennese and Hesitation waltzes like professionals," she continues. "Now — as there are so many of you and only one of me, I've arranged for a particular treat this year. Some of your more senior classmates have agreed to come today and give you a demonstration."

All the blood in my body rushes to my face. I tug again at the folds of my uniform while trying to hide behind George. *Please, please,* I think, *don't let the instructing student be William.*

When the door opens, I'm relieved only for a moment. Because the alternative isn't much better.

Eliza strides through the door, and George immediately stands straighter at the sight of her. She's in the pleated skirt and starched, crisp white blouse of the school uniform. Next to the masses of our lumpy gray gym outfits, she practically glows. Following her is Chase Peterson.

"Mr. Peterson, Miss Patton, why don't you give the class a demonstration of what their end goal looks like?" Mrs. Percy says. She sashays over to the stereo and sets a record spinning until the notes curl out from it in ribbons. Chase extends his hand to Eliza, and they begin to glide across the floor in three-step counts.

"One, two, three; one, two, three," Mrs. Percy dictates. "Gentlemen, look at how Chase leads. *Excellent* form, Eliza. Ladies, see the posture of her back?"

"What do you know about her?" I whisper to George.

"Eliza? The 'Face of Sterling'?" George cracks his knuckles again. "She's a Patton. Rich as anyone — even the Clifftons. She and Will have been friends since they were little. Everyone's always thought it was inevitable they'd end up together."

I try to pretend that this doesn't make my heart suddenly plummet like a stone.

I'm paired to practice with Chase, and it sinks even lower.

"Hello, Will's little houseguest." Chase's hand finds my waist. A mole lurks under the dark stubble on his shaved head. His teeth are white and straight, but his smile is more like a smirk.

When I don't respond, he guides us through the strand of dancing students to where Eliza has been paired with George. I'm not sure how he can talk and dance at the same time. I'm using all my concentration to count steps in my head and avoid landing on him. "I saw your mother last weekend," Chase says to Eliza when we approach. "She's gracing you with her presence this week?"

Eliza shrugs. "Not to worry," she says, sounding bored. "She's off again tomorrow."

"Is she coming back before Disappearance Day? Or staying clear of all the . . . unpleasantness?" His eyes glitter at her, and she narrows hers back at him, as if she's trying to unearth another layer of meaning behind his words.

"Aren't we curious today?" she says, moving George's arm to a different angle, her voice becoming icy and prim. "She might be back. She might not. She's attending an auction. And my sister has a performance."

She sniffs. I'm trying not to look at her skin. It is dewy and creamy and looks as if it has never seen a blemish. Meanwhile, I can feel a pimple preparing to make yet another appearance on the left side of my chin.

"Ouch!" Eliza cries, jumping back. George's latest step has landed on her foot. "Oh, good." She yanks George's arm back into the proper dancing position. "It's not as though I needed those toes anyway."

Chase's sudden laugh sounds like glass breaking. Freckles burn across George's face.

And then Chase turns his attention to me.

"So, new girl. What's Cliffton like at home?" he asks. "Do you stay up late drinking Shirley Temples and painting each other's nails?"

George's embarrassment still lingers, heating the air around us. It infuriates me that we're both being batted back and forth between Eliza and Chase like pathetic little mice.

"Actually, Will prefers to pour cocktails while I teach him how to French . . ." I say. Chase's mouth drops open. *"Braid,"* I add sweetly. I send Eliza a look that I hope says *You do not scare me.*

Chase lets out a short whistle. "This one's got some moxie, doesn't she?"

Eliza narrows her eyes and looks me up and down. As if she's miscalculated and is now reevaluating me.

Chase's hand drops a degree lower on my back.

"So, Aila," Eliza says eventually, cocking her head, "there was *no one else* willing to take you in but the Clifftons?" Her voice takes on an exaggerated incredulity. She tuts. "Isn't it sad how history repeats itself."

My breath comes a bit faster, and I stop myself just in time from tripping over Chase's feet. I'm not quite sure what Eliza is getting at. Which gives me a growing sense of dread.

"Whatever do you mean?" Chase plays along.

"Hey Eliza—" George says, valiantly trying to change the subject.

Eliza ignores him. "Don't you know?" she says to Chase. It's as if George and I aren't even there. "Her mother was an orphan. She didn't have anywhere else to go, either, so Eleanor Cummings took her in."

Eliza's words land like stingers, throbbing on their marks.

"You don't know what you're saying," I answer sharply. I falter on the dance steps again and push Chase's hand away. "My mother wasn't an orphan."

Eliza's jade eyes widen. A short laugh of disbelief cracks her perfect rosy lips.

"She didn't tell you?" She seems genuinely surprised. *She's lying,* I think. My mother would have told me something that important about herself.

A cruel voice inside my head mocks: *Like she did about everything else?*

"Next thing you know, she'll say she's never heard her mother was the Catalyst," Eliza says under her breath.

"All right—" George says at the same time that Chase says,

"Bold words from a *Patton*," but Mrs. Percy has stopped the music and is walking toward us.

"Wasn't that helpful?" she chirps. "Let's thank the upperclassmen for joining us today. We can learn so much from those who have gone before us."

"It's always *such* a pleasure," Eliza says, raising an eyebrow. "I love teaching people things they never knew before." With a final wave, she and Chase leave, buoyed by the applause of the class.

Something acidic is rising in my throat. I gulp down a breath, trying to pull out the seeds Eliza has left scattered behind her.

But I can already feel them sprouting as I practice steps with George for the rest of class. "Don't listen to her," George says, attempting to cheer me with spot-on impressions of Principal Cleary. I smile weakly at him, but by the time gym is over, Eliza's seeds have sprouted roots and split into branches: one of doubt, the other of bitterness. For Mother. For Eliza.

For me and my endless naïveté.

I am standing in front of the tournament sheet when George catches up to me. He wisely doesn't say anything about the tears running down my cheeks. I dab at them angrily with the heels of my hands.

Aila Quinn, I write at the bottom of the list under "Stars."

CHAPTER FOURTEEN

That night at dinner Miles and I are both quiet. We push the food around on our plates and give such halfhearted answers that soon Mrs. Cliffton stops attempting to draw us out. Will stayed late at the library to work on a group project, so he is not there to fill our gaping silences. I find myself wondering when he will be back. And if Eliza is there, too.

"Well, I have some work to catch up on anyway," Dr. Cliffton says in response to our silence. "Maybe we'll hold game night tomorrow." So we each retire to our rooms as soon as dinner is over.

I brush my teeth in front of the blank wall, thinking about Miles's silence at dinner and wondering if someone at school has gotten to him, too. I throw on my bathrobe, tie the sash firmly around my waist, and head down the hallway to rap on his door.

"Who is it?" he calls.

"It's me. Can I come in?" When he doesn't answer, I push the door open anyway.

He is sitting on the floor, drawing.

"Is . . . everything okay?" I close the door behind me.

"Yeah."

The tip of his pencil is flaming orange, but the lines that appear beneath it are nothing but a sooty gray. He keeps drawing more lines, as if the color will start seeping out after a rusty start.

He tosses the orange and pulls out a deep teal, the one he always uses for the ocean or mixes with gray when he's drawing my eyes. It leaves a smear down the page as dingy as old, dirty snow. The red pencil yields something more like smoke.

"Those aren't the ones Will bought for you at the Marketplace, are they?"

He shakes his head. "No. These are from home." He reaches his hand under the bed and retrieves a wooden box. "These are the new ones." He opens them and pulls out a red. He uses his old pencils to draw the stick figure of a girl, then opens the new one and gives her deep red hair. Mother's hair. The Variant pencils are brighter than I ever remember the original colors being.

"You want to talk?" I ask.

He shakes his head again.

"Okay. Come find me if you change your mind."

He doesn't look up. "'Night." He's returned to his old pencils, drawing streaks of gray over and over across the page.

But it's Miles's knocking that wakes me in the morning.

"Come in," I call groggily, not moving from the warmth of my bed.

He slips through the door, then stands next to it, squirming.

I squint toward him. "Do you need to go to the bathroom or something?"

He ignores this. "Do I have to go to school today?"

"Of course. Don't be silly." I flip the pillow over to find the side not heated by my skin. But I look up at the sound of his sigh and catch the flicker of something in his face.

"Come here, Miles." I sit up and pat the bed beside me. "Why don't you want to go to school today?"

He sighs again, his small shoulders raising and falling. Sleep is crusted at the edge of his eyelashes. "Some kids say things about Mother," he says, scowling. "That she was a witch and she's the reason things are bad here."

I pull my hair up into a knot, not bothering to hide my ear from Miles. "Yes," I finally admit. "People say things to me, too. But you know it's not true, right, Miles?"

I think of Eliza's confident smugness about Mother being an orphan.

At least probably not everything *they say is true.*

He shrugs, but his shoulders lose some of their angled stiffness.

"That's all that matters," I continue. "We knew her. They didn't. So what they say doesn't count. Not even a little bit."

He does something strange with his mouth, twisting his tongue all around while he considers this. There's a gap where a tooth should be.

"Heya!" I say. "Did you lose something?"

He reaches into his pocket, and then the white stump of a tooth is nestled in his palm.

"It came out last night," he says. "I woke up, and it was in my mouth. I almost choked on it."

"Yuck." I wrinkle my nose. And then he laughs.

"Aila?" He starts to squirm again. "Mrs. Cliffton says nobody is supposed to have dreams." He rolls the kernel of tooth in his hand. "But last night, I had one."

I keep my face blank, but my stomach rolls. Will's words return to whisper in my ears. *Your mother was different than everyone else.*

I bite down on my lip.

"What was the dream about?" I ask, to buy myself more time.

"It was a nightmare," he admits. "It's going to sound embarrassing when I say it out loud. I don't even know why it scared me."

"I used to have night terrors about a black cat that wore jewelry," I say. "So . . . proceed."

"There was a little bird," he says, "and I knew that it was sick. It was living in a dark room all day long, with the curtains closed. And there was a beautiful, healthy little bird there, too, who flew in and out. But the sick bird hated the healthy one. And then they switched places, and the healthy one died in the bed, and the sick one grew stronger and came to our front door, and—" He reddens. "I don't know why, but it made me afraid."

"I'm sorry," I say. "I'm glad you told me." I give him a half squeeze, half pat on the shoulder—not quite a hug. "But don't tell anyone else about it yet, Miles. You and I will figure it out."

"I know *that*. I'm not a dunce." He pauses. "And I'm not supposed to say anything about the Disappearances to Father?"

"Just for a little longer," I say. "It's too difficult to explain in a letter. And we don't want him to worry. We'll tell him one day."

Miles actually turns and grins at me then. His cowlick sticks up. His smile is less familiar because of the gap left by his tooth. "It's not that hard, is it?" he says. "Pretending?"

"No," I agree.

Pretending is the finishing word.

Pretending is a better word than *lying*.

When he leaves, I dress, fighting against the strangest wave of jealousy. I haven't dreamed for as long as we've been in Sterling. Does this mean that Miles, like Mother, is different somehow?

And, I think, tucking Mother's necklace under my collar, *does it mean that I'm not?*

"Where's Dr. Cliffton?" I ask over breakfast.

"Malcolm's spending the day at a museum in Cheshire to research the stars Variant," Mrs. Cliffton says, pouring herself a cup of coffee. "He wanted to get an early start, and I doubt we should expect him before dinnertime." She glances at the clock. "The rest of us should get going."

Miles and Will follow her out to the car, and I'm a step behind them. When I reach the foyer, I pause at the cracked door of Dr. Cliffton's library.

What was it Chase said to Eliza in the gym? She'd accused Mother of being the Catalyst, and he'd said *Bold words, from a Patton.*

I've made the decision before I can second-guess myself—I dash into the library, open the bottom drawer, and take out the history of Sterling. I slide off the cover of my biology textbook and put Dr. Cliffton's book inside it. It's a perfect decoy, and I head out to the car with the book, and my hope, secreted away in my bag.

CHAPTER FIFTEEN

Morning, Beas," I say when I arrive for Digby's lab. She is still half asleep, examining a sheet of paper filled with lines of her own music. I can tell by the occasional tilt of her chin that the notes are playing in her head. George stands at the chalkboard. His neat, tight writing details our findings from yesterday's experiment.

Thankfully, it seems my classmates are not watching my every move anymore. My intrigue as the new girl is beginning to wear off. I fish the book from my bag and find the index again, shielding the pages at an angle only I can see.

First I look up Mother. She warrants only a small paragraph midway through the book. Behind the safety of my hair I examine her picture. Her large gray eyes are the same as mine but with a glint of playful mischief that is more Miles. I take in her clear skin, glowing with youth, her pointed chin and high cheekbones. Her picture bursts from the page, but the accompanying text is spare.

> Juliet Cummings, orphaned at birth and raised by Eleanor Cummings, is the only citizen of a Sister City who has been able to regain her senses upon leaving. On March 20, 1925, she arrived in Sterling declaring that her senses had returned outside the town's borders. Trailing a hopeful crowd behind her like the Pied Piper, Juliet led them to a lake just beyond Sterling and pointed.
>
> The only face the water reflected back was hers.

Juliet was unable to offer any explanation, and the town was divided over whether she was genuinely surprised or had plotted some form of cruel trick. Tempers flared. She fled the town shortly thereafter, never to be seen again . . .

Whispers remain in her wake, and the biggest mystery is still unsolved: how Miss Cummings managed to overcome the Disappearances — only to then all but disappear herself.

I sink my teeth into the soft wood of my pencil and hurriedly turn to the index. I trace down the list of names again until I find "Patton, pages 3, 9, 54–56."

On page 54, a black-and-white photograph of a woman looks back at me with the proud stare of an aristocrat. The caption identifies her as "Victoria Antoinette Patton." With her pinched lips and high cheekbones, the woman resembles Eliza, except that her fierce gaze is softened by delicate webbed lines at the corners of her eyes. The taste of hot metal returns to coat the inside of my mouth. I suck on my cheek and begin to read:

THE PATTON POSSIBILITY
The Patton family boasts a long and illustrious history in Sterling. In addition to being one of the original founding families, the Pattons are known as dedicated patrons of the arts — something truly exceptional for a town of Sterling's size.

I roll my eyes. Did the Pattons write this book themselves?

Notably, Victoria Patton (pictured) spent her lifetime acquiring the most famous of the Patton family's collections, including some of the first-known hieroglyphics, an Egyptian sarcophagus, and two golden goblets reportedly dating back to ancient Babylon. Clara Patton, her daughter, plans to orchestrate a tour for these pieces to be shown to the outside world on a rotating basis.

But one piece will be notably absent. The most infamous one of all — the one some believe might have instigated the Disappearances. The Blooming Sapphire.

I straighten. My heartbeat flares.

The Blooming Sapphire, a tiara encrusted with diamonds and sapphires in the shape of a lotus flower, is a piece the Pattons sought for decades to complete their prized collection of Russian jewels.

However, in 1905 the piece wound up in the hands of a family from Corrander by the name of Rabe. After several months of negotiations, Victoria Patton brokered a deal to trade the Blooming Sapphire for something that had great sentimental significance to the Rabes: a garden of glass flowers, crafted centuries ago by their distant ancestors.

The deal went off without a hitch — until three months later, when the Rabes discovered that while a select few of the flowers were genuine, many had been faked.

The fallout was immediate. The enraged Rabes demanded that the Blooming Sapphire tiara be returned.

The Pattons argued that they purchased the glass flower garden for a hefty sum specifically to facilitate the exchange. They put the Blooming Sapphire under lock and key. Several months of mounting frustration, accusations, and aggression followed, until the Rabes became so angry that they left

Corrander forever. They have not been seen or heard from since.

The proximity of this event to the first Disappearance has led many to believe it is the Catalyst for the landslide of troubles that followed. The Rabes were always an unusual family, and there were whispers of their dabbling in dark arts. But perhaps the most incriminating element of this theory is a look at the Rabes' fascination with the glass flower garden. A near-perfect imitation of nature, the flowers are said to be so realistic that the only way a human being can tell that they are not real is by their missing scent.

An interesting coincidence, to be sure . . .

Dr. Digby walks into the room just as I return the book to my bag. I can't help but grin. Everything is starting to make so much more sense now. Why Eliza took to hating me so easily. It is about Will—but not entirely. To hate me is to deflect blame from her own family.

"So . . ." I say as casually as I can to Beas. The opening bell rings out through the halls, and Dr. Digby shuts the door. "You're friends with Eliza Patton?"

"Mmmhmm," Beas says absently. She clenches her pencil between her teeth, still looking over her music.

"That's interesting."

She raises her eyebrows. "What do you mean?"

"I guess I'm just a little surprised."

Beas takes a deep breath and removes the pencil from her mouth. "Sorry, Aila. Keep me out of it," she says simply. "I'm not interested in being caught in the middle. I know Eliza can be ridiculous sometimes, but we've been friends since kindergarten. And you'll learn that if there's one thing I value, it's loyalty."

I purse my lips and scratch at a freckle on my arm. "Of course." A dull flush begins to creep up my neck. "You've known her forever. I wasn't trying to make it about choosing sides," I add hurriedly. "It just seems like somehow I've already wound up on Eliza's bad one."

Beas fills in the empty oval of a note. "Yes," she concedes. "Being on Eliza's good side is the safest place to be. And I don't think you'll be getting there anytime soon." She pauses. "Not as long as you're sleeping down the hall from Will, anyway."

Or as long as Mother can be used to draw any blame away from Eliza's family. The Pattons must have found it very convenient that their scapegoat could no longer defend herself.

That is, until Miles and I showed up.

I bend toward the wall, curving away from Beas. When I've finished writing, I tap Beas's foot under the table, drawing up the hem of my skirt.

My guest, if aught amiss were said, I've written along the top of my knee, *forgive it and dismiss it from your head.*

Beas reads the scrawled words of my Stevenson quote and lowers her face so Dr. Digby can't see her amusement.

"I knew I liked you," she says, and goes back to drawing a symphony of notes across her page.

When we return home after school that afternoon, Dr. Cliffton's car is parked in the driveway.

And his book is still in my bag. My stomach drops.

"Want to study together?" Will asks, and we push open the door to Dr. Cliffton's library. Will sinks into the plush leather armchair. I sit on the floor and lean my back against the paisley loveseat, watching the sun cast shadows across the rug and my knee. Trying desperately to think of a way to get him to leave.

"Aren't you supposed to be working your apprenticeship with Tuck today?" I ask.

"He's meeting with Cleary about a stage for the Harvest Fair."

The Harvest Fair. Sterling's polite euphemism for Disappearance Day.

Will opens his notebook. "Twenty days left," he says, staring out the window.

The resignation in his voice reminds me of when Mother was ill and we were starting to grasp that she might not get better. I understand how Sterling feels, straining against a countdown it can't escape. Watching the time run out, then being forcibly turned upside down and reset.

To distract us both, I stand and fiddle with the knobs on the radio, adjusting the settings until Judy Garland's voice fills the room. She barely masks the sound of Dr. Cliffton's shuffling walk, his weight against the cane. I start to squirm. My bag lies on its side on the rug, not three steps from our feet.

Will's dark eyebrows raise as his father enters the library. "Well? Did you have success?" he asks.

"Success in that I've determined a few more things that *won't* bring the stars back," Dr. Cliffton says, and smiles good-naturedly. He pushes his glasses from where they've fallen down his nose. "But I'm afraid I'm still as stumped as ever on this one." My apprehension grows as he makes his way, slowly, to his desk.

He opens the first drawer, then the second, as if he's searching for something. My stomach knots. Why didn't I leave the book there? What happens when he realizes it's missing and then it turns up in my bag? I edge back to my seat and pull out my homework.

His hand moves to the final drawer.

"Dr. Cliffton!" I blurt out, scattering my papers to the floor. "Would you tell me how you invented the first Variants?"

Dr. Cliffton releases the drawer handle and straightens. His eyes light with interest. "You'd like to hear the story about the discovery day?"

Will puts his feet up on the ottoman. "My guess is she wants the *abridged* version," he says, his mouth twisting.

Dr. Cliffton places his glasses back on the bridge of his nose and gives us a wry look. "The abridged version? I'll do my best." I sigh in relief as he turns to examine the row of books closest to his desk and pulls out a large volume called *An Encyclopedia of Herbs, Spices, and Botanical Cures* from the shelf. I've bought myself a little more time.

Dr. Cliffton brings the book to his desk and splits open the pages like an axe falling into wood. I abandon my homework and rise to get a better look. The image he navigates to is not what I was expecting: it is a spindly, ugly little flower with straggly green leaves and a puffed head of spikes in a bright magenta.

"Unassuming, isn't it?" Dr. Cliffton asks, as if he were reading my mind. He clears his throat. "I stumbled upon the Variants quite by accident. I was in high school at the time. Matilda and Juliet and I were in the library one day, studying, and during our short breaks I often found myself looking through the plant encyclope-dias—"

Will gives a short laugh and unfurls his legs. He comes to stand next to me. "In case you were wondering, Aila," he says, "that means he was reading an encyclopedia *for fun.*"

"I suppose we can thank polio for ruining any chances I had at athletic interests," Dr. Cliffton says, but his voice is entirely void of bitterness. "Otherwise I might not have found the encyclopedia to be my idea of a good time. And perhaps," he says, "I might never have found the Variants at all." He touches his neck in the exact way Will does.

"Now, Aila, I was getting closer, but I was still on the wrong path," he continues. "I was intrigued by a plant I'd found called kesidang. Its common name is bread flower because of the aroma it gives off in bloom. I was researching how I might acquire its seedlings.

"But my sister Marjorie found me in the library that day. She was growing concerned about our mother, who had taken ill weeks earlier and never regained her appetite. Marjorie wondered if I had any ideas for getting her to eat. Because I had the encyclopedia open, I happened to stumble upon this."

He taps the page. "Holy thistle. Also called blessed thistle, or God's cure-all, because it treated all sorts of maladies even back to the Middle Ages. It was used in poultices and as an astringent, prescribed to aid digestion, lactation, even fight the plague. And naturally, it can be used as an appetite stimulant.

"I suggested it to my sister. 'But where will we find thistle this time of year?' she asked.

"Juliet said she could get us some. The next day, there she was, bearing a pouch spilling over with thistle birdseed."

He laughs. "Of course I couldn't very well serve my poor ailing mother a cup of birdseed. So I took it to my mortar and pestle."

He gestures to a stone bowl perched at the corner of his desk. I'd always been so busy looking for the Sterling book that I thought it was a paperweight. But now I realize it's a mortar and pestle, hewn from rough, speckled granite and engraved with five words: "To seek . . . always to seek."

"I ground the thistle into dust so fine I could sprinkle it over my mother's food. At that point she was eating nothing but bread and water." Dr. Cliffton's eyes are shining and far away, as if he is about to make the discovery all over again. "Well, how do you describe what it is like to smell something—anything—for the very first time? The water, of course, didn't smell like anything. But the bread . . ." He trails off. "It smelled like it had just been baked in the oven, warm and soft, and it reached my mother's room before I did. She was sitting up in bed by the time I came in, and she kept smiling and lifting the bread to her face until I finally made her eat it. She swore up and down that the Variant version was even better than what was in her memory."

I touch the coarse, round neck of the pestle. "So that was it? You ground thistle, and it somehow unlocked all the scents?"

"Unlocked the scents," he repeats. "I like that." His blue eyes twinkle behind his glasses at my expression. "This story isn't what you expected? You were hoping for something magical?"

"Well, maybe . . ." I admit. "Something a bit more like magic."

"So, perhaps it is," he says. "After all, what is magic? Just a term we use for the unexpected, resulting from the right elements in combination. Perhaps you've only thought of it as the correct words in a spell, or mixture of ingredients in a pot."

I think of my mother's Shakespeare book. " 'Double, double, toil and trouble,' " I say, and smile.

"But really, aren't there bits of magic everywhere we look?" Dr. Cliffton continues. "We've just stopped seeing it that way."

I hesitate. "I'm not sure I know what you mean."

"I mean—cake," he says wryly. "Why does the perfect combination of ingredients put together at just the right temperature become a fluffy, airy cake? Why do water molecules sometimes turn into flakes of snow and sometimes rocks of hail? Why is it that two people coming together in love can create life"—I blush and avoid looking at Will—"and yet the volatile combination of another two can end it?"

He closes the book. "So, yes. When just the right things come together, there is always a bit of magic. And when just the wrong combination of things do . . ."

"There is tragedy," I finish softly.

"But you didn't even tell her the best part of the story," Will cuts in, leaning the weight of his arms on the desk. He turns to me. "After my father discovered the first Variant, he went to find my mother—because even back then he carried a bit of a torch for her." He smiles. "And she was with Juliet. So the three of them crushed the rest of the thistle together and took the Variants to the bakery. Then they passed out loaves of bread to practically the entire town."

"That was very much like your mother, you know," Dr. Cliffton says. "She was always trying to help people."

My face warms, picturing Mother. Young and beautiful. Handing out the golden loaves to giddy, outstretched hands. It makes me proud that the very first Variants were created from the thistle she supplied.

Dr. Cliffton's head bends again as he flips to a page entitled "Lamiaceae Herbs," and I notice for the first time that his brown hair is pricked with gray. He points to an illustration of evergreen needles, with tiny blue flower sprigs nestled between.

"Shall I stop? Have I hit the limit of your interest? As Will is well aware, sometimes I forget that others aren't quite as fascinated by the Variants as I am—"

"No, please," I say quickly. "I like it."

The Variants. They are like Sterling's North Star: one bright spot to orient them against an ever-advancing darkness.

"These, the Mind's Eye Variants, were another stroke of luck," he says, and I can tell that he is pleased to continue. "I was actually in search of a Variant for our missing dreams. However, that one has proven to be very elusive, even to this day." He wets his fingertip to skim through the pages.

"I'd already experimented unsuccessfully with a number of things—Saint John's wort, peppermint, white periwinkle—when I stumbled across a passage on the legends of the Middle Ages. It said that people would place sprigs of rosemary under their pillows to ward against nightmares. But of course, rosemary is also associated with memory." He smiles. "I could have just looked at *Hamlet*. You'd be amazed at how many hints I've found within Shakespeare's pages."

My head shoots up, and Will looks at me. I can tell he remembers my asking about it, and he gets a funny look. "Huh," he says.

"Shakespeare?" I prod Dr. Cliffton.

"Yes," he explains. "I've found that with the Variants, most—not all, but a good portion of them—have roots in literary clues."

So another piece of the puzzle slides into place. That's what Mother's markings mean: she was looking for literary clues to help solve the Disappearances. It's exactly the sort of thing she loved. A real-life riddle. She probably saw it all as a big game.

" 'There's rosemary, that's for remembrance,' " Will says, holding the mortar and pestle in front of him like a skull. " 'Pray you, love, remember. And there is pansies, that's for thoughts.' "

"If becoming Sterling's first athletic champion woodworker doesn't pan out, you could always find work as Hamlet," I say, nudging him gently with my elbow. Then I drop my arms rigidly back to my side.

Am I *flirting* with him?

"Or Ophelia, rather," Will corrects. He grins and nudges me back when he sets the pestle down.

Is he flirting with *me?*

"It seems so obvious to me, now," Dr. Cliffton says absently. "I guess that's the way it is with most things when we are looking at them with new eyes."

He bends to his desk drawers again, and I tense. But he opens the second drawer and, reaching underneath a stack of papers, retrieves a small vial. It is round and squat, with a glass stopper.

"The very first batch of Mind's Eye I ever made," he says. He pulls the stopper and lets me peer inside at the swirling mist that is the same lacquered, shell-like color as the one I saw in the Market. "This Variant is most potent when used as a paste on the eyelids," he says. "When I discovered it, I found that I could recall the very first conversation I ever had with Matilda. I could see the blue cotton dress she had on, down to the detail that it was embroidered with white flowers on our first day at Sterling Elementary. I was able to relive the exact details of an event that had disintegrated in my memory almost thirty years ago."

My throat tightens. "On the days you find something you thought was lost forever," I say, "it must feel like bringing it back to life again."

Dr. Cliffton nods. "I think there are a lot of things in Sterling we appreciate now, more so than we ever could have before they disappeared."

I think about this, rolling it around in my mind like a marble throughout the rest of the evening. I think of it when I replace Dr. Cliffton's book in his desk drawer in the moments after everyone is called for dinner. When I slip off Mother's necklace, lay it on the nightstand, climb into bed, and pull the quilt up to my chin.

I sleep soundly until the light of the next morning nudges me awake. When I open my eyes, it takes a moment for my vision to focus.

Then I jolt up. Panic explodes in a spray of fireworks within my chest.

I reach out to my nightstand. Its surface is smooth and empty.

My mother's necklace is gone.

CHAPTER SIXTEEN

Date: 3/14/1941

Bird: Killdeer

To protect their nests from an approaching predator, killdeer will attract attention to themselves by flapping in fake distress and dragging one of their wings on the ground as if it is injured.

Once the predator has moved away from the nest, the killdeer ends the act and flies away.

Phineas doesn't start by teaching me how to rob graves. Those are messy and exposed. Instead, we start with bleach and locks.

"If cleanliness is next to godliness," he says, pouring amber glass bottles into the washtub, "then sloppiness is the fastest way to a jail cell."

He throws a soiled handkerchief into the bleach water, and we watch it turn as white as snow. Like magic. "Ten years of my life," he says. "Just disappeared because I got careless one day. So learn this first and learn it well: dirty work always requires the cleanest hands."

We spend the next week on locks. Door locks. Safe locks. Skeleton keys, hairpins, hex wrenches. Some locks take movements as small and fine as threading a needle. Others are heavy and blunt. He teaches me to turn my wrist, to apply just the right amount of torque until I hear the faint click of the pin. How to gauge entry points of houses and wrench open coffins. Which shovels to use for hard clay and which to use for loam.

"You're quick," he grunts after a particularly grueling day. His affirmation awakens an insatiable sort of hunger in me. I hadn't lied. I've always been good with my hands, and I take to Phineas's skills as naturally as claiming my birthright.

What's funny is that after a lifetime spent trying to strengthen my legs, I slip back into my old limp. People would rather avert their eyes than look at a cripple. So I shuffle on and off to my advantage, so that no one ever gets a good look at my face.

And to think that before this I'd always thought that not being seen was a bad thing.

The first woman I rob owns underwear that is silky and cold in the drawer. Behind it, predictably, is her jewelry case. Holding gold rings, a garnet brooch, an antique watch.

For once, my courage doesn't desert me. It flows through me in a rush of beating heart and nerves. But I bang my shin against the coffee table on the way out and find myself wishing for a smear of Night Vision. It is the first time I've thought of Sterling in ages.

The Variants. The Variants. My bag of loot hits against my leg in a rhythm as I walk home in the shadows. The memory of the Variants remains a nettle in my side. It had been my thistle, after all. Juliet had asked me for the birdseed, and I had given it to her without question, right out of my own stash. But no one seemed to remember that when the three of them were together, handing out the bread and warming in Sterling's adoration. I should have been up there with them.

Without me and my thistle, it's possible the Variants never would have existed.

The sun is rising by the time I reach home. Phineas calls me to the porch. I dump the contents of my bag onto the table for him to sift through. He grins at me with teeth that are growing ever more gray.

"Good," he proclaims, pawing over the loot.

A surge of pure euphoria hits me then. That I've done it. Pulled off my first job.

Phineas observes me with the hint of amusement. "Proud of yourself?"

"I'm good at it."

Phineas lights a cigar. "You come by that honestly. It's in our marrow."

His next words come out in smoke. "I miss that feeling. It's practically coming out of your skin. Wish I could bottle it." He knocks the ash from the cigar tip.

I have the flicker of an idea then. But it is still dim.

The Variants. Bottled. Euphoria.

Then Phineas erupts into a coughing fit so violent he has to stub out his cigar. When he hacks into his hand, the sound is unmistakably wet. He looks down. Tries to hide it.

But he isn't quick enough. At the sight of the unmistakable rust that is left on his palm, the flicker of my idea falters and fades away.

turn my room upside down. Run my fingers across every surface and nook in the bureau drawers, sift through the sheets, check
the drains. I consider asking for an unsanctioned use of Mind's Eye
to check my memory, but I don't need it. I can see myself unhooking
the clasp and coiling the chain as I always do, placing the necklace on
my nightstand so that it doesn't wrap around my neck while I sleep.

I know, even as I strip the cases from the pillows one last time,
that Mother's necklace isn't here.

A chill works its way down my spine like fingers playing a piano.

Someone came in and took it. While I was sleeping.

I throw on a crumpled wool dress that I'd left lying on my floor
and fling open my door.

Miles. Of course. It had to have been Miles.

I head for the back garden, where he's spent the last week playing with a model airplane he built with Dr. Cliffton. But now he
stands beside the garden's western stone wall, the airplane overturned
in the grass, with one wing crooked, like a broken arm. He is cupping
something in his hand, and a silvery thread of hope shoots through
my veins.

But when he turns, it is only the remnants of flower petals. He
is pulling out delicate clusters of pink and white turtlehead blossoms and beheading them from their stems. They are Mrs. Cliffton's
favorites.

"Miles." Hope is hammering in my chest. I won't even be mad at him — not *that* mad — if he has it. Though I've only had it for a few weeks, I've grown used to the weight of it against my skin, and I feel strangely off kilter without it. As I walk toward him, my head starts to throb.

"What?" He hides the petals behind his back. The rest of the evidence remains strewn like tattered rags around the Clifftons' garden.

"Did you take my necklace?" I ask. "The one with Mother's ring?"

"No," he says. But he won't meet my eyes.

"Miles, don't lie to me," I say sharply. I take another step toward him.

"It's probably somewhere in your room." He squints down at the petals at his feet. "Maybe," he smirks, "it's with your dart and your ribbon and all your lovey-dovey poetry about Dixon Fairweather."

I grab his shoulders and shake him hard enough to make his teeth rattle, realizing that it's the first time I've touched him in ages. "This isn't funny," I hiss. "Stop being your painfully annoying self for one single minute and tell me the truth."

He looks at me as if I've struck him. "No," he says softly. "I don't know where it is."

I release my grip on his small shoulders, and as soon as I do, he runs. I watch the swirl of his cowlick until he reaches the hens and sends them flapping and squawking away from him. When I close my eyes, I can almost see Mother's displeased expression: she would have gone after him, and I would have retreated to my room to add another line to my floor.

Tears prick my eyes. Miles and I will always stay the same, no matter what else changes around us.

I find Mrs. Cliffton in the sunroom, canning beans in a row of gleaming glass jars. "Can you help me?" I ask. "I've misplaced my necklace."

She and Genevieve help me unmake and remake the bed, lift the mattress, push the dresser out from the wall. Dr. Cliffton and Will join in to search the other rooms of the house. "I'm so sorry, dear," Mrs. Cliffton says eventually, standing from where she'd knelt to look under a table. Her palms push back the wisps of her hair. "I know it has sentimental value. I'm sure it will turn up."

"I probably just set it down somewhere," I say. It's a lie, but I don't want her to think that I'm making any accusations. I bite back tears, then let myself out into the garden.

I examine the weathered bricks of the house and the tree, its large limb reaching right up to my window.

My necklace didn't just disappear. Which means that either a thief broke into my room in the night and stole it while I was sleeping or someone in the Clifftons' house is lying to me.

At the moment, I can't decide which is worse.

When I reach the school field for my first Stars practice, Mrs. Percy is already there, shielding her face from the sun, balancing a rectangular metal box under the crook of her elbow. My head pounds with a headache that has persisted ever since Mother's necklace went missing three days ago.

"Let's set up," Mrs. Percy says. I help her level something that resembles an archery target at the edge of the field. There are six lines blooming out from a bull's-eye in the center, and I breathe a small sigh of relief. If Stars are anything like darts, there's a chance I could be good at them.

But then Mrs. Percy starts hanging thin wires in front of the target. She slips a silver and red candle into the first wire knot and two glass vials of water in the knots on either side. They are light enough to swing loosely in the breeze.

"Shall we begin?" Mrs. Percy asks. At my nod, she presents me with a pair of thick white gloves. "Precautionary measure," she explains. "Don't want any fingers to be accidentally sliced off on the first day."

She winks. I shift my weight from one foot to the other and laugh nervously. I'm already starting to sweat. No room to dwell on Mother's necklace now. Not if I want to keep all my extremities intact.

"I'm afraid I don't know much about Stars," I admit. "Maybe you should start from the beginning."

"It's simple, really." Mrs. Percy pulls on her own gloves, a light lavender color, then cracks open the metal box. Inside is a neat array of silver Stars, each roughly the size of my palm. Their edges glitter, as sharp as razors.

"There are three rounds, with three Stars thrown in each round," she says. "That means you have nine chances to collect points. You receive points for each Star that hits the target, and the value increases the closer you get to the bull's-eye."

I nod.

"But the real prize is to hit the hanging candle with enough force that the Star slices through the wax, causing the candle to fall and light the fuel below the target. A direct hit to the bull's-eye is fifty points. If you successfully light the fuel, it's one hundred and fifty.

"In all honesty," Mrs. Percy continues, squinting at me, "don't count on that happening. It's only been done twice in the history of the tournament. And you'll need to avoid hitting these vials of water that hang on either side of the candle. If those shatter or spill, you'll lose points — and likely the candle flame as well."

"Got it." I work my fingers to the tips of the gloves. "I've never heard of this game before."

"This version of Stars originated in Corrander," Mrs. Percy says. "The tournament favors traditional games with a bit of a twist."

Makes sense. It's a description fit for the Sister Cities themselves.

"Oh, and one more thing," Mrs. Percy adds. "In the third round, the target will be moving."

My mounting concern must be apparent because Mrs. Percy quickly lines me up in front of the target and demonstrates the proper throwing motion.

"It's all in the aiming and the snap of the wrist," she explains. "You want to grab it by the tip and put as much spin on it as you can when you release it." She demonstrates a few practice snaps before letting the first Star fly. It slices through the air and into the target.

"We'll have to experiment and find out which style works best for you — over the shoulder or from the side, near your waist."

Mrs. Percy hands me a Star. It's heavier and sturdier than I'd imagined. Nothing like Father's small, weighted darts that fit into my hands like skipping stones.

I carefully touch the point of the Star with my gloved finger. "These seem" — I hesitate — "like they could be dangerous."

The look that crosses Mrs. Percy's face is not exactly comforting.

"Yes, most definitely," she says. "If thrown at a person—in self-defense, of course—they could even be fatal."

In self-defense.

"Now," says Mrs. Percy, and I step up to the line. "Let's begin."

During our card game on Thursday evening I notice that Miles has lost another tooth. I still feel bad over confronting him about Mother's ring, and he hasn't spoken a word to me since.

"Miles—" I say, wanting to make amends after the game is finished, but he ignores me and shuts the door to his room. I get ready for bed, take an aspirin for the headache that won't seem to go away, and feel under my pillow to make sure the Star I wrapped is still there. Which gives me an idea.

I pull out Mother's book. While I'm waiting for Miles to go to sleep, I scribble a few more notes in my new list:

Scents:
Thou losest thy old smell. — As You Like It

Eyes without feeling,
feeling without sight,
Ears without hands or eyes,
smelling sans all. — Hamlet

When the moon is low and bright between the oak branches outside my window, I sneak into Miles's room with a nickel in my hand. He hadn't called attention to his new missing tooth, and I'm not sure that Mrs. Cliffton noticed. Maybe a contribution toward a new

Sub-Mariner comic will help mend things between us. I carefully tear out a sheet of paper from the notebook that lies open on the floor next to his bed and write:

Forgive me? ☹
Love,
Your Sister

Miles is sleeping, his mouth turned down and drooping, his hair smashed against his forehead. His hand is curled around the edge of his blanket. When his mouth twitches, I wonder jealously if he is dreaming.

Thankfully, he's a deep sleeper. Sliding the coin and note under a pillow weighted by his head isn't as easy as I thought it would be. I feel a tooth there, just as I'd hoped, and pull it out in exchange.

On my way out the door I pause over his sketchbook. Now that I've torn out the front page, I can see a drawing and writing underneath. I bend for a closer look.

I'm relieved to see that the first drawing is something other than Mother's grave. Instead it is a sketch of a winged tooth fairy. She carries a satchel spilling over with teeth, and she's riding in a carriage made from a hazelnut shell.

I turn the page.

Mother, he's written. *I don't know if you can see this from where you are now. But I thought you'd like this riddle.*

He's drawn a small, lifelike frog, with mossy shades of greens and browns. Underneath he's written:

Why are frogs so happy?

(They eat whatever bugs them!)

What is a frog's favorite drink?

(Croak-a-cola!)

Croak-a-cola. It's so . . . *stupid.* I choke on a sob that comes out of nowhere. He's drawn the little frog so carefully with his Variant pencils—Mother would have loved it. And I'd forgotten about the hazelnut shells. Anytime we found an empty nutshell in the garden she'd tell us that a tooth fairy must have left it there. The tears flow over my cheeks, and my breath is hitching because I'm trying to cry without making any noise.

I want her ring back.

I want *her* back.

I close the notebook and return to my bed, where I lie down and cry straight into my pillow. It feels good, and it hurts, as if something tight and thorny is coming unknotted in my chest. I finally sit up, and I am drying my face with my sleeve when there's a soft knock on my door. I hastily finish running my sleeve over my cheeks and nose. Then I throw a blanket around my shoulders and, at the last minute, grab my Star from under my pillow.

"Yes?" I open the door only a crack.

Will stands in front of me, dressed all in black. His hair is short again.

"Oh—are—" He's taken aback when he looks at my eyes, which must be bloodshot and red-rimmed. "I'm sorry. I can come back later."

"No." I attempt a smile and open the door wider. "It's fine. What do you need?"

He remains in the hall but cocks his head and gives me a long look.

"Do you want to go somewhere with me?" he asks finally. "It's relatively safe and not entirely allowed."

I sniffle. I want to be anywhere but alone in this room. "Yes," I say.

"Get dressed, and I'll come back for you in ten minutes." His mouth cracks into a grin. "And I'm glad you're up for it. Your room happens to be my escape route."

plait my hair around my head, dress in trousers and boots, and pull out the coat I found hanging in my closet earlier in the week. It's a deep cherry red in a thick-knit wool. Mrs. Cliffton said it was one of hers that was too small, but I know that's not true: I saw it hanging in Finch's tailor shop on our first day in town.

I open the door at Will's light knock, and he steps into my room.

"Too bright. You should take it off," he says immediately, closing the door behind him. "The coat, I mean," he clarifies, flushing. "To help us blend in on the road."

"Oh." Reluctantly I return it to the closet, running my hand one last time over the red sleeve. Will shuts off the light, so that all we can see is the mottled brightness of the moon, more yellow than white. Then he pulls a pouch from his pocket.

"Embers," he explains, and dusts some over my head and arms. "No coat needed."

Next come the Night Vision Variants. He opens the stopper and puts some of the sparkling paste on his fingertips. "Close your eyes?" He steps forward until he's standing close enough for me to feel his breath. He smoothes the Night Vision over my eyelids. A pleasant thrill shoots through me at the feather-light touch of his fingertips, which lingers even after he applies his own Night Vision and stoppers the vial again.

He climbs onto my window seat, hoists open the window without a sound, and leaps onto the outreaching arm of the tree branch. Then he turns and holds out his hand to me.

I blink at him in wonder, looking around and past him as my eyes adjust to the darkness. I can see everything in a silvery cast, a shade lighter than shadows and outlines, as if the world has been dimly backlit.

Will smiles, and it is as bright as day.

"Are we going to use the Tempests?" I whisper, taking his hand and stepping onto the branch. I have to press up against him so that he can pull my window all but closed again.

"Not yet," he says, and my disappointment must show, because he adds, "I promise you can try them soon."

We shimmy down the tree, and I'm glad I spent so much time scaling the oak that towered over Mother's garden in my backyard. "You really can climb," he says when I jump from the bottom branch.

"Impressed?" I ask, but hope he's not so impressed that he won't try to take my hand again.

We stick to the shadows, and Will finds the shortest part of the garden wall for us to hop over. We head in the direction of town and school. The night air is chilled enough to pull my breath out in white puffs, but the Embers are working nicely. I have a sense of warmth that glows, as cozy as if I were wrapped in a blanket at the foot of a fire.

We move quickly on foot. "Where are we going?" I eventually ask.

"This way," Will says, and we take the fork that heads away from town. "There's a clearing just a bit beyond school."

"And we're going there in the middle of the night?"

"Just us, and a few dozen of our closest friends." He squints. "And rivals."

"Do you often meet up with large groups of people in the dead of night?"

"I do when it means getting to race with the Tempests."

"The Tempests that have been outlawed, you mean?"

He cocks an eyebrow at me. "Not outlawed. Strongly discouraged."

"Hence why we're sneaking out without telling your parents . . ."

"Yes," he says, "although I think they know more than they let on. So far they haven't said anything. But if I come to breakfast with a broken limb, I'll be in it for sure."

We pass the school, which is huge and dark and looming in the night, and cut through the adjacent orchard. Apples hang heavy on the branches like oversize ornaments. "Midnight snack?" Will plucks a few as we pass and tosses me one.

"It's our tradition," I tease, and bite into it. It is sweet and crisp, and with my night vision its white flesh practically glows.

Someone drops down from the shadows to greet Will, and I stop myself from shrieking just in time. "Carter," Will says, slapping him on the back. "Thanks for keeping watch tonight."

Carter nods and pulls himself back up into the branches of a tree. "Just do me a favor and win. Larkin's already been running his mug."

"Sounds about right," Will says. We keep moving through the trees, and others are coming behind us. Everyone is dressed in black. "Almost there," Will says. Beyond the orchard the trees give way to a clearing, and then we come upon a still, dark lake.

I can make out some of our classmates — the hulking shadow of Chase Peterson, the girl from dressmaking who always walks on her tiptoes — gathered on the strip of pale beach that rings the lake. My heart rises at the hushed sound of Beas's laugh, but I can't tell exactly where it's coming from. We walk toward the students, who are clumped in patches between two long docks that bookend either side of the beach.

Eliza is at the head of the nearest group, shaking her hair, smiling with her white teeth. My stomach twists as Will leads us over to her. *Please, no,* I think.

"Hey, 'Liza," Will says as we join her. "You and Aila know each other, right?" he asks, but his eyes are already on a row of others lining up along the beach.

Eliza shrugs. I don't say anything at all.

"I'll find you after," Will says, leaning toward me. "Do you know what a kazoo sounds like?"

"Yes," I say, amused despite the fact that he is about to abandon me with Eliza Patton.

"That's the warning sign. If you hear it, run and hide. Pick a tree or something — now that I've seen you climb." And with a smile, he leaves to find his friends, who are warming up on the beach.

I stand awkwardly beside Eliza, playing first with my hair and then with my hands, searching the crowd for anyone familiar. I finally glimpse Beas, and she waves, looking surprised to see me. I try not to feel hurt that we spent all of biology together this morning and she never mentioned anything about this.

"A!" she says, walking over to me. "You came!" She grins. "You're a bit more of a rebel than I'd pegged you for."

I smile back and decide that whether Sterling is temporary or not, I actually want to be real friends with Beas. There's something about her that reminds me of my mother. Perhaps it's the way she refuses to march to everyone else's beat.

Or maybe she's just hearing a different one altogether.

"Hey, 'Liz," Beas adds, pronouncing it like *lies*. She links arms with us both. Eliza rolls her eyes.

"Guess what? Thom's coming tonight," Beas whispers. "I know the race is very hush-hush. But . . ." Her giggle is throaty. "I invited him anyway."

Eliza releases Beas's arm and sits. "You're playing with fire," she says, examining her nails.

Beas drops down next to her on a slab of driftwood. "Anybody got any Embers?" she asks, ignoring Eliza. Tonight John Greenleaf Whittier peeks out from the hem of her skirt:

Are these poor fragments only left
Of vain desires and hopes that failed?

By the time George slips through the trees, there are around forty of us on the Sterling side and almost as many gathered for the opposing team. The sky is an abyss without the stars, and my night vision makes the lake look like a dark silver mirror that reflects nothing at all.

"Aila?" George asks in surprise when he spots me. He dips his head to make sure. "Are you running tonight?"

I pat the rough hunk of log next to me. "I hadn't planned on it."

"You should," he said. "I'm not. But everyone should have this experience at least once in their lives." George sets his bag at his feet and plops down, his freckles glowing like constellations.

"And what experience is that?" I ask, but I'm startled by Beas suddenly leaping to her feet. She throws herself on an approaching figure, laughing her throaty laugh, muffled by the kisses she is planting all over his face and neck.

She leads a tall boy with dark eyes toward us, her face flushed and her eyes shining.

George reaches out a hand to shake, and Eliza offers a wan smile. "Oh, hi, Thom," she says casually before returning to her nails.

"A, this is Thom," Beas says. "Thom, this is that girl I was telling you about." She wrinkles her nose at me. "*Good* things," she assures me.

"Any friend of Beas —" he says, grinning.

I dip my head at him. "Nice to meet you." He is tall and broad, and Beas just fits into him, her dark head barely grazing his chin.

"Here, have some Embers," she says, and reaches on her tiptoes to sprinkle a handful over him.

"I have to leave by two to get home." He sits where the sand meets the grass.

"Let's not talk about it," she says, nestling into him before she leans forward to start stretching out her calves.

The crowd is filling in, settling onto the logs and driftwood that ring the beach.

"Race seems early this time," a boy comments behind us, biting into an apple as large as a fist. "The last one was barely a month ago."

"You know why." A girl with a handkerchief tied around her head turns to look at him.

"You mean because of Disappearance Day?"

"There are only two weeks left. Everyone could use a distraction."

"They think if we come out here and run around, we'll just forget about it all for a while?"

"Fat chance," George mutters.

A girl I recognize from my history class, Nell, is acting as some sort of official. She has a slight lisp and deep dimples. To draw our attention, she blows into a horn that sounds like a muted owl's call.

"Welcome, all," she says, extending her hands. "And a special welcome to our guests from Corrander tonight!" She nods at our muted clapping. "The girls will go first. Racers, line up in the sand and get your armbands."

Beas and Eliza start removing their shoes. "Are you going to race?" Beas asks, knotting her hair up into a ponytail. She pulls on a pair of trousers under her skirt, which she promptly drops into the sand. Thom gives a low whistle, and she winks at him.

"Do I need Tempests?" I ask.

She laughs as if I've asked something hysterical.

I shrug.

"Next time, then," she says, and she and Eliza grab hands and run to the line drawn in the sand. They are fitted with black bands that snake around their upper arms, and the bands are dusted with Glimmers until they take light. The racers' left arms glow either crimson for Sterling or gold for Corrander. But the bands on their right arms are lit with individual colors. Eliza's becomes jade as she leans down to stretch, and Beas's is lavender.

"Racers, take your places," Nell instructs. The crowd around me responds by stomping their feet in the sand, which manages to convey enthusiasm without making too much noise. I'm looking around, wondering where the finish line is. There are ten girls lined up to face the lake.

"Ninety seconds to go," Nell announces, "starting on my count."

The sprinters each loosen the tie of a pouch that's hanging around their necks. A Corrander girl pours out a handful of Variants, and the moonlight catches them in the crease of her palm.

And suddenly, watching Eliza crouch in the sand to ready herself, I understand.

The Tempests aren't going to help them run beside the water.

They're going to help them run *on* the water.

CHAPTER NINETEEN

Hey." Will suddenly drops down behind me. "Quick. Would you want to race?"

He pushes his hand through his hair and then extends something out to me with a flattened palm.

It's the pouch of his Tempests.

"I measured it again, and I think I've got just enough for two," he says.

"Sixty seconds!" Nell calls.

"Do it," George says, shoving me. "You can't come to Sterling without a Tempest race." I hesitate for half a moment. Then I leap to my feet and grab the pouch from Will's hand. My heart immediately starts to ricochet.

I kick off my shoes and run barefoot to join the other girls on the beach. Feel the sand, wet and cool, under my toes. *What are you doing?* half of me screams. *What if these run out in the middle of the lake and you sink like a stone?*

When I reach the line, someone steps forward and wraps two bands around my arms. With shaking fingers I open the pouch of Tempests.

"Thirty seconds," Nell calls.

I'm dusted with Glimmers, crimson on my left arm for Sterling, a greenish-blue on my right.

I haven't even warmed up. I'm probably going to pull a muscle and promptly drown.

"Yes, A!" Beas says, shooting me a thumbs-up. "This is going to be such a blast."

"Fifteen seconds," Nell says. "You may ready your Tempests now."

I pour the Variants into my hand. They are softer than I expected, finer even than grains of sand. I glance up at Will, and at his nod, I lift my arm and shower them over myself. They fall softly around me, like flakes of ash in my hair, dissolving on the tips of my lashes.

"Five," Nell says. "Four." The crowd joins in the countdown. I crouch down into the sand, feeling a tingle take hold along my skin, amping through my blood like a coil ready to spring.

"One," Nell says. At her whistle, the girls around me take off like a shot.

And then I leap into a running step. The wind clutches my hair and unfurls it behind me, and my breath comes almost too quickly for me to catch it. I send up two sprays of sand before I reach the lake. The sound of my feet hitting the water is more like the splash of a shallow puddle than wading into the depths. For half a second I expect to sink, for my feet to give way to the water's surface.

But the girls flanking me each become streaks of light as the water turns to road beneath them. It is like running in parallel with horizontal bolts of lightning. Though the lake stretches on for the length of at least two football fields, within a few breaths we are already almost a quarter of the way across it.

I'm flying as if the water itself were pushing me forward; as if running were the most natural thing I've ever done. It's easier even than breathing. The dull sky spreads out overhead, void of stars, flat and polished like a stone. I can feel my hair, wild and cold, and my cheeks are warm and red. I feel more alive than I have for as long I can remember. Nothing matters — not my fight with Miles, not my missing necklace. I can't stop laughter from pouring out of me. I'm being too loud. I look like a fool. I don't care at all.

When I reach the other side, I'm a half step behind everyone else, and I never do catch them. They are a rainbow of colors just beyond me as we turn back across the lake, and by the time I reach the starting line again, I feel nothing but euphoria, even though I'm dead last. I step onto the beach, grinning and perfectly dry. The crowd claps as Nell steps forward to declare the winner. I'm last, Beas is fourth, and Eliza comes in second, barely behind some girl from Corrander. Eliza glares in the way of someone summoning a death wish and straightens her hair, but then her attention is drawn to the water's edge. I follow her gaze.

Something is brewing between two boys whose arms glow with competing bands of crimson and gold. They exchange words I can't quite hear, and then a brief shout rings out as the Corrander boy slams into the racer from Sterling. I squint my eyes at the figure stumbling backward from the blow. *Figures,* I think. It looks like Chase.

He splashes thigh-deep into the lake but rights himself instead of falling.

"That's for whatever disappears next," the Corrander player growls. Someone near me responds with a low boo, and then a sense of unease passes through the crowd, as distinct as the wind rustling cornstalks around the burned shell of Mother's house.

"You think *I* have something to do with it?" Chase's voice catches somewhere between surprise and a sneer.

"One of you. Sterling's got more possible Catalysts than us and

Sheffield combined," the Corrander player says. Eliza's back suddenly stiffens. "And it sounds like that number keeps growing."

My face reddens in the dark. Because now they're talking about me.

Chase takes a step closer. The dark water moves from his knees to ring around his ankles.

"Oh, Roger," Chase drawls, as if he's talking to a small child. "Maybe we've been thinking about the whole Catalyst thing all wrong." He adjusts his armband, which is the color of a glittering bruise. "In fact, perhaps we should be grateful. Because now none of us have to worry about smelling you and your gross sister."

Roger jumps onto Chase and starts pounding his chest. Chase wrestles him off, thrashing about until they both fall with a loud splash. By the time Chase stands, dripping and spluttering, his armband extinguished, Will has placed himself in the center of the fight with arms extended. A Corrander player holds Roger as he struggles to break free.

"All right, then," Nell says nervously. She claps. "Let's move on. Chase, Roger, you're disqualified. Boys' round starts in ten minutes."

The crowd dissolves, and we return to our pieces of driftwood, where George and Thom hold court over our shoes.

"Roger and Chase are disqualified?" George asks. He looks at Thom. "That improves our odds on Larkin versus Cliffton."

"Should we up the ante?"

"It's definitely going to be between the two of them."

Eliza sniffs. "You better not pick against Will."

"I'd never pick a Larkin over a Cliffton," George says. "That's like aligning with the darkness."

"I don't get it," I whisper to George, settling back into my seat.

"Oh," George says. "Leroy Larkin's father invented the largest number of Variants, after Dr. Cliffton. So the sons of the two most prolific Variant inventors are about to face off."

"Victor Larkin actually invented the Tempests," Beas adds. "But their families aren't exactly chummy."

"Because they're competitors?" I ask.

"Because Dr. Cliffton's always careful about which Variants he introduces. They're usually subtle and harmless," George says.

Eliza smoothes her hair. "And we can't always say the same about what the Larkins have brought us," she says cryptically. I think again of the Variants that were left off the list at school.

"Well, with that," George says, picking up his bag, "I'm going to find a nice secluded spot in the woods to take a whiz."

"Try not to get murdered by someone from Corrander," Eliza says sweetly.

"We're going to go find a nice secluded spot, too," Beas says, pulling Thom's hand and grinning.

When Eliza realizes that this means we are going to be left alone together, she pointedly picks up her bag and leaves without another word. By the time I turn my head again, she has vanished into the crowd.

A hint of chill hits me, as if the Embers are starting to fade away. I settle back onto my log, wishing I had my red coat as one more layer between me and their world.

I'm still sitting alone when the murmuring starts. There's a rustle of papers being passed, the wheel-turn of silence, and then reactions of gasps and giggles. I pretend not to notice as heads raise to glance in my direction. And then, one by one, they all look away. As if I'm not what they were searching for.

The moon moves out, full and bright, behind the dark smear of a cloud. I hear something that sounds like "Margo's here tonight" and "Who found this?" and "It's always been ripped out of the copies I've ever seen." By the time the papers are passed to me, I'm filled with dread.

It's hard to tell where the stack came from. No one is walking around to distribute it — it's just distributing itself, passing from person to person like sparks catching. I take the papers and glimpse the heading — "The Mackelroy Misfortune" — just as George returns, whistling.

It takes me a moment to understand what I'm looking at. The title is printed in the upper right corner. *"The Legends of Sterling, 203–208."* It's the same pages that were torn out of Dr. Cliffton's book.

I look up at George and cringe.

"Whatcha got there?" he asks, and takes the stack from my hand.

He chews on his bottom lip as he reads it, but otherwise his face doesn't change.

"My mother would flip her wig if she knew this got out" is all he says. Then he looks around to see people's heads bent over the mimeographs. He hides the remaining sheets away in his bag. "But . . . too late now, from the looks of it."

He thinks for a moment, then folds one of the copies from the top and slips it into my pocket.

"I don't want —" I say, even though I'm deadly curious.

"Just take it," he says. "Let's just be in it together."

I don't look at the sheet, but I feel the pointed fold of its crease in my pocket whenever I move. The crowd parts, and I can see Eliza laughing with someone. Glancing our way.

How convenient that she disappeared with her bag just moments before the papers started circling.

"I can't imagine who might have done this." I look toward Eliza. "Will she stop at nothing to make sure the spotlight isn't on her?"

George almost looks amused. "You think?"

"I guess you and your girlfriend have a lot in common, Mackelroy," someone jeers, throwing a crumpled copy at George's head. A spectator from the Corrander side of the beach sets his sheet on fire and taunts, "Mackelroy, I know you're over there . . ."

George leans back stoically on his elbows as people around him skim through the words. I slip the folded piece of paper deeper into the crease of my pocket.

"Let's get started," Nell calls, drawing everyone's attention back to the water. Beas and Thom return to settle in behind me, their lips and cheeks splashed red and blotchy. Smiling, dazed. Fingers interlaced. I take a soda bottle from George and pop off the top, wondering what it would feel like to ever be that happy.

Nine boys line up at the water's edge, visible by the red and gold of their armbands.

Will's is a marigold yellow that makes his arm looked ringed with fire.

He rocks on the balls of his feet, looking long and lithe. The bubbles from the soda fizz on my tongue. Out of the corner of my eye I can see Thom playing with the ends of Beas's hair.

"Leroy's the one with double gold armbands," George whispers, and I find him easily.

"Race starts in three . . ." Nell says, "two . . ."

She sounds the signal. Will throws a handful of Variants over his head and leaps from the dock. He and Leroy take off, their lights practically colliding as they fight to take the lead. They are evenly matched, carving across the water in tandem, their lights reflections of each other.

They reach the other side in a handful of breaths, slightly ahead of all the others, and simultaneously turn back toward us. For a moment they become a single bright smudge in the distance. Then they separate into distinct lines again as they rocket back across the lake.

From this distance, Will's spark looks like Mars next to Leroy's crazed sun. Leroy edges dangerously closer to Will, and I wonder if anyone has ever gone down into the black water before. How difficult it would be to find them once their armbands hit the surface and were extinguished. My stomach twists.

They shove into each other and ricochet apart. A murmur goes through the crowd, but somehow neither of them goes under.

We rise to our feet as they near, and the closer they get to the beach, the closer they get to each other. Both sides of fans are yelling, our attempts at quietness forgotten, and one of Leroy's golden bands reaches out toward Will. But Will sidesteps the shove at the last possible second, a move that appears to catch Leroy off-guard.

A second before they reach the finish, Leroy loses his momentum and splashes into the water. He emerges, sputtering, as the other racers dodge to avoid running right over his head.

Will steps triumphantly onto the beach, his arms still ringed with blood and fire.

A loud cheer erupts that I'm sure anyone within a mile radius can hear. He's taking large, measured breaths, as if his lungs were wings expanding under his ribs. Leroy emerges from the water a moment later, his shirt slicked to his chest. Scowling, he accepts a beach towel and a handful of Embers from one of his teammates.

I hang behind George as the crowd pushes toward Will and knocks him around in congratulations, ruffling his hair, punching him in the arm.

But just before he's hoisted into the air and carried away, he searches through the crowd until he catches sight of me. Grins until his crooked tooth shows. And I think that for the rest of my life I will never forget this night — when under an empty ink sky, a boy who shone brighter than the stars stopped long enough to smile at me.

The crowd scatters into the night, leaving apple cores and soda bottles and tattered copies of "The Mackelroy Misfortune" strewn in the sand, but a few of us stay behind to hide the evidence of the race.

George collects the abandoned Mackelroy papers and then digs a hole to set them alight. He douses the flames with lake water until the words are dark ash blending into white sand.

"I better get going," he says. "Don't want to risk the wrath of Agatha Mackelroy." He bids us all goodbye and lopes off into the trees, as if he doesn't have a care in the world.

Beas and Thom crouch near the lapping water, stalling for time, drawing in the sand with the edges of sticks. "So when will I see you again?" Thom asks.

I'm not *trying* to eavesdrop, but their voices carry.

Beas bends to draw half a dozen notes in the sand. She pushes her hair behind her ears. "Probably not until after the next Disappearance. My parents are being extra nuts lately."

"When's that again?"

She looks at him as if she can't believe he would forget. "Two weeks."

"Do you . . . have any guess for what might disappear?"

She shivers, then searches in her pocket for more Embers. She drapes them over him, then herself, and shakes her head.

"I hope it's not something big," he adds.

"Is there something in particular that would break the deal for you?" Her voice is suddenly brittle and high, and so unlike her. She tosses her stick in the sand.

"What do you mean?" he asks.

"Nothing," she says. "I don't want to do this now. It's been such a nice night."

"No, really, what do you mean?"

She blows up the fringe of her bangs. "I mean, what happens if it *is* something big? I'm going to keep losing things, and you're not. Our lives are going to keep looking more and more different." She says softly, "*I'm* going to be more and more different."

He comes up behind her, hugs her to him. "It'll be all right," he says. "Maybe it won't be a bad one this time. Maybe it will hardly matter at all."

"You should find someone else, Thom," she says softly. "There is someone else out there who would be better for you, and I know that."

"But I love you, Beas. I don't want someone else. No one else is *like* you."

I move away from them, suddenly not wanting to intrude on their moment anymore. I walk toward the dock, toward Will. But I stop short when I see Eliza approach him. She cocks her head. Runs her hands through her long, glowing hair.

"Congratulations," she says. She smiles. "Remember what you told me on the afternoon of December seventeenth when we were fourteen?"

"Um, no," he says, and laughs a little.

"Well, I do," she says coyly, and hands him something in a glass globe.

Then she melts into the shadows of the trees until I can't see her anymore.

"Ready?" Will asks after we've returned the beach to the way it looked before.

"Ready," I say. Beas and Thom have slipped away without saying goodbye, and I wonder if they've broken up. But I see them kissing again in the shadows as Will and I walk by, and I smile down at my boots.

Will takes a deep breath. "It's peppermint air."

"What's that?"

"When it was this cold when I was little, I used to say it felt like a peppermint on the back of my throat when I breathed."

"Peppermint air," I repeat. "Cute." The wind has blown wisps of my braid free, and I begin to unwork the rest of it. "How did it feel to win? I think the Clifftons are truly Sterling's golden family now," I say, shaking out my hair so that it falls down my back.

He smiles shyly. "I have to admit I don't think anyone's ever looked at me that way. I mean, I've seen that expression before. It's just always been for my father."

"Has he ever seen you race?"

Will gives a short laugh. "No. And I doubt he ever will. He'd bust my chops if he found out I've bought Tempests and given money to the Larkins." He clears his throat. "I don't want to pull the wool over his eyes. He just doesn't really understand, you know—with the cane and all—how it feels to run like that." He falls silent for a minute, and all I can hear are our footsteps on the leaves. "We've sort of always just missed each other—because I'd rather be running or building, and he's perfectly happy to read about plants all day." He clears his throat to change the subject. "But you enjoyed yourself?"

"I think I still have a buzz." The words brighten out of my mouth like fireflies. "Can I go again? When's the next one?"

"Usually every couple of months," he says. "More frequently during the summertime. Or like tonight, when we all needed a distraction."

The moon has disappeared behind the clouds, and I have no idea what time it is. Thunder rumbles distantly. "We'd better hurry."

We climb over the garden wall and creep along the edge of the house until we reach the tree beneath my room. Will kneels to give me a leg up, and I grab on to the curve of his shoulder. I want time to stretch on so we can stay here, in this perfect night, for longer.

I'm halfway to the first branch when a light twitches on.

My stomach drops, roiling even further when the front door opens.

Dr. Cliffton motions us inside without a word.

"Straight to your rooms," he says when we're in the foyer. "And you can expect I'll be speaking to both of you first thing in the morning."

CHAPTER TWENTY

A little less than six hours later, the morning sunlight pours through the window onto Dr. Cliffton's closed door. I wait anxiously outside of it, running my fingertips over my ugly ear, feeling as though I'm five years old again. Wondering just how much trouble I've gotten myself into.

And all this time I thought it would be Miles who got us kicked out of Sterling.

I sit down in the chair Will made and feel the paper folded in my trousers pocket. To distract myself, I pull it out.

THE MACKELROY MISFORTUNE

The Mackelroys first arrived in Sterling a quarter century after the town was founded. They were farmers, weavers, and tradesmen, representing the hardworking middle class for generations. In fact, they were the very portrait of the average man — that is, until Lorna Mackelroy was born.

Lorna Mackelroy was the most beautiful girl of her generation. She had long, golden hair, a complexion as pure as cream, and eyes the color of the sea. When she was sixteen, she became engaged to a young man from Sheffield named Charlton Templeton. Their love was young, passionate, and all-encompassing — the kind you hear about in fairy tales — but her parents were firmly against the match. The family's hope at a better life and elevated status rested solely on Lorna and her chance beauty. They expected her to marry high above her class and bring the rest of the family with her. Lorna was caught between her love for Charlton and her duty to her family's wishes. She promised to marry Charlton once he set off into the wider world and made his own fortune.

And make a fortune he did — eventually. But empires, especially those of the shipping trade, are not built in a day. There would be long stretches where Lorna didn't hear from her fiancé, but her love for him never faltered. Many suitors came to marvel at her beauty and ask for her hand, but she always remained faithful to her one true love.

In the twelfth year after Charlton set off from Sheffield in search of his fortune, Lorna received no news from him for nine months. She had not seen her betrothed in more than three years. Lorna was still a beauty, but the requests for her hand had quietly died down with each passing year. Everyone in the town told her that time had run out; Charlton had given up and was never coming back for her. Her family's distress mounted with each day that brought no news from him.

An entire year passed. Heartbroken and convinced that Charlton had either forgotten her or been killed at sea, Lorna agreed to marry Lars Cousins, a neighboring farmer from Sterling. When Charlton finally returned, richer than anyone in the town had imagined he could be and ready to claim his bride, it was too late — she had married Lars just three days earlier. Lorna soon learned that Charlton had been shipwrecked on an island in the Pacific for months before he was finally rescued. When they realized what had happened, both Lorna and Charlton were devastated.

Because memories of Lorna overwhelmed Charlton in Sheffield and Sterling, he retreated to Corrander, married someone else, and promptly died from typhus, leaving his new wife with wealth beyond measure. However, people always said that he haunted Sterling, and there are a number of reasons why the strange Disappearances could be born from this tragedy.

This theory would explain why the Disappearances affect all three towns of Sterling, Corrander, and Sheffield.

When Charlton returned and found Lorna married, a fierce change came over him. He is rumored to have stormed to the Mackelroys' home and declared that they had, in effect, forced him to "buy" Lorna's love. In the final hours of fever, he was inconsolable and said that it was "an abomination to put a price on the few things in life that are the free right of every human being."

Of course, it is this last point that is the most chilling. People believe that Charlton's revenge was to curse the towns with a punishment that fit his crime: forcing them to buy things that the rest of humankind experiences without cost.

I quickly fold the paper away. I still can't hear what's being said behind the thick wood of the door, only the low murmur of voices —almost entirely Dr. Cliffton's, with a few interjections from Will. I hear snippets of — "dangerous . . . you could have been hurt . . . this is her home for now . . . inappropriate . . . out together . . . watch yourself."

Then the door swings open and Will emerges, looking sheepish.

He raises his eyebrows at me, and his face relaxes. "You look terrified," he says. "Don't worry. He knows it's entirely my fault."

I walk into the library, my heart skipping, and face Dr. Cliffton.

"Sit down, Aila."

I sit.

"I am your guardian," he says. "And I take that very seriously."

"Yes, sir," I say miserably. I bite into my lip and wait. I've never seen him look so stern.

"I suppose I never *explicitly* told you that you couldn't leave the house in the middle of the night. So I do not plan to say anything about this to your father," he says, "but I don't want it to ever happen again. So consider this a stiff warning."

I nod fervently as a wave of relief douses my nerves.

"If anything were to happen to you . . ." He removes his glasses, sets them on the desk, and rubs his eyes. "Just don't be out at night," he says finally. "Especially this time of year."

He looks so concerned for me that I want to pat his hand and assure him that I'm all right and I'll never do anything dangerous again. I feel so wretched, sneaking out with his son and breaking into his library and stealing his book. I clasp my hands together in my lap and want to do something to make it all up to him.

So I offer him an olive branch in the form of a small confidence.

"Dr. Cliffton?" I say. "There's something else I think you should know."

He squints at me. Then he places his glasses back on his face, as if he's putting on a coat of armor. "Go on."

"Miles had a dream."

Dr. Cliffton's eyebrows shoot upward.

"Did he, now?" He sits back in his chair, and his fingertips meet one another, then separate so that he can pull at one of his eyebrows. He shifts into a different mode, as if changing gear: less paternal, more clinical.

"How many?" he asks. "How often?"

"Just one that I know of." I open my hands helplessly. "But I can't be sure. We haven't . . . spoken much of late." I wonder if he has found the nickel and note yet.

"Did he say what the dream was about?" Dr. Cliffton asks, and when I recount the nightmare of the two little birds, his eyes become glassy. He squints, as if he is reaching for something just barely beyond his grasp.

"Was there anything special about the night before? Or did he mention anything out of the ordinary that morning?" he asks.

I think back to our discussion, with the sun soaking through the drapes, to the troubled look on Miles's face.

To the gap in his mouth.

"He lost a tooth," I say. "He said it came out in his sleep. He almost choked on it."

Dr. Cliffton chuckles and claps his hands together with a loud crack. A look of realization dawns across his face.

"Of course. *Of course.*" He shakes his head. "I've heard rumors over the years of children around this age possibly having dreams. Granted, their parents weren't eager to speak up about it." He smiles sadly. "Considering how families with 'exceptions' can be treated here." He pushes his glasses back up onto his nose and hurries on. "But now — thanks to you and Miles — I finally know what must have happened."

"I'm still in the dark," I admit.

"Let me explain. If you had to guess, what would you say is the most common of dreams?"

I touch the upholstered buttonhole of the armchair. "Falling?" I guess. I shrug. "Flying?" I remember the Tempests last night, the lake lightening under my feet, and am glad Dr. Cliffton can't read my thoughts. "I'm not sure."

"All good guesses, but no. It's the loss of one's teeth," Dr. Cliffton says. "Imagine for a moment that in the middle of a dream, you open your mouth and feel that all your teeth are lost. Nothing but gums left." He stands up and begins to pace, his excitement growing. "Losing teeth in dreams is a well-documented subconscious projection of anxiety. It's one of the most common dreams — if not the most."

He stops in front of the window and looks out at the horizon. Then he faces me.

"So when it comes to finding a new Variant, we always must look at things inversely." He smiles. "Variants are like that: one big riddle. So now, when it is the dreams that are lost, we find them in a tooth."

So Miles isn't special. Relief washes over me. *Not like Mother had been.* He just happened to lose a tooth in the night, like many other children in Sterling before him. Perhaps the whole thing could have been solved so much sooner if parents hadn't been so afraid to admit that their children had seen something disappeared. I start laughing with relief and can't stop, even when we go to wake Miles and tell him that beyond all odds, an eight-year-old child of Juliet Quinn's is the one who has finally brought dreams back to Sterling.

Dr. Cliffton needs teeth to test his theory about the Dream Variant, so I give him the one I plucked from Miles's pillow last night. We all agree not to mention the theory to anyone until there's more proof, and Dr. Cliffton gleefully sets to work. He manages to procure a few more teeth while we're at school, and then he spends all of Saturday working with one of the local farmers to find a tool and method for crushing the small white jewels into a fine powder.

Dr. Cliffton tries the first Variant batch himself and then applies a second over Mrs. Cliffton in her sleep. She wakes on Sunday morning telling him of the most beautiful place she visited in her mind. We celebrate with poached eggs and cinnamon pears.

There's one Variant portion left. Will offers it to me and Miles, but we let him take it. The next morning, we all look up as he appears at the breakfast table.

"So?" Dr. Cliffton asks. "What did you think?"

"Good," Will says. He reaches for the coffee.

"Are you going to tell us about it?" Mrs. Cliffton asks.

"No." He brings the mug to his lips to hide a grin. "Not a chance."

That evening, Dr. Cliffton takes the news to the Sisters' Council. He is gone so late that I don't even hear him come home.

"The Council is thrilled," he informs us in the morning. "They voted to approve immediately. I already have a list of orders from the voting members, and they're asking me to seed the Variant into the Market as soon as possible."

The news of the Dream Variant has broken by the time we leave for school. It's too sensitive to appear in the *Sterling Post,* but it spreads like wildfire anyway. Cars drive by the Clifftons' house for the next several days, leaving parcels of potatoes and fresh brown eggs and even precious bags of sugar at the gate. The phone rings until Mrs. Cliffton tires of answering it and simply takes it off the hook.

"Miles," she says. "A classmate of yours called today. Wants to have you over after school next week."

He beams, even at me. It seems as though the discovery of the Variant, and the part that we played together, will be enough to thaw the last remaining tension that has lingered between us ever since I accused him of taking Mother's necklace.

"You did it," I whisper to him over dessert.

"Kinda you, too," he says back, and that's when I know we are okay again.

Dr. Cliffton begins a waiting list for orders and sends out a request to the town that he'll pay an entire dollar per tooth. "Legitimately lost teeth only, please," he reminds a group of Corrander boys who show up at the door with a few suspiciously bloody baby teeth and younger siblings lagging close behind.

It is just the thing to distract everyone as preparations launch into full force for Disappearance Day. With one week remaining, groundskeepers set to work on the orchard and school lawn, trimming grass, stringing lanterns, and clearing brush from the paths. Beas has extra rehearsals every day for an orchestra performance at the Harvest Fair. Will spends time with Tuck the carpenter constructing a stage, a podium, and additional seating.

My gaps in Cass's letters are growing larger. I mention nothing of this when I write to her on Saturday. Nothing about Miles's discovery, the Variants, the Marketplace, the Tempest race, or Disappearance Day. How I've finally stopped searching for my reflection when I walk past windows and mirrors. "I have practice now for this new game called Stars," I write. "It's similar to darts." I force my pen across the page. "I miss you and Father, and Mother most of all. Some days I'm so anxious to be back home with you again."

But there are some days, like the next afternoon—when I'm sitting outside with Will and Miles under crimson leaves pattering with rain, feeling warm under a cloak of Embers and Veils, and watching raindrops slide over my opened palm—that I find I'm not quite as anxious as I used to be.

Mrs. Cliffton opens her daytime scheduler at the breakfast table before school. "Let's talk about what still needs to be done before the twenty-ninth."

"The twenty-ninth?" I ask, my head jerking up.

"Yes," she says, "the Harvest Fair is on the twenty-ninth."

"Every year?"

She nods, then continues on with her list. "We'll pick up some honey and figs. And Malcolm will need to bring his telescope."

But I'm not listening. My mind is traveling back to three years ago, when Miles was five. The first year he insisted we do something special for birthdays other than his own. He helped Father and me make a lemon sponge cake topped with glazed strawberries. Talked Father into getting us all tickets to the cinema to see *The Wizard of Oz,* even though the flying monkeys gave him nightmares for weeks after. At the end, Miles had the whole theater sing to Mother. The way she smiled let me know she was doing it for us, not because she enjoyed it. In fact, she'd never really liked her birthday, and I'd never understood why.

But I do now.

My mother's birthday was October 29, 1907.

She was born on the first Disappearance Day.

CHAPTER TWENTY-ONE

Date: 7/28/1941
Bird: The Fulmar
Means "foul gull" in Norse.
Nauseating smell acts as a defense against predators.
But it's a poor defense, as many birds can hardly
smell anyway.

I can tell that Phineas is starting to sense that something is off. There's the cut on my cheek I can't see. I nicked myself shaving and didn't realize. "You slice yourself?" he asks, gesturing to his own whiskered mouth one morning. I probe the crusting of dried blood with my tongue until it starts to bleed again.

"Don't know how I missed it," I say lightly. Phineas fetches me a bandage. Carefully covers the cut himself.

The gesture startles me. It's the first time in years someone has touched my face.

There are bloody tissues in the waste bin again, folded beneath other trash. I find them when I'm emptying the can. There are too many to just be mine.

My mind keeps going over it while I grate potatoes to make hash for our dinner. I put the first few on the stove to fry and turn to grate another. My eyes begin to burn and smart. As if I'm cutting onions. I don't stop to think about why. I'm still mulling over those bloody tissues.

When Phineas appears in the doorframe, I look up just in time to see his face change. Go wide and wild with shock. "What the devil?" he yells.

I turn to see flames behind me, yellow and blue. It wasn't onions that had bothered my eyes. It was smoke.

I snatch a pan cover and drop it over the blaze. Throw a handful of salt on the flames that are escaping around its edges. Like fire-dousing Variants, *I think blurrily. The smoke is like gravel in my throat. Makes me cough like Phineas. He flings open the window, sending the smoke rushing out into the cold air. The flames in the pan finally weaken and go out.*

When the smoke clears, I can see what I've done to Phineas's pristine kitchen.

Black singe marks shoot up the wall behind the ruined back stove burner. Flakes of white ash settle around us like snow. I managed to contain the flames just before they reached the curtains.

The apology I attempt sends my lungs into a fresh coughing fit.

But Phineas isn't listening. He is looking intently at a spatula that sat near enough to the heat to melt into a pool of rubber.

I think I read somewhere that melting rubber smells horrible. All of a sudden I can't remember. Especially when Phineas fixes his eyes on me. Glittering and cold.

He ignores the mess and pours two glasses of blood-red claret. Sets the larger one in front of me and gestures for me to sit.

"Talk," he commands.

"I can't smell anything." I bow my head in confession, like this is somehow my fault. "I haven't been able to since the day I was born."

Phineas rights the chair again and sits down heavily. Heaves a sigh. Rubs his temples with the knuckles marked for each year that he was behind bars. I gulp down the wine, wondering what he's thinking. If the fallout from my Disappearances will be worse than I'd feared.

But he suddenly opens his palms to me in a gesture of admission, clean and white against the background of the blackened stove. When he shrugs, my understanding dawns.

"You . . . can't either?" The wine, the realization . . . they make my mind spin.

He gives a single curt nod. "Anything else unusual ever happen to you?" His voice has grown dangerous and low.

"The Disappearances," I breathe. I check them off my fingers, and his eyes darken with each one: the lost colors and dreams, the starless nights, the missing reflections. Something new vanishing every seven years, like clockwork.

He's chugged two glasses of wine by the time I finish. "All this time," he says, his voice already slurring, "I thought it was only me."

I fight the strangest urge to laugh. "You and the population of three other towns."

"What do you mean?" His voice is too loud. "Which towns?"

"Sterling, Corrander, and Sheffield."

By this point we're both drunk on a bottle of wine and no dinner. But I can tell he is thinking hard about something. Like a puzzle he is trying to figure out.

"I left a ring with you. A stone," he finally says. "With a teardrop in it." The corners of his lips are stained.

"Yes, I remember," I say, leaning a steadying hand against the table. "But I don't have it."

Phineas strokes the stubble on his chin. It is no longer pricked with gray, but is being consumed by it. Or maybe the color is simply draining out of him. "Then who does?"

My voice is hoarse. "I'll get it back."

The room spins slightly off its axis, as if Phineas were swirling it along with the wine at the bottom of his glass. "Everything is forgiven," he says, vaguely nodding at the destruction I've caused. "Just get that stone for me."

CHAPTER TWENTY-TWO

What can it mean, that Mother was born on Disappearance Day?

Her incriminating ties to the Disappearances are growing harder to dismiss. I flinch every time someone mentions the Harvest Fair. October 29.

Stop being ridiculous, I tell myself. *Stop being disloyal.* Maybe being born on Disappearance Day isn't incriminating — maybe, in fact, it's the reason why she was able to leave.

Yes, I think, glancing up from the words she's circled in her Shakespeare book. Maybe that's all it was. Some supernatural transaction, some magic in the air that made her immune because she was born the same day it happened — something akin to being struck by lightning.

I scratch out another entry to my growing list. Either way, I don't want anyone else to know the connection. Mother must have been quiet enough about it growing up that people didn't know — no one's said anything about it yet, and even the entry in the Council book made no mention. I'm certainly not going to call attention to it.

But the realization makes me even more anxious for Disappearance Day to be behind us.

Four more days.

Less than twenty-four hours before Disappearance Day I make my way to the courtyard picnic table where I always meet George for lunch. I pull out my peanut butter sandwich and my copy of *Underwoods* with the missing cover, when suddenly Beas sits down beside me. "May I join you?" she asks.

"Please." I nod, and she pulls out her brown lunch bag.

"What are you reading?"

I show her my tattered copy of Robert Louis Stevenson. "Looks well-loved," she says. She digs into her own bag and retrieves a book by John Greenleaf Whittier.

"I've never read that one," I say. "Want to trade?"

"Sure." She slides her copy across the table. "It's fun to know someone who's keen on the same sorts of things." The sunlight dapples her face like freckles. "A friend," she adds.

I bite back a pleased smile as George joins us. "Ladies," he says, unwrapping his own peanut butter sandwich. He eats it in approximately three swallows.

Beas bites into a jam tart. "You haven't been wearing that necklace lately," she says to me. "The pretty glass-looking one."

"Oh," I say, my fingers finding the empty space where the stone would normally hang, just between my collarbones. "This sort of odd thing happened, actually." I tell them about waking up and finding it gone.

A look of horror crosses Beas's face.

"The Disappearances only happen on Disappearance Day, right?" I'm only half kidding. "Other things don't randomly go missing in the night?"

"No," Beas says. "That's unsettling. Stuff like that never happens here. We don't even lock our doors most of the time."

"Who could have taken it?" George asks.

I shrug. I don't like dwelling on it. It still disturbs me enough to keep my Star close at hand all the time. Most days I keep it wrapped up and tucked in the pockets of my skirts and trousers. Just in case.

And then, from out of nowhere, a ball flies toward George's face. He gives a little yell and jumps out of the way, but it nails him in the arm hard enough to redden his skin.

"Watch out!" someone calls lazily. "Almost another Mackelroy misfortune."

There's a snicker, and then two boys from the crowd at the Tempest race move on into the orchard.

"Hilarious," George mutters, wrapping up the rest of his lunch. "I should be working on my Variant Innovation, anyway." He waves at us and ambles away, his shirt untucked, his hair smashed at the back of his head as if he just woke up from a nap.

"Kind of unfortunate for George, isn't it?" Beas says.

I nod. Not that I want the Catalyst to be tied to George, of course. But it feels treacherously nice, on days like these, to be in the honey warmth of the sun instead of Sterling's shadow.

"I'm glad I got to meet Thom at the race," I say. "He seems swell."

"He is," Beas agrees.

"But he's not from here," I say hesitantly. "So . . . how was he allowed to come?"

Beas laughs. "You're a real rule follower, aren't you?"

"Not *always*," I say. "But, I guess, mostly."

She smiles down at the cellophane she's unwrapping from another jam tart. "Thom used to live just over the border. He found out about the Disappearances when we were younger, and he never breathed a word about it, even when he moved two towns away. Over the years he's gained our trust."

"And also because you're in love with him."

"Yes."

"So there are exceptions."

"Sometimes." She takes another bite. "I mean. Look at you."

"Do you think you'll end up with him?" I ask, crossing my ankles under the table. "Do you think it's possible for . . . people from different places to be together?"

She looks at me with a slight frown. Then she sighs. "I don't know. It gets more complicated every seven years."

"It's not so bad here," I say. "Thom could live here and use the Variants. It's not that big of a sacrifice."

"Oh yeah?" she says. "Would you do it? Be willing to forfeit things you don't even know are going to disappear? We could live through ten, eleven more Disappearances. And maybe when enough gets taken, it adds up to not be worth it."

I stay silent. "But the Variants. They replace the missing things eventually."

"There's no guarantee that Variants will be found for everything that's going to disappear. Sometimes it takes years. For some things, it could be never." She pauses. "I don't want to ask Thom to make that choice."

"Would you ever consider leaving here for him?"

She laughs a short laugh. Looks down at the napkin crumpled in her hand. "I want to tell you I would. But at least here I get a chance to have some of those things back with the Variants. If I leave, I really lose them."

I want to argue with her vehemently. To convince her that maybe Thom could be worth it.

"Then we'll just have to find a way to end the Disappearances, won't we?" I say lightly.

"Sure," she says, her mouth turning down into a wry smile. She unwraps her last tart and hands it to me. "I thought that's why you were here."

CHAPTER TWENTY-THREE

October 29, 1942
Disappearance Day

At half past two on Disappearance Day I pull on my red coat and knock on Miles's door. He sits cross-legged on the floor, sketching.

"Ready?" I ask.

He's wearing gloves that are huge on him, loose and bunching around his fingers in drooping folds even as he clutches his Variant pencils.

"Aren't those a little big for you?" I ask.

"They're Will's," he says. "He *gave* them to me," he adds purposefully. I don't fail to notice the chill in his tone.

"Everything okay?" Things have thawed between us in the wake of the Dream Variant discovery, but now Miles stands and pushes past me without answering.

I sigh. He's just like Mother, with his impossible moods. Maybe he's as anxious as everyone else about what the day will bring.

"It's too depressing to be home tonight," Mrs. Cliffton says when we climb into the car. She sprinkles Variants over her compact and applies a deep red lipstick. "So with the Harvest Fair, we make it into a celebration. We rise up to meet it."

Sterling is hosting the fair this year, so we park the car and join the line snaking into the high school. Dr. Cliffton lugs his telescope case, and Will balances Mrs. Cliffton's platter of cheeses. A large sign with imposing letters hangs on the front door. It says HARVEST FAIR— TICKETS REQUIRED. STRICTLY ENFORCED. Mrs. Cliffton nudges Will, her hair flaming like cinnamon against the fall sky. Her eyes crinkle. "It's peppermint air," she says, inhaling.

We hand over our tickets and enter the long hallway of the school, our footsteps echoing past darkened classrooms, and we leave our coats on a set of empty desks. Mrs. Cliffton's deep blue dress, belted at the waist, has a full skirt that swishes at her knees. I have on my best dress, short-sleeved and moss-colored, with a high collar that used to perfectly hide Mother's necklace. I try to fix Miles's cowlick, but he shoves my hand away and glares at me.

"What?" I ask.

But he sets his jaw and doesn't answer.

Dr. Cliffton sprinkles us with Embers and we step outside. Paper lanterns swing from the orchard branches, and strains of live music filter from somewhere in the distance. Trails are lined with glass mason jar luminaries and flowers. We pass a cluster of hens pecking seed, a pile of pumpkins, children spilling out of a hayride. The mood is more festive than I expected; there is a current of energy, or maybe relief, that the day is here. That the unknown is almost known.

"There are some of your friends, Will," Mrs. Cliffton says, waving. "Do you want to join them?"

Will acknowledges them, and my heart rises with happiness when he says, "I'll find them later."

Together we drop off our provisions and head toward the lake. Punting boats slice through the water, which has a different mood entirely today, choppy and blue instead of the black glass of the other night. People perch on picnic tables and sprawl on blankets in the grass, eating golden-fried doughnuts rolled in cinnamon. A girl with strawberry blond hair is nestled between the roots of a tree, reading a book. Her glasses are too big, and every so often she lifts her face to smile at the sky. Younger children scamper up the branches above her, sending down sprays of blood-red leaves. Their hands pluck apples from the topmost branches, the only ones that remain.

Dr. Cliffton leaves us and joins three men who are fishing from the near dock. He struggles with his cane in the sand, and the men hurriedly make room for him to take a seat on the hunks of drift-wood. One says something that makes him laugh, and they offer him a fresh catch still sizzling in butter over the flames from a sandpit. A few of my classmates are roasting Betty Lou marshmallows until they puff out in crisp pillows. A young boy with large brown eyes sits in the sand nearby, letting it fall through his fingers, blowing intermit-tently on a silver whistle. On any other night I'm sure someone would tell him to stop. But tonight no one does.

We leave Dr. Cliffton and continue on through the rest of the grounds. There are tables of rich food everywhere—apple butter slathered over thick biscuits, squash soup with fresh cream, savory meat pies with scored crusts that Mother would have loved, loaves of lemon and lavender cakes dusted with flower petals, bottles of wine and mugs of spiced cider and dark hot chocolate. Miles never takes off the gloves, yet he reaches out to touch everything: the bark on the trees, the tassels hanging from tablecloths, an iridescent wind chime carved from mother-of-pearl. Melted ice cream streaks across the gloves like comets.

Even in the midst of the excess, there are signs that everyone's provisions have been pooled for this one night. As Dr. Cliffton assembles his telescope to offer glimpses of planets, a flush of small children run by, their baskets filled and shirts upturned to hold their candy. One of the littlest ones takes a tumble, her stash scattering along the ground like marbles, and everyone around her bends to help collect them again.

I straighten at the distinctive sound of a candy cracking into shards under a shoe.

"Malcolm," says a voice.

Dr. Cliffton stands from where he had crouched to inspect one of the little girl's sugar-coated almonds in the fading light.

"Victor." Dr. Cliffton nods curtly to the man in front of us. There's a boy standing next to him who looks vaguely familiar. They both have a sharp look to their faces and pointed chins, though the boy lacks the small mustache that makes his father look almost like a rat.

"I suppose it's off to the races again tonight," Victor says to Dr. Cliffton, and the words jar my memory. I recognize the boy now. Leroy Larkin. The one Will raced against that night on the lake. "No rest for the two of us when the Disappearances keep coming," Victor continues. He smiles, but it is all teeth, no warmth.

"Best of luck to us all," Dr. Cliffton says stiffly. He doesn't return Victor's smile. "That the next Disappearance is something minor and the Variant can be found quickly."

"I heard Cleary is planning a run for Sterling's next mayor," Victor says. "But maybe you'd be better suited for the job. A little change of pace, perhaps, Malcolm? Find another way to be the people's savior?"

"Have a good night, Victor," Dr. Cliffton says pointedly, turning back to his telescope.

Victor Larkin squeezes his son's shoulder. "Come along, Leroy," he says. "Matilda," he says, tipping his head to Mrs. Cliffton.

Will mutters something under his breath, crouching to find another candy. I bend to help him look, even though the young girl with the basket is long gone.

"That's the other Variant inventor?" I ask quietly.

Will grits his teeth. "I wouldn't really put Victor Larkin and my father in the same sentence," he says. "Mr. Larkin invented some of the Enhancements. The Tempests, for instance. But he also came up with the Hypnosis Variants. They're outlawed everywhere, but that doesn't stop him." Will shoves his hands into his pockets. "He doesn't seem to have any problem selling his integrity to the highest bidder."

"Hypnosis Variants?" I ask, but I'm interrupted by Miles.

"So when is it supposed to happen?" he asks, popping one of the girl's forgotten almonds into his mouth. "The Disappearance, I mean?" he adds in a loud whisper.

Dr. Cliffton clicks the last part of his telescope into place and checks his watch. "Anytime. At the original fair it wasn't until close to six o'clock. One year it was around two o'clock, another four. It seems later in the day when Sterling hosts. So now we just wait, and watch."

"Maybe nothing will disappear this year," Miles says, crunching on the candy. "And then it will all be over."

And the way Mrs. Cliffton's back suddenly straightens like a rod, the way the excitement builds as the hours pass without a Disappearance tells me that this is exactly what everyone is hoping.

When the sun begins to set, the luminaries and lanterns flame with fire and Glimmers. I buy a flower necklace from Viv, the woman from the Marketplace, and a woven flower crown from one of her daughters. The girl wears them stacked along her arm like floral bangles. The one she places on my head has peach dahlias, orange lilies, and sprigs of delicate white buds that look like dots of pearls. I can feel Will's eyes on me the moment she pins it into my hair.

Up ahead a man sits playing the banjo on a low branch that stretches parallel to the ground. A father and his young daughter are dancing together to the spirited music, she laughing as he swings her around, and my crown feels heavy when I turn my head away from them.

That's when I catch Mrs. Cliffton slip something into a woman's bag. The woman is wearing a colorless dress and has a handkerchief pulled around her unwashed hair. She is so focused on chasing after a young boy without dropping the wailing baby slung over her arm that she doesn't notice what Mrs. Cliffton has done.

"Aila!" Beas breaks through the crowd. She holds a pumpkin cinnamon roll wrapped in a napkin, dripping with icing. "I wanted to make sure you got one of these." She hands the roll to me, still warm. Eliza follows her, delicately eating a candied apple on a stick. "Oh, and you should get in line early for one of the Babcocks' baked cinnamon apples," Beas instructs. "I'd wait with you, but I'm supposed to be warming up for the concert." She wears the deep woven purple strap of her violin case like a purse.

"See you, Beas," Eliza says, taking another prim bite of apple.

She wears a body-skimming costume that drips with red and silver beads, and a younger boy with the same bright green eyes as hers trails a half step behind her. He smiles widely when he sees Miles.

"Hello there, Miles," he says, stepping forward. Miles kicks at the dirt in response. "Hi," he mutters.

"Mrs. Cliffton," Eliza says brightly, "my mother was thrilled to hear about the new Dream Variant. She wants to have you and Dr. Cliffton over for dinner when she returns in a few weeks."

"That would be lovely," Mrs. Cliffton says, but she is distracted, waving to a man, giving him a small pat on the shoulder as he passes, discreetly dropping something into his bag with her other hand. I've gotten a better look this time. It's a Variant pouch.

My understanding dawns when I see that Will has some, too. So many they are practically spilling from his pockets. The Clifftons are using the chaos of the crowd and the shadows to sneak Variants into people's bags. Bestowing anonymous gifts on those whose clothes and faces show signs of wear, on the night they will be most in need of some cheer.

This is who I am finding the Clifftons to be. Eyes open, watching for the need around them, and quietly meeting it. Like new coats for Miles and me.

Like Miles and me ourselves.

"I'm performing later," Eliza says, gesturing at her costume. "It's the routine that won in the Sisters Tournament last year. I couldn't bear to turn them down when they asked me to do it tonight."

"They wanted my older sister, Cassandra," her brother interjects. "But she has a *real* performance. Where Mother went. To see her."

Eliza's eyes blaze. "*Thank you,* Walt," she says through gritted teeth. Then she touches Mrs. Cliffton's arm. "I hope you'll make it," she says, and her smile broadens into something real when she looks at Will. "I'll look for you."

"I'll look for you," her brother mimics silently behind her, making a face.

"Nice to see you, dear," Mrs. Cliffton says noncommittally.

"William, Carter was looking for you," Eliza says. "I'll help you find him. I think I saw him over there."

When Eliza pulls Will and her brother along with her, Mrs. Cliffton reaches down for Miles's shoulder and mine. She gives me a small squeeze, an acknowledgment of how much she understands and will never say.

"Come on, you two," she says dryly.

I purse my lips into a line to hide my smile. The Clifftons, whether they are trying to or not, are making inroads straight across each fault line of my heart.

I'm pleased when Miles finds two of his classmates and melts with them into the crowd. Once the sun has fully set, there are two false reports of Disappearances in quick succession: the first when someone bites into a mealy, tasteless apple, and the second when Mr. Babcock declares the rum in his flask has become water. After a few tests, both claims are refuted, and everyone disperses back into the night with a sigh of relief.

I find George in line for Dr. Cliffton's telescope. We take our turns looking at cratered shadows of the moon and a burning red Mars, and then we join a crowd gathering at the lake's edge. Leaves crinkle like parchment under our feet.

"Let's hope he's feeling uncharacteristically brief today," George says as Principal Cleary clears his throat from the podium. "Welcome to the eighty-fifth annual Harvest Fair of Sterling," Cleary begins. His deep voice echoes across the water. The fires shimmer along the beach. "We extend a very cordial welcome to our friends from Corrander and Sheffield here tonight."

He clears his throat again in response to the smattering of half-hearted applause. Then he holds a monocle over one eye and reads from the cream-colored papers in his hand.

"Our forefathers — rest their souls," Principal Cleary intones, "never knew what momentous double meaning this fair would some-day hold. Yes, we gather to celebrate the bountiful yield of the past year. And while some might say that much has been taken away, we always must remember how much we've been able to regain through a bit of hard work and applied intellectual prowess."

"Oh, here we go," mutters George. "This is a warm-up for him running for mayor."

"We think tonight, and every night, of our brave men fighting, and I'm sure their thoughts are with us on this significant occasion as we recount the beginning of our humble struggles, thirty-five years ago to the day."

There is no applause this time. It is quiet enough to pick up the ragged sound of Principal Cleary's breathing, the crisp shuffle of the papers in his hand. I glance at the crowd around me. Wonder again about Mother's ring. If perhaps the person who took it is here tonight.

"So what do we come together to celebrate on this most bitter-sweet of days?" Principal Cleary hurries on. "Yes, we celebrate our harvest, but we have something even greater to observe: that the people of the Sisters are strong, resilient, and, most important of all, resourceful. We have all persevered — no, I dare say, *thrived* — admi-rably, humbly, worthily, all in the face of an unparalleled challenge."

George blows a thick piece of sand-colored hair from his forehead. "This is actually one of Cleary's favorite days," he says. "This and graduation. And the Christmas Ball. Really, anywhere he gets to orate and get his photograph taken."

I'm about to remark on Principal Cleary's unfortunate choice of bow tie when I catch something out of the corner of my eye.

"Be right back," I say instead, and slip away.

Miles stands alone, twenty yards behind the crowd, his eyes trained on the dirt at his feet. When I draw nearer, I'm startled by the tears that fall like rain on his one gloveless hand. Something about that bare hand makes my chest constrict and then open, until the hollowness makes my rib cage seem too small.

"Miles — what's wrong?"

He looks up at me and hastily brushes the tears from his face. "I'm not crying," he says angrily.

"I didn't think you were," I lie.

"You forgot, didn't you?" he says. "She hasn't even been dead for that long, and you already forgot that today was her birthday."

I step back, touching my cheek. So this is why he's been distant today.

"I didn't forget," I say.

"Don't lie. You didn't even mention it once," he continues.

"I didn't forget," I insist. "I'm sorry, Miles — I should have said something. I just didn't know what." My knee is almost touching someone's overturned ice-cream cone that is melting in the dirt. "What happened to your glove, Miles?"

His face fights against crumpling.

"I lost it somewhere."

"Let's look for it. I'll help you."

I take his hand in mine then. It is cold, like stone, almost as cold as Mother's always was in the dream I used to have. He lets me hold it for half a minute. Then a sudden burst of applause marks the speech's end, and he pulls it away again.

We retrace Miles's steps across the grounds, past the booths of pies and snuffling piglets and confetti left like pieces of gold glinting in the mud. The crowd drifts toward the orchard, settling into seats with glasses of wine and steaming mugs before the concert starts. Beas sits in her chair, glancing over her music one last time. A woman walks over to her, and Beas nods as they speak. I look more closely at the woman, who wears a sharply pressed skirt and has ruby nails and a severe hairdo. I recognize her. It's the lady from my first day in town. The one who put the note into my bag.

The woman reaches out to tuck Beas's hair behind her ear, and my stomach curls. It's the kind of touch only a mother would do.

And then Eliza springs up to them. She is flushed and too giddy to play at being aloof. The beads on her costume hit against one another, shimmering.

"Let's see if the school has a lost and found," I say to Miles, edging closer to the orchestra seats. Curious to know what has suddenly made Eliza so happy.

"Guess what?" Eliza clutches Beas's arm.

"Let's see . . ." Beas says wryly. "All *three* of your tournament events have already forfeited to you?"

"No." Eliza's voice gets higher. "William asked me to go to the Christmas Ball with him!"

I stop walking. The air thins, and my heart feels like a fist clenching. At any minute it's going to crumble in on itself and become dust.

Mrs. Fogg turns around and sees me and Miles. I hurry past the three of them, into the darkness of the school, with Miles on my heels.

Just find the blasted glove. Don't think about anything else.

"Where did you last see it?" I ask, forcing my voice to brighten. Blinking back tears when the guard at the front door tells us that no one has returned a missing right glove.

"I went on the hayride with my friends," Miles says hopefully.

"We'll check there next." We cut through the crowd and to the front of the line. I ignore the displeased mutters and hoist myself onto the wagon. The wooden boards creak, and for one moment I catch myself waiting for the dry, sweet smell of the hay bales.

And then I see it: one black cotton finger, barely visible between the bent tufts of straw.

"Aha!" I jump down from the wagon and hand the glove triumphantly to Miles. His face shines at me, and I resist the urge to smooth his cowlick. "Don't lose it this time."

I see Will walking toward us. He smiles, lifts his hand into a wave, but I pretend not to notice. Instead I pull Miles along in the other direction.

"What happens if we make it to midnight and nothing has disappeared?" someone asks to my right. "Does it mean it's over?"

"Don't say it out loud," someone else hisses. "There's still hours left."

"Even then—remember the year the dreams went?" a third voice interjects. "We didn't realize for days."

"Aila!" George grabs my arm. "Where'd you go earlier? You just disa— Oh, never mind. Poor choice of words."

"Hey, George," I say. "This is my brother, Miles."

"Miles?" George says. "Not Kilometers?" He grins at his own joke.

Miles sighs heavily and shoots me a look. "Never heard that one before," he says dully.

"Well, anyway, nice gloves," George says. "And — oh — uh, hide me, will you?"

He ducks down between us.

"George . . . what are you *doing?*" I ask, glancing around. Will has vanished into the crowd again.

George cocks his head and squints up at me. "Did you read the paper I gave you at the race — about the Mackelroys?"

I glance at Miles. He doesn't know that I snuck out to see the Tempest races. And I don't want him to.

"Yes," I say, drawing out the word and shooting George a look.

George straightens and peers around again. "Remember how it said that Charlton Templeton married someone else, instead of my ancestor Lorna? One of his heirs is a girl our age, from Corrander. Her name is Margeaux Templeton." He runs his hands through his hair. "My mother wants me to make amends with her. Show a united front so people won't think our families are behind the Curse."

"I see. Making amends seems to be going *very* well," I say, grinning obnoxiously. I steal a handful of his kettle corn.

"Well, Margeaux makes it a little hard," he says, swatting my hand away. "She always looks as though she's planning ways to bump me off."

I casually scan the crowd. There is a girl glaring in our direction. She's wearing a jeweled headband perched atop curly mouse-brown hair. She might have been pretty if not for the perpetual scowl. It's hard to tell.

"Ah," I say. "I think I found her."

"See? She's downright scary."

"I bet you could buy her affection with this kettle corn." I plunge my hand in for another fistful. Send pieces flying when I put it in my mouth. "It is *that* good."

"Be nice," George says. "I think it's a rule that you have to be on my side."

"So how does your mother want you to make amends?"

"I'm pretty sure she wants me to propose."

I choke on a popcorn kernel.

"Or . . . at least ask Margeaux to the Christmas Ball," he continues.

"Sounds like a more reasonable place to start," I say, recovering. With Miles in tow, we find a place to sit in the grass, which is silvered and cool in the moonlight, tickling my bare leg. From this vantage point we have a good view of Beas's row.

"Oh, well, um, about that . . ." George says. His freckles darken. He lowers his voice so Miles won't hear. "I was kind of thinking it would be more fun, if maybe . . . *we* went to the ball together."

"Oh!" I say, and, in a moment of panic, stuff another handful of popcorn into my mouth. I spot Dr. and Mrs. Cliffton a few rows away. She is leaning against him. The breeze rustles her hair. I do not look for Will. "Okay," is all I can think to say.

"Great," George says, settling back into the grass.

The conductor, Mr. Riley, taps his baton on the music stand and lifts his hands in the air. The orchestra members draw their instruments to a ready position, like strands of a web tied to the tip of his baton, and the crowd around us quiets. Mr. Riley's arm flashes down, and at his signal the strings section comes alive with notes.

The music is so rich and full that it seeps into the depths of my chest, blurring the line between pleasure and hurt. Maybe it is both. Maybe it is shimmering them together into something new. I close my eyes and listen, thinking of what Dr. Cliffton said about combinations coming together to make magic.

I turn my face to Beas as she begins to play. Her eyes are closed, and the music is flowing through her and out of her so that she seems to be made of it. The seconds are dripping from clocks that everyone is trying not to watch. Beas's violin crescendoes into the height of her solo, her chin pointing up as her bow slices down.

And then her notes stop, as sudden as a record scratching. As if we are hearing her through the radio and the plug has been ripped from the wall.

Beas's arms keep moving, but there is only the rasp of horsehair sliding along the steel strings and, from somewhere in the audience, a slight cough.

Someone titters uneasily, and then there is a gasp, followed by a low moan. George sits up, his hands gripping his knees, his knuckles colorless.

"No!" A young girl's wail cuts through the silence. The musicians test their own instruments and then stand, knocking over their chairs and setting down their bows in a daze. Family members run forward from the crowd with outstretched arms.

An old woman stands next to me and, in a broken voice, says, "Please. Make it anything else."

In the midst of the chaos, I frantically seek out Beas.

She hasn't moved from her chair. She stares down at the sheet of notes in front of her, wiping tears from her face before they can fall onto her lowered violin.

CHAPTER TWENTY-FOUR

Date: 10/27/1941

Bird: Canaries

Canaries do not sing in the fall. The singing parts of
their brains die off.

They grow anew over the winter months, to sing once
more come springtime.

"What do you want me to work on today?" I ask Phineas. I pick up our
dishes to rinse them in the sink. Dew beads in glassy pebbles along the window. "I could replace the hinges on the front door."

He clears his throat. "I think the odd jobs are pretty much done," he
says carefully. I scrub at the crusted egg yolk on my plate, realizing what
that means. Now that I've brought home money and fixed the house, I have
outstayed my usefulness.

My throat tightens, as thick as if I'd swallowed cotton. I hope he comes
straight out with it. It will be so much worse if he dances around it, dropping hints.

Maybe I should just announce that I've been planning to leave anyway.
I scrub at the plate so hard I worry it might crack in my hands. I take a
shaky breath. Set the plate on the rack to dry. Purposefully leave little pieces
of the egg clinging to it in a filmy ring.

Phineas folds his napkin. "I was thinking you could stay on anyway.
To live," he announces, pushing back from the table. "But we'd need a new
stove. So why don't you stop and pick up another one?"

"Oh," I say casually. "All right."

I pick the plate back up from the drying rack. Scrub it again, until it gleams.

The bell tinkles overhead when I enter the hardware store. I weave through the aisles, past grinders and vises, Singer sewing machines and lawn mowers, to examine the stove models under blinding overhead lights. After picking out the most expensive one and arranging for delivery, I return to the sewing machines. Some of the needles look hefty enough to stab someone with — to gouge out an eye, pin a hand into a wall or a table. I pretend to examine the number 2 compass saw that narrows into a rapier point. I can't tell if the mirror hoisted in the upper corner is showing me, but I palm the thickest package of sewing needles anyway. Slip them into my pocket, all while keeping my eyes trained on the saw.

I have the money for them, of course. Taking them is just for fun.

Ironically, a salesman is talking to the owner about a new lock system when I sail past them with the needles in my pocket.

The salesman slides his business card across the counter just before I walk out the door. "The question is, how much would you pay for peace of mind?" he says to the owner.

That's when the flicker of my idea comes back to me. Catches flame.

How much would you pay?

Variants. Bottled. Euphoria. Peace of mind.

I consider it as I return home to Phineas. As I carve out an empty place in the belly of my wooden bird. I jimmy a lever like a corkscrew inside, so that when I twist the bird's head, a needle descends.

The Variants, the Variants. The discovery that should have been at least partly mine. The Variants recapture or enhance senses. Physical experiences.

Why hasn't anyone thought beyond that? Extrapolated to another level? Is it possible to bottle emotions? Capture states of mind?

If people will pay money for a temporary improvement to the physical world — even something as fleeting and insignificant as a scent — how much would they pay for something that goes infinitely deeper than that? What price could be placed on the ability to apply a mental state on command, from a pouch or a bottle?

Peace.

Joy.

Courage.

Even the very thing I feel rising within me as I twist my needle back up inside the bird.

Hope.

Not Variants, I think. But Virtues.

CHAPTER TWENTY-FIVE

The Monday following Disappearance Day is familiar but not, like the slightest wrist turn of a kaleidoscope. The lab table scored with crosshatches, the row of bottles the color of sea glass, the glint of cold sunshine through the window, and the scrape of my chair as I take my place between George and Beas. Beas doesn't look up. Her eyes are swollen, and for once there is no music in front of her. She's not doodling notes along the page margins or humming under her breath.

She slides her head down into her arms and says through them, "I broke up with Thom."

"What?" George and I both say.

"Honestly, I don't see the point," she says. "And that's all I want to say about it."

"All right." George's eyebrows raise. After a beat he says, "I heard Eliza's sister is coming home."

"From the opera?" I ask.

"Well, how's she meant to sing now?" Beas asks bitterly, not raising her head. Even Dr. Digby leaves her be, and she doesn't say another word for the rest of class.

I'm trying to remember the words to Whittier's "At Last" to write for Beas, when the bell rings and she abruptly stands. "Beas—" I say. I scramble to gather my books and head after her, but Eliza is waiting at the door. She takes Beas by the arm.

"I know you can't see it now, but there's someone better for you *here,*" Eliza assures her as I walk past them. Beas lays her head on Eliza's shoulder and doesn't look at me. Eliza continues, making a point to raise her voice. "That's why people from Sterling belong with other people from Sterling—and not with outsiders."

I walk toward my locker. That's what I will always be to George and Beas and Will. Someone who can leave at any moment and will never truly understand. I fiddle with the lock, wondering if my attempts at comfort over the Disappearances will ring hollow. Or worse—patronizing. This is the first time I can see the Disappearances for what they really are. A disintegration. Methodical and relentless. They tangle together in a jumble of hooks and splinter outward.

When I open my locker, a folded note flutters out. I reach to pick it from my shoe with dread. It is a boy's handwriting, cramped and small.

I bet you can hear it.

Can't you?

I crumple the paper. It could be from anyone.

Of course I can't, I want to scream.

I take a deep breath.

Temporary, I tell myself. I watch Beas's and Eliza's retreating backs. *Temporary for me.*

And me alone.

The hallways at school remain eerily quiet for the rest of the week. The atmosphere is one of stunned defeat—in the gymnasium as

I hurl Stars, at home as I sort scrap metal with Mrs. Cliffton for the war effort. Will lopes off with his toolbox in his hand, mumbling about finding something to fix. On Thursday, one week after Disappearance Day, Beas shifts in her chair next to me in lab and I glance at her knee. For the first time ever, there is nothing inked across her skin.

More silence, everywhere.

"Do you think the Clifftons would mind if I came home with you?" George asks as we're packing up our books. "I have some Variant ideas for the music that I want to run by Dr. Cliffton."

"I'm sure it's fine," I say. I hesitate. "Beas, do you want to come?"

"No thanks," she says, and slides off her seat to the door.

Mrs. Cliffton's car isn't where it normally is, parked along the curve of the side lane. My muscles ache with a dull hum from yesterday's Stars practice. I'm so sore I can barely pull on my coat. I scan the emptying lawn. "Do you see Miles anywhere?"

"Shh," George says tensely. I hear it now, too: a boy's voice, sneering just out of our sight. It's coming from the orchard.

"Maybe some of your teeth will solve this new Disappearance, too," the voice threatens, followed by the sound of scuffling. I drop my bag in the dirt and start running, my heart pumping between rage and fear, my fingers curling into fists as I turn the corner.

But Eliza beats me there. She flies out from the side door of the gymnasium and reaches our brothers first. Yanks hers, hard, by the elbow. When he turns, I recognize him from the Harvest Fair.

"Yow!" he whines, and I stop short.

"Walt," Eliza says in a voice that could wither a stone. "He's *a baby* compared to you. At least pick someone who can put up a good fight. Without a worthy opponent, you're nothing more than a bully."

She lets go of his arm roughly. "You're a *Patton,*" she says with disgust. She sniffs. "That's beneath you."

She turns away, and when she notices me standing there, she glares at me with an intensity that could melt glass. But I'm grateful that she defended Miles, even if she did it in the most insulting way possible. And—I wonder vaguely—did she just admit that she sees me as her equal?

She stalks away, calling to Walt over her shoulder, "And you'll be lucky if I don't rat on you to Mother for being such a little pig."

Walt follows after her, chuffing. He glares at each of us in turn and kicks plumes of dust into the air to curl back on us. It settles along my teeth as grit.

George brushes off his schoolbag. "He's a peach," he mutters.

Miles doesn't try to shield himself from the dust cloud. He bends to examine the stones studding the dirt at his feet, and the dust collects in his hair.

He wouldn't want me to fuss over him. So I stand still, a safe distance away from him. "You okay?" I say, and when he nods, I thrust my hands into the pockets of my coat. Finally Mrs. Cliffton pulls around the bend.

"Sorry!" she calls to us, rolling down the window. "I got caught up in a phone conversation I could not end for my *life.*" She pinks when she sees George, and I know who must have been on the other end of the telephone line.

George either doesn't pick up on this or doesn't care.

"Could George come over to study?" I ask Mrs. Cliffton.

"Only if he agrees to stay for dinner, too."

"Thank you," George says. He lowers his voice as we walk to the car. "Who would have thought today's knight in shining armor would be *Eliza?*" He looks carefully at Miles, as if gauging whether he's truly gotten away unscathed.

Miles looks small and innocent when he climbs into the front seat without saying a word. But I am all too familiar with the set of his jaw as he squints out the window, rubbing the stones smooth between his fingers.

I know my brother. And I think they've all underestimated him.

At home, George and I spread our books out on the kitchen table near the warmth of the oven. Genevieve is rubbing a rainbow of spices into the chicken she's preparing, trading out glass pans of au gratin potatoes and green beans for the loaves of bread she's baked fresh for dinner. She clucks her tongue and fusses like a hen, complaining that we're in her way, that we prattle on worse than two old women, but she keeps a steady stream of cookies and sandwiches appearing on our plates.

"Do you think Beas will be all right?" I ask George, cupping the crumbs into a line on my plate.

"She will," he says, his mouth full. "Give her a few more days."

But I know this Disappearance has cut her deeply. The absence of music is like a necklace that has snapped, scattering its collateral damage like wayward beads. I want to collect them all again—the dancing and singing, records and concerts and balls—and find a way to give them back to her.

"So what do people think is happening?" I ask.

"Theories abound," George says. "That it's some sort of curse. That it's a change in brain or sensory function—something passed down through families as a genealogical trait. We've explored the idea of it being something in the air or water or soil. That we were all having a psychotic break. Or maybe," George muses, squinting, "maybe it's just something random and unfortunate, like being struck with a disease."

"George—" I hesitate, still seeing Walt's attack on Miles. "Why do people keep targeting me and Miles when there are so many other possible Catalysts?"

I've seen the Council book, I think. *I know about the others.*

"Let me ask you this," George says. "Why do you think Eliza's so determined to be Miss Sterling everything? Have you ever noticed that?" He twiddles a pencil between his fingers. "Why do you think my mother is always in the middle of everyone's business? The thing is, Aila, that your mother left. She got the chance to get out, and she took it. And people feel like she deserted Sterling, and that only proved her guilt." His face softens. "Anyone else who could be a Catalyst is doing whatever they can to show they're the opposite of what she did."

I bunch my skirt in my fists under the table.

We're interrupted by the sound of the front door opening. We gather our things and meet Dr. Cliffton and Will in the foyer.

"Hello, George," Dr. Cliffton says with surprise. I cringe as he and Will pause at the sight of George and me standing side by side, as if trying to determine exactly what's going on between us.

"Dr. Cliffton," George says, stepping forward, "I know you're looking for a Variant for the music, and I was wondering if you might be open to a few ideas I have?"

"Certainly," Dr. Cliffton says. "Your mother has mentioned that you have quite the scientific mind. Perhaps with it, we'll reach the answer in half the time." He turns to Will. "Can we finish that discussion another time? Or would you care to join us?"

Will looks at George, then back at me. He scratches at his eyebrow.

"No, that's okay," he says.

Dr. Cliffton reaches into his bag to show George a book stuffed an inch thick with notes. "I've collected ideas for a decade in anticipation of this. Almost a thousand so far."

George holds up his single sheet of paper. "I've come up with . . . this."

"Excellent," Dr. Cliffton says, taking it from him. "We'll add it." He stuffs it into the book and gestures George into the library. "I feel strongly that it must be in here. Let's get started."

The door closes behind them.

Will and I are left standing in the foyer. It's the first time we've been alone since Disappearance Day. Since he asked Eliza to go to the Christmas Ball.

"Hi," he says, setting down his toolbox.

"Hello," I say stiffly.

He reaches into his back pocket. "I stopped by the post office on the way home," he says. "This came for you."

He hands me a folded envelope inked with Father's handwriting.

I rip it open on the spot and skim through his words about noon mess and calisthenics and jellyfish and a sun so bright it's sent men to the infirmary with burns. I can barely imagine how far away he must be from me now — here, the clouds hang low and gray with threatening snow. Still, I slump against the railing with relief.

Will lingers next to me. "Is everything all right?"

I give him a short nod and turn away without elaborating.

"Swell . . ." This time, his tone returns my coolness.

I'm heading upstairs to leave the letter on Miles's bed when there's a sudden knock on the door.

Beas stands just outside, shifting her weight.

"I changed my mind?" she says, shrugging, and I smile and throw the door open wide to let her in.

I give Beas a tour of the house, and we settle on the floor of my room. She hands back my *Underwoods.* "It was good."

"Pick another," I say, gesturing at my meager shelf. She examines my worn copies, and when she selects Yeats, I pull out my mother's Shakespeare book.

Occasionally we hear the library door open as Genevieve brings tea. "I've already crossed off these twelve," Dr. Cliffton says. "And I'm organizing the rest by materials we need to procure."

George is starting to read down the list when my eyes fall back to *King Henry the Eighth.*

"Bid the music leave."

I lean forward and read the words again as I uncap my pen. I add a circle around the words, as if I'm wreathing them with a crown.

Then I unfold the list I've made and add my latest find. It joins my last entry from *The Tempest,* the one about everything on this great globe dissolving, fading, leaving not a rack behind.

"What are you doing?" Beas asks, peering over my shoulder.

There are so many circled passages. All the things Mother found, and more that I discovered after her. My list now stretches to two pages. Taken altogether, laid out like this, a picture is starting to emerge.

"Dr. Cliffton said that most of the Variants seem to have literary clues," I say vaguely. "Many found in Shakespeare."

I flip through more pages, my eyes skimming through the words as fast as I can take them in. Beas returns to her homework. "I like the Bard, but sometimes the Elizabethan English feels like trying to run through mud."

"It gets easier," I say, distracted, moving on to *Much Ado About Nothing.*

My eyes flit over the words until I reach what Mother has circled next.

A funny sort of tremor runs through me.

She's marked:

Beat.: I am stuffed, cousin, I cannot smell.

Marg.: A maid, and stuffed! there's goodly catching of cold.

Beat.: O, God help me! God help me! how long have you professed apprehension?

Marg.: Ever since you left it. Doth not my wit become me rarely!

Beat.: It is not seen enough, you should wear it in your cap. By my troth, I am sick.

Mar.: Get you some of this distilled Carduus Benedictus, and lay it to your heart: it is the only thing for a qualm.

Carduus benedictus.

Benedictus I recognize. "Blessed," in Latin, the dead language Mother had once insisted on trying to teach me. Why did that sound vaguely familiar? It takes me a moment to place it.

My heart takes off, as if I'm nearing the edges of something I've been missing.

Then I abruptly close Mother's book and snatch my list. "Beas," I say, "I have an idea."

I knock on the library door, my excitement dazzling the higher it climbs. "Come in," Dr. Cliffton calls.

Beas and I step into the library, which is aglow with lamplight and the searing of the sun as it sets. George and Dr. Cliffton are leaning over a pile of books, the covers all open and layered on top of one another. They look up at me with polite expectation.

"I've been reading something of my mother's," I begin. "A Shakespeare volume. And I have a theory about the Disappearances."

Dr. Cliffton straightens. "Go on."

"I just came across this passage." I show them my circled words: "Bid the music leave." I flip to another page. "And here — when Beatrice says she can't smell, Margaret recommends trying *Carduus benedictus*. It reminded me of when you solved the first Variant."

I pluck out the plant encyclopedia he had shown me earlier. Navigate to the little spiky magenta plant.

The caption underneath says *"Carduus Benedictus*. Blessed Thistle."

"You said yourself that you can find so many of the clues in Shakespeare's pages," I remind him. I unfold my lists and smooth them out across his desk. "I've been working on this. What if — what if *all* the Disappearances are found there?"

Dr. Cliffton furrows his brow as he looks over my work.

"This is an impressive compilation, Aila. Truly." He taps on his chin in thought. "I suppose what you say is a possibility. Let's think this through, though."

He runs his fingers down my hastily scrawled columns.

"There are a fair number of things still missing—both from a Disappearance standpoint and a Variant one. Off the top of my head, I don't see the Embers or anything about the missing stars."

"Yes," I say, pointing to my list. "See, here—I thought the stars could be 'overcast the night,' from *Midsummer Night's Dream.*"

He pauses, thinking. "But we can still see the moon at night, so it seems a bit of a stretch."

George peers over his shoulder. "And what about Miles's Dream Variant, with the teeth? That's definitely more along the lines of Freud. Hundreds of years after Shakespeare."

"W-well," I stammer. I wasn't prepared to have to defend my theory as if it were on trial. "I haven't finished looking through all the pages yet—"

"And the biggest question that remains for me is—why?" Dr. Cliffton muses. "Why would this happen now, and here? Why would it affect us so far into the future—punishment for people and towns that didn't even exist when Shakespeare lived?"

"Well, I'm not sure," I admit.

"As impressive as Shakespeare was, he didn't have the power to see into the future—as far as we know." He chuckles. "And there's no historical tie between us and Shakespeare, or even between Sterling and Stratford-upon-Avon."

I nod. I hadn't quite gotten around to thinking about *why* Shakespeare would be involved in a curse on three towns he'd never visited, hundreds of years after his own death.

"I think there are naturally a lot of ties to be found here," Dr. Cliffton says. "He was quite prolific, of course, and one of the most influential authors in the history of literature. But I don't think this is quite able to stretch large enough to give us the whole story."

I nod, feeling deflated. They've punched gaping holes in my theory. If it and my ego were made of cloth, they'd both be in tatters.

Seeing my face, Dr. Cliffton says gently, "It was a good thought, Aila. Keep thinking along these lines. Maybe you'll find something."

"No, you're right," I say. "It doesn't hold."

"I better go," Beas says, looking as deflated as I feel. I show her to the door and watch her walk away through the first flakes of snow.

Then I close Mother's Shakespeare book and push it into the shadows under my bed, feeling foolish that after thirty-five years of Sterling's mystery, I actually believed I would be the one to solve it.

CHAPTER TWENTY-SIX

Date: 11/11/1941

Bird: Red-breasted Nuthatch

Nuthatches build nests in holes of trees, then spread pitch around the entrance to guard against predators.

Every time they return to their nest, they risk death.

They must choose the right angle and fly straight in or become caught in their own traps.

The Virtues are only an idea.

But so were the Variants, at one point. So were all great inventions: nothing but a conception. So I start feeding the idea by reading everything I can find on the brain. Anatomy. Psychology. Emotional development. Even Aristotle's works on ethics, virtues, and vices.

I read all day and ruminate at night when I'm deep in the mud of graves. I scratch out diagrams behind the pages of my bird drawings. The wisp of my idea grows.

It's not so hard. I'm used to teaching myself the things I want to know.

I ask Victor Larkin to meet over scentless coffee in a café just outside Sheffield. It annoys me, the way he counts the money under the table and immediately glances down at his watch. He spoons a cube of sugar into his coffee. "I'm a little unclear why we needed a meeting," he says crisply.

"I heard you invented something that might be of interest to me."

Victor's spoon stills, but the coffee keeps swirling around it. "And what would that be?"

"Hypnosis Variants."

His head shoots up. I've caught his attention now. "How did you hear about that?" he hisses.

I lower my voice. "I grew up in Sterling. I know all about the Disappearances."

He inhales deeply. I reach into my own pocket for my wooden bird. Set it on the table, easily within my grasp. "I'm not looking to take any control away from you. I'm looking to help you expand it."

Victor sips his coffee and motions for me to proceed. "I'm a bit of an inventor, too," I say. I stroke the wooden back of my bird. "I'm creating something to inject into the brain to separate out Virtues like Joy, Peace, Courage. Make them rise to the top like cream. Then skim them off and bottle them up, to sell. To use for later." I relish the way his eyes grow wider, his coffee forgotten and growing cold on the table. "An extrapolation, if you will, of the Variants."

"You realize something like this could even surpass Malcolm Cliffton," he says. "That self-righteous bastard won't have anything to do with me." He rubs at the hair on his chin. "What do you need to get started?"

I tell him as he pays our tab.

"I'll get it for you," Victor says, holding out his hand. "Stefen, I have a feeling it's going to be a pleasure doing business with you."

When I get home, Phineas is in his room.

"Where were you?" he asks. He is pacing, fumbling with his hands. He seems agitated. I slowly set down my bag. "Settling with Victor."

"Have you tracked down the Stone?"

"I'm working on it," I say. "But I've got this great id—"

I stop. Suddenly notice the maps spread around him. Maps he's drawn hastily, over and over, marked with X's. Maps of Corrander, Sheffield, and Sterling.

"What's going on?" I ask him slowly.

"Stefen," he says, "I think I caused the Disappearances."

CHAPTER TWENTY-SEVEN

Eight days after the music disappears, Principal Cleary strides into the cafeteria during our lunch hour to announce that the Christmas Ball is canceled. It is so quiet when he leaves that his footsteps echo all the way back down the hall.

"He's not even going to give us a chance to find a Variant in time?" George grumbles, pushing his food around his plate.

"How long does it usually take Dr. Cliffton?"

George sets his fork down on the table. "Well—" he admits, wiping his mouth. "Usually? Years."

Someone sticks out a foot and trips me on the way out of the cafeteria, but George catches me just in time.

"Sorry," I mutter. "Clumsy." George's hand lingers one half second longer than necessary on my arm. He flushes and pulls away with a look that leaves me feeling suddenly confused.

I'm still thinking about that look hours later, at Stars practice. Wondering if it's possible that George has started to think of me as more than a friend.

My toes graze the line Mrs. Percy has taped along the wooden slats in the floor. I wind up, picturing George's easy smile, his rumpled shirts, his hair that sticks up and reminds me of Miles.

Throw.

There's no tingling electricity, no heightened senses or

self-awareness that I always feel whenever Will is near. But . . . could there ever be?

Throw.

It would make much more sense on paper than Will and me. That and the fact that Will seems to like Eliza anyway.

Will probably thinks of me as the sister he never wanted.

Extra hard throw.

I stand back and look at my work. All three Stars have hit their marks and stuck, shearing in deep. My practicing is starting to pay off.

I take an extra step back from the throwing line, my shoes scuffing against the wood in the bright warmth of the gymnasium. My final Star zips through the air and catches its teeth in the white space, just edging the bull's-eye.

Mrs. Percy erupts into applause so sudden it startles me.

Then the doors to the gymnasium burst open and Eliza strides through, past the wall of trophies encased in glass. She is accompanied by another student and is dressed in a fencing jacket, with a mesh mask under her arm.

Mrs. Percy waves at her. "Plenty of room for you and your sparring partner, dear."

Eliza nods and brandishes an epee.

"And room for one or two more, I do hope?" a woman says, following on Eliza's heels. She's dressed in a sharp skirt suit, and her hair is pulled into a black chignon. She beckons to a skinny man bearing a large camera.

"Hello, Daisy," Mrs. Percy says. "How are things at the *Post?*"

"Busiest time of the year. The interest is already high for how things are shaping up for the tournament." Her mouth turns down. "Perhaps because everyone wishes to take their minds off of other more . . . unpleasant developments."

Daisy sniffs, then points to a spot on the floor.

"Darien, set up here," she directs the photographer. "Get some shots of Eliza. She won two events last year, riding and dance, and this year she will fence in addition. Is that right, dear?"

Eliza nods in agreement, her face fresh and pretty.

"No one from Sterling has ever won three events in the same year?" Daisy continues, her inflection somewhere between a statement and a question.

"That's what I've been told," Eliza says.

Daisy writes this down in her notepad. Darien adjusts his tripod. I throw another Star.

"You're quite driven?" Another statement-question from Daisy.

"I thought—why not? Why not try for something that's never been done before? Really, anything I can do for Sterling, to lift people's spirits during a trying time," Eliza says graciously.

Daisy notes this. "Wonderful," she says. "Well, carry on with your practice. I want to get some action shots to run with the article—we'd love to show the dedication that leads to local history being made."

Eliza's blond ponytail bobs with a nod. She puts her mask on and steps forward in short strides until she finds a blind spot in her partner and jabs.

I hurl three Stars in quick succession, pretending not to notice that anyone else is there.

"Good, good," Daisy says. "I want a clear shot of her lunging."

As Darien's camera clicks, I pluck my Stars from the target. Walk back to the line, careful to avoid their razor-sharp edges.

"And you — what is your name?" Daisy calls.

It takes me a minute to realize she's speaking to me. "Aila Quinn," I say. "Aila *Cummings* Quinn," I add, after a pause.

Daisy doesn't react to this. "And you'll be competing in Stars this year?" She flips to a fresh page in her notebook. "Darien, when you have that shot, move this way. We haven't had a representative for Stars in *ages*. What prompted this attempt?"

She looks up at me expectantly, as if she is waiting for something profound. My mind, predictably, goes blank. "I just . . ." I start. Look down at the Star in my fingers. "I saw something I thought I might be good at, and wanted to do what I could." My eyes flit to the back of Eliza's head. The mask is pulled down over her face, but I can practically feel her rage at Daisy's diverted interest. "I hope I can contribute something for Sterling this year."

As Daisy writes, I push away the silky voice of hope I recognize. The one that used to whisper *Your mother will get better. Your father won't be drafted.*

William will notice you.

Sterling will embrace you.

"Well, I'd *love* to see what you've got," Daisy says. "Darien, be sure to get a few good shots of Aila practicing." The tall, skinny man who is Darien moves closer to me. A few students, their uniforms wet with the sweat of their own practices, have trickled in and are now watching.

I toe the line, my nerves buzzing. If a crowd this small makes me nervous, what will happen when all of Sterling is watching?

I wind up and throw. My first Star tears through the air and lodges in the target. There is some obligatory clapping. I don't turn around. "Yes," Daisy says to Darren. "I think we'll definitely want to do a piece on this one."

At that, Eliza begins jabbing at her poor sparring partner with everything she has. The gathering students clap at Eliza's small victories, and Daisy's attention swings back to her.

"We should expect quite a showing from you this year, Miss Patton," Daisy says. "You're such an accomplished young woman. Some see you as the unofficial representative of this town's youth. What is it that drives you?"

Eliza's gloved fingers adjust their grip on her epee. "Growing up here, being a part of this community — it's a sense of pride and belonging that I just can't explain," she says pointedly. "That's what drives me. I'm flattered that so many want me to represent them in that way." Eliza pauses to take a sip of water and waves winningly at the small crowd.

I shoot another Star at the target. It barely lodges at the outer edge. I have to walk past Eliza to retrieve it.

"Looks like someone needs more practice." Eliza twirls the epee in her hand. "Out of curiosity, do you even know whom you're going up against?"

I yank the Star from the target fabric and don't respond.

Eliza stores her epee. "Because if you did . . ." She trails off. "I think you'd find a better use for your time."

Her eye catches something at the door. Will is leaning against its frame, watching. Just one look is all it takes for me to know that it's still him, will always be him, who I want.

I tuck my practice Stars away. My muscles have begun to ache pleasantly.

"I think I just did," I say, and walk to where Will is waiting to accompany me home.

pull the red hood of my coat over my hair and follow Will outside, where snow is falling in thick wet clumps. Will dusts me with a handful of Embers. The cold recedes, and we walk in a halo of pleasant warmth.

"You and Eliza look pretty good in there," Will says.

"Thanks." I glance at him and smile. I'm tired of nursing my grudge against him for liking Eliza, and it's nice just to be near him, talking again. He seems to relax, too, realizing that I'm done with freezing him out. A gust of wind sweeps my hood back and finds the uncovered skin at the base of my neck, but it is devoid of chill.

"Can I ask you a question?" Will plunges his hands into his pockets. "What is it that you and Miles are always saying to each other? Something about Finland?"

"Finland?" I look at him, confused.

He adds, "Or Finnish words?"

It takes me a moment to put it together, and when I do, I start to laugh. I laugh and laugh until my stomach hurts, harder than I have in ages, and probably harder than I should, but I always feel a little lightheaded around him anyway.

When I'm able to speak again, I wipe away a tear. "You think they teach us Finnish in Gardner?"

"All right, rag on me all you want." He rubs the back of his head, the line of hair that fades into his neck. His hair is short again.

He must have just cut it. I like it best when it's starting to grow out, a week away from the way it looks now.

"It's called the finishing word," I explain. "*Finishing*—like last, final. It's just a silly game we used to play with my mother. Sort of a bridge she invented between her interests and mine. She liked puzzles, and I liked words. So if you were able to come up with just the right word for a situation or a person, it was like fitting in the finishing piece of a puzzle."

"The game applies to people, too?" He cocks his head. "Does that mean that I have a Finnish word?"

Yes, I think. *It is captivating. Considerate. Unattainable.* "Wouldn't you like to know?"

He flashes the crooked tooth at me, and a thrill shoots up my back and out into my fingertips.

"My mother used to make the winner a crown out of dandelions," I say, twisting my tingling fingers out together in front of me. "I had a perpetual yellow stain on my forehead two summers ago. Basically, I won so much that it made me a loser."

His laugh materializes into a puff of air. He clears his throat. "Do you miss it? Gardner, I mean?"

I think of Cass's attic nook. Mother in the garden. How horrible the quiet was after she was gone. "I miss what it used to be."

"I think about what it would be like to leave here sometimes." Will makes it sound like a confession. "More than sometimes. Not for forever or anything. Just to see what else there is. We used to go places when I was younger. The coast. The mountains. And that time my mother took me to visit you in Gardner." He exhales. "But we leave here less and less now. It gets harder, I guess, with each Disappearance."

He shrugs. The snow swirls around us. I don't say anything. I let the silence build between us so that he will keep talking.

"At the strangest moments, even when I'm racing on the water, I find myself worrying about everything I haven't seen yet," he says. "Because who knows what will go next? The taste of food? The sight of all colors, beyond just our paints and pens? Living here is like being inside a ticking bomb."

His eyes are a dark, marbled blue. His voice carves into the air with a sudden edge. I nod, encouraging him to continue. "If I had a fortune," he says, "I'd rather spend it traveling the world than building a big house or having a lot of things. I'd rather build memories instead. Because those are the things you carry with you always, everywhere, things that can't be destroyed or taken." His face flushes with something more than cold.

I want to tell him I've never heard someone else's thoughts come so close to my own. To reach for his hand, intertwine our fingers. Instead, my breath billows out, white and soft. "Yes" is all I manage.

"But it's kind of nice to have a dream to chase," he says. "Something to look forward to, I guess."

I nod. "Better than always looking back."

"So are you chasing something, then?"

I think of Mother's past, how its branches always seem to be reaching up to touch my own future.

"Maybe," I say. "Maybe something I'm not sure I want to catch."

"How intriguing." He turns to face me, teasing now. "Maybe your Finnish word should be *guarded*."

"I prefer *reticent*," I say. I lean toward him, closing the distance between us to say something in his ear.

"You like a good chase, do you, William Cliffton?"

He nods, his right eyebrow raising. His eyes have returned to their regular blue.

"Then why don't you catch me?" I ask, digging my boots into the powder beneath our feet. "Variants are cheating!" I add, taking off.

I can hardly believe my own boldness. Especially when I see Will's smile just starting to bloom behind the sprays of my pure, white snow.

CHAPTER TWENTY-NINE

Date: 1/13/1942

Bird: European White Stork

Chicks unhappy with the provisions of their parents will abandon them and try to sneak into another nest.

I rent a small abandoned cabin with a cellar in Sheffield for my experiments. I line my pockets with money from the robberies Phineas sets up; then I travel to Sheffield and watch the cages teem with mice bodies, hating the way they shudder and whimper, the way their nails catch in the cage wire. I'm glad no one witnesses my first attempt at extraction. Jumping and sweating like a faint-hearted coward.

They're just mice, I tell myself, and hold the first one, squirming and soft, as I pick the spot to insert my needle. But I save one mouse. I name her Vala. She climbs the length of my arm and nestles into the space below my ear. I like the soft warmth of her, the feel of her tiny breath and beating heart.

I return home after a week with a bag packed full of my failures. I throw the dead mice from the cliff for the birds to pick apart. Then I join Phineas on the porch as evening falls, and I ask, "Where were you when you realized the scents had gone?"

"I'm not really sure." He sits back. Puffs on a cigar until he is engulfed in a wispy cloud. "It all happened around the same time. Losing your mother. Becoming a father. I was in such a daze. Heartbroken, acting sloppy and careless. The cops caught up with me not long after." He snorts. "Not being able to smell in prison wasn't much of a curse."

He is quiet for a long time. "They took me away when you were just a baby," he says, "and I knew you might not even want to know me. But I was always planning to come back for you."

I become so still I can hardly breathe. Look out through the screens I hung at waves as black as pitch. Moon like metal overhead. "But I was still in jail when I realized that whatever was happening to me was going to keep happening," he says. "I woke up in my cell one day and couldn't see my reflection."

The porch has grown so dark I can hardly see him. "That's when I knew I couldn't come back for you anymore. Thought I was going mad. Or that I ran afoul of someone who had cursed me. Not so hard to believe when you've spent years doing what I did."

What a waste. To spend all those years waiting for him. And all along he had been trying to protect me from a curse I was already under.

But something inside the inky, clotted part of my heart melts at those words. To know that he had stayed away to protect me. It almost burns at first, the warmth returning where frostbite had long ago set in. Then it begins coursing thick and gold in my stomach. Like I've taken a deep swig of alcohol.

I pet Vala that night as I'm falling asleep. A few days later I return to my experiments.

In Sheffield, the pile of mouse bodies grows.

It takes almost three months to track down Juliet.

"She's in Gardner. Connecticut." My contact repeats the address twice, and I promise to do his next job for free.

"Dear Juliet," I write. Gritting my teeth.

"I know things ended badly between us.

Can we put it in the past?"

It is a lie, of course. There was too much damage done too long ago. As *immutable as fossil by this point. But Phineas wants the Stone. He thinks he started the Curse. He thinks he might know how to end it. I'm not convinced. Even more — I don't know if that's even what I want.*

But I'll go along with Phineas for now. See where this takes us. After all, I think, smiling a little at my joke as I slide my needle into the next mouse.

Patience is a Virtue.

CHAPTER THIRTY

With the snow falling outside and the fire sparking from the hearth, Christmas is both cozy and muted. The tree smells rich with pine and sap but only for the short time after we've sprinkled it with Variants. No carols play. None of Mother's drawings are sketched across stark brown wrapping paper. None of her riddled clues were hidden around the house, leading to a single present for Miles and me to open on Christmas Eve. My father doesn't come down the creaking staircase to make waffles for breakfast in his red pajamas and a beard of shaving cream.

But sitting around the fire with the Clifftons, exchanging gifts and overstuffed stockings, eating ham ringed with pineapple, green beans sprinkled with almonds, mashed potatoes layered with cheese, and vanilla meringues that are lighter than air, I find a strange sense of hope where I had feared would be only a gaping sadness. It feels half like a betrayal and half like the deep exhale of a breath I've been holding for too long.

I glance around the table at the faces that surround me. I think of my father, how I don't even know where he is right now, and consider how much difference a single year can make. I never would have chosen this. Yet somehow there are hints of green coming up through the scorched earth.

We exchange gifts, but there's a conspicuous lack of one from Will. I bought him a model set of the Golden Gate Bridge, something full of intricate pieces he'd have to construct. It admittedly cost much more than I spent on anyone else. "Until you get there—" I'd written on the tag, and I knew I'd done well by the way he flushed when he opened it.

I unwrap the final gift with my name on the tag, a pair of soft gloves the color of butter that Mrs. Cliffton must have picked out on Father's behalf. They are beautiful, and I look down at the mountain of torn paper at my feet and tell myself it's silly to feel disappointed.

We're cleaning up the paper, gathering the ribbons to save for the next celebration, when Will brushes my arm.

"I do have something for you," he says, and he runs his hands along the hair at his neck, almost as if he is nervous. "It's not done yet. But it's probably close enough. Do you want to see it?"

We put on our coats, and he leads me outside through the gardens and tells me to wait as he disappears into the shed. Our feet leave deep prints in the snow. It takes me a moment to figure out what I'm looking at when he comes out. I walk toward him, playing with the sleeves of my coat, my hair tangling with the wind.

"Merry Christmas, Aila," he says.

It's a wooden box with beautiful bronze hinges. "To hold Variants someday," he says. "Or letters."

He's carved a word into the bottom, swirled into it where the wood looks like cream. I squint at it to make sure I'm reading it right.

LUMOAVA, it says.

"What does it mean?" I ask, running my gloved fingertips along the grooves.

"You'll figure it out," he says with a devious little smile that thrills me in a tangle of hope and confusion. "Eventually."

"Thank you," I say, clutching it, and that single smile is all it takes for me to decide that maybe I don't hate riddles as much as I thought.

CHAPTER THIRTY-ONE

Date: 4/21/1942

Birds: *Vultures, buzzards*

Carrion birds are carnivorous scavengers. Can be found near the decaying flesh of animals and, occasionally, poorly tended graveyards.

My mother's gravestone is polished granite that's stuck into the grass like a comb. ADA BLYTHE SHAW. How strange to see my own beginning, the date of my birth, etched there as her ending. The one day on earth we shared.

I stand next to Phineas and fidget with my hands. Look around at the things I've been taught to notice about graveyards. The newer gravesites, where the earth is still tilled and brown without the shawl of green grass. The graves so carefully tended that someone would surely notice if they were disturbed, and the ones whose wilted, shriveled stalks scream of neglect. I never knew how much Phineas had loved my mother until I saw her gravesite.

If anyone touched it, he would know.

"How did you meet?" I ask.

"We grew up together," he says. "I'd loved her since she was five years old, and never anyone else."

I think, of course, of my own little red bird.

"She was buried here?" I ask. "Not in Sterling?"

"She was originally," he says. "But I wanted her closer to me." And he leaves it at that.

A pair of song thrushes fly over our heads.

"Good thing she died before she could see all that happened." His voice thickens as he scrapes his fingers along the soil. "She would miss the stars, especially."

I nod, thinking about how his head is always down, looking at the dirt, while my eyes train skyward like my mother's. He reaches down and rubs the earth until his hands are as dark as the crude tattoo marks nicking his knuckles.

Then he sniffs. Straightens. Walks past me.

"I'm sor—" I start to say, but he interrupts me.

"When did the whole thing with the birds start?" He turns his eyes from the dirt at our feet to the endless blue of the sky.

"I got a bird encyclopedia for my tenth birthday," I say, stumbling over myself to change the subject. I'd almost forgotten—that first encyclopedia had been from Juliet. I have a sudden picture of her eyes lighting up, pushing her hair behind her ears. She'd sent me on a treasure hunt to find it. "You would have liked it, actually. I had to follow a series of maps to get it." Juliet had buried my bird encyclopedia under a tree. I looked at it so much over the years that some of the pages had fallen out of the binding.

I try to brush that memory of her away like an itch.

"Have you heard?" Phineas asks. "About the Stone?"

"No." I toe the grass. "But I've been thinking—what if the Disappearances could be made into something beneficial? I know you think you caused them, but I've been working on something—"

Phineas raises his eyebrows. "Don't waste time with that. It's not as important as the Stone. Just get the Stone."

"Why?" I ask, my annoyance flaring. "Of course what I'm doing is important. Why do you care so much about the damned Stone all of a sudden?"

"Because." His eyes are calm. "I'm dying, Stefen." As if it were the most obvious thing in the world.

The air around me shrivels. I gape at him.

"That Stone might be nothing," he continues, weaving a path back through the graveyard. "Just a piece of meaningless rock. But it might be much more than that. It might have the power to save me."

As we walk back past my mother's gravestone, I notice for the first time the space that's been left there next to it. It is meant for him. My old anger at Juliet suddenly rages up, unchecked. Juliet, hoarding the very thing that could keep Phineas with me.

Phineas is right. The Virtues are secondary. And I am going to get that Stone from her.

Even if I have to rip it from her lily-white fingers myself.

CHAPTER THIRTY-TWO

When Miles was five — young, but still old enough to know better — he started knocking his drinking glass over. Mother was patient at first. Sopping up his tears first and then the spilled milk.

After a dozen more spills, though, she began to get mad. Made him clean up his own messes. Demanded that he stop being so clumsy. But spills kept seeping across the table as if Miles had brought them to life: rivers of water, moons of milk, paisley splashes of juice. He even broke a glass once when it rolled off the table and shattered in a cacophony of shards on the floor.

Mother became livid. He was clearly doing it on purpose. She'd threatened, in a moment of passion, to cancel his birthday. July 28. His favorite day of the year.

After that he'd gone three days without a single spill. Then Father had come home from work, and Miles, in his eagerness, jumped up from the table, sending his glass sailing. He'd frozen. Turned to Mother, his eyes full of fear. Because even though Miles was Mother's favorite, there was a line you could not cross with Juliet Cummings Quinn.

But she hadn't yelled that time. A line *had* been crossed — for the first time, he hadn't actually been trying to spill the glass, and it struck her as incredibly funny. She'd laughed, trying to smother it with a dish towel, and Father had come into the kitchen and loosened his necktie, his eyes crinkling and lighting up the way they did when she laughed like that.

I'm thinking of that when Miles brushes his hand against his glass on New Year's Day and reaches to catch it just in time. I try to meet his eye, to exchange a smile, but he doesn't look at me. It makes me wonder if he even remembers those days at all.

Will's jaw faintly twitches when George pulls out a chair to stay for dinner again and volleys ideas to Dr. Cliffton over the table.

"Perhaps we look at something to do with Linus? Greek mythology?"

"Or the Chinese? Ling Lun?"

"Ah, yes, bamboo pipes?"

"Could you pass the rolls?" Will says.

"Did you see in Father's letter about the pineapple spigots?" I ask Miles, trying to draw him out. He doesn't look at me, so I turn to Will. "They stopped at a pineapple factory in Hawaii and filled up glasses of juice in spigots straight from the wall."

"Hawaii," Will says, his eyes lightening. "I wonder what it's like there."

Miles glares at me. "That letter came weeks ago."

He bangs his spoon down and leaves the table. I flinch at the distant sound of his door slamming.

"Sorry," I mutter. He and his moods, just like Mother's. I stand to follow him, but Mrs. Cliffton says, "Perhaps I should go," and folds her napkin on the table.

Will turns his attention to George. "Are you doing something for the Sisters Tournament?" he asks, interrupting his father mid-sentence. I pass him the dish of latticed pear tart, and he thrusts it at George without even looking at it.

"Variant Innovation," George says, his mouth full. He shovels food onto his fork. He's been talking so much he's barely touched it. "You're playing ball?"

Will gives a short nod. "So what did you invent?"

George swallows. "Really I haven't had much time to work on it. This," he says, gesturing toward Dr. Cliffton's library, "seems more important."

"Yes," Will says, "I suppose it does." He abruptly pushes out his chair and leaves the table.

Then it is just me, eating pear tart, silently listening to George and Dr. Cliffton, who don't seem to notice that everyone else has left. But I understand why the Variant consumes them. I feel it, too — as though everyone's attention has turned toward the Clifftons' house in a spotlight of expectation.

Snow falls quietly beyond the window, blanketing Sterling.

We've been back at school for only three days when Mrs. Cliffton draws me aside an hour before dinner. She's smiling, but there is something in the tightness around her mouth that causes me to tense.

"Aila!" Her voice is bright, but she twirls her wedding ring around on her finger like it is circling a drain. "Can I speak with you? Somewhere private?"

Fear steals my voice. I nod, and lead Mrs. Cliffton to my room.

Mrs. Cliffton closes the door behind us. "What I need to say is a little difficult."

I sit down on the edge of my bed. "What is it?" My mouth tastes like paper.

Father. Please don't let it be about Father.

"I met with Miles's teacher today," Mrs. Cliffton says. "I'm afraid that he has been . . . causing some trouble at school."

"Oh," I breathe, my panic falling from me like a blanket. "This is about *Miles*." I take a deep breath to slow my pounding heart, and my alarm shifts to annoyance. "What kind of trouble?"

"Well . . ." Mrs. Cliffton hesitates. Her hair corkscrews wildly away from her face, and I notice the fine lines branching out from the corners of her eyes. "A classmate's missing shell collection was found in Miles's desk. He was disinvited to someone's house. And today he started a fight with another boy, though the teacher was unsure exactly what caused it."

"I see." Heat spreads across my face. "I'm truly sorry that he's causing trouble." I suddenly want to place my hand on top of Mrs. Cliffton's, to apologize. Do something to show her my embarrassment and sincerity. Instead I keep them clasped in my lap. "I'll talk to him," I say.

"I know this has been a challenging time, with so many changes. And he's still so young," Mrs. Cliffton says. "I want to do what I can to help him. But Aila—" She breaks off, as if pained. "If he were asked to leave, there simply aren't any other schools in Sterling for him to attend."

"I understand," I say, suddenly wondering how much influence the Clifftons must have wielded to get Miles and me to Sterling against the Council's wishes.

But even the Clifftons' clout must run out at some point.

"I felt it was only fair to tell you. I hope that was the right thing to do."

"It was," I insist. "Thank you. I will speak to him."

No, I will wring his neck.

I find Miles in the sunroom, surrounded by paper, sketching with his Variant pencils.

"Miles." My voice is quiet. And dangerous.

He looks up at me through golden lashes with such scorn, as if he knows what is coming. His hands are swimming in the oversize folds of William's gloves again, and he can barely hold the pencil. The picture appearing on the paper is our house in Gardner. I grit my teeth against the words I want to say. Everything that I can't take back, that is dangerously close to exploding out anyway.

"Listen to me. And take off those gloves. You look ridiculous."

He folds his gloved hands across his chest in defiance.

"What is this about you stealing things at school?" I say. "And now you're getting into fights? What are you thinking?"

"You would have wanted me to fight him, too." Miles's pencils scatter across the floor when he rises to his full height — already half an inch taller than he was when we arrived just a few months ago. "Walt and the others are always coming at me, saying everything is Mother's fault. I'm tired of people calling her a witch and a liar."

I want to scream. At him. At everyone.

"Yes," I say through my teeth. "He sounds like a jerk. That doesn't mean you can fight him. Next time, go tell the teacher." Miles rolls his eyes at this suggestion.

"And stealing, Miles?" My voice is rising. "Don't you know they might make us leave?"

"I don't care." His voice climbs to match my own. "Who cares what they think?" His fury builds in waves. "You would just let them say those things about her, wouldn't you? If you really loved her . . ." His lower lip curls, and I blink for a second, wondering if he might cry.

Instead, he narrows his eyes. With the aim of a perfectly thrown dart that would have made Father proud, he spits out the words:

"The finishing word is *traitor.*"

It's the final push that sends me over the edge, as if he's done it with that small gloved hand.

"If I really loved her," I say coldly, "I would do whatever I could not to embarrass her memory. Do you hear me, Miles? *You are embarrassing her.* And you embarrass the Clifftons. And you embarrass me."

He is silent, and for a moment I think I've won. But then he says the words quietly, just under his breath, almost to himself but not quite.

"She loved me more than you."

It pricks me to the core. Because I've always known it to be true.

I hurry out of the sunroom and plow straight into Will. "Sorry," I mutter, my hand finding the bump of my ear. His blue eyes are so soft and warm when he looks at me that I wonder how much he overheard.

I run to write Cass, the ink pouring out my frustrations all across the page. It feels so good to write her the truth about something. I can tell her about Miles, and I know that out of everyone, she will understand. She can take my side without losing her affection for him.

I'm signing my name under three long pages when I hear the muffled noise of Miles crying in his room. The sound of it wrenches my heart, even as I watch his second chance to start over in Sterling unspooling in front of me.

Another glass he's tipping over, just beyond my reach.

CHAPTER THIRTY-THREE

Date: 5/16/1942

Bird: Bearded Vulture

The bearded vulture finds bones to drop from heights and break apart so the marrow is exposed. Unlike other vultures, the bearded has a revulsion to rotten flesh. It wants fresh prey, so it will sometimes attack things that are still living. Even by pushing them off cliffs.

I knew Phineas was sick. But it took so long for us to find each other and finally get on our feet. There should be a balance to suffering. And I've paid more than my share already.

It is as though Juliet can sense these thoughts and my anger building like a storm. Even after all these years.

"I'm so happy to hear from you," she writes in response to my letter.

I have no idea if she means it. I skim over the rest—the parts about how she's married. Has two children now.

I shove my desk clean and sit down to reply. At the end I inquire about the Stone. I don't tell her about Phineas's theory of the Disappearances. I just ask if she'd be willing to send it back.

After I post the letter, I cannot sit around hearing the coughs that are sucking Phineas's insides out. He resists any of my research on alternative treatments for him. So I hire a maid, Laurette, who clomps around like a small horse, dusting and vacuuming and driving Phineas crazy with her constant complaining. Then I set off for Sheffield and throw myself with *renewed vigor into finding something in my experiments. Anything to live for other than Phineas.*

There are days when I think I am creeping closer to it. I inject collections of chemicals, herbs, narcotics, vials of different mixtures and potencies into the mice. Sometimes they convulse, mostly they die. But sometimes, with my latest tweaks, they become very, very calm and peaceful. Attain a state that's almost dreamlike. That's what I want to isolate and remove. I want to act like a sponge, soaking it all up and out of their minds to wring out whenever it proves most useful.

As the weeks pass and I creep closer to the answer, I find that I no longer mind descending into the cellar. Even on the mornings when the sun is shining and the birds chirp madly in the trees.

A part of me might have actually come to enjoy it.

When Juliet's response comes, I rip into it without leaving the post office.

"I'm sorry for my delay in responding," *she writes. Her handwriting is the same and yet older, somehow.* "I've actually been rather ill — can you believe it?"

As if I could forget how she'd hardly been ill a day in her life when we were younger. Always the opposite of me, in every way.

But reading those words is the first time I ever associate her miraculous health with wearing the Stone. The first time I wonder whether that Stone actually does have some power in it after all.

"She still has it," I tell Phineas, and his face becomes brighter than I've ever seen it. "She sent it to be polished, and then she'll put it in the mail to us."

Hope threatens to open long-shuttered wings inside my chest, but I push them back. Hoping makes it harder to breathe. I notice how eager she sounds to do anything that would make things right between us again.

I wonder if I could even forgive Juliet for all her past sins. If she does something unselfish for once and helps me save Phineas.

That night I creep down the hallway and peek into his room. The light falls across him as he lies motionless in the bed. His skin is papery and faded into the pillow. My heart catches for a moment at the silence.

But his chest still rises, falls. I stand and watch its movement until my own heart returns to a normal rhythm.

Some nights I want to lie down on the floor next to him and hold on to his sleeve, as I had so long ago with my school uniform.

As if that is all it would take to make sure he is still there in the morning.

I wait for the package from Juliet, the one that will carry the Stone. A week. Then another. Then another. She is certainly taking her time to send it.

No—she is taking Phineas's time. From him.

From me.

My rage builds and burns. I write her one more time. Suggest that I could even come get it myself.

The day before I plan to jump on a train and confront her over her silence, her response finally comes.

I know with one glance that it is too small, too thin. I slit it open with trembling hands. Wondering what excuse she is going to give. If I would actually have it in me to kill her.

But I don't find her effusive scrawling. Only the tight handwriting of her husband, Harold Quinn, and a newspaper clipping folded inside.

Dear Mr. Shaw:

I'm sorry to tell you that Juliet has passed away.

Forgive me for not inviting you to the funeral. I'm only just now making it through all of Juliet's old mail. I've included her obituary.

We buried her yesterday.

CHAPTER THIRTY-FOUR

The week that passes after my fight with Miles does nothing to cool my anger. I'm trying to help Mother's reputation in Sterling, and he's done nothing but make it worse. It feels strange to be in a new year without her — as if I'm walking through a door into a new room, leaving her behind, and the next year will be another room, and another, and I don't want to go.

Cass's response to my letter about Miles is so laced with reassurances and shared history that I could cry, but the days pass with no mail at all from Father. I sit in the library and halfheartedly look through Austen and Shelley for possible music Variant clues while George steadily crosses off more lines in Dr. Cliffton's black book.

"No closer?" I ask as he packs up his things.

"Every wrong answer eliminated is a step closer to the truth."

"What does the truth even matter," I say, suddenly bitter. "People are just going to believe whatever they want to believe." I think of Mother's desecrated house. "Or what is most convenient for them."

"Of course it matters," George says, closing his book, and his voice is sharper than I've ever heard it. I think of his steady hands peeling the onion, of the way he documents each finding in our labs with something between a child's excitement and a scientist's precision. "Something happened that set this whole thing off, and we don't get to *decide* what it was. If our premise is wrong, then we'll keep moving in the wrong direction, looking for the answer in the wrong places. And we'll never be able to set it right unless we know which Catalyst was the true one."

I shrug at him.

"Let me ask you something." George examines me with the blazing intensity normally reserved for his microscope. "What exactly is it that you're looking for? I mean, what do you want out of all this?"

I shift uncomfortably. "Of course—I want the truth—" I stammer. "Then maybe people will stop being so awful. I mean, *you* should understand now. Didn't it make you angry that night at the race? With all those copies of 'The Mackelroy Misfortune'?"

He laughs a short laugh. "Who do you think mimeographed those and sent them around for everyone to read?"

"What?" I blink at him, dumbfounded. "Are you saying *you* did that?"

George sighs. "My mother is very resourceful, especially as head of the Library Preservation Society," he says. "She got to almost every copy of the Council book first and tore out the pages. If she knew that I hid one and made copies, she would ship me off to boarding school." He pushes his hair up from his forehead. "I'm not sure what compelled me. It just made me feel . . . right somehow, doing that."

"Even if the Catalyst does end up being tied to you?" My throat clenches. "Even if people *hate* you for it?"

"We're all in it," he says. "We all have those questions, and we're all hoping that it isn't us. Shouldn't that make us more empathetic when the truth comes out?"

I follow him to the foyer, where we almost collide with Will. He nods good night and climbs the stairs, and as I watch his retreating back, I want to ask George, *How can you be so unafraid of the truth?* *Even truth that is inconvenient or damning or not what you want it to be?*

"Well, it *should* make us empathetic," George says, his voice rising at my silence. "So you know what?" He flings his arms out wide. "If it's my family, then so be it. I just want to find out and end all of this. But know this, Aila. You can't search for the truth with integrity if you're only looking to find the kind that benefits you."

I set my jaw, stung.

"I'm sorry," I say, softening. "You're right. When I first got here, I guess I *did* just want to clear my mother's name." I look at him. "And that was selfish. But now I want to find out the truth. For everybody's sake."

His mouth twists into a smile. "All right," he says simply. "I believe you."

Then he lifts the front window curtain and peeks out. "Look."

Mrs. Mackelroy is parked on the drive, craning her neck out the window for any glimpse into what's going on inside. George throws open the curtains and waves at her with both hands. She dives back into the shadows, laying on the horn in her haste. It blares a short, shrill blast.

George lets the curtains fall again and shrugs. "Covert Operations keeps trying to recruit her."

He's broken my sullen mood despite myself, and I open the door into the cold night. "You're a really good friend, George."

"You too, Aila," he says, and I fix the latch behind him and hurry up the stairs to catch Will.

I call his name in a low voice just as he reaches his room, and his hand pauses on his doorknob.

He turns to me with a look that betrays the slightest surprise.

I make my way down the hall until I've left too little room between us, probably, for being alone in the dark hallway. I could take a step back, but I don't. Neither does he. Lights are twinkling within his eyes, blooming, fading as he looks at me in the darkness.

"Can I help you with something, Miss Quinn?" he asks formally, his hand still on the doorknob, but his voice is scratched and smoky with whisper, and heat curls beneath my skin.

"Will," I say quietly. I look up at him, almost close enough to feel him breathe. "Do you think you could you build me a target?"

There are things I have started to notice about Will: things like the smooth grooves that run over his palms like water, the slight scar just above his lip that appears only in a certain light, and how sometimes at breakfast I catch myself staring at his mouth and wondering what it feels like to kiss someone. It is a secret I don't dare speak to anyone. Even to Cass.

Even to Beas, when I meet her in the back corner of the school library and we sit near the heater, the sky hanging gray and cold just beyond the window. She can actually practice her violin there now while I study or read one of her poetry books. Today she's lent me Alfred Lord Tennyson. *In Memoriam.*

I like to watch her over the edge of the pages when she thinks I'm not looking. She refuses to let the Disappearances ripple outward and also rob her of her ability to play, so she perches over her music sheets, her arms furiously moving the bow over the strings, as if she could force the notes out from sheer will.

I startle when, without warning, she suddenly flings her bow and then scatters her sheets of music onto the floor.

I close my book. "Want to talk?"

I move to retrieve her bow and hold it out to her as an offering.

She sighs and takes it from me. "I want music the way I would crave food if I was beginning to starve."

"Do you ever hear it in other things?" I crouch to gather her music sheets. "Sometimes I think I almost do, in the wind, or a train horn."

"I hear it in everything," she says, bending to help. "The rhythm of footsteps. Doors closing. Even flies buzzing and tapping the windows." Her mouth turns down into a half smile. She hesitates. "Aila, I've always wondered. Do stars . . . sound like anything?" Her voice turns almost shy. "I've only seen them in pictures."

"No," I say. "At least, if they do, we can't hear it on earth."

"I wish I could see them." She sets her violin into its plush velvet case as though she's tucking in a baby. "Sometimes I imagine what it would be like if there was music in everything. If stars could sing, or shadows scraped along where they fell. Or if the wind made leaves tinkle like wind chimes."

I clear my throat. Now it is my turn to be shy. "When you're in love . . . Is — um. Doesn't that kind of make everything sing?"

She smiles in a way that is both wide and sad. "Yes," she says. "And when it's over, everything gets disjointed, until some days I can hardly find the music in anything anymore."

She leans over to pick up her violin case, and I think, *That is what grief feels like, also.*

At dinner that night, Will's hand is only a whisper away from mine. He catches my eye and smiles.

I want to tell him that I miss the sound of his singing through the wall.

I want to tell him, *Sometimes I almost think I can hear the music again, whenever I'm with you.*

Beas catches my arm in school the next day as I'm walking out to Mrs. Cliffton's car. She pulls me into a side classroom and thrusts a book in my hands.

I turn it over.

Shakespeare: A Biography.

I cock an eyebrow at her.

"I know you're not really looking at Shakespeare anymore," she says, her voice hushed. "But look at this . . ." She flips to a section called "The Disappeared Years."

"There are no records of Shakespeare at all during this period of time. No one knows what he was doing then—he simply vanishes." She bites on her lower lip. "People think he was searching for something. Do the math, Aila."

1585 to 1592.

"Seven years?" A smile begins to dawn across my face. "Shakespeare had seven *disappeared* years?"

I look at her. She looks at me.

"It could be nothing," she says, taking the book back from me.

"It's probably nothing," I agree.

But I slide into Mrs. Cliffton's car with a new sense of lightness, and before I fall asleep that night, I crouch down on my hands and knees.

Reach through the gauzy cobwebs and pull Mother's book back out from under my bed. I work through *Othello, A Midsummer Night's Dream, Winter's Tale.* My pen nub scratches against the page, transferring Mother's notes to mine, and I realize how much I *want* this theory to be true. I want my mother to help solve this mystery from the grave. To not have abandoned the people of Sterling. To redeem their memory of her. And to redeem mine.

CHAPTER THIRTY-FIVE

Date: December 15, 1942

Bird: Potoo

Known as "ghost birds" for their ability to blend into a dead tree stump. Can remain perfectly motionless. Eyelids feature a slit for the bird to see out, so that whatever the bird is looking at has no idea it is being watched.

Once I know Juliet is dead and the Stone isn't coming, Phineas's cough begins to rattle my bones through the walls at night. I take more and more jobs so I won't have to hear it. I try not to notice the stripe of bone peeking out from his sleeve. How sallow his skin has become.

But I do not stop pursuing the Stone. When Juliet's husband ignores the letters I send to his house, I decide to pay him a visit in person. No one is at the house when I knock. I snoop around the outside windows, looking for an entry point, until I catch the next-door neighbor spying on me. I leave empty-handed.

Of course Juliet could play games and thwart me like this. Even from the grave.

I return to my cabin in Sheffield with the strangest sense of anticipation trilling over my skin. I slip on my gloves. Tut my tongue. The cage of mice rustles in response.

I move to the darkest corner of the cellar, where I always keep a single mouse in an empty cage. The unlucky mice. Nameless, plucked out by chance, to know little more than cold, starvation, and isolation throughout their short lives. The one in there now has patches of fur missing, a ripped ear. It knows enough to tremble when I come near.

I throw it a piece of rotting celery as I set out my row of instruments. Check my logbook. Retrieve Vala from my quarters and bring her down to the stark cellar. She nestles up into her place under my ear. I push back the small twinge I feel at her warmth; she is nothing but a small sacrifice for a greater good.

"Goodbye, pet." I cradle my carved wooden bird, switch out the sewing needle for a syringe in two clicks. I fill it with my most promising formula.

I insert the syringe into her body and empty it entirely.

What I withdraw from her is less than a thimbleful of thick, swirling liquid.

Vala slumps in a heap. She crouches there, unmoving, in the swell of my hand for a long moment. Barely breathing air into her own small lungs. I bring her to the nameless mouse's cage, and when I open the door, it trembles and looks at Vala as if she could be something to eat.

I set Vala inside. Watch her with curiosity for a moment. She is nothing more than a heap of warm fur. I do not pet or soothe her. But her body does not stay still for long.

After a moment she begins to shiver and shake uncontrollably. She stands, becoming rigid, and lets out a high-pitched sound of agony. Then she begins to run in circles. Banging up against the edge of the cage with her head, as if she is trying to beat something out of it.

I pause to note this development in my log.

Then I take the unnamed mouse in a firm grip as it squirms and tries to escape. The mouse with the mangled body and ripped ear. And I give it the greatest gift of its short, miserable life.

I insert the contents of the vial I extracted from Vala straight into its bloodstream.

At first, when the mouse stops trembling and squeaking, I'm certain I've killed it. Just like all the others.

But then.

A sense of anticipation trills along my skin without warning. I pause. Take another look at the cage.

The unnamed mouse raises its head, cocked and curious. Its muscles, always so taut through its starved body, suddenly relax.

I watch the mouse warily. Set my wooden bird and the empty vial down on the counter. After a moment I open the cage and extend my arm.

The nameless mouse doesn't hesitate. It scampers confidently up the crook of my elbow. Past the curve of my shoulder to the prized spot just below my ear.

I begin to stroke the mouse's patchy fur with great care until I swear it is almost purring.

CHAPTER THIRTY-SIX

The Clifftons usually hide the newspaper, but on Wednesday morning I find it spread wide across the breakfast table.

ROOSEVELT FLIES TO NORTH AFRICA: TEN-DAY PARLEY WITH CHURCHILL MAPS TOTAL DESTRUCTION OF AXIS.

Perhaps this means the war is almost over.

On Saturday I lie on my stomach on my bedroom floor and write to Father again, with Mother's book open beside me. I lean to scribble a new line in my notebook. I have several lists now: lines of Disappearances and Variants. A section on Shakespeare's life: marriage, twins, collaborators, death. Recurrent themes in his work that I will scour later for clues: ambition and loyalty, herbs and flowers, greed, blood, disturbance of corpses, plays on words, appearance versus reality.

My list is growing longer every day.

"Aila?" Will knocks on my door.

I close my books and follow him outside.

He's made a buttress. The frame is made of wooden planks and covered with chicken wire. It's packed tightly with what looks like rags, scraps of carpet, and quilt batting. As I watch, he secures a taut piece of canvas across its front. He tests the resistance of the wood, the security of the bolts. "Like it?" he asks.

I bend to the buttress and smooth the face of the canvas with my palm. "It's exactly what I wanted," I say. I try not to beam. "What do I owe you?"

He pops open a can of gray paint and says, "That look is more than payment enough." When I flush, he laughs and hands me a paintbrush.

"My father built a target for me once," I say. "He taught me to play darts when I was younger." I sweep my hair out of my eyes. Glance away as soon as I feel the unexpected threat of tears.

I clear my throat and dip my brush into the gray abyss of the can. "We haven't had a letter in a while."

Will draws his brush along the edge of the target to create the outermost lines. "Maybe it simply got lost."

I nod. Focus on filling in the bull's-eye with quick, sharp strokes.

Will moves to paint the final concentric circle, and so do I, and we paint until we meet in the middle. At one point our hands almost collide, but at the last instant we skim through the air past each other.

"Wouldn't you . . ." he pauses. "Wouldn't there be a telegram if something had happened?"

I've thought this, too, a hundred times. *But would they know how to reach us here?*

"I'm sure he's all right," Will quickly says with a lopsided smile. He gestures to the target as if to draw my attention away from my thoughts. "Good job with the bull's-eye." He turns the buttress so that the wet paint will fully catch the sun. "I made a tripod to hold it, too. You can try it out as soon as it dries."

Will heads upstairs to change his clothes, but I hesitate in the kitchen, where Miles is finishing a plate of eggs and swinging his legs under the table. Miles and I have barely spoken two words to each

artists since the dawn of time?" Dr. Cliffton looks years younger than he did at dinner last night.

The music begins to sputter and fade. But even in the silent spaces between it, the air around us feels changed. "I'll give you a hint," Dr. Cliffton says. " 'Fled is that music: Do I wake or sleep?' "

I don't even have to think. "That's Keats. 'Ode to a Nightingale'?"

Keats, I think with a sharp pang of disappointment. *Not Shakespeare.*

But it's hard to feel anything but joy when George opens his grasp to reveal a single nightingale feather, silky and russet brown, the promise of music now resting in the palm of his hand.

We celebrate for the better part of an hour. Genevieve dances into the room with glasses of punch and egg salad sandwiches. Then we all sit together in the library, drinking in the sparkling punch and the music as if it were nectar.

Dr. Cliffton makes several phone calls to inquire about ordering large quantities of nightingale feathers. "Yes, *nightingale,*" he repeats, enunciating and pressing the telephone closer to his mouth. He hesitates. "Larkin? I'd prefer to work with someone else. Nothing underground. Keep everything aboveboard, please."

Mrs. Cliffton turns to Genevieve and me. "We should host a party," she says, her hands clasping. "We could surprise everyone. Align it with the Sisters Tournament so no one will suspect anything."

Dr. Cliffton blocks the telephone receiver with his palm. "That would give us time to make enough Variants so that people could have them that very night instead of having to wait."

Mrs. Cliffton finds a notepad and starts making a list.

Dr. Cliffton and George spend the rest of the afternoon grinding the remaining feathers, and at the end George is rewarded with two small midnight-blue pouches shot through with silver threads.

"You know where we have to go, don't you?" he asks me. We put on our coats and slip out the door together. "Be back soon," I say to Mrs. Cliffton.

"Home before dark, please," she says. Will doesn't look up.

George and I walk the mile to Beas's house. Knock on the door, which is wreathed with boxwood and ribbon.

"You two look like the cats that swallowed the canary," Beas says, narrowing her eyes when she opens the door.

George holds out his hand. The pouch sits in his palm like a robin's egg in a nest.

Her mouth falls open. Eyebrows twitch with the first spark of hope.

"Shh." He brings his fingers to his lips. "You can't speak a word yet. But . . . Do you happen to have a violin lying around?"

Her eyes turn to stars. She fetches her violin and leads us outside. We walk deep into the cushioning silence of the woods and sit on moss-covered rocks next to a brook. Beas closes her eyes when George dusts the freshly crushed Variants over her violin.

And then, from memory, she sets her bow to the strings and plays us the most beautiful song my ears might ever hear.

CHAPTER THIRTY-SEVEN

Date: December 16, 1942

Bird: Jay

Upon discovering a deceased one of their own, jays group together and sound alarm calls. They do not leave the carcass for two days, even to eat. Instead they sit and attend their dead.

Just before dawn I tuck the broken mouse under the collar of my coat and use the Tempests to run on the train tracks until I hit the edge of Sheffield. When the sun begins to rise, I jump on a train and ride two hours home.

"I could market Peace as a fresh start for an anxious or drug-addicted mind," I explain to Phineas later that morning. "Joy to combat a broken heart. Courage to inject like a shot in the arm."

We sit together on the porch, eating eggs. I drape a blanket over Phineas's legs and feed my broken mouse a piece of cheese.

"And you think you can do this in humans?"

I swallow. "I do." The mouse's teeth catch my finger, enough to prick the smallest drop of blood. I press my fingers together to staunch it at the same time that Phineas presses his gray lips together.

"You're a hustler. You remind me of a younger version of me." And then he barks a laugh that turns into a fit of coughing. His spine knocks hollowly against the back of the chair. "Just don't lose focus on the Stone," he reminds me. "Juliet's husband still doesn't respond to your letters?"

I shake my head.

"Perhaps you need to pay another visit to Gardner."

I nod, fingering the vial of Vala's Peace.

"Now, admittedly, comes the hardest part," I say. "Finding a human to . . . practice on." It's a turning point, the edge of the knife. I consider the mouse bodies that mounted in piles over the months of my failed attempts.

Phineas cocks his head toward the clanking of the sour-faced maid in the next room who is scrubbing splotches from the stolen silver.

"I doubt anyone would miss her," he says, lighting a cigar.

I stand. Push back the small voice in my head that pleads reason, pleads restraint. Push it back until I simply can't hear it anymore.

"Laurette?" I call, reaching into the cabinet for Larkin's chloroform. "Can you help me with something in the cellar?"

CHAPTER THIRTY-EIGHT

February 4, 1943

Keats. Keats for music.

And Freud for teeth.

I crumple the list I've made about Shakespeare's disappeared seven years — that he was looking for something valuable, that he was ill or escaping punishment for illegal poaching. But I can't quite bring myself to put Mother's book away again. I like the way the pages look covered in her handwriting and mine, as if our words are holding hands.

"Aila!" Mrs. Cliffton calls me to the kitchen.

"Tea?" she asks.

I nod, rubbing my hands together.

"Put some water on for us, would you?"

Genevieve has the night off, but she's left a big pot of stew simmering on the stove. Mrs. Cliffton brings a ladle of it to her lips, then sorts through an array of spices. A flowering sprig of rosemary sticks out from her bun.

"Aila, how does Miles seem to you lately?" she asks as I light the stove under the kettle.

"Better," I say. "Though it's hard to be certain."

"Things seem to have quieted down," Mrs. Cliffton agrees thoughtfully. "Do you know what the trouble was about at school? He seemed hesitant to tell me."

I pick at the crescent of my thumbnail. "It was about Mother. The things people say."

Mrs. Cliffton sighs. "I figured as much." She sets out two mugs for us. Through the window I watch Will disappear into the garden shed and leave with his toolbox. My old curiosity sparks.

"Your mother wasn't perfect," Mrs. Cliffton says, paging through the rows of tea bags. "But she did a lot of good here." She curls her fingers around the white threads of two mint teas. "I want you to know that."

"I think you're the only person who believes it," I say. A cluster of burrs appears at the back of my throat.

"You probably never knew this, but your mother set me up with Malcolm." Mrs. Cliffton plucks the kettle off the stove just as it starts to howl. "We might have wound up together anyway, but Juliet was the one who recognized that we had feelings for each other and pushed to make it happen." She smiles. "So I suppose that without Juliet, there's a chance Will might not have even existed."

I take the steaming mug from Mrs. Cliffton. The burrs recede a bit.

"And, as I think Malcolm told you, your mother had a hand in creating the first Variants. She found us the thistle."

I watch the tea bleed into the water.

Mrs. Cliffton returns to stirring the pot. Her hair shines as though it's reflecting the pans hanging in a rainbow of copper behind her.

"I know some people think she was the Catalyst," I say boldly. "Do you?"

Mrs. Cliffton doesn't turn around. She just keeps stirring, for so long that I wonder if she heard me. "I think Juliet was *a* catalyst," she says finally. "I don't think that word always has to be a bad one."

I'm silent. The steam whispers up from my mug.

When Mrs. Cliffton turns to face me, her eyes are bright.

"I'm glad you've come to Sterling, Aila. It's too easy to vilify a person who no longer lives and breathes in front of you." She reaches into her pocket and sets a glass globe of pearlescent Mind's Eye on the table. "Don't tell Malcolm I've given you this before you're Of Age. But Juliet was a dear, lovely friend to me. She was a good mother." Mrs. Cliffton pushes the Mind's Eye to rest in front of me. "And I want you to remember her that way."

There are so many secrets I'm keeping.

So many secrets between all of us, really. Big and little, silly and significant, weaving together into something that I want to believe is a safety net. But in some lights, it looks more like a web.

Every day I conceal from Will how I really feel about him.

There are other secrets, too.

The biggest are the ones I try to keep from myself.

I watch Miles from the second-floor window. He's in the yard beyond the gardens, kicking a ball to himself, volleying it in short spurts on his knees and then chasing after it. Will has been working with him to practice, and he's improved.

I want to ask him if he ever resents Mother sometimes, too. For lying. For leaving us. If he ever wonders whether Father could have fought the draft harder in order to stay with us.

If he ever wishes I were different than I am, the way I find myself wishing he was. Easier to be around.

Easier to love.

I watch him for a long time. Then I let myself out the back door, walk straight for him, and hug him without saying a word.

"What was that for?" he asks.

For being infuriatingly, inescapably mine, I want to tell him. For having echoes of Mother and Father pumping inside you even though they aren't here. For knowing what it was like to have Juliet Quinn as a mother, and what it was like to lose her.

Instead I just shrug. "Sorry for fighting," I say. "I know it's been a hard year. I miss her, too."

He juts his jaw. Blinks up at me a few times, as if he's deciding something.

"Aila, I have something to show you." The look on his face is fierce, but his lower lip betrays a twitch of nervousness. "Don't be mad."

My heart leaps when he motions for me to follow. Because suddenly I am sure what he is going to say.

He leads me along the garden path to the outer side of the stone wall. The sun is setting, and a light snow is beginning to fall. Miles kneels down and brushes off the few flakes that have collected like breadcrumbs along the top. Then he reaches his gloved hand into the crack, where it forms a perfect small shelf, enough to keep whatever is hidden there dry.

I close my eyes. *We all have secrets from each other.*

"I thought I missed her more. You don't show it that much." He takes a deep breath. "But I'm sorry for what I said. Because she loved you, too."

And from the hidden crack in the wall, he draws it out:

Mother's ring.

CHAPTER THIRTY-NINE

Date: 2/11/1943

Bird: The Great Gray Shrike

A songbird related to the common crow. It looks innocent.
Doesn't even have talons. But do not be fooled. It mimics
the calls of a songbird to lure it close. Then it hammers it to
death. Drags it to the nearest thorny plant or wire fence and
impales it.

In the end, creating the Virtues turns out to be just like working with locks.
It takes time and practice and making careful adjustments. I already have
the equation from Vala. I just have to find the right dosage for a human to
unlock what is inside.

Once I get Laurette to Sheffield, the vial I extract from her is a brown
liquid, small and unappealing. It adds up to be little more than the tip of my
finger — but it is enough to render Laurette basically useless. I know I've done
it when she starts to remind me of how Vala had been by the end. She quivers
in the corner, her eyes wild and unfocused, muttering under her breath and
shaking so badly that the simplest of house chores becomes impossible.

When we return to Phineas's, she shatters a serving plate on the ground
and then screams until she is hoarse. I send for her sister.

"A stroke, possibly? Or perhaps some onset of schizophrenia," I suggest
when the sister comes to collect her. I feel the smallest flicker of sympathy.

Then I call Victor with the news that I have the first vial of Peace for
him to try.

"Is there someone who would make for a good test beneficiary?" I ask, holding it up to the light.

"Yes," Victor says. "I know a man desperate for something that could help his son. His mind is consumed by addiction to opium."

"What I have isn't much," I admit, tapping the vial with my finger. "And likely not of the best quality. But it's enough for this first experiment. To work out all the kinks."

Then I hang up with Victor and place an ad in the newspaper for a new maid.

But that isn't where I will find my next candidate for the Virtues. I don't want a maid. I need someone who has led a charmed life, unlike Laurette's. Unlike mine.

Someone whose Peace is actually worth something.

Juliet's house is quaint, tucked onto a quiet street, with icicles dripping from the gutters. I knock three times, then break in through a ground-level window as thunder rolls overhead. Despite everything that happened between Juliet and me—even though her garden is overgrown and wilted—I take care not to step on her flowers. I can tell that once, not long ago, they were tended with great care.

My steps echo on the staircase, which slants heavily to the right. There is a thin line of dust on the bureaus in the bedrooms, as if no one lives here.

Juliet's house betrays her touch at every turn. I focus on keeping myself detached from feeling anything when I see the figurines she collected. The bed where she slept. The clothes she wore, still vibrantly colored but in more mature fashions than when we were teenagers. It doesn't seem possible that her time has run out while mine ticks on. I rifle through her things, thinking, Where does a dead woman hide what might have kept her alive?

But the Stone isn't here.

So I find a shovel in her garden shed and walk to the center of town. Push through the small white gates of the cemetery. Wind through the aisles of graves in a thick, cold rain.

These are the twists and turns that have brought me here. I look at the name engraved on her tombstone, barely visible in the sleet, and try to muster the old anger I once felt. All the simmering resentment. But now I just feel empty.

How ironic, that all my training with Phineas has prepared me for this.

I use her own shovel to dig. The rain helps to loosen the frozen ground, but I'm drenched when I finally crack open the shell of her coffin. I am careful not to look at her face. Something in me doesn't want to.

Instead my eyes slide down to her hands, folded and white. Like marble. The Stone is not there, where it has always been on her ring finger.

Sometimes it feels like my whole life has been a cruel game. In the years when it would have been easy to take the Stone, I'd never known I would need it. And when I finally tracked it down and had it within my sights, it vanished again.

I'm close to the kind of laughter that will make me come unhinged.

Because of course I should be used to it by now. Something I want just disappearing.

I close the casket in the rain and surprise myself when I leave my hand for a moment on the wood. As if there's any room to feel grief over her.

I hoist myself out of the grave.

Cover her and my memories over until they are both buried again deep within the earth.

When I shift, I feel Phineas's maps folded in my pocket, marking the places that could end the Curse. The very thing that would make the people of the Sisters finally love me, and render Malcolm, Victor, and my Virtues useless.

But love isn't what I thought it would be. It's nothing but a currency that's far too easy to spend—and still end up with nothing in return.

I'm losing Phineas. Without that Stone I've already lost him.

I pull out the maps he gave me. I could use them to heal the Sisters and play the hero. But that's not really what I want anymore.

I look at the X marked on each of the Sisters and then fold the maps. Chilled wetness curls its way up the legs of my pants.

What I want now is to twist the knife and make the Sisters hurt even more.

CHAPTER FORTY

February 15, 1943

'd almost forgotten the weight of Mother's ring around my neck. I find myself reaching to touch it, the smooth glass of it behind my clothes. I do not take it off even to shower. I tell Mrs. Cliffton that I found it buried at the bottom of my schoolbag, and for the moment it's even restored the precarious balance between Miles and me. Other than no word from Father, everything feels almost right again.

The feeling lasts for barely a week.

After school and Stars practice I join everyone for dinner. The sun is just starting to set. When I take my seat, Mother's ring slips out from behind my dress.

"Aila!" Dr. Cliffton says. He places his napkin in his lap. "You've found your necklace!"

My eyes flicker to Miles. He stares down at his plate.

"I found it in my schoolbag —" I start to say, but then Mrs. Cliffton's face blanches. "Mrs. Cliffton," I pause. "Are you all right?"

"Malcolm —" she says, her voice trembling. Her face is ghastly white. "I can't hear you."

"What?" Will's hand freezes on the serving spoon. "What do you mean?"

"Matilda?" Malcolm says, blinking at her. He gestures to his ears. "I can't hear your voice. But — I can hear the others."

Will looks between them. "You can't hear each other?"

"I don't understand." Mrs. Cliffton's breathing starts coming faster, her face flushing with color again as she bunches her napkin on the table. "What does this mean?"

"Can you hear me?" Will asks, and at the same time they both answer, "Yes."

"And me?" I ask.

"And me?" Miles asks.

They both nod. Dr. Cliffton is still clutching his silverware in his hands.

I can hear everyone.

Then Mrs. Cliffton whispers, "Me?" and Dr. Cliffton pales and shakes his head.

"What about me?" he asks. His voice rings clear to me, but Mrs. Cliffton's eyes fill with tears.

The phone shrills from the library, and Dr. Cliffton stumbles toward it, his foot dragging in his haste. We hurry after him. Miles steps on my heel.

"Hello?" The crease in Dr. Cliffton's brow sharpens as he listens. "It's happened to the Parkers," he informs us. "They can hear everyone but each other." As soon as he replaces the receiver, it rings again. He picks it up.

"And the Silvermans," he confirms. He hurries for his coat and his cane, and then he stops. Strides toward Mrs. Cliffton and pulls her into an embrace. She lays her head on his chest and he kisses her forehead, then turns her so that she can see his face. His lips. "We'll find the answer," he says to her, and her eyes fill with tears.

"But we just had a Disappearance," she says.

"It can't be that," Will insists. "We're not due for another seven years." His voice falters. "Right, Father?"

The phone rings again, shrilly, making us all jump. Mrs. Cliffton quickly takes it off the hook.

"Stay with your mother," Dr. Cliffton says to Will, me, and Miles. Miles's eyes are wide as he leans against the doorjamb.

"Where are you going?" Will asks.

"I'm calling an emergency Council meeting to find out what the devil is going on."

Then he slams the door so hard that the window glass rattles in his wake.

He doesn't come home until breakfast the next morning. When he bursts through the front door, his eyes are bloodshot. At the sight of him Mrs. Cliffton immediately sets down her coffee cup and stands. He kisses her cheek, then gestures for us to follow him into the library.

"Clearly something significant has happened," he says, wheeling out a chalkboard. He searches along the rim for a slice of chalk.

"Husbands and wives can't hear each other anymore?" Will asks.

"That was our first theory." Dr. Cliffton pushes his glasses up his nose, looking weary. "It evolved as the night went on. While the phenomenon was happening to most spouses, it wasn't true for all of them. And then we'd discover it was happening among other sets of people who were seemingly unconnected."

For Mrs. Cliffton's sake he writes in a quick, methodical hand, "All three Sisters reporting inability to hear voice of person they love."

He fiddles with the chalk in his hand and turns back to us. "*Romantic* love," he clarifies.

"So it is a Disappearance," Will says, aghast. He sits down heavily, as if someone's shoved him.

"Yes." Dr. Cliffton nods and clears his throat. "It does appear that way."

"But it hasn't been seven years yet!" Miles protests, stomping his foot at the unfairness of it all. "It's not following the rules!"

Dr. Cliffton scrawls for his wife, "Town in uproar."

"It's causing all kinds of additional chaos," he tells us. "Mrs. Doyle can hear Mr. Doyle, but he can't hear her. Mr. Stevens can't hear Mrs. Doyle, but he *can* hear his own wife." He drags his hand over his eyes and groans.

"Will," Mrs. Cliffton says, "ask your father how we will communicate."

Will relays the message, and then his father's answer: "Lip reading? Carrying a pad of paper everywhere? We can learn sign language. We'll devise a system. Until I can find a Variant." Though Dr. Cliffton looks exhausted, he says, "I'll start looking now. This very morning."

Mrs. Cliffton's lips tighten, and her eyes fill with tears. "Another one? Another rabbit to chase?" She plays with her wedding band, twirling it around her finger. "This is never going to end, is it?" she murmurs, and the look on her face gives me the same tumbling feeling as though I've just missed a stair.

"I'll find it, Matilda," Dr. Cliffton says, his brow creasing. He takes her arms and holds on to them as though he's tethering her, as if she otherwise might simply float away. "I promise," he says fervently, tilting her chin up toward him. "I won't stop trying until I've found it."

"I'll do whatever I can to help, too," I say. "Me too," Miles says. "And I will, too," Will vows, his jaw clenching. I clasp my hands together, hard, in my lap and put up a front of bravery for the rest of them. But I'm thinking that if hope has escaped even Mrs. Cliffton, now there is really reason to be afraid.

"A new Disappearance is bull manure," George mutters the next morning in Digby's lab. He halfheartedly measures a blue-tinted liquid into a beaker. The room around us is quiet, with students huddled wordlessly over their experiments or speaking in voices so subdued they blend with the scratching of pencils on paper. I sit on my stool and watch the dust sparkle across a sunbeam.

"Things don't just happen for no reason," George insists to Beas and me. "Something's *changed*. Something set this off." He looks up at us for acknowledgment.

"Maybe you solved the music Variant too quickly," Beas whispers sardonically. She draws a music note that has the base of a skull. "Maybe the Curse didn't think we had *suffered* quite enough."

"I suppose that could be a possibility," George says thoughtfully. "I mean, it *is* another auditory Disappearance. Maybe we're supposed to take that as some sort of warning."

George swivels to grab a glass slide and knocks the edge of the beaker with his elbow. It tumbles to the floor in slow motion and shatters.

For an endless moment we all just look at it.

The room has fallen so still that we can hear the sudden ricochet of steps moving down the hallway. They grow louder and faster as they approach, and then the door to Digby's lab bursts open and Chase Peterson enters.

"Mr. Peterson, excuse me—" Digby begins, turning from the chalkboard.

"Have you heard?" Chase says breathlessly. "The Disappearances have hit a fourth town."

A sudden gust of air sends Dr. Digby's stack of papers to the floor, scattering in large white tiles. George rises, slowly, from where he has knelt to sweep the glass. It crunches like gravel under his weight.

Dr. Digby's voice is strained. "Class, you are dismissed."

"Why?" George asks, slamming his hand down on the picnic table. His breath puffs out in angry billows. His hands are already turning red and numb with cold, as if he's too distracted or defiant to use the Variants.

His mother, of course, has already collected every scrap of available news by the time he reaches her on the telephone. "She heard that the Disappearances struck Charlton," he relays.

"Where's that?"

"It's the town just beyond Sheffield."

"Today?" I ask.

"Yesterday. Around the very same time as our Disappearance."

My chest lightens a little at the sudden sight of Will, his hands shoved into his pockets. He approaches our table and stops there, leaning his weight against it. Beas is a half step behind him. She slides onto the bench next to me.

"Just the voices disappeared in Charlton, then?" I ask George.

"No," George says. "They got every Disappearance we have. It hit them all at once."

"That's even worse than what happened to us," Beas says, picking at the pills on her wool gloves. "Not our gradual descent. Just

—one day you have everything, and the next . . ." Her gloved fingers flutter.

"I heard the Council is heading to Charlton to brief them about what we know—" Will begins.

"They're bound to be a bit disappointed that we haven't solved it in the past thirty-five years," George mutters.

"—and to see if they have any clues that could help us . . ." Will continues.

"And to make sure they stay quiet about everything, I'm sure," Beas says.

"Your father is going?" I ask Will, and he nods.

"This has to be making the Council nervous. The Curse almost seems to be mimicking a virus or an infection now," George says absently. "To spread like this, in such close quarters?"

"Why jump, suddenly, to a new town?" Will says. He squints away from us. "And why disrupt the cycle of seven years?"

"This deviation should not be happening. Everything up until now has always been so ordered," George says. He fumbles in his backpack for his Variant research notebook. "Do you reckon this means . . . the Disappearances will start speeding up?"

I clasp my hands together and rub them under the table. To me the Curse is acting less like an infection and more like a fox I'm trying to hunt. Every time I think I've caught a scent, it veers off and loses me again.

Beas shivers and scoots closer to me. "I never realized there was something rather comforting about the seven years," she says. "Depressing, yes, because we knew it would just keep going—"

I try to brush off the settling doubt and focus on what Beas is saying. "Maybe a new pattern will emerge now. Something new that could help us solve it for good," I say, trying to sound hopeful.

"Or maybe it's just warped into something unpredictable, with no sense of rhyme or reason anymore." Beas fixes her gaze on something beyond me, far in the distance. She whispers, "That would be the most terrifying thing of all."

When I come out of Stars practice that afternoon, it's the first time in three months that Will isn't standing there waiting for me.

All over town, the same debate is happening in waves: whether the tournament should be held is argued in the halls of the school and in Council meetings. At home, the Clifftons scribble notes to each other between bites of breakfast, wondering whether they should cancel their tournament party.

Perhaps we should just announce the music discovery now.

Today?

People would like to hear it.

I suppose it would give some encouragement.

I leave for school before they reach a decision.

"The Clifftons might cancel their party," I tell George and Beas.

"Hmm. Wonder if Eliza will cancel hers, too." George opens his folder, and I glimpse an invitation addressed to him.

I pause. "Eliza's having a party?"

George's mouth falls open, and he hurriedly tries to close his folder, but I snatch the invite from the flap before he can.

It's handwritten in script.

To George Mackelroy: You are invited to a Patton victory celebration after the closing ceremonies of the tournament.

"Sorry, I shouldn't have said anything," George says. "I just thought, if she invited *me,* she invited everyone." He squints. *"The entire human race."*

"A victory celebration?" I scoff, handing the invitation back to him. "That's taking confidence to a new level. Even for her."

"So just win," Beas says wearily, resting her head on her outstretched arm. "She can't turn a Sterling victor away from a victory party." She nudges me. "You could do it, you know. You could beat everyone. Even Margeaux Templeton."

"Margeaux Templeton?" I ask. So that's who I'll be up against. The name sounds familiar, and it isn't until George groans that I remember why. The girl who glared at him on Disappearance Day, the heir to Charlton Templeton's shipping fortune in "The Mackelroy Misfortune."

"My vote is that nobody cancels anything," Beas says, shoving her books into her bag. "That's what we do. We go on. Life *has* to go on." She looks at me meaningfully. "They're not canceling tonight, at least," she whispers. "See you later."

"Much later," George adds.

Another Tempest race, then. I nod, trying to forget the promise I made to Dr. Cliffton back in October. My heart sings at the thought of a moonlit night alone with Will.

At least Eliza can't prevent me from coming to that.

But he isn't there again when I come out of the gym doors. As I walk home without him, it seems longer and colder than it usually does. *Maybe his practice let out early or ran late,* I think. *Maybe he went to the soda shop with Carter.*

"Is Will here?" I ask Miles when I walk through the door, shaking free of my coat.

I can see half-chewed bites of sandwich in his mouth when he answers. "He left a while ago. With his toolbox."

Hmm.

"Hey. Where were you today?" I ask Will casually when he walks in the front door an hour later. I'm lounging on the couch in his father's library, doing my homework where we usually do it together. He's without his toolbox, I notice.

"Oh. Nowhere in particular," he says. "Just had some things to do."

I raise my eyebrows and loudly flip the page of my textbook. Underline a note in my notebook. My stomach prickles when he sits down next to me, and I keep waiting for him to mention the race. Some sort of sign or look, a note slipped to me when no one is looking. But we study together alone in Dr. Cliffton's library and still he stays silent. My excitement dims as we sit down for dinner. Maybe he simply isn't going to race anymore, just as he told his father he wouldn't.

Mrs. Cliffton makes the final decision on the tournament party over our dinner of pork chops ringed with golden pineapple.

"We've decided to have it," she announces, setting down her fork. "And we'll invite the people of Charlton, too. We need to gather together at times like this." She looks to Dr. Cliffton, and he nods in agreement. In a matter of days they've already become better at reading each other's lips.

"Everyone could use a bright spot at this bleak time," Dr. Cliffton says, dishing salad onto his plate.

"These last six months have certainly been wretched, haven't they?" Mrs. Cliffton asks. Then she flushes bright red. "Except for

having you and Miles here, of course, Aila—I—I didn't mean—"
she says, but my stomach twists in a knot, and her words hang in the
air over us for the rest of dinner. As if everyone's attention has suddenly been drawn to the very same realization.

How exponentially worse things have become for Sterling in the
short time that Miles and I have been here.

CHAPTER FORTY-ONE

That night, I tell everyone to sleep well and close my bedroom door, but instead of my nightgown, I pull on a black sweater and trousers. I spend close to an hour examining a magazine photograph of Gene Tierney, trying to set my hair in a glamorous wave like hers by feel alone. Then I sit on my bed with a poetry book opened in my lap, trying not to think of what Mrs. Cliffton said, reading the same stanzas again and again.

At just past eleven thirty my ears prick with the sound of Will's footsteps. He must think he's being quiet, but I can hear the soft padding of his feet as they sink into the hallway rug. I close my book and stand, my heart ascending. His steps pause just outside my doorway, and I wait for his knock.

But then, after a long moment, the padding continues on down the hall, fading into a single creak on the stairs. It takes the slightest whisper of the front door closing before I can admit to myself that he has left. Without me.

I sit for a long moment, clutching my hands into fists in my lap.

What just happened?

Is it because he suddenly realized how much worse things became with Miles and me here? Or because he was tired of me tagging along? Has he been kind out of pity while secretly finding me a burden? With horror I think, *Maybe he wants to be alone with Eliza and I would have been in the way.*

The bump at the top of my right ear burns, as if Dixon

Fairweather is whispering into it again. I strip off my dark clothes and hurl them into the back of my wardrobe. *It doesn't matter,* I think fiercely, changing into my nightgown. Raking my fingers through the wave I set until it is limp and flat again.

Before I return to the warmth of my bed, I open my window and let my curtains wave out into the night like white flags of surrender. He'll see them when he comes home and know that *I* know that he didn't invite me. It's childish and spiteful, and a move more punishing to me than to him. I'm shivering considerably by the time he returns almost two hours later.

I hear him scale the tree outside my window, and he knocks quietly at the frame before he climbs into my room. He closes the window behind him without a word and then turns to face me, his cheeks flushed with cold and his hair wet and darkened with sweat. He is breathing heavily, as if he ran all the way home.

I cross my arms over my chest. "Have fun?" I ask pointedly.

"I didn't realize you needed me to invite you," he says stiffly. He stands rigid and straight. "I figured George or Beas did."

It's like a knife to the heart. "I told you last time I wanted to go with you."

"And then you promised my father you wouldn't."

"So did you," I retort. My cheeks blaze.

"I'm sorry." He looks away. "It just gets complicated. With us living in the same house. With you not being from here. I wish things could be different."

"Do you?" I ask cruelly. "It seems like things are working out pretty well for you and your family just the way things are."

"Okay, Aila," he says, his jaw setting in that way it does, letting me know that I've stung him just where I wanted to. Making me feel as though I've both won and lost when he leaves, closing the door to my room soundlessly behind him.

My head and chest ache all the next day. "Where were you last night?" Beas whispers at lab. "I was looking for you."

"Didn't feel good," I mumble, and barely say another word to anyone the rest of the day.

After practice with Mrs. Percy I don't even bother waiting for Will. I start walking in the breath-catching cold, the sun shearing through the clouds overhead, remembering what Mrs. Cliffton said about different sorts of Catalysts. I can feel the curve of Mind's Eye in my pocket and the sharp corner of the Shakespeare book poking through my bag. I think about how someday soon we can go home again and leave this wretched place behind us.

I keep my head down until I turn onto the long lane that soon becomes dirt. An early March snow has fallen between the rows of harvested corn, white and raked as evenly as part lines.

Mother's house appears earlier than it had in the fall, its dull gray peeking out from behind the grove of naked trees. I steel myself for the onslaught of slurs across the decaying boards. But the shadows are falling in such a way that for a moment, I can't see them.

I walk closer, my bag heavy with books and hitting against my leg with enough force to leave a bruise. The trees rustle like summer rain. I stop and listen. Blink, and blink again as I look toward the house.

It wasn't a trick of the shadows. The words simply aren't there anymore.

The house has returned to a smooth, single layer of gray paint.

My heart springs open like shutters.

The snow is cleared from the ground. The word *Catalyst*, once carved everywhere in the dirt, has been raked away. Edges for flower beds are marked off with a small rudimentary fence. The craggy ends of the boards are smoothed. Even the chimney's waterfall of bricks have been collected and mounted into a smart, finished bench. Mother's house no longer looks desecrated and condemned. It looks more like a memorial.

Who did this?

I sit on the brick bench and drop my bag heavily into the dirt, my face burning at the memory of Will sneaking off all those times with his toolbox.

I don't understand him. One minute I think he's flirting with me, the next he's treating me like a pariah. He invites Eliza to the ball, but then sometimes he almost seems jealous of George.

And now this.

I do think he's come to care for me. I'm just not sure in what way.

I survey the grounds and consider which flowers I will plant here in the small flower beds, which seeds I will push down deep into Sterling soil to bloom whether I am still here to see them or not. I pull Mother's Shakespeare book from my bag. *She would like mountain laurel,* I think. I trace my fingers absently along the name she has written. The note I found on that very first day on the train.

Stefen. I will always love you.

There, in the resurrected shadows of her house, I have a sudden thought. I reach into my bag and pluck out the vial of Mind's Eye Mrs. Cliffton gave me. Put the smallest whisper of it on my fingertips and touch it to my eyelids.

Stefen, I think.

A string of memories floods in front of me, short and clear, like water droplets spilling onto my eyelids and casting ripples. In one I'm nine, standing next to a younger version of Mother as she looks at her reflection in the chipped vanity, brushing her cheeks with rouge as she calls out "Stefen" and then corrects herself to call for Miles; another she's out in the garden, her hair long and tangled, her eyes haggard with sleeplessness as she chases my brother as a toddler. There are only five of these memories altogether: just a series of her calling Miles by the wrong name, and the last one of her at the sink, talking to herself under her breath as she scrubs the dishes and watches a blood-colored cardinal out the window.

I'm no closer to understanding who Stefen is. But I almost don't care.

Because I can *see* her.

A deep chill is snatching the feeling from my fingers, but once the images fade back into blackness, I dab one more touch of Mind's Eye on my eyelids. *Frogs and fish,* I think, and take myself back to us in the garden. She laughs in the gray morning, the ring glinting on her finger, her skin glowing and as ripe as a peach in its prime. I want to stay and watch her this way, and I try to hold on to it until my tears have washed all the Mind's Eye away.

I wipe my eyes, and the wind rustles the pages of the book, still open in my lap, to a poem we've both marked. Had she kept making these notes long after she left Sterling? Had she stayed up late into the night circling these passages, still haunted by this mystery? Stalked by guilt, and wondering why she alone had been set free?

My love is strengthened, though more weak in seeming;
I love not less, though less the show appear;

That love is merchandized whose rich esteeming
The owner's tongue doth publish everywhere.
Our love was new, and then but in the spring,
When I was wont to greet it with my lays;
As Philomel in summer's front doth sing,
And stops his pipe in growth of riper days:
Not that the summer is less pleasant now
Than when her mournful hymns did hush the night,
But that wild music burthens every bough,
And sweets grown common lose their dear delight.
Therefore like her, I sometime hold my tongue:
Because I would not dull you with my song.

I pull my hands out from where I've tucked them into the warmth of my sleeves. My heart lifts in tandem with the cluster of dried leaves at my feet. They swirl and rise, spun into new life by the wind. Because I suddenly see the thing I'd missed before. The most important one of all.

Philomel, I think. Of course.

I run straight to Beas's house and ring the doorbell. Mrs. Fogg scowls when she sees me but calls, "Beatrice, that Aila Quinn from school is here."

Beas brings me to her room, which is cluttered with post-cards, record sleeves, hair clips, glass cases, and a poster on the wall of a woman in a corset playing a violin. Her bookshelf is full of poetry, and her violin case stands in the corner next to a collection of bows. We sit on her bed, and I throw my frozen toes under the covers.

"Philomel," I tell Beas, throwing Mother's book open on my lap.

"In a poem Shakespeare wrote about songs restrained and music held back. Don't you see? Philomel! It's Latin for nightingale!"

There's a sudden beating rush in my ears. My theory was always just a hunch, but there is an undercurrent of something more now. A flash of pure revived faith.

She squeaks and pushes her hands together. "I *knew* it. I *knew* you were onto something!"

She pulls out two bottles of Coca-Cola she has hidden under her bed. They fizz when we open and clink them.

In her throaty voice she says, "So now you just have to find the rest of them. Ooh!" she claps. "Let me help!"

I raise my soda to meet hers. "Cheers, Beas. Let's divide and conquer."

On Thursday she passes me a note in class when Digby's back is turned.

VEIL VARIANTS:
To dry the rain
on my storm-beaten face

On Friday I pass her back:

hypnosis
DOCTOR: You see, her eyes are open.
GENTLEWOMAN: Ay, but their sense is shut.
— Macbeth

Her eyes widen, and she gives me a thumbs-up.

"Tomorrow — bring everything you've been able to find," I say.

"What are you two whispering about over there?" George asks, peering up from his microscope.

"Boys," I say.

"Margeaux Templeton," Beas says at the exact same time, and sticks her tongue out at him.

On Saturday morning I beat Genevieve to the door when Beas rings the bell.

"First things first," I say, leading her up to my room. "You have to have one of these."

We settle onto the floor, surrounded by books, paper, and pens, and I hand her one of Genevieve's creations rolled in cinnamon and sugar. "A dirt bomb."

She exchanges it for her notepad. "Here's everything I found in the sonnets."

I take her list and begin to compare it with mine.

"You?" she asks, biting into the doughnut with a shower of cinnamon and sugar.

Warmth and hope are seeping through me with every row of her finds that I add to my list. "I was looking for the two things that threw me before," I tell her.

"Right. Freud's teeth. Did you know there's something about a snake's tooth in a paragraph about dreams in *Macbeth*?" she says. She closes her eyes as she takes another bite. "And did you know that I'm kidnapping Genevieve for these?"

"I found something better for dreams and teeth in *Romeo and Juliet*," I say.

And in this state she gallops night by night
Through lovers' brains, and then they dream of love;

On courtiers' knees, that dream on curtsies straight;

O'er lawyers' fingers, who straight dream on fees;

O'er ladies' lips, who straight on kisses dream.

"It's describing a fairy midwife who rides in a chariot made from a hazelnut," I say.

"The tooth fairy?" Beas grins.

"And remember when Dr. Cliffton said my 'overcast the night' was a stretch for the Disappearance of stars?"

"Because we could still see the moon."

I nod and show her my list, where I've struck it out. And in its place I write triumphantly:

Stars, hide your fires — Macbeth

Then I toss my pen onto the covers, and Beas's eyes grow huge as she looks through the pages and pages of my notes. My pulse begins to hum.

"It's here," she says. *"It's all here."*

DISAPPEARANCES:

scents

Thou losest thy old smell. — As You Like It

Eyes without feeling,

feeling without sight,

Ears without hands or eyes,

smelling sans all.

— Hamlet

reflection

And since you know you

cannot see yourself

so well as by reflection. — Julius Caesar

Two glasses, where herself

herself beheld

A thousand times,

and now no more reflect — Venus + Adonis

dreams

My love and her desert;

that canst not dream. — All's Well That Ends Well

colors

Your mistresses dare

never come in rain,

For fear their colours

should be washed away. — Love's Labour's Lost

stars

Overcast the night — A Midsummer Night's Dream

Stars, hide your fires — Macbeth

music

Bid the music leave. — Henry VIII

VARIANTS:

dream

O, then, I see Queen Mab hath been with you.

She is the fairies' midwife, and she comes

In shape no bigger than an agate-stone

(tooth fairy?)

Her chariot is an empty hazel-nut

Made by the joiner squirrel or old grub,

Time out o' mind the fairies' coachmakers.

And in this state she gallops night by night

Through lovers' brains, and then they dream of love;

O'er courtiers' knees, that dream on court'sies straight,

O'er lawyers' fingers, who straight dream on fees,

O'er ladies' lips, who straight on kisses dream . . .

— Romeo + Juliet

ember

And see thy blood warm when thou feel'st

it cold. — Sonnet 2

fragrance

I cannot smell.

Get you some of this distilled

carduus benedictus → (holy thistle)

and lay it to your heart.

It is the only thing for a qualm.

— Much Ado About Nothing

glimmers

All that glisters is not gold — The Merchant of Venice

hypnosis

DOCTOR: You see her eyes are open.

GENTLEWOMAN: Ay, but their sense is shut. — Macbeth

looking glass

And if my word be sterling yet in England

Let it command a mirror hither straight

That it may show me what a face I have

— The Life + Death of Richard II

When Phoebe doth behold Her silver visage in

the watery glass

Decking with liquid pearl the

bladed glass — A Midsummer Night's Dream

mind's eye

There's rosemary, that's for remembrance.

— Hamlet

Crush this herb into Lysander's eye.

— A Midsummer Night's Dream

night vision

When most I wink, then do mine eyes best

see, For all the day they view things

unrespected;

But when I sleep, in dreams they look on
thee, And darkly bright, Are bright in dark
directed. —Sonnet 43

nightingale

There is no music in the nightingale
— Two Gentlemen of Verona

It was the nightingale, and not the lark,
That pierced the fearful hollow of thine ear.
— Romeo + Juliet

Philomel in Sonnet 102

tempest

Then should I spur, though mounted on the
wind; In winged speed no motion shall I
know — Sonnet 51

Swift as a shadow, short as any dream,
brief as the lightning in the collied night
— A Midsummer Night's Dream

veil

To dry the rain on my storm-beaten face
— Sonnet 34

"Holy mackerel, Aila," Beas breathes at last, spreading the sheets out
beneath her fingers. She covers her gaping mouth. "You did it."

"It was my mother," I say softly. "I just picked up the bread-crumbs she left and kept going."

"So what does this mean?" she asks, her low voice rising higher. "Aila, what does this mean?"

"It means," I say, swallowing, "that the Sisters are living in a curse taken *entirely from Shakespeare's own pages.*"

"Do you know that this is the closest anyone has come to a lead like this in decades?" Beas leaps to her feet. "Come on, let's tell the Clifftons! Let's tell everybody!"

"Wait!" I say, grabbing her arm. I fight my own urge to fly down the stairs and triumphantly pound on Dr. Clifton's library door. "We still don't know why the seven years are significant, or why it's happening here, at this time period specifically. I don't think we should tell anyone until we can answer those questions."

I don't mention the other question that continues to haunt the back of my mind:

Why was my mother the only exception?

She pouts a little, but then she grabs my arm and we both squeal and jump. Because today is the mark of something that has changed, a corner we've turned. We can both feel it. Something big. Something new.

"All right," Beas agrees. "We won't tell anyone yet. We're going to fan this little theory of yours until it's strong enough to catch fire all on its own."

"Exactly," I say, folding my list away.

And then we're going to watch it blaze.

CHAPTER FORTY-TWO

Date: 2/20/1943

Bird: Albatross

The albatross mates for life, yet in that lifetime it flies millions of miles alone.

Larkin's done his job well. The buzz about the Virtues builds along the clandestine pipes of the underground. It's mostly just rumors. Victor wants the clamoring to reach a fevered pitch before we auction off bits of Virtue for more money than either of us have ever imagined.

But we have to find that stock, first.

All along I've assumed that Harold took the children on some sort of trip. Believed that with the house still and with all their things in it, they must be coming back. With the Stone. One of them must have it, and if I had to guess — my money's on the girl. Because history always repeats itself.

But it is as if they themselves have disappeared. The dust is disturbed only by me. My shoes leave footprints on the wood that I have to sweep away. Being inside that abandoned house, surrounded by the smiling faces of their photographs, makes me feel like I'm going mad. Like I've entered into a family of ghosts.

I can tell the Quinns' neighbor is suspicious as soon as I knock on the door. Something about me always seems to set people on edge.

She opens the door a crack and squints out at me, with her windswept hair and her overly rouged cheeks. Reid, it says on the mailbox.

I paste a smile on my face. "Mrs. Reid," I say —

"Who are you?" she asks. "I've seen you creeping around. What business do you have with the house next door?"

"Juliet and I grew up together," I explain.

"I didn't see you at the funeral," she says, pursing her lips.

The old taste of rot fills my mouth, and I clear my throat. "We'd . . . lost touch until recently."

She remains unconvinced. My patience is wearing thin.

"I need to get in touch with her family. If you could tell me where to find them —" I take a step forward.

"Don't know where they are," she says, and closes the door in my face.

I hear the click of the lock — an easy one I've picked a hundred times before. I'm almost certain she's lying, and I half consider barging in and drugging her with the chloroform in my pocket. I could get her to a Sister City and collect a new Virtue. See how much Victor can get for it.

Instead I turn away with a weary sigh. It's too much effort for such a grumpy old bag. I need someone young. Someone closer to childhood, when life is easy and carefree and joyful. At least — it's supposed to be.

I glance at Aila's window one more time.

I flip up the collar of my coat to conceal my face and turn back toward the train station, my head swimming with thoughts of Juliet, and I can't think of the few bright spots of my youth without thinking of the one person who created them. The girl I fell in love with when I was all of ten years old — her, and no one else ever again.

Matilda.

Juliet's best friend.

My little red bird.

I duck my head into the wind and feel my limp come back ever so faintly when I start to jog.

Even now. Even still, I love her. Ever since the endless winter I was ten years old and my foster mother, Eleanor, wouldn't let me go outside. I sat all day by the window, though the heat from the fire fogged up the panes. The world beyond them had started to seem like nothing more than a muted photograph.

But then one day Juliet and Matilda spilled through the front door, and I did not turn to see them shake the snow from their hair. Their cheeks would be flushed where cold and skin met, both of them so full of life. I kept looking down at my bird book, and I jumped when Matilda came up behind me.

"Do you like to watch the birds?" she had asked kindly. "Juliet said you watch them from the window."

For a moment I couldn't find my voice. "Yes," I finally said. "But there aren't many to see in the winter."

"Which one is your favorite?"

"Matilda!" Juliet had called, her voice spinning down, already halfway up the staircase.

"Coming!" Matilda called back.

But instead she turned, expectantly, to me.

I stuttered, flipping through the pages until I found the one I loved to look at. The bleeding shock of colors of the painted bunting. I showed it to her, shyly, as if it were a part of myself.

She'd studied the image for a long time, her red hair falling into her eyes until she brushed it away.

"Matilda?" Juliet called.

But she stayed next to me. Used her fingertip to trace the outline of the bird in the fog of the window.

"Until the spring comes," she whispered, and her touch lingered long after the frost melted away.

CHAPTER FORTY-THREE

Before Beas leaves, she dusts me with Embers, and I head outside to pull the tarp from my target and unpack my Stars. My heart sings from our discovery, and I'm pleased at how comfortable the pieces have come to feel in my hand over the last six months. How the throwing motion has molded my muscles so much that flipping the Star from its tip doesn't require as much concentration. I practice my throws over and over, from greater distances, until they regularly sink into the target's center, until the afternoon wanes and my body aches.

Miles and Mrs. Cliffton don't return from town until after dinner. I'm already dressing for bed when Miles knocks on my door.

"Aila," he says, "there's a letter."

I throw open the door, and as soon as I see my father's handwriting, my eyes fill with tears.

I rip into it. I wonder what he looked like when he wrote it. If his stubbly beard has grown out without anyone to protest that it feels scratchy.

This, out of everything today, is the best news of all.

Miles leans against my door as I fold it back into the envelope. "Are you still grumpy?" he asks.

"I'm not grumpy," I say. "I've never been better."

"Well, you *were* grumpy. A frightful grump, this whole week."

"Funny how quickly everything can change," I murmur, running my fingertips over the letter again.

He sits down on my bed. "Were you mad because everyone is saying that we came and then an extra Disappearance happened?"

I raise my eyebrow at him. "Who is 'everyone'?"

His eyes glint. "All the kids at school. But Walt started it."

"Eliza's brother?" I huff. I narrow my eyes at Miles, suddenly noticing his bouncing knee. "Why are you so giddy right now?"

"Because I have something for you. It was meant to cheer you up." He jumps from my bed and digs in his pocket. "I took this in town today."

He hands out a small folded white paper. The corners of his mouth twitch.

"What is this?" I ask. "A telegram?"

He nods. "From Mrs. Patton to Eliza and Walt."

"Miles!" I drop it as if it has burned my fingers. "You can't take someone's mail. It's against the law!"

"You aren't going to read it?" he asks, eyes wide and incredulous.

I don't answer. The telegram has landed in my lap, where it smolders like a coal.

"Fine. I'll tell you what it says anyway." He rips it back. " 'No longer able to make tournament due to significant auction. Stop. Postpone party with my apologies. Stop. Sending gifts to make up for regrettable delay. Stop.' "

Something in my stomach curdles. As if I've taken a swig of sour milk.

Miles is growing restless at my silence. "It was easy," he says. "I swiped it when we were in the telegraph office and no one was looking." He examines my face for a reaction. "And they deserve it," he adds quietly. "I saw the way she was with you at the Harvest Fair. Let

Eliza and Walt see how it feels when they can't explain everything about their mother."

Scowling, I reach for the telegram. Feel the ridged edges with my fingertips. Clearly the right thing would be to deliver the message to Eliza, as it was intended. I know this. But I really, really don't want to. How could I get it to them without confessing what Miles has done?

If anyone finds out that he's stolen from the Pattons, there will be consequences. It would embarrass the Clifftons. It could get Miles kicked out of school. And then where would we go?

Not to mention that I would have to eat major crow in front of Eliza.

I can feel Miles looking at me. Part of me wants to kill him.

At least he took only the telegram, I think darkly, and not the gifts Mrs. Patton promised.

"I suppose no one needs to know," I say slowly. "Maybe the telegram just got lost, or didn't come through." I rip it into tiny, unreadable shreds before I can second-guess myself. "I won't tell if you won't," I promise.

He rewards me with a lopsided smile, a rare seal of his trust.

"And Miles," I warn, "if you ever steal anything again, I'm going to rip your arms right out of your body."

"All right, Aila," he grumbles. "I was only trying to make you glad." He finds something else in the depths of his pocket and throws it at me. A pouch of his Dream Variants. "For not ratting on me," he says. "May your dreams be filled with stars and not with shadows," he says. And then he is gone.

I sigh and flop back onto my bed, uncertainty working its way through me like a drop of dye in water. I suppose I just have to see it as choosing sides between Eliza and Miles. So of course I was right to pick Miles. He is my own flesh and blood, and it's my job to protect him. That's how you're *supposed* to be with family.

But a small voice within me nags, *Even when they've done something wrong?*

I ignore it and turn toward Miles's other gift.

I know how dreams work. They're a bit of a gamble, conjuring up the loveliest visions or the darkest nightmares, forcing me to confront the deepest fears that only I know exist. I wonder if there's any control over it, the way there is with Mind's Eye.

I dip my hand into the pouch, cover myself with the Variants, and close my eyes, trying to prod my mind in the right direction.

Even though it hurts, I let myself picture the night of the Tempest race, of walking alone with Will in the cool darkness. Of him stretched out lazily in the grass, watching me throw my Stars at the target he made. My heartbeat slows. I drift to sleep.

When I open my eyes, I don't see Will at all. I'm alone in the school gymnasium. Sunlight streams through the high windows, bright and warm. I look down, feeling a sword in my hand.

As soon as I glimpse Eliza striding across the floor, I know my mind has betrayed me.

She's wearing my red coat, and I'm wearing her costume from the Harvest Fair. I touch the beads, shimmering like raindrops against my fingers. I feel naked.

Eliza suddenly lowers her mask to protect her face and charges toward me with an epee drawn. I struggle to pull down my mask and then realize with horror that I don't have one. I instinctively raise my sword. But it hasn't the lightness of an epee. It's a real sword, heavy and razor sharp.

I struggle even to lift it, my balance shifting as I try to defend myself. But Eliza continues advancing, the tip of her epee stinging me again and again until I'm pushed back against the wall. Then I see my chance: one bare spot at Eliza's neck.

I raise my sword to strike. I hesitate.

In that moment the dream dissipates, and Eliza is gone.

There is a beat of darkness. A minute might pass, or an hour. And after the darkness fades again, I see the flowers.

There are hundreds of them, bright and gorgeous, just as I remember them when Father had cut and arranged them in colorful pockets around Mother's bed. During the final weeks he picked them every morning, refreshing any stems that drooped or wilted. He began to bring the garden in to Mother when she could no longer bring herself out to it.

Her room is dim, and I'm drawn to the flowers. I pick up the nearest vase. Inhale the white puffs of hydrangea. My brain has not forgotten what they smell like; I drink it in.

But this is less a dream and more a memory. I *remember* this scene. It was the last time I saw Mother alive. Here is the rain, pattering on the window. Mother's face is so drawn and haggard, her wide eyes too large, her small frame barely making a dent on the pillow. But even then I can see the fighting spirit that still flickers. In the dream, Mother's voice is muffled and distorted. It all comes rushing back. All the things I had wanted to say that day, and what I said instead.

"Aila." Mother's voice is threadbare. "Take care of your brother. You will always be tied to each other. Don't treat him in a way you will come to regret." Her next words are blurry and barely formed, as if I'm hearing them through thick glass. "It doesn't always come right away," she whispers.

I take Mother's hand in mine. It is pointed and bony.

"I'll take care of Miles," I promise. "I'll look after him."

I look down at our hands and think about how many things die when a person does. Not just her body, but the scent of her and the sound of her voice, the way that her esses whisper off the tip of her tongue and the sound of her singing, always singing, when she washes dishes in the kitchen sink. The question feels like thorns on my tongue, but I don't ask it now, just as I hadn't then.

What will the world be like without you in it?

Now I know.

It is a world that is emptier, more tired, often dulled. It is gray where there used to be endless color. It is nights without the guiding compass of stars. It is surviving some days solely by the kindness of others. It is fighting, always fighting, to find all the beauty that is still here, even after the worst Disappearance of them all.

The finishing word, I want to tell her, *is* brokenhearted.

"It's going to be all right," I whisper. She drops my hand and reaches for my hair. Tucks it behind my ugly ear. "I love you."

I love you, I love you, I love you.

I don't know if it's the dream or my true memory, but Mother seems to be trying to say something else. She struggles to form the words, but they are slipping away from her.

I grab for her hand again, but it has suddenly turned to the marble of all my other dreams—so achingly, bitterly cold. I clutch at it and listen to a distant sound that is pure distilled sadness.

I don't recognize it as my own sobbing until the door opens and

Will is suddenly there, his arms wrapping around me, pulling me up and out of the suffocating mist of the dream.

"It's all right," he says, his hands gripping my shoulders. "Open your eyes. It's not real." I look at him until I can finally grasp what he's saying. "It's not real. *This* is real."

He waits until my eyes can focus again on the light streaming in from the hallway, on Mother's picture looking back at me from the bureau, on the muted, constant yellow of my bedroom walls.

When my breathing returns to normal, he lets go of my shoulders.

"Thanks." I wipe my eyes with the backs of my hands. "I'm okay now."

"Good," he says.

Then he lies down on the floor next to my bed without another word and stays there with me until the light of morning comes.

CHAPTER FORTY-FOUR

The next morning, I eat toast alone in the kitchen and wander through the hallways until I find Mrs. Cliffton in the sunroom. She is surrounded by boxes of nightingale feathers, and a ledger is open in her lap.

"Morning," I say, stepping into the room. I blink in the sunlight. My sadness from last night still hangs around me like a veil.

"Good morning, dear." Mrs. Cliffton looks up. "Did you get something for breakfast?"

"Yes," I say. I pause. Toe the line of the cool tile floor.

Mrs. Cliffton sighs and sets her ledger aside. "Aila, I wanted to apologize again for what I said the other night. I'm afraid it all came out wrong, and I wish I hadn't said it." She tilts her head. "It's true that parts of these months have been harder than usual, but you and Miles have been a bright spot for me — and I really am so glad you've come."

I clear my throat and push through an unexpected wave of shyness. "I was wondering —" I say. "Did my mother ever know someone named Stefen?"

Mrs. Cliffton turns sharply. "Stefen?"

I've caught her off-guard, and there's a look on her face I've seen once before, months ago. When she was beginning to explain about the Disappearances. It is a look of trying to tread carefully.

I steel myself and press on. "Who was he? A friend of hers? Something . . . more?"

"Well, Aila," she says, shifting, "they grew up together. They were both raised by Eleanor Cummings."

One more time, it's as though the air has been knocked from my lungs. I unclench my hands as if they have pulled up roots. Roots tangling into more roots, branching secrets coming up with every tug. How will I ever know when I've reached the end of them?

I sigh and sit down on the loveseat. "She never said anything about him," I say wearily. I close my eyes and whisper, "Why would that be?"

I open them again when Mrs. Cliffton sighs, too. "Stefen was an unhappy person," she says. "More so the older we became. He was always very sweet to me, but I think he often resented Juliet. They had a troubled relationship, especially at the end."

"What made him so unhappy?"

"He was dealt a tough hand in life, it's true," Mrs. Cliffton says. She pauses. "But we each still have a choice in the matter when it comes to how we respond." She looks at me. "Of course, bitterness is usually easier. And I think it's possible to very much understand why people make the choices they do, even though they are the wrong ones."

I think of the telegram Miles stole, the shredded pieces of it hidden upstairs in my waste can. "So what happened to him?"

"He left Sterling not long after Juliet did, and no one ever saw him again. Juliet tried to find him for years, but I think eventually she gave up. The last I heard, she was starting to believe he was dead."

But he must not be, I think. He must be very much alive. Because Mother was planning to send him the book with her ring in it, and she had been wearing it right up until she died.

"I'm growing so tired of these surprises," I tell her, my voice suddenly shaking. "Is there anything else? I don't even know what to ask anymore. I just want this to be the very last time I feel this way."

She looks down at her hands, and with a deep breath I steel myself for whatever is coming.

"Juliet wrote me just before she died," she says, pulling out a handkerchief. "Aila—" She hesitates. "The Disappearances did come for your mother, in the end." She folds and unfolds the cloth into a little square in her lap. "At first she thought she couldn't smell the flowers because she was ill. But then . . . she asked your father to bring her a mirror." Something tightens in my chest. "I didn't know if I should tell you," Mrs. Cliffton continues. "I didn't think it would help anything for you to know. But maybe there have been too many secrets around here. And that is the very last one I know of."

When I look up, I am taken aback to see Mrs. Cliffton's eyes bright with tears.

"I watched a memory of her the other day," she says. "I never thought I would again. I thought it would hurt too much."

"I dreamed of her last night," I reply. "And it was good to see her again." I blink back sudden tears. "But it was hard, too." I pause so my voice will stop wavering. "I don't want to forget her."

"I remember how difficult it was for me to lose Juliet when she left Sterling, and that was just because she moved away. You've already faced more loss in your young life than most people. And your mother . . ." Mrs. Cliffton does a funny little laugh and uses the handkerchief to dab at her eyes. "She would be so proud to see how well you've done. She would just beam with it."

Mrs. Cliffton offers me the handkerchief, and I swipe at my

threatening tears. "Could you tell me about the memory of her?" I ask. "If it's not too personal?"

"It was something Juliet said the last time I saw her, when I came to Gardner and brought William with me. It made me happy because it was one of those riddles she always used to love. Want to take a guess?"

I nod.

"What grows most in darkness?"

Mother's riddles. Always her riddles. I think for a moment.

"Secrets?" I venture.

Mrs. Cliffton smiles and shakes her head. "Hope," she says.

I surprise myself then by laying my head on her shoulder. Though the heat of our skin grows sticky and her hair faintly tickles my neck, we do not speak or move for a long time; not until the sorrow from last night finally falls away, and I feel rest.

Will is waiting to walk me home after Stars practice the next day —leaning against the wall, just like all the times before. As though our fight never happened.

He's showered, and his hair is slicked back and he's changed into the shirt with the cuffed sleeves that always makes his eyes look the bluest.

"Hi," I say to him.

"Oh!" he says, straightening. "Um. Hi." A strange look crosses his face.

"Thanks for what you did the other night," I say, and he is still looking at me with an expression I can't quite read. We start walking, and after a moment I bring my fingers to wipe my mouth and ask, "Is there . . . something on my face?"

"What?" he says. "Oh. No." He seems distracted.

"I'm sorry about what I said to you," I tell him, flushing. "After the race. It was uncalled for, and I didn't even mean it."

He has just started to respond when a car passes us on the road and someone with a scarf covering everything but his mouth leans out the window. "Go skip town like your mother did!" he yells. "And this time, take the Curse with you."

A flash of anger instantly darkens Will's face, and he picks up a rock and hurls it at the car, but it's already disappeared in a cloud of dust around the bend.

"Everyone here is such a hypocrite," he mutters. He tightens his fists at his sides. "Like they wouldn't have done the exact same thing if they got the chance. They would. All of them."

"You wouldn't," I say quietly.

He looks at me. "I would."

He gestures toward the road, and we start walking again. "My father would stay, actually. He's found a way to help people, to have some sort of use." He clears his throat. "I admire him. I wish I were more like him. But I don't blame your mother. If I had the chance to run, I would take it." He glances away. "And I would never want to be anybody's reason for missing that chance."

The look on his face makes my heart twitch. "Your father would fight hard to stay with you," I say, the words suddenly spilling out from where they've been stuffed down and hidden for months. I can already feeling the tightness building in my throat. "But my father didn't even try." I choke on the words. "In some ways," I say, picking up my pace, suddenly angry, "going off to war was easier than facing life with us."

"I'm sorry, Aila," Will says, reaching out a hand toward me and then pulling it back. We walk in silence for several minutes.

Just as the trees begin to clear again, we pass a massive house with a bright red door. "Who lives there?" I ask, pointing.

He glances at my finger. "Guess," he says.

"The Pattons?"

He nods.

"Why do they have a red door when no one else does?"

"Imported it. Paid for it to be painted and brought in from another state. Most people here don't have that kind of money to spend."

I raise an eyebrow at him. "*Your* front door is gray."

He raises one back at me. "If my father had a finishing word, it would be *solidarity*."

The finishing word. I laugh, but his face suddenly flushes, and with it I remember his Christmas present. We walk the rest of the way in comfortable silence, and I wait until Will has climbed the stairs to his room before I slip into Dr. Cliffton's library. I close the door and skim through the stacks of books for a collection of foreign language dictionaries. Pull one in particular from the shelf.

I sit down in the corner and open it. My heart starts pounding, my fingers flying faster as I flip through the pages and come upon the entries of *L*'s.

The word Will carved in the wooden box, the riddle he left for me to discover at Christmas. *Lumoava.*

It means "enchanting."

In Finnish.

Heat burns along the bows of my rib cage. My heart takes off in a spray of paper wings that doesn't slow until I see Will at dinner that night. Then it trips a beat and takes flight anew.

I sit down in the seat next to him, which is a mistake.

He has to ask me three times to pass the green beans before I realize that I can't hear him anymore.

cannot hear Will Cliffton.

This is bad. My thoughts race. *This is bad.*

I practically throw the green beans at him as I stammer an apology that I was lost in thought. It's convincing enough that no one suspects the truth.

I think.

And now I have to hide.

I leave the table and immediately shut myself in my room.

"Do you want to play cards?" Miles calls through the closed door.

"I'm not feeling well!" I answer.

It's not a complete lie. My head is pounding, and my stomach is turning itself into knots over the newest riddle I have to solve.

How am I supposed to hide from Will *in his own house?*

I have to keep us from speaking for as long as I can. Even though I desperately need the Stars practice, I'm able to feign illness for two full days before Mrs. Cliffton says she's calling for the doctor. On the third morning I rise earlier than normal, throw on my school uniform, and stuff my face with toast in the kitchen in front of Mrs. Cliffton and Genevieve. "I'm really feeling so much better," I say, grabbing for one more slice. "Need to catch up on what I've missed. Do you think it would be all right if I borrowed Will's bicycle?" Then I pedal away from the house as fast as I can.

After school I ask Miles to tell the Clifftons I'll be staying late. "I want to use the school target," I lie.

"What's wrong with the one Will made?" he asks.

"His doesn't move," I say with impatience. "Besides, it will help me visualize being here for the tournament." And then I dart to the back stacks of the library and emerge only when Mrs. Cliffton's car pulls away with Will inside.

I weave more plans as I practice hurling Stars at the target.

"Miles is driving me crazy," I tell Beas the next day, and then George the day after that. "Would it be all right if I came over for dinner?"

Each night I return home and head straight to my room, so that I manage to barely even glimpse sight of Will for five days.

I pull the covers straight up over my head and feel utterly exhausted. Knowing, stomach curling, that there is only so long I'm going to be able to keep this up.

Solving the Curse has reached a critical level now. More urgent even than the tournament, which is less than a week away. I throw Stars at the school target until my arms burn, then take Miles to town and ask Mr. Fitzpatrick to order a new Shakespeare biography for me: the most detailed one he can find. I know better than to hope that Dr. Cliffton will solve this voice Disappearance quickly. He hasn't spent years preparing for it, the way he had when the music disappeared. So each night I rush through my homework and then find myself falling asleep in the early-morning hours with Mother's Shakespeare book open in my lap.

I'm so tired by this routine that three days before the tournament, I doze off in the middle of Dr. Digby's lab and Beas has to elbow me awake.

I open my eyes to glimpse the quote she has written across her knee.

Affection is a coal that must be cooled;
Else, suffered, it will set the heart on fire.

"Like that one?" Beas asks when she notices me looking at it. "I wrote it partly in your honor."

I half choke, thinking that she's somehow guessed about Will, until I recognize the words. They're not about my Will. They're by Shakespeare. I sit up and rest my chin in my hands. "Is it getting easier?" I ask hopefully, gesturing at her knee. "Getting over Thom?"

"No," Beas says simply, and covers the words with her skirt. "It's not."

Then she kicks me under the table: "Find anything to tie Shakespeare to this one?" she asks.

I pull out a piece of notebook paper.

Speak low, if you speak love.

&

CLAUDIO: Silence is the perfectest herald of joy. . . .
BEATRICE: Speak, cousin; or, if you cannot, stop his mouth
with a kiss and
let not him speak either.
— Much Ado About Nothing

There are problems with my theory, gaping holes that can't be explained, but I just know I'm on the right track. I feel it like a string vibrating. As if my mother were whispering in my ear. And if I fill my thoughts with Shakespeare, they won't be filled with Will—and maybe, if enough time passes, my feelings will dim.

But I feel a surge of euphoria, terrifying and addictive, every time I think of him. It's almost like being hit with a Variant: a pure shot of joy, bottled and shimmering, multiplying even as I try to empty it from my hand. I doodle *lumoava* in the margins, wondering at how the Curse can dull every one of my senses.

Yet somehow love still makes them feel more alive than they've ever been.

I've completely forgotten about the interview I had with Daisy from the newspaper until the day before the tournament, when I finish my final practice with Mrs. Percy and swing by Fitzpatrick's to pick up the biography I ordered. It's one more excuse to stall before going home to help the Clifftons prepare for tonight's party.

Mr. Fitzpatrick rings me up and nods toward the display case. "Don't you want a paper?"

I turn, and my own face confronts me from above the fold. The headline screams NEW RESIDENT AILA QUINN SETS SIGHTS ON STARS. I'm hurling one of my Stars directly at a picture of Eliza brandishing her epee, as if we're getting ready to do battle.

I pick up a copy and can tell by the first paragraph that it's steeped in small-town drama, a story that aims to pit us against each other, with a current of subtext running just beneath the surface. Two girls with something to prove.

The perennial favorite versus brand-new blood.

It's apparent from the photographs whose side the paper has chosen. Eliza is cast in a soft light that makes her look so gorgeous she almost glows. The shadows on me are positively garish, and I look as though I'm getting ready to break into a snarl.

"They could have found a better photograph," Fitzpatrick acknowledges, echoing my thoughts. I put the paper back so the images are hidden, hoping that Will never lays eyes on either one of them. When Fitzpatrick gives me my change, he whispers, "But my money's still on you."

"Thank you," I say, surprised, and his words make my veins light with renewed confidence. "Are you coming to the Clifftons' party tonight?"

"I think so." He pushes the Shakespeare biography across the counter.

"I really wouldn't miss it," I say with a meaningful look. "It's going to be one to remember."

Then I tighten my grip on the book and run the whole way home.

CHAPTER FORTY-SIX

Date: 3/5/1943

Birds can sense storm patterns before we can.

By the time we even start to sense brewing danger, they have fled their nests and disappeared.

I slide into the booth at a back-alley diner in Corrander that's filled with the sort of people who are too busy looking for their next fix to care who I am or what Larkin and I are discussing.

Victor holds out a stained menu. "Do you want eggs?"

"No." My head throbs. "Anything but eggs."

He orders bacon. I order burnt toast and coffee.

"Thought you'd like to see some of our potential customers," he says as he nods toward the rest of the diner. He takes a sip of coffee. "Partner."

I survey the people around us. Heavy-lidded. Dead-eyed and gray-skinned, slumped against cracked leather seats and walls coated with old smoke. People for whom the natural world doesn't hold any more beauty or promise.

"Do you understand what I'm saying, Stefen?" When Victor smiles, every angle in his face sharpens, like a mirror breaking. He slides an envelope bursting with money under the table. "Even that meager hit of Peace from the maid worked. The father is eternally grateful. We have to get more."

"It worked?" I ask. The diner suddenly brightens around me. The smoke peels clean from the walls. Success. Glory. Eureka. Malcolm Cliffton has never done anything so big and so meaningful. What I have done dwarfs the Variants by comparison. I echo Larkin's smile and scrape off the blackened surface of my toast. "Breakfast's on me, then," I say, and he laughs.

"I have another already lined up," Victor says. "He's ready as soon as you get your hands on some more." He turns to his papers. "Good timing, with the tournament this weekend. While everyone's distracted."

My eyes fall to the front of his newspaper. I take a bite of my toast, and flakes of it fall like black snow on my plate.

I immediately start to choke.

"Can I see that?" I rip it from his hands.

AILA QUINN, the headline shrieks. Right there on the blasted front page.

"That's my niece." I'm still coughing, pieces of toast lodged in my throat. "I've been looking everywhere for her."

And all this time she's been in Sterling. The very last place I would ever expect for Juliet to send her own children.

"I'm sorry—what?" Larkin says, sipping his coffee. "You're Juliet's brother?"

I nod.

He shakes his head. "I didn't even know she had a brother."

I clench my jaw. "Juliet never really wanted anyone to know about me."

Victor looks faintly amused. Then he leans forward. "So why are you looking for the girl, then?" His eyes narrow. "This wouldn't have anything to do with the Virtues, would it?"

"She has something sentimental I want back. But she might be able to serve more than one purpose."

A thought nags at me like a hangnail.

My foster mother, Eleanor Cummings, died years ago. And Juliet burned almost every bridge she had in Sterling when she fled.

"Where are the children staying?" I ask carefully.

"At that bootlicker Malcolm Cliffton's house. He married Matilda. Matilda Fine. You remember them, don't you? Won't have anything to do with me. They're both even more insufferable than they were growing up."

My heart tightens at the sound of her name, even now. I keep my face vague. "Yes. I think I know who you mean."

They are the last two people in this world I want to see. The man who stole the Variants. The woman who stole my very own heart.

But I need the Stone before it's too late for Phineas.

"They're hosting a big party tonight," Larkin says. "Too many people. But tomorrow . . ."

I scrape at the dried food with my knife until the plate gleams.

My little red bird, I think. It seems as though fate means to bring us together again, one last time.

CHAPTER FORTY-SEVEN

I 've just finished placing the final white slabs of Variant soaps —the tart brightness of lemon, the softness of lavender—in the bathrooms for the party when Mrs. Cliffton calls for me, and I follow her voice up the stairs. Miles is coaxing away the last dust bunnies, and Will is helping Genevieve set out rows of thin crystal glasses. The waxed floors shine.

"I have something for you, Aila." Mrs. Cliffton draws the curtains over the large windows of her bedroom and vanishes into her closet. She appears holding a hanger cloaked in black tissue. "I won't take offense if you don't like it," she says, bringing it forward. I unwrap the sheets one by one to uncover a satin gown dyed a glacial blue. I gingerly touch the tiered chiffon of the skirt and feel my face flush with pleasure.

"Is it all right?" Mrs. Cliffton asks anxiously. "Mr. Finch still had your measurements on hand, so it should fit. But if you don't like it . . ."

For a moment, my throat closes. I'd been planning to wear an old dress of Beas's that mostly fit. "It's beautiful," I manage to say. "Thank you," and then I hurry to my room to try it on.

I unbutton my shirt and slip the gown over my head. It falls like water over my shoulders and down my back, tightening into a slightly fitted corset around my waist. Small white pearls lie on the fabric like drops of frost, and the dipped neckline leaves Mother's necklace exposed bare against my breastbone. I take it off and hold it in my hand, considering whether I should leave it hidden somewhere in my room. In the end I return it to my neck and turn the chain around so that it falls down my back to gleam between my shoulder blades.

"Mrs. Cliffton?" I ask, knocking on her door. She opens it, dressed in a midnight blue satin ball gown with short sleeves and a dipping neckline, and I think I've never seen anyone look so elegant.

She smiles widely when she sees me. "Oh, dear. Do you like it? Have you seen yourself? You look stunning."

She leads me to the bathroom and flicks her wrist toward the mirror. My reflection swirls and materializes. I step forward.

The dress sets off the auburn in my hair in a river of dark copper, and Mrs. Cliffton uses a curling iron to form large, soft waves at my shoulders. Then she pins them with a sprig of silver flowers. My eyes stare back at me, gray and bright in the mirror, and though I wish for a more dramatic curve along my chest and waist, the corset helps. I suppose it's because I don't spend much time seeing my reflection these days, but the girl looking back at me seems older, somehow.

Mrs. Cliffton applies bright red lipstick to her lips and a dab of Vaseline, then offers them to me. As soon as she finishes blotting, our reflections fade back into blank glass. She turns to me for a look of approval as the doorbell rings.

I just nod and grin at her, and it makes her smile.

"William!" she calls. "Can your father get the door?"

I return to my room for my shoes and then peek over the balcony. Eliza has arrived, wearing a scarlet dress that falls in chiffon drapes, with a spray of silver sparkle around the neckline, almost as if she is dusted with Glimmers. Her hair is piled in an updo that must have taken half the day, and her shoulders peek out from beneath a stole. She laughs, a high, tinkling sound, at something Dr. Cliffton says, and sips from a flute of sparkling cider Genevieve serves on a silver tray. "Thank you," she says. "My mother bought it for me."

I wait until Mrs. Cliffton has gone downstairs to greet Eliza and act as a buffer. I grip the banister, keeping my eyes trained on the stairs to avoid falling. When I reach the landing, Eliza and Will are lined up next to each other for a picture. Will is in a black suit and tie. His eyes are a searing blue, his eyebrows arched and dark, and even though I tell it not to, my heart aches.

"Smile, William — a real smile," Mrs. Cliffton prods, and at the moment the camera flashes, his face turns toward me. Then George strides through the door, followed closely by his mother.

"See, Georgie," Mrs. Mackelroy trills. "I want the ivy to climb up the face of the house, just so — just *exactly* as the Clifftons have done. And the lights everywhere — Matilda, what you've done is simply marvelous," she says, reaching out for a glass of champagne. "It's inspired, really."

George whistles when he sees me. His tie is Sterling crimson and silver, latticed into a plaid. His hair is combed and his freckles are barely visible. There's an air of confidence that's new since I saw him that first day outside the doors of the high school.

"Aila and George, line up by Will and Eliza and we'll get a picture," Dr. Cliffton says. "In honor of the ball that never was." I hesitate, then end up between George and Will, trying not to meet Will's eyes while also keeping my face turned toward his mouth in case he says something to me. His hand comes to rest on my hip. I wonder what he smells like.

In the hallway, Miles sits on the chair that Will made, his hair slicked back and his bow tie only slightly askew, as if he started to pull it away from his neck and stopped himself.

"Let's get a photograph for your father," Dr. Cliffton says to us, and I bend to Miles's level. The shutter clicks, and just before I stand again, Miles whispers in my ear, "The finishing word is *lovely*."

"Oh!" I say. "Thank you, Miles." My surprise goes straight to my head, as golden and sparkling as the bubbles of Mrs. Mackelroy's champagne. I wear Miles's unexpected compliment for the rest of the evening like a spray of perfume.

More guests begin to arrive. The Mackelroys are followed closely by the Babcocks, the Fitzpatricks, the Percys, the Petersons, several other families of my classmates, and Viv, the woman who sells the flower necklaces. The house swells with people, and we spill out into the backyard, where the Clifftons have erected enormous tents. There is still an early spring chill in the air, but the tent begins to buzz with the warmth of our bodies and there is a basket at the entrance lined with pouches of Embers for people to take as they need.

Looking for Beas, George and I weave through vases heaped with pink and orange snapdragons and coral nerines, their colors rich enough to drink. I find her at the end of a long table, filling her plate from the spread of cheeses drizzled with honey and figs, sliced meats, fruits, tarts, and sweet cakes. A crystal bowl of punch crowns the end of the table.

Beas's gown is silver, with beads that rim along the hem, and white satin gloves reach halfway up her arms.

"Aila, that dress," Beas says, her mouth full. She daintily runs her gloved hands over her lips. "So much better than the old one of mine you were going to wear."

"Yes, you look pretty," George says, but he's distracted. "Margeaux Templeton is here? Why?" he groans. "She's glaring this way again. Maybe she's here to take you out before the competition tomorrow."

My stomach flutters with nerves.

"Let's not talk about it," I say.

Will and Eliza emerge from the house, and she takes him by the arm and leads him around the crowd to make conversation and shake hands, as if they are running for office. Will laughs, listens, and gets Eliza a glass of punch, but when he thinks no one is looking, he slips away to walk the back garden paths alone.

Beas catches me watching them.

"You know he made a promise to her when they were fourteen that he would bring her to a Christmas Ball," Beas says, taking a sip of punch.

"What?" I ask, instantly flushing.

She raises an eyebrow. "And, with Mind's Eye, there's no getting out of old promises."

I'm beginning to splutter that I don't know what she's talking about when Dr. Cliffton clinks his knife against his glass and gestures for George to come to the front of the tent.

The buzz of the party fades as George makes his way forward, and Dr. Cliffton's voice cuts through the clear night. Mrs. Cliffton stands beside him, her eyes sparkling.

"Welcome, everyone," he says. "Matilda and I are so pleased you all could join us tonight."

"Hear, hear!" someone from the crowd calls.

"It is a bittersweet thing to welcome the people of Charlton to be with us tonight. But we believe that tragedy and hardships allow us a unique opportunity to draw together. Strengthen one another. Lift one another's spirits." He pauses. "I think this might help."

He pulls a cover from the Victrola, and a hush settles when he opens his palm to reveal a Variant pouch. "The man who found these will do the honors," he says, and pushes George forward with the pouch. As George measures out a handful, the air takes on the sudden weight of held breaths and mounting expectation. Someone in the crowd whispers, and someone else shushes him.

Dr. Cliffton sets the needle on the record player.

George dusts it with Variants. Then they both step back and wait. Beas squeezes my hand. I squeeze it back.

For a few long seconds there is only silence and tension. But then the first notes begin to infiltrate the crowd like sunlight through water. The people around me, dressed in finery and dripping with jewelry, strain forward to listen, eyes alight. Hands fly instinctively to mouths, and conversations hush. Then someone drops a glass on the bricks of the patio and it shatters.

A large cheer goes up when the music suddenly swells. The horns come to life in Benny Goodman's "Jersey Bounce," the air brightens with it, and people turn toward it in a wave. Some draw closer to the record player. The rest grab someone and start to dance, creating an improvised stage in the grass.

I'll never forget, for the rest of my life, watching the intimate moment when a Disappearance is returned. Some stand with eyes closed or hands clasped, some sing along with the words, still others sit alone on a bench or at the edge of the fountain, wiping silent tears. George salutes Mrs. Percy when he takes turns bringing me and Beas out to the dance floor. "Not such a clod anymore, am I?" he asks us.

"You're a regular Fred Astaire," Beas says, and he beams at us through the steady stream of people coming up to clap him on the back.

Eventually the music turns drowsy, slow, romantic. I turn away from Will and Eliza, who are dancing near the tent's center. I find Miles, and we sit together in the grass, under the starless sky, eating hard candies. I juggle them for him, the way I used to, until the song is done.

Every time the music ends and a new tune begins, the crowd bursts into applause. I make my way to the edge and catch Will's eye from across the party. He raises his hand in a wave, and I wave back. "Hi," he mouths.

"Hi," I say from a safe distance, across the crowd. I know him well enough now to recognize when he is truly happy. His eyes are bright, his jaw is unclenched, and for the first time tonight I'm certain he's no longer pretending.

The hour grows later, but the guests show no signs of leaving. It's clear how much they all want to stay, to soak up the last notes of music, to gather it in the folds of their dresses and take it home in their pockets. In a way, they'll be able to, because I've seen the small pouches set out in rows near the door—from the looks of it, enough for at least one song for each guest. I stifle a yawn and consider stealing upstairs to my bed. But when I near the staircase, I catch a curious look pass over Mrs. Tripplehorn's face as she speaks with Mrs. Fitzpatrick. It's the kind of look that makes me suspect they are talking about me.

I'm instantly awake again. I creep closer, hugging the wall to stay in the shadows.

"She really does look just like Juliet. So much so that it's unsettling," Mrs. Fitzpatrick says.

My instinct was right. I crouch down behind a planter and fuss with the strap of my shoe.

"It's the eyes. I will say, Juliet was always kind to me, but whenever I spoke to her, I always felt like she was looking right through me. Such a pity for the poor children, to lose their mother so young." Mrs. Tripplehorn clucks her tongue.

"So much sickness and death in that family, now that I think of it. It almost seems to follow them around."

You're wrong, I think. Mother always said how she was barely sick a day in her life as a child. "I saw her once," Mrs. Tripplehorn continues, "with that strange boy. Do you remember?"

I hold my breath. A strange boy. They must mean Stefen.

"Oh, yes. The one in the wheelchair? I'd almost completely forgotten that. He was so gaunt, always something wrong with him. Such a poor, odd little thing, wasn't he? I wonder whatever happened to him."

"Aila, what are you doing crouching in the corner like that?" Mrs. Mackelroy says, a little too loudly. She sways, as if she can't quite keep her balance. The women clam up at the sound of Mrs. Mackelroy's voice and exchange knowing looks, then change the subject.

"Nothing," I say, standing. "Just minding my own business." I gather the folds of my dress and turn for the stairs. "You might try it sometime."

"My, my," Mrs. Mackelroy titters. "Lovely to see you, too, dear." She drains the rest of her champagne flute. As I'm climbing the stairs, she asks no one in particular, "Now, where did that charming fellow go with all the cocktail shrimp?"

I climb the stairs and leave the bright, humming noise of the party for the darkened shadows of the hallway.

I've reached my door when I hear footsteps behind me. I whirl around at the touch of a hand on my arm.

Will.

Oh.

"Is everything all right?" I watch his lips form the words. "Did I do something wrong?"

"Of course not," I say quickly.

"Then why are you avoiding me? I've hardly seen you in weeks, and just now I was almost yelling for you."

I swallow. Mind clicking, and clicking. "I—"

There's a flicker in him at the first hint of realization. His smile tilts up, briefly. "Are you—you can't . . ." his lips say, trailing off, his eyes wide and unsure. The air around me is humming. I take the deepest breath, fill my lungs with it. I can't hide it anymore. So I shrug and tell him everything there ever was with the smallest shake of my head.

"Aila," he says. Takes a step toward me. Hesitates. My heartbeat is a breaking wave, climbing, crashing.

Then he leans down and kisses me.

His mouth is warm and soft, and my heart leaps up to graze my breastbone, and everything inside of me begins to bloom and glow and hum, and I kiss him back, first softly and then more, more, bringing my hand up to touch that place on his neck the way I've always wanted to, for all the times I've wanted to draw him to me and all the words I've wanted to say, and I can feel his breath hitch, his heartbeat exploding between us.

We pull away and flush, push into my room, close the door silently behind us, my skin lighting and tingling as he touches my elbow, grazes the curve of my waist. He motions for a piece of paper and then writes, "I can't hear you either."

I read the words over and over, my heart bursting. "Since when???" I write.

He smiles and scrawls, "Awhile."

"I've been hiding from you," I write back.

We cover the pad with notes: "I found what you did at my mother's house." "What are we going to do? No one can know, my parents might send you back to Gardner." We can hear the murmur of the party below us, Miles's footsteps on the stairs, and Will folds his hand into mine.

"I have to go," he mouths.

"You have to go," I repeat, but instead he leans and whispers in my ear; secret words I'll never know, that fall and melt, his breath light as snowflakes when it touches my skin. And I am happiness, and joy, and soaring, and heat. I run fingertips across the ridge of his cheekbones, the sharp curve of his jaw, and confess to the air, "I would do it all again to get to this moment with you."

And then he is laughing, his eyes shining like they've been lit with fire, and he looks at me as though he can't quite believe it when I bring my lips to his one more time.

CHAPTER FORTY-EIGHT

An egg that's been cracked is irreparably broken.
And it means the birth of something new.

Death is not quiet or peaceful, but filled with horrible sounds.

I'm summoned to Phineas's room by a cough that doesn't end. It just becomes wetter and thicker until he is choking on it. I call for the doctor to come. Phineas's eyes grow wide and panicked, but he forces himself to calm and gather his breath.

His room is stark and gray, but he is surrounded by his books. His maps. And me.

I am glad that he is not alone. I am glad that I found him, and that he let me.

"Stefen," he says. His eyes are focusing and unfocusing again, as if he's not sure it's me. "I gave my whole life for that one Stone."

I know this story, at least the parts he's told me before, and I've guessed the rest of it. But he's delirious. Maybe he thinks this is his last confession. Maybe he's seeking comfort.

So I will help him tell it. I want him to know that the ending will turn out all right.

"I heard rumors of it," he says, his breath laboring. "A Stone, rumored to have power to heal. Protect" — *he wheezes* — *"life."*

"Yes. It was coming from England. You went to meet the ship at port."

"Most people thought it was . . . nonsense . . . But your mother was dying. I would have done anything."

"So you borrowed the money," I say, touching his hand, "to get it for my mother."

"More than I could ever pay back in a lifetime." His skin is as colorless as a Sterling door. "I should have realized how anxious the seller was to get rid of it. Should have walked away when he made his final terms." He erupts in a coughing fit.

"The doctor is coming," I say. "Soon."

He shakes his head. "Everyone else dropped out when he brought out the second box. 'Package deal,' he said. 'You take this with the Stone or you take nothing.' At first I thought it was a hatbox." He almost laughs. "But it was as heavy as lead."

"No one else was willing to take it. But you didn't back down," I say. I bring a glass of water to his cracked lips.

"What did I care?" He swallows, choking the water down. "My hands were already dirty. It's almost as if it was meant for me. I took the Stone. Took the box. The seller was so nervous. Made me swear I'd hide it well enough so no one would ever find it. So I scattered its contents on the way back. Buried them deep, in three different places. But when I got home . . ."

It was too late. My mother had died in childbirth.

"And then," — he rakes the handkerchief across his mouth — "I got sloppy." He closes his eyes wearily.

"I was young," I say, keeping my voice even. "I don't remember when the police came for you. I don't remember going to live with Eleanor."

"I left the Stone with Eleanor. In case you needed money."

"And now you've left the maps," I say.

He closes his eyes, his head slumping. "You have everything you need to fix it."

"But Phineas — I don't want to fix it." I lay my hand on top of his shriveled one. "I've found a way to make it useful. The Curse is your legacy. It's going to take care of me."

Even after you're gone.

I tighten my fingers around the vials in my pocket. The Curse will keep on taking, each time breeding more despair. Making people desperate for the kind of Peace that only I can provide.

Phineas starts coughing so much that he can barely speak. But he's trying to tell me something, so I grab a piece of paper and pen from his desk, knocking everything else to the floor in my haste. I place the paper in front of him, and he writes in a spasming hand, so jagged I can hardly read it,

"The Curse is not my legacy, Stefen," he writes. "You are."

I bury Phineas myself. Under the birdfeeders I'd strung along the house, in the loamy soil he loved. Next to the cliffs where we had sat and watched the ocean. A place I will never need a map to find.

For the first time, I am giving something precious back to the earth rather than taking it out.

When the sun rises harsh and glaring in the sky, I stand under the shower and let the scalding hot water wash the dirt of his grave from my skin. Some of it remains under my fingernails. I leave it there.

I pack my carved wooden bird with a new syringe, several empty vials, my pouches of Hypnosis and Tempest Variants, and the gun I find in Phineas's drawer. The Stone can no longer save Phineas. Now I will get it for me.

The train horn calls to me as I near the station. The sound of something ending, something else about to begin.

"Where to?" the ticket agent asks.

"Sterling," I say. I push a handful of folded bills toward him. "I'm going home."

CHAPTER FORTY-NINE

The Sisters Tournament – Opening Day
March 6, 1943

Why, I wonder as I look out at the endless, undulating faces of the tournament crowd, had I ever thought this would be a good idea?

The first day of the tournament is blue and warm, with the promise of spring. Everything seems loud and alive after the muffled stillness of winter. I shield my eyes from the sun and pull at the bottom of my uniform shirt. It's a crisp white, with a single silver and red patch embroidered over my heart. I skipped the opening ceremonies to warm up, and Beas came to find me, brandishing a kohl liner.

"Good," she'd said, lining my eyes. "Now they look like steel."

I step out onto the grass before my event and look for her. She's halfway up the stands, sitting next to George. She lifts her fingers to her mouth and whistles. I resist the urge to feel the knot of my ugly ear and instead wipe my palms inside the pockets of my uniform.

The school band plays a medley of the Sisters' fight songs under a dusting of Variants as I make my way to the center of the field, fervently hoping that Genevieve's good-luck breakfast doesn't make a second appearance. I'm fairly sure the only thing worse than crashing and burning at my event would be upchucking in front of the greater population of three towns.

Sterling applauds for me, its first Stars competitor in years, and my eyes flit through the stands. George gives me a deadpan salute. Eliza is in the front row, clapping politely without a smile. Will is a few rows behind her, sitting with Carter and Chase. I flush beet red, remembering the feel of his mouth on mine, and quickly look away from him. I spot Mrs. Mackelroy, wearing dark glasses and weakly clapping while she sips a bottle of Coca-Cola. It's strange how quickly these faces have become so familiar. The Fitzpatricks. The Foggs. Members of the Council.

When I find Dr. and Mrs. Cliffton and Miles, I wave, and my eye suddenly catches a mark on my arm: a small heart, drawn with Miles's sure hand, just inside the crook of my elbow.

I stare at that heart for long enough until I remember how to breathe again.

My competitors flank me on the field: Shirley Beaudry from Sheffield, and Margeaux Templeton, who enters to the most raucous applause of all. Her uniform matches mine except that her patch is threaded with gold and purple. She wears a headband covered with tiny sparkling golden stars, and she seems shorter than I remembered from the Harvest Fair. She waves dutifully at her section of the stands, but she steals a few nervous glances at the Sterling crowd. At my friends. Almost exactly where Beas and George are sitting.

I narrow my eyes, instantly on guard. I watch Margeaux more closely as she takes her place on the field. She sneaks another glance. Why does she keep looking there? What could possibly be drawing her attention back, again and again?

And suddenly, in the bright sunlight, under the watchful eyes of almost everyone in Sterling, I understand what George doesn't. It's the way Margeaux's hand subconsciously finds her hair, the way she looks up without trying to appear that she is doing it, the studied nonchalance I've seen in Will when he is trying to hide the fact that something is hurting him.

Despite my nerves, I fight the urge to burst out laughing. George has completely misread the reason behind Margeaux Templeton's glares at the Harvest Fair. She doesn't hate him — it's the opposite.

The trouble is how difficult it can be to tell the difference sometimes.

But there is no more time to consider this. "Competitors," the announcer says, "take your places."

I steal one last glance at my ink heart and step up to the throwing line.

Shirley and I go first. Within five minutes we've each zipped our three Stars through the air. I watch her and she watches me, and by the end of the first round it's clear that we are a fairly even match.

Then there is Margeaux.

Her Stars are custom cast in Corrander gold and purple, and they sing through the air, cutting a path directly to the target and leaving a metallic echo in their wake. My second throws are solid, but my Stars seem to hang heavily by comparison. They all find the target except for the last — an outlier that feels wild leaving my hand. It bounces from the target rather than sticking and drops me even further behind Margeaux's established thirty-point lead.

I look up at the scoreboard and force myself to take a deep breath. Shirley leads me by ten points, a slim margin to hold for the final round. But Margeaux's score is fifty points beyond that, and I have only three more chances to catch her. My blood courses with adrenaline. I've spent too many hours practicing, sweating, aching, dreaming, to lose like this. I have one more chance to make those months of work worth it.

Mrs. Percy flips me a discreet thumbs-up from the sideline. At the urging of a shrill whistle, the target springs to life and begins to move along its tracks.

Shirley steps to the line for her final throws, and her hand shakes when she reaches for her Stars. The first hits the target along the outer rim, but the second leaves her hand violently, flying past the target to land in the grass like a heavy jewel. She picks up her final Star with the air of someone who has already conceded her loss, and she throws it without conviction. Her final score isn't enough to meet even Margeaux's second round.

Which just leaves me to catch her.

"Final round for Aila Quinn, from Sterling," the announcer says, and gestures me forward to the line.

I am still in this, I tell myself. There's still the smallest possibility I could win.

But the tingling feeling I sometimes get, the one that tells me my next throw is going to be good, is missing. I try to summon it as I watch the target move along its path. There's a cool breeze on my face. Someone in the crowd coughs. The Stars feel heavy in my hand.

I try to call to mind my mother's face.

But suddenly I can't.

I frantically search for memories of her, any of them, but all I can picture is little more than a blurred shadow. She has just slipped away, like sand trickling between my fingers. *Like everything in this cursed place,* I think fiercely.

I turn without really looking and hurl the remaining three Stars from my hand at the same time.

They soar through the air and rock the target almost simultaneously.

The crowd gasps, and I turn to look.

The first has landed on an inner ring, just to the right of the bull's-eye. But the second and third have sunk in almost to their hilts, centimeters away from dead center. Two bull's-eyes.

My breath catches in my lungs. Their force is making the candle swing lazily, back and forth, as if it's trying to decide whether to fall.

After an endless moment the candle finally slows and returns to resting. Its fuse, holding one hundred points within it, remains unlit.

Sterling's crowd jumps to its feet anyway, chanting my name in unison when my points are posted and I vault into first place.

I step back, and a tiny sprout of hope shoots up. I try to push it back down, but there is no stopping it.

Margeaux suddenly seems much less sure of herself. She moves to her line, mouthing something under her breath. The banners flutter as the crowd quiets. She steals another glance in George's direction and steels herself. Then her arm cracks like a shot as she sends her Stars rocketing through the air.

The first one hits the outer edge of the target, narrowly avoiding a complete miss. The second falls nearer to the bull's-eye, but still in the outer ring. I watch her score tick up on the board, calculating the difference. Her final throw has to be a good one, or else I've won it. I fix her with my steel eyes, willing her to let me have this. Suddenly wanting it as much as I've ever wanted anything before.

Margeaux winds up and hurls her final Star. It arcs through the air in a straight shot, as if the target is drawing it there by force, and every eye in the stadium watches it hit the candle. It slices through the wax, hard and clean.

This time, the candle does not hesitate.

Its lit wick topples forward and catches the fuel in the grass, and the word *Corrander* blazes and pops in the ground just beyond my feet.

Margeaux's fans shriek and raise hundreds of tiny flags in the air, a field of violets and marigolds. The red and silver flags wither as everyone from Sterling sits back down.

I blink numbly at the candle. The tiny sprout of my hope is ripped out, all the way down to its roots. I can't believe that after all this time, in only a handful of seconds, I've lost.

I force myself to go to Margeaux and extend my right hand.

"Congratulations," I say. Before she can respond, the Corrander fans surround her, lifting her above their heads, and I seize the opportunity to slip onto the sidelines.

"Aila!" Mrs. Percy pulls me behind a corner of the stands where we can't be seen. "You did well," she says. "It was a very good showing for your first time, and you've made us all proud."

She hands me the final Star. The one that had just missed the mark — that caused the candle to sway but not fall.

"Thank you," I say, taking it, and then George barrels over and throws an arm around my shoulders.

"Ya did good, kid," he says. "And so Beas and I would like to cordially invite you to a bonfire at Chez Mackelroy tonight. I can't guarantee any fancy food, drinks, or entertainment. But" — he lowers his voice — "you *did* only win silver."

I punch him in the arm. "You don't have to do this, I'm really fine," I say.

"Do you need the speech? Because, you know, sterling for Sterling is actually really much better than *gold* for Sterling —" George says.

"All right," I snort. "I'll come."

"Six o'clock," he says, and as soon as he's gone, a hand pulls me deeper into the shadows of the stands. I whirl around, and in the instant I realize it's Will, he's kissing me. All my disappointment instantly evaporates, and for one stolen moment I am filled with pure light.

I'm still feeling dazed when he rolls up his sleeve and shows me his arm, where he's written "Next year." Then he grins and ducks back out into the sunshine.

I smile and close my eyes, and I can suddenly see Mother again, exactly how she would have appeared if she had really been here, her laughter reaching its too-high octaves, shouting my name, not caring for a moment what anyone else thought.

Don't let them crush you, her voice whispers in my ear, and the iron grip of Sterling's approval suddenly loosens.

I tuck the losing Star into my pocket and head back onto the field, thinking that perhaps I've won a victory today, after all.

CHAPTER FIFTY

The closer the train draws to Sterling, the harder I begin to sweat.

I shift in my seat, pulling my collar from where it suffocates my neck. "Are you all right?" an elderly woman asks, leaning toward me.

"Fine," I snap, and she mutters something and returns to her newspaper. I pull my hat down a notch to cover my face.

The train glides right by that horrid lake, the very one that falls just beyond the border of Sterling. I catch sight of the water, gray and sheening, and feel a literal pain in my side. As if Juliet's ghost has come back to stick a small knifepoint right between my ribs.

Everything, everything changed on the fateful day Juliet saw herself in that lake.

We were seventeen, and it had been years since we'd been close, whispering stories to each other in our shared room. Since the nights I had fallen asleep to the sound of her breathing.

Word swept through Sterling in a frenzy that Juliet Cummings had seen her reflection — but by the time the news reached me, the crowd at the lake had already begun to dissipate. Two men were shoving each other in a fight that had just started brewing. Juliet was nowhere to be found. There was something heavy in the air. I realized soon enough what it was.

Hope. Freshly soured.

I remember leaning over the water. Holding my breath. The sinking feeling when there was nothing before me but silver water, clear enough to see ink drops of tadpoles against the sand and silt.

I'd trudged back to town, my legs tiring and as heavy as lead. But then

I'd seen Matilda, and everything had suddenly felt so much lighter. Brighter. The air, my legs, even the future.

She had been alone. Beautiful, beautiful Matilda, with her hair fluttering like red feathers.

"Have you seen Juliet?" Matilda asked, her eyes wide with panic. "I'm worried about her."

"No," I said. My mouth was dry, as it always was when I was near her.

"What's wrong?" Matilda knew me well enough to notice. She even reached out and touched my arm.

I looked into her eyes, green and speckled with gold. I would have told her anything at all, if she looked at me like that. I licked my dry lips. "I couldn't see my reflection," I admitted.

"Don't feel bad. Neither could anyone else," she'd said kindly. "No one but Juliet. That's why we need to find her."

"But why *her*?" The question exploded from me with such fierceness that Matilda dropped my arm and took a step back. "It doesn't make any sense," I said, softening. Wanting her to close the distance between us again. "If Juliet can, then why can't I?"

"What do you mean?" she asked. Confusion had crossed her smooth, pretty face.

It should have been obvious.

"Because—because I'm her brother."

"But . . . you're not related by blood . . ." she said.

I gaped at her, unable to breathe.

"Is that what Juliet told you?"

And something inside me snapped then. As if I were a lock. Finally coming undone after just the right combination of clicks.

CHAPTER FIFTY-ONE

Beas's bicycle is leaning against the fence by the time I arrive at George's. I find them both in the clearing behind his house, laying a kindling foundation for the bonfire.

"Did you *walk* here?" George asks, eyeing my muddy shoes as he breaks a stick over his knee.

"I needed to stretch my muscles," I say.

"How very Elizabeth Bennet of you," Beas says. Her hair is pulled up in a knot on her head, her bangs poufed in a wave that grazes her eyebrows. They stand and clap for me as I set my bag in the grass. "Stop," I laugh, waving them off.

George rolls up a newspaper and sticks one of Daisy's articles about the tournament between the slats of kindling.

"George, I saw you making amends with Margeaux today," Beas notes, sharpening a stick with a Swiss army knife. "Did you manage to bury the hatchet?"

"Hardly. I'm pretty sure she still wants to cut me," George says, stuffing in another tight ball of newspaper.

"I'm pretty sure that's not what she wants to do to you," I mutter under my breath.

"What?" Beas breaks out into hysterical laughter. "Are you serious? Margeaux Templeton is keen on George?"

"Almost certainly," I say, settling on the stump of an old tree.

George's jaw falls open. "You think Margeaux is stuck on me?"

He taps a book of matches against his palm, then adds thoughtfully, "She's actually kind of cute, I guess . . ."

Beas and I catch each other's side glances. I smother a merciless burst of laughter.

"So are you ready for Variant Innovation?"

"I wanted to do the music Variant, obviously, but working with Dr. Cliffton disqualified it. So I have something else," he says, lighting the match to the paper. "Underwhelming."

Beas raises her stick threateningly toward him. "Show us, Mackelroy."

George pours us two mugs of tea from his thermos and spreads several pouches of Variants at our feet before picking one up and dusting it over a sprig of mint. When he dips the mint into the tea, it instantly hisses and crackles, like ice cubes clinking together, and the mugs become frosted and chilled. "*Voila*," he says. "Mint iced tea. Try it."

Beas and I clink our mugs together and then take a sip.

"Mmm," I say.

"Amazing, George," Beas echoes.

"It's really just a glorified version of ice," George says, kicking the dirt. "But I'm hoping to make a version for human use. A companion to the Warming Variants, for cooling off in the summer."

"Impressive. How did you do it?" I ask.

"Mint root," he says.

"Mint root," I note. I've taken to hauling my Shakespeare book with me everywhere, and I pull it from my bag. "I bet I'll find it in here."

"Really, this again?" George says, and Beas shows her loyalty by poking him in the side with her stick.

"Yow," he says, rubbing his shirt. "Don't get sand in your eye. I just mean—why are you so stuck on the Shakespeare thing?"

"Because she's found *every single Disappearance* there . . ." Beas says proudly. "*And* all the Variants. And a seven-year connection— well, really I found that one. But she might have told you earlier if you hadn't been so quick to shut her down the first time."

"All right, all right," George says, throwing a stick into the catching fire. "So catch me up. You really found them *all?*"

I nod, and they both look at me expectantly, settling into their seats. The fire catches hot and bright, throwing shadows onto their faces.

"It started because I wanted something of my mother's," I tell them, remembering my last day in Gardner all those months ago. "I ended up taking this book."

I open the cover. "She'd written all over it," I say, showing them the pages. "She was planning to send it to someone she grew up with in Sterling. I actually found her old ring hidden here—" I slip my fingers into the fold of the back cover. That first day, I'd felt only the smooth surface of the stone. But there is something else in there now. Something I'd missed before.

My fingers graze the edges of a small folded envelope.

I fish it out.

"Go on. So what's that?" George asks. But I don't answer him. I see the name "Stefen Shaw" written as the sender, my own familiar Gardner address scrawled across the front.

My hands betray the smallest tremor as I open it. There are two items folded inside: a handwritten letter and a sketch page that's old and warped with creases.

I'm vaguely aware of Beas and George coming to stand over my shoulder.

"*Dear Viola—*" the letter starts, and I think, *Why Viola?* again —the same name Mother had used in her letter to him.

Some time has passed since your last letter, which I'll admit has me curious. Phineas and I have been very eager to hear from you.

Well, perhaps this will inspire a response. I have a riddle for you, for old times' sake. Something I've been working on, similar to the Variants. Something big. I'll give you a hint as to what it is. Find it within the pages of "our" play.

"What does thou mean? . . . I did think, by the excellent constitution of thy leg, it was formed under the star of a galliard."

I pause. My mother has solved the riddle. She's scrawled next to it, Our play → Twelfth Night. → Missing line: Is it a world to hide virtues in?

And then she's written: → Virtues???

If you send me your guess, I'll tell you if you've gotten it right. Maybe you could send it along with the ring you promised. Phineas is growing quite anxious for it. Just for sentimental reasons. It reminds him a great deal of our mother.

You should know, Juliet, that he isn't well.

So please follow through on your word and send it soon. Or I can come get it in person if that would be more convenient. I could meet your family. Perhaps Phineas could even come along, too, and meet his grandchildren.

Although it might not be possible with his worsening condition. I think seeing the stone would greatly help his spirits.

Very eager to put all of the past behind us. Sending the ring would go a long way. Please be in touch as soon as possible.

Your Sebastian

My eyes flit over to the drawing, which is terribly faded, as though Mother has had it for a long time.

It's dated 6/11/1923, and it shows two birds. One is healthy, with wings stretched across the width of the page, so wide that it almost obscures the other. The half-hidden bird is cowering, and looks sickly, as though it is wasting away.

"The rarest of occurrences," the caption reads: *"the egg with two yolks. A fight to the death; in most cases, one embryo outcompetes the other, and only one survives to hatch."*

In tiny, almost illegible letters at the bottom, the same hand has written a chilling promise: *"Someday you will hurt like I hurt."*

The hair on my arms prickles. This drawing of the two birds. Just like what Miles had seen in his nightmare.

"Aila?" Beas asks, putting her hand on my arm. "Are you all right?"

My mind is firing, making connections, but they're branching off in directions so quickly that I almost can't grasp what is right in front of me.

"Our" mother. "Our" play, the letter said.

Phineas could meet his grandchildren, Stefen wrote.

His grandchildren. He means me and Miles.

Viola instead of Juliet. Sebastian instead of Stefen. I know these names. They are the twins from *Twelfth Night* who hid their true identities from everyone else—in the book open right in my lap.

And then that horrible drawing with two birds and one egg.

There is a click in my brain, and everything comes into focus as clearly as George twisting the knob on Digby's microscope.

Mother and Stefen hadn't been foster siblings.

They had been flesh and blood *twins.*

My breath starts coming fast, and I reach up to feel Mother's ring. Stefen had wanted this stone. He sounded almost desperate for it. And Mother had been planning to send it to him before she died and couldn't follow through with her plan. Has Stefen been trying to find it all this time?

Has he been trying to find *me?*

My head is pounding. Something about this isn't right. I stand and send the book tumbling to the ground. "I have to go."

"Aila—" George says.

But I'm no longer listening. One of George's pouches lying in the grass is the vibrant purple of Tempests. I grab for it and empty it over myself, and I'm already halfway across the clearing before George and Beas can draw another breath.

CHAPTER FIFTY-TWO

When I step from the train, Larkin is waiting for me, his hat pulled low. We board a bus shuttling tournament visitors to Sterling and sit in different rows. He takes off when we reach Sterling, and I hurry to keep him in my sights. It is jarring to follow Larkin through the center of town, as though the present is overlaying the past like a slab of warped glass. There is the gas station. The tailor where I got my ill-fated uniform. Fitzpatrick's General Store. A new cinema and soda shop stick out like sores. The quiet sidewalks I remember are packed with visitors for the Sisters Tournament. We blend in better than I ever could have hoped.

The crowds thin the farther we get from town, and we cut into the woods to stay off the main road. I hurry to keep up with Larkin, who is moving quickly, and when we finally emerge out onto a dusty back road, I have to stifle a cry.

I recognize the house—even now, even though it's mostly burned. Something dark rises in my chest, into my throat. I never wanted to be here again.

This was the last place I ever saw Juliet alive. The site of the last conversation we ever had.

I turn my face away as we pass.

"Stefen?"

I blink. I can almost hear the fear in my foster mother Eleanor's voice when I'd burst through the front door, probably looking murderous. I'd run all the way home from the lake that day, still burning with fury over what

Matilda told me in the road. Once again, Juliet had something I didn't. She'd gotten her reflection back.

But it was worse than that. She had disowned me, denied that we shared the same blood. Even to her closest friend in the world.

"Is everything all right?" Eleanor had asked.

I'd ignored her and flown up the stairs. My legs were shaking badly after the run. Even after years spent strengthening them, they still threatened to fail me.

Juliet startled when I entered her room. Her suitcase was pulled out onto her bed. When she turned to me, I noticed a fresh scratch on her cheek.

She smiled when she first saw me, but then her face fell at my expression.

"Have you come to join the witch-hunt, too?" she asked bitterly, turning away. "In case you haven't heard, everyone hates me."

She'd thrown one of her dresses into the suitcase.

"Well," I croaked, my throat as dry as sandpaper, "maybe you deserve it."

"Stefen!" A pile of freshly laundered shirts had tumbled from her hands. "What could you possibly mean?" She was looking at me with a wounded bewilderment that was maddening. I ground my teeth together.

"I mean, I know we haven't been as close lately—" she started, turning back to the suitcase again, but I couldn't listen to another condescending word from her.

"Do you know what it was like to grow up with you?" I asked, steadying myself against the wall. It felt dangerous to get this close to it. The packed-in, pent-up years of my rage, as hot and dense as coals. "You never even considered what it must have been like for me." Day after day, waving goodbye to her from behind the window as she skipped off to school. Spending her days laughing with friends and learning from real teachers. Running home on her perfectly strong legs. "It was hard enough to grow up as an isolated cripple, without you parading your life in my face at every turn."

She gaped at me. "I . . ." She sat down heavily on the bed. "Where is this coming from?"

"But that wasn't enough, was it?" I continued. "You took my thistle for the Variants." The shock just kept deepening across her face. As if she hadn't even remembered where that thistle had come from. "That thistle could have been the thing that finally made people see me. But you needed that all for yourself, too."

"Stefen—"

"And then, Matilda." I moved a step closer to her. Balled my fists so hard that the next day they'd been bruised.

She shook her head, playing dumb. Juliet was a lot of things, but dumb wasn't one of them. "What could this possibly have to do with Matilda?" she asked.

Matilda, sweet Matilda, the girl who had come home with Juliet so often that she'd practically grown up in our house. The only person outside my own family who had ever really spoken to me. The only person, including my family, who ever really listened to what I said.

I would have loved her. Treated her so well.

But Juliet had taken it upon herself to push Matilda right into Malcolm's arms. "Tell me, then, my dear Viola." I practically spat at her. "Why does Matilda think I'm your foster brother?"

Juliet had frozen. The brief flash of guilt on her face confirmed everything I had already known. She'd hidden who I was to her. Because even since we were very little, she'd been ashamed of me.

"It wasn't about—you—" she stammered, as if she were reading my thoughts. "I didn't want people to know about him. Locked up. For being a grave robber." She twisted her mouth in disgust. "So I said I was an orphan, and I took Eleanor's name. But you kept the name Shaw." I'd taken the slightest satisfaction at how flushed her face was growing with her own misery as she tried to explain herself. "Everyone just assumed we weren't related. You weren't in school; it didn't seem like it would matter when I didn't correct them. But—I should have. At least with Matilda. She would have understood." Her eyes pleaded with me. "Can you please understand?"

"I don't ever want to see you again," I said, and though I didn't know it was about to come true, I meant it. "So maybe it isn't everyone else in Sterling who is wrong," I said, trembling. "Maybe we're all exactly right to hate you."

"Stefen." Her face was ashen. "I'm so sorry. I was never trying to hurt you."

But she didn't mean it enough. Because once she packed her bags, she took off and never looked back. My very own twin. She'd cut me with the little nicks of a thousand different betrayals over the years, but that one went the deepest of them all.

"You coming?" Larkin says, turning back to me at the fork and interrupting my thoughts.

I hadn't realized how much my steps had slowed.

"I've lost track of where we are," I say. I reach to feel the steadying shape of the bird in my pocket. Run my fingers over the smooth grain of its back. "I don't even know where the Clifftons live."

Larkin places a pouch of Hypnosis Variants in my hand and smiles. "I do."

CHAPTER FIFTY-THREE

The Tempests I took from George wear off after barely a mile. As the sunset swells across the sky, I return to a regular pace, which now feels akin to running through water.

I wish someone would drive down the road, someone who could get me back to the Clifftons' sooner. I want to be safely inside the house with the doors locked and a fire going. To tell Dr. and Mrs. Cliffton what I've found out about Stefen. To reassure myself that this strange, choking fear is just my nerves overreacting after a long day.

And then I see that someone *is* there, just beyond the bend, her long blond hair streaming from underneath a hat, her aggravation apparent even from a distance. She leans against the curves of a black car, examining her nails, while someone — a driver? — crouches next to a loosened wheel.

"Eliza," I call out. My voice sounds hoarse, and I wave maniacally until Eliza stops examining her nails and looks at me with a mixture of suspicion and amusement.

"What are you doing?" she says, taking in my mud-streaked legs and raising her eyebrows.

"Do you have any Tempests?" I ask, ignoring the question. A stain of cold fear is still seeping across my body. "Please," I say urgently. "I need them. It's really important."

"No," Eliza says, now looking at me strangely. "If I did, I'd be using them to greet my mother when she gets off the train. Instead of standing here." She adjusts her hat and shakes her hair into a blond wave. *"Obviously."*

My stomach drops a knot further. I had forgotten all about the telegram. Eliza still believes her mother is returning home today.

You don't have to tell her, a strangled voice says inside my head. *No one would ever know. Don't waste time with her. Get home and make sure everything is okay.*

I obey the voice and turn toward the direction of the Clifftons' house without another word.

But I barely take two steps before I whirl back around. I can't do it.

"Eliza," I blurt out. "I have to tell you something."

This wasn't how I'd pictured it all happening. I had wanted Eliza to hurt the way I hurt, to know what it felt like to have a mother disappoint and embarrass her. I realize with horror how much I want this part out of myself now — the part that chooses bitterness. The part that makes me more like Stefen and less like Mother or the Clifftons.

I feel the grit of the road in my mouth, and I'm starting to shake. "Your mother isn't coming," I confess. "She sent a telegram, and I . . . I took it. She said an auction came up and she's not coming. I'm so sorry."

Eliza studies me coldly.

"What?" she asks.

The last bit of my pride struggles against me as I try to choke it down.

"I know. It was horrible, and I don't know why I did it. I'm sorry," I repeat.

Eliza's mouth sags open. I have actually rendered her speechless.

"You were right about a lot of things," I say. "I hope someday you can forgive me."

Before Eliza can regain her composure, I turn and begin to sprint again, running until I can't see her or the broken-down car anymore. A piercing pain hitches in my side.

But I force myself on.

I slow to a half jog when I glimpse the iron gates of the Clifftons' property. The setting sun throws golden pinks and oranges in streaks above my head. I'm limping by the time I make it up the curving gravel drive.

I know, already, that something is wrong. The house seems strangely silent, as if it is holding its breath. The chimney isn't smoking. The lights are off. Everything is too dark.

I'm climbing the last stair to the front door when I hear it, coming from the garden.

The air splitting apart with the sound of Mrs. Clifton's scream.

I bolt for the garden. When I round the corner, I stop short.

Will stands just beyond the stone wall. His expression doesn't change when he sees me. A man is between us, dressed all in black, with his back turned to me. He's holding dark, glittering Variants in one hand, and in the other is a carved wooden bird. I can't see his face, but I know who he must be.

He has found us, just like the bird in Miles's dream.

Juliet's twin.

My uncle.

Stefen.

I drop down behind the wall just as he begins to turn in my direction. My lungs burn, but I hold my breath so that I don't make a sound. Suddenly I can't remember: Did I tuck the final, losing Star back into my pocket or is it lying uselessly on the floor of my room?

I must have hidden myself just in time. Stefen's voice turns back in the other direction, away from where I'm crouching. I scoot closer to the wall, running my fingers soundlessly over it until I find a peephole.

I peer through it and will myself to come up with a plan for what to do next.

"Matilda," Stefen says softly. "Malcolm." His voice turns hard. "I'm going to ask you one more time, with an added incentive to cooperate." He gestures to the Variants in his hand. They are slate-colored ones I don't recognize. But I watch as Will freezes at the sight of them. "There's no need to threaten anyone, Stefen," Dr. Cliffton says. A faint glisten of sweat appears on his forehead. His glasses have ridden down the slope of his nose. "Now, I'm going to ask you to leave my property before I call the police."

My fingers fumble in my pocket for the Star, and my heart sinks. I feel nothing but fabric. I want to scream.

Where is Miles?

"Of course," Stefen says to Dr. Cliffton. "I understand." He closes his hand over the slate-colored Variants and returns his hand to his pocket. How odd, to see the flashes of Mother in him when he turns his face in profile — features that always meant softness and protection in her, now jagged and distorted on his face. For a second it seems that he's going to leave. That maybe it's all going to be that easy.

But then he turns back around. Whips his hand out of his pocket again, and before I can even cry out, he's thrown a shower of Variants into the air.

They hit Mrs. Cliffton straight in the face.

"Matilda!" Dr. Cliffton yells, and the sound of her name echoes, and I think numbly, *She can't even hear him.*

Mrs. Cliffton blinks several times. Her eyes turn glassy, as if she's just wakened from a deep sleep and she's still caught somewhere between waking and dreaming.

Oh, I realize. The slate-colored dust. *Hypnosis Variants.*

"Matilda!" Dr. Cliffton charges toward Stefen, giving Will a hard shove. "Will, run! Go!"

But Will doesn't run. He regains his balance and bolts toward Stefen, just behind his father.

Stefen is too quick for either of them.

He throws another blast of slate-colored Variants over Dr. Cliffton and Will as if he were casting a net. Will stops running. The dark blue of his eyes lightens and then becomes blank. Something inside of me slips, like an anchor coming unmoored.

"Stay there and be still," Stefen directs Dr. Cliffton and William, and they instantly obey. I am frozen in place, watching in horror. I cover my mouth so that I won't make a sound.

Where is Miles? I could sob with relief when my fingers feel a prick, sharp enough to draw blood. It is the beautiful, saving point of my Star, coming out of its binding. My heart leaps as my hand closes around it.

I'll kill him myself before he gets to Miles.

"Malcolm," Stefen asks. "Tell me now. Where is the girl?"

He answers immediately in a monotone voice: "The Mackelroys' house." I draw in a sharp breath.

"And do either of the children have the Helena Stone in their possession?"

Dr. Cliffton blinks. "I do not know what that is."

The Helena Stone? I fumble with the ring, feeling the metal under my clothes lying hot on my breastbone. Why is Stefen so desperate to have this? It has to be more than a simple trinket if he is willing to go this far to get it.

Which means I have to make sure that he never does.

"Never mind," Stefen says with impatience. "Victor, where is the Mackelroy house?"

"I'll show you," a second voice says. A man steps from the shadows.

It's Victor Larkin.

I have to hide my mother's ring. And suddenly my thoughts clear, and I know exactly where to put it. I have to find Miles's perfect hiding spot, where it lay for months. I begin frantically feeling along the wall for the shelf. Terror scrapes down my spine like the serrated edges of a knife as I fumble along the stones with my fingers. I feel a break, but when I reach my hand inside, it is too shallow. My pulse throbs as I keep looking.

It's been a minute, maybe more, when my blood suddenly chills. I know, instinctively, that it's been silent beyond the wall for much too long.

I scramble back to my peephole.

They must have asked William a question, and I couldn't hear his answer.

The Clifftons are standing in a row, as still as dolls.

And they've all turned to stare straight at my hiding place.

"Hello at last, Aila," Stefen says softly.

He is standing right behind me.

I pivot and scream, scrambling away from the new handful of the Variants he's drawn from his pocket. He advances on me, and I stumble when I catch a glimpse of his left ear.

One final horror for me to find.

There's a knot at the tip, in an exact mirror of my own.

It's the last thing I see before he covers me with the Hypnosis Variants, and they fall around me like flakes of ash, and I know, then, that he has won.

CHAPTER FIFTY-FOUR

"Did she see me here?" Larkin growls. "No one was supposed to see me here."

"After tonight it won't matter what she's seen and what she hasn't," I mutter.

I try to hide the shudder whenever I glimpse Aila's face. The same gray eyes, pointed chin, dark auburn hair. It is like Juliet, back in time.

As soon as her eyes glaze, I order her to join the others. She doesn't move quite as quickly as the Clifftons had. "Go!" I bark at her. She takes her place at the end of the line, and I examine her hands. She is the spitting image of Juliet, except for the finger where she always wore the ring.

It isn't there.

I curse. Something red starts beating behind my right eye.

"Where is the Helena Stone?" I shake her so hard that her head snaps back. "Where is the ring your mother always wore?"

I almost think I see a flicker of something in her eyes, but that's impossible. She swallows and answers in a monotone voice, "Father has it. He's at war."

I resist the urge to scream.

But—I tell myself—at least if the Stone is far from here, then it can't end the Curse. I blink away the red and am trying to decide what to do next when a light suddenly flips on in the kitchen.

I scramble for my last pouch of Hypnosis Variants. Pour them into my cupped hand, ready to throw, and drop the emptied pouch in the grass. I turn to welcome our final player.

"Mrs. Cliffton?" a young boy's voice calls out, cracking with fear as he opens the back door. "I think there's something wrong with Genevie—" He sees us and stops short.

I stare at him. If Aila is Juliet, then this child is me.

"Miles," I say quietly, "come here," but his eyes suddenly go wide. He's seen something behind me, and I instinctively flinch. Turn just in time to see a hurtling flash of silver.

I bring my hands up to shield my face, straight into the path of something sharp. The razor edges of a Star bite through my hand.

I scream. There is a searing, burning pain like I hadn't known existed.

I force myself to look down. See without understanding where three of my fingers used to be. They are now somewhere on the ground. Along with the last of the Hypnosis Variants. Spilled and useless.

And then there is blood, so warm, and a pounding in my ears.

My hands, I had told Phineas. I've always been good with my hands.

I don't let myself look down again. I don't want to know how bad it is.

How? I think blurrily. How did the girl slip through the power of the Hypnosis Variants, like no one ever has?

Larkin is wondering the same thing. His face darkens as he advances toward Aila, and he growls, "How did you do that?"

She lets out a cry of terror, and he wrestles her across the lawn to tie her to a chair. Straps her into it with his belt and tightens the notches so her breath starts to hitch.

Everything is like a dream, and I stand for one stunned moment, reeling in the pain, and then rip off my coat and wrap it around my hand to staunch the bleeding. "Miles, it's going to be all right," the girl says, over and over, until Larkin finally covers her mouth with a hankerchief.

"We gotta get your hand back together. She got you pretty good," he says to me. "Good thing she didn't hit your jugular."

"I need to see a doctor," I say.

"Then let's get what we came for," Larkin says nervously. He picks up a vial. "I can't risk anyone knowing I was here."

I fish out my bird and return to nursing my hand. "You'll have to do it."

But when I look up again, he hasn't moved toward Aila.

He's standing next to Matilda.

She smiles the sweetest smile and starts to say something I can't hear, but he doesn't let her finish. He plunges the needle into the side of her neck and empties it.

Something inside of me simultaneously withers and explodes when he pulls the syringe back to fill the vial with her Peace. It isn't the thin brown of Laurette or the mottled yellow Larkin described from the addicts. Matilda's Peace is so pink it's almost golden. I'm woozy. Blood is streaming down my arm.

Aila's cry is smothered when she strains against the chair, and tears slip down her cheeks.

"Aila, don't cry," Miles begs, his own voice wavering, and seeing him is like looking back through the years at myself.

I wasn't expecting him to look so much like me.

I take a staggering step. This isn't how it was supposed to happen. I was going to love Matilda, not destroy her, even though she destroyed me, and Juliet was supposed to send the Stone, and Phineas was supposed to live.

My beautiful Matilda, my little red bird, lying on the ground.

"What have you done?" I snarl at Larkin.

"Don't worry, Stefen," Larkin says. He sets the first vial in the grass and reaches for another. "I'll find you a good doctor."

I've only ever loved three people in my entire life.

Now two of them are dead.

And Larkin just made the last one disappear forever. Her Peace swirls like galaxies from the vial in his hand.

"Matilda," I say, my voice breaking. "If only you'd chosen me, this all could have been so different."

Then I turn and shoot Victor Larkin in the heart.

CHAPTER FIFTY-FIVE

As soon as the bullet enters Victor Larkin's body, Stefen drops the gun.

I can hardly breathe around the handkerchief, Larkin tied it so tight. *Stefen shot him.* Victor Larkin, who just did something to Mrs. Cliffton, and now . . . I squeeze my eyes shut and then force them open.

Stefen is going to kill us all.

But instead he abandons the gun and crawls toward Mrs. Cliffton.

My Star glitters in the grass, tinged with red. Stefen had turned and intercepted it before it hit him in the neck. I might have killed him. For my brother.

Suddenly Miles is next to me, working on my bindings, his hands shaking, and when he frees my mouth, I whisper to him, "Don't look over there." A bloodstain is soaking into the grass around Larkin's body.

"What do we do?" Miles whispers, his eyes wide pools of terror. He works at the last knots around my hands. I look at Dr. Cliffton and Will. See a twitch of muscle in Dr. Cliffton's forehead. Will blinks rapidly. Stefen's hold on the Hypnosis appears to be dissolving.

"As soon as you untie me," I whisper. "You run."

Dr. Cliffton's eyes dilate first, then Will's. They come awake, their muscles twitching. Then Dr. Cliffton sees Matilda.

He cries out.

Dr. Cliffton shouts at Stefen, "Stay away from her!" and Will yells something else. He takes one jerking step forward.

Mrs. Cliffton opens her eyes. Blinks at the sight of Stefen. He hovers over her, and she gives one wild, hollow laugh.

It abruptly turns to a soul-piercing scream.

I wish I could shelter my ears from the horrible, unending sound. *Why isn't Stefen running away?* I think numbly. His hand is bleeding heavily, streaming down his arm, but he is ignoring it. Trying to staunch it with the fabric of his coat while also tightly holding something he's taken from Larkin—something glass, almost like a vial. He crouches over Mrs. Cliffton, fumbling with it, his hands shaking, when Will suddenly launches across the grass to tackle him.

Dr. Cliffton is one step behind him, but Stefen doesn't try to defend himself against them. "Don't break it," he gasps as Will wrenches his arms behind him and slams him face-first onto the ground.

Miles frees me, and my arms spring forward, aching, burning from being tied.

Dr. Cliffton yells, "Aila! Call for help!" His voice is urgent. "Hurry."

I run for the telephone, pulling Miles along with me just as Stefen recovers the breath that's been knocked from his lungs.

"I'm the only one who can help her. Please—" he chokes. "Let me try."

By the time the police and the doctor arrive, we've moved Mrs. Cliffton inside to the bed. Restraining her takes the combined effort of me, Will, Dr. Cliffton, and even Genevieve, who had been knocked unconscious by the Hypnosis on the kitchen floor. We hold Mrs. Cliffton down on the bed, thrashing and screaming, until the doctor arrives with something strong enough to sedate her. She collapses back into the bed. Whimpering until she's silent, and only occasionally twitching.

Will paces near the foot of her bed. Wipes away a tear with the heel of his palm.

"What have you done?" Dr. Cliffton asks quietly.

Stefen sits in a chair in the corner. The doctor has bandaged the stumps of fingers on his hands, and they are now handcuffed behind him. Three policemen ring him, hands on their guns.

"I invented something," Stefen says. "Something new. An extrapolation of your Variants, Malcolm." He looks up through a long fringe of hair. "Something so much bigger than them, though. I call them the Virtues."

Dr. Cliffton inhales. "Virtues?"

"Peace, to start." Stefen shifts in his chair. "I found a way to extract it and store it," he says with an edge of pride. "I was working on others. Courage. Joy."

"For what purpose, exactly?" Dr. Cliffton's voice is shaking.

Stefen pauses. "I'm sure you know."

"To sell it?" Dr. Cliffton asks. The words are quiet and filled with horror.

Stefen stares back at him with defiance.

"You've taken Matilda's own Peace from her? Are you such a monster?" Dr. Cliffton thunders.

"*I* didn't take it from her," Stefen says fiercely. He bangs his handcuffed hands on the back of his chair, his bravado dimming. "Never from her."

"We should finish the rest of the questioning in a holding cell, Malcolm," the police chief begins, taking a step toward Stefen.

"Wait," Dr. Cliffton says. He holds up the glass vial between shaking fingers. "I need to know if he can fix this."

Stefen clenches his jaw. "This is all very new. I've never tried to reinsert someone's Peace after it's been removed from them. I've only ever had two successful transfers of Virtues."

"Out of how many attempts?" Will growls.

Stefen doesn't answer. Eventually he says, "If I don't try, this will assuredly remain permanent."

Dr. Cliffton takes a long breath. Then he gives the police chief a curt nod.

Stefen is released from his handcuffs, and he holds up a strange-looking syringe. At the end of it is a carved wooden bird. He draws the full vial of Peace up into the syringe, fumbling with the thickness of his bandaged fingers, and then tenderly brushes back Mrs. Cliffton's hair.

"Shh," he says, his voice barely more than a whisper, pressing the needle to the side of her neck. Then he slowly empties the syringe.

"All right," he says. He sets the drained vial on the nightstand. "Wake her."

It takes a minute for the sedation reversal to work its way through her veins. Her eyelids flutter. She attempts to sit up, but she is held back by the restraints we've fit over her bed. She takes one look at our faces, and her eyes widen with fear and horror, and I feel it spread to my own face when I realize that she doesn't recognize any of us.

And then she starts to scream again, a sound I am certain is going to haunt me for the rest of my life.

Dr. Cliffton's mouth twists. He covers his face with his hands as the doctor rushes to sedate her again.

Stefen's voice breaks. "I'm sorry."

He flinches when Will slams his fist into the wall.

And then they take him away.

The sun rises like melted wax over the fields behind the Clifftons' house the next morning. Miles has slipped into my bed, and I'm grateful for the warmth of him. I watch him sleep, free from both dreamed nightmares and living ones.

Mrs. Mackelroy arrives shortly after dawn with George, two casseroles, and all the news from town. She immediately sets to work organizing the influx of food and flowers that are already piling up outside the Clifftons' closed gates, and she whispers to Dr. Cliffton.

The double tragedies of the Larkin and Cliffton families have rocked the Sisters.

The rest of the tournament has been canceled.

"People are panicking. You'll want to lock away any of the Variants you have," she continues in what is likely the lowest voice she can muster. "There was a run on the Marketplace, and every last one of them is gone. Malcolm — some people out there are angry," she warns, and looks meaningfully in my direction.

Dr. Cliffton inhales and rubs his eyes wearily. He turns to me.

"You and Miles are not to leave the grounds of this house," he instructs me. "Not for any reason."

So I slip out the back door. Rain showers have slicked away any traces of blood in the garden. The grass is a lush spring green, and the silent flowers are starting to erupt from the ground.

Miles and I never should have come here. We led Stefen right to this house.

I sink down and start gathering the flowers. Armfuls of lilies and peonies. Pinks, oranges, yellows, whites. I bring them inside, and Genevieve helps me arrange them all in vases. And then, just as Father did for my mother, I bring the garden in to Mrs. Cliffton.

I open the curtains so that her bedroom feels less like a grave. Now her eyes are closed, her breath rising and falling in her chest. Her red hair flares out on the pillow, wild and untamed around her pale face. I arrange the flowers in a colorful wreath to surround her.

"I'm so sorry, Mrs. Cliffton," I whisper.

Miles knocks softly. "Have you eaten?" he asks. I can see the blue of his veins running under the skin of his wrists, carrying Mother's blood and Stefen's. Guilt splays out like fingers pushing against my chest. Why is it that whenever our family touches Sterling, it seems to be the wrong things coming together, a combination that always ends in tragedy?

"I'll come down in a little," I say. He turns to go.

"Miles —" I say, and he pauses. Waits in the doorway.

"What?"

"I love you," I tell him.

"I know," he says. He makes a grimace at me, but just before his back is turned, it becomes the faintest smile.

I take the picture in the silver frame from my room and place it next to Mrs. Cliffton's bed, like a guardian to watch over her. I look at the image one last time, at the two women who have loved me as mothers. I have found the handprint I was looking for, shimmering on the glass — the real Juliet Cummings Quinn, between all her brightness and shadows. I think of how much she knew and didn't know, and all she tried to shield us from. How greatly she failed. How I still love her, even so.

I turn away, and a sob catches in my throat. The flowers, the bed — it is too much like the last time I saw her. A new echo of my nightmare, all over again.

I reach for Mrs. Cliffton's hand as though I'm following a script. But this time, when I touch her skin, I find that it is still warm.

The guilt and sorrow that swirl within me are replaced by something else. Resolve. It suddenly tightens in my chest like a steel fist.

I'm not going to run from the Curse, the way my Mother did.

I'm going to stay here. And I'm going to end it.

"Can you come at nine tomorrow?" I ask Beas over the telephone, repeating the same words I've just spoken to George.

" 'Hope is the thing with feathers,' " she says. "See you tomorrow."

As soon as I replace the receiver, there's a knock on the front door.

Genevieve's steps pause. "Who is it?" she asks.

There's a muffled answer, the sound of the door opening. "Aila?" Genevieve calls. "Someone's here for you."

I look with hesitance at the phone, where I've just finished speaking with both George and Beas. Then I rise and peer around the library door. Eliza stands in the foyer, wearing awkwardness as though she's never experienced it before, shifting under the weight of a large satchel.

My stomach knots.

When I slip out of the library, she says, "Hello," as if the word tastes odd in her mouth.

"Hi. I can . . . go get Will?"

"No," she says quickly. "I'm here for you."

I close the library door behind me, remembering our encounter on the road. Bracing myself for whatever she's come to say.

"I'm . . . sorry to hear about what happened." Eliza steps forward to offer me the oversize bag hanging heavily from her shoulder. "These are for you."

I take it and glance inside warily. The clasp is practically popping open to reveal stacks of plump purple velvet sacks tied with gold ribbon.

It's layers and layers of Tempests.

"These are the last ones," Eliza says. "On the road, when I saw you . . . You said you needed them."

I gape at her, remembering what else I said on that road. "These must have cost a fortune," I finally say.

Eliza shrugs. "I traded for them. My mother sent me some earrings to make up for her missing the tournament and everything." She picks at her fingernails. "They were huge and hideous, and I never would have worn them anyway."

I close my gaping mouth. "Why . . ." I start. *Why would you do this for me, after everything I did to you, and we did to each other?* I close the clasp of the bag, heavy with Tempests, and stop myself from throwing my arms around Eliza: this girl who is the most unsolvable riddle of all. "Thank you," I say instead, hoping it sounds as genuine as I feel.

She turns to leave without another word, and I hesitate. "Do you want to come back tomorrow?" I blurt. "George and Beas will be here at nine. We'll need all the help we can get."

"You know, it really doesn't come easily, wanting to help you," she says. She looks up at the chandelier, and the light falls in diamonds across her small nose, her perfect skin. "But I want to help Sterling, and I want to help William. And I think, right now, you might all be tied together."

"So is that a yes?" I say.

She smiles and pulls the door shut behind her.

When dawn breaks the next morning, I wake to a strange, unsettling sense of cold air seeping into my room and a sharp rap on the front door. The kind of sound that conveys urgency and the weight of bad news.

I'm instantly awake, and I leap out of bed to crack open my door. Poke my head out into the hallway and strain to hear the hushed exchange between the police chief and Dr. Cliffton.

"*Stefen*—" I hear.

"I'm sorry, Malcolm, we don't know how he did it," the police chief says.

"What do you mean, *gone?*" Will's voice. Furious.

"Somehow he managed to slip every lock we have."

I close the door to lean my weight against it and then turn, slowly, as I become faintly aware of a new sound. A sound coming from my window, which was closed when I finally fell asleep last night.

And now is not.

I hadn't imagined the stream of air I'd felt on my face when I woke. My mouth goes as dry as bones. There's folded paper stashed into the open gap of the sill, fluttering with each gust of wind.

I'm over to it in two bounding steps. I can already tell it's Stefen's handwriting. I recognize it from his letter. My hands shake violently as I unfold the pages.

You'll find what you need here. Maybe it could help Matilda.
Get the Stone and finish it. Before I change my mind.

The pages behind it appear to be maps. Four in all. Sterling, Corrander, Sheffield, and Charlton. One for each of the Sisters.

I clutch them against my chest, my mind and heart racing. Glance around my room, shuddering when I think of him being here last night while I lay sleeping and unprotected. He'd had the opportunity to do and take whatever he wanted, from any of us. Why didn't he?

But then my eye catches Eliza's satchel at the foot of my wardrobe. It's thrown open. I kneel beside it. It had been bursting with Tempests before.

Now there's barely a single row left.

I picture Stefen stooping to fill his pockets with the Tempests. Enough for him to whip through the Sisters last night, all the way through Charlton, and then disappear forever.

I clutch the maps he left in one hand and feel for the weight of the Stone with the other. It is still safely hidden under my nightgown. The Helena Stone: the thing Stefen was searching so intently for and never found.

But if I already have the one thing Stefen wanted, I think, my fingers tightening around it — *then what are these maps for?*

At nine sharp, we gather in Dr. Cliffton's library for one final search party. Me, George, Beas, and Will.

George tries to hide a look of surprise when Eliza slips in just after nine, wearing reading glasses, her hair pulled back in a tight knot. She sits down next to Beas and opens her notebook with a freshly sharpened pencil. I pour her a cup of coffee, and we get started.

"There are two questions we need to answer," I say, standing to address them. "One: Why would Stefen leave this series of maps, and two: Why would he go to such great lengths to get this Stone?" I look around the room and take some semblance of comfort in our steaming coffees, the steeled resolve, the togetherness in figuring out what we will do next.

"Let's start with the obvious question. Why don't we just follow the maps he left and start digging?" Beas asks.

"Well, for one, Beas darling, we don't even know what we're looking for," Eliza says. "And it could be a trap."

"Or it could be something that helps us." I watch as Will clears his throat. "And helps my mother."

"We're going to do every last thing to help her," George assures Will. "I just think we should have some idea of what we're looking for first."

"Any idea what we could find there?" I ask. Every face looks back at me blankly. The clock in the corner ticks out a minute of silence.

"We'll come back to it. Let's talk about the Stone, then," I say, fishing it from behind my blouse. The four of them examine it, glinting between my fingers.

"Maybe it's some incredibly valuable gem?" Beas asks. "Stefen wanted it because it's worth a lot of money?"

Eliza rolls her eyes. "It's not exactly a diamond, is it?" she says skeptically. "No gemstone that I recognize, anyway. It almost looks like glass. Where did you get it?"

"Her mother gave it to her," Will says.

"Well—actually," I say, "I found it. Hidden in my mother's Shakespeare book."

"And where did she get it?" Eliza asks.

"I don't know." I hesitate. "But I think it has something to do with Shakespeare, now more than ever. Not only because of where I found it." I spread out my notes in front of them. "But because Stefen called it the *Helena Stone*."

I turn to Dr. Cliffton's chalkboard to catch Eliza up to speed. "We've found other connections that trace back to Shakespeare, too." I hand her my evidence. "Every last Disappearance is in his pages."

"And seven years are mysteriously missing from his career, which has inspired all sorts of theories," Beas says. "One of which is that he traveled Europe and Africa looking for something of great value."

"Let me guess," Eliza says. "You think it could be that Stone?"

"There's one way to find out," I say. "That's why I need your help." I display every volume of Shakespeare the Clifftons have and three different Shakespeare biographies, including the new one I ordered from Mr. Fitzpatrick. "Let's see if there's anything in here called the Helena Stone."

I hand *A Midsummer Night's Dream* to George and *All's Well That*

Ends Well to Will. "These both have Helenas in them," I say, "so let's start there. Eliza, Beas, and I will take the remaining biographies."

We each crack open our books and dig in.

The room settles into silent concentration, rustled only by the quick flipping of pages, the pouring of more coffee, until George closes his copy of *A Midsummer Night's Dream* with a sigh. "I'm sorry. I don't see anything," he admits. "You guys have something?"

"I think I do," Will says, jabbing his book. "Here. This one has a Helena and a plot about a ring. Listen to this. Helena is described as some sort of healer."

I read the words over his shoulder:

> *"I have seen a medicine*
> *That's able to breathe life into a stone.*
> *Quicken a rock, and make you dance canary,*
> *With spritely fire and motion,*
> *Whose simple touch is powerful to araise King Pippen."*

"Yes!" I say. "And look at this." I bring out a pen to wrap a dark circle around another passage:

> *"Plutus himself,*
> *That knows the tinct and multiplying medicine,*
> *Hath not in nature's mystery more science*
> *Than I have in this ring."*

Will hesitates and then leans forward to pick up the Stone from around my neck, my skin heating at the brush of his fingers. I watch his lips carefully as he speaks.

"If this Stone has the power to make someone better by its touch," he says, "to heal like 'multiplying medicine,' then no wonder Stefen wanted it."

He holds it to the light, shining through clear and sharp to illuminate the teardrop suspended inside, and I remember, suddenly, how off I'd felt at first when Miles had taken it. The persistent, pounding headache. And that was only after wearing it for a month.

"That could maybe explain why the Hypnosis Variants didn't work on you," George says.

"Why my mother was never sick growing up," I add softly. I take the Stone back from Will with fingers that betray the slightest shake.

"And," Will says, "maybe that's why she could leave, even though she was from here." He gestures to demonstrate his point and make sure I grasp it. "Because she was wearing that Stone."

It protected her, I think. *Until the day she must have taken it off to send it to Stefen.* I close my eyes. It lines up with when she'd become ill. And why the Disappearances finally caught up to her.

"So maybe someone stole that Stone from Shakespeare," Beas muses. "And it released some sort of Curse from his very own pages."

"But—wait," Eliza says. "This still doesn't make sense. The Helena Stone might have been what helped Juliet leave. But that doesn't explain why *we're* still cursed."

"Right. Why wouldn't the Curse have just followed your mother?" George asks. "And why would it affect so many different towns? If the Curse is on the Stone, then the Disappearances should have ended here and started up in Gardner."

I sigh. Every time I think we've glimpsed the end of the maze, we run straight into another wall.

Think.

"Let's take a break," I say. Will leads us to the kitchen, where we ring around the wooden table, making sandwiches on crusted bread and eating Mrs. Mackelroy's casseroles. I can't help but notice that Will barely touches his, and suddenly I'm no longer hungry, either.

I take a plate to Miles in his room. He tries to hide what he's working on, but I see it anyway. He's crushing seed packets of lilies of the valley, mint tea bags, fir needles. All of Mrs. Cliffton's favorite things. He sees me looking at his piles, his attempts at little make-shift Variants. "I'm going to find a way to bring her back," he says fiercely. I can tell he's been crying.

I hesitate. Set the plate down on the desk. Touch his arm gently before I leave. "Me, too."

When I return downstairs, the rest of them have finished lunch and traipsed back to the library. I sink down into my seat with newly blazing resolve, and George hands me a plate of cookies.

"Where did we leave off?" Eliza asks.

"We think the Helena Stone is somehow related to the Curse, but it's not the whole thing. There's still something particular about the Sisters," George says.

I tick off my fingers: "Something is still here, something that's related to Shakespeare, something that has even more importance than this Stone."

George's brow knits. "After all, even the ring doesn't protect you from the Disappearances when you're inside the borders," he says to me. "It's as though it gets overpowered when you're close enough to the Curse's source."

"So that's what the maps are going to lead us to, right?" Eliza ventures. "Something still here, that Shakespeare would have cared enough about to put this horrid Curse on us all."

"And we're just going to jaunt out and dig this cursed thing up, huh?" George says. "Hmm. Sounds reasonable."

"Maybe it's buried treasure?" Eliza suggests, her eyebrow cocking with irony. "Heirlooms from a royal family?"

"Or maybe the addresses of a family line descended from a lover who scorned him?" George adds.

Beas is studying something in the biography I gave her, and she suddenly makes a noise in her throat.

"This biography says that Shakespeare always feared that someone would dig up his grave and disturb his bones. Enough that he had this sign engraved near his tombstone."

GOOD FRIEND FOR JESUS SAKE FORBEARE,

TO DIGG THE DUST ENCLOASED HEARE.

BLESE BE YE MAN Y SPARES THES STONES,

AND CURST BE HE Y MOVES MY BONES.

She flips the page toward us.

"I think I know what we're going to find at the end of those maps," Beas says.

I whisper, "We're going to find his bones."

George says, "He put a curse on his own grave?"

"With words taken from his own pages," Will says.

CHAPTER FIFTY-SIX

Though neither of us speaks of it, the tension between Will and me mounts as the clock creeps closer to midnight. Every nerve inside me tingles. So many things depend on whether we're right tonight. My mother's past. His mother's future.

Dr. Cliffton barely speaks through the entire day. He looks old and exhausted. I want to tell him that it's all right to sleep. That broken hearts are heavy. That before you learn the weight of grief, even the simple act of living feels impossible. But we do learn it, eventually. I'm just not sure whether the weight of it gets lighter or we get stronger.

He lies next to Mrs. Cliffton in the bed through most of the day. He never stops holding her hand. When he finally goes downstairs late in the evening, I slip into Mrs. Cliffton's bedroom and lay the Helena Stone over her heart. Let myself hope, for one moment, that it could be enough. But she continues to whimper, as if she feels haunted even under sedation. I kiss her cheek, take the Stone, and return to my room, where I dress all in black.

Miles has fallen asleep with his clothes on. I dust him with a heavy dose of Dream Variants from Will to ensure that he doesn't hear us leave. I bend to brush my lips over Miles's hair. He looks angelic, his skin smooth, his lips puckered. It's so easy to love him when he's sleeping.

At five to midnight there's the lightest tap on my door. Will steps into my room, and I give him a nervous smile. "Are you sure we shouldn't tell your father?" I scribble on a notepad. He traces my eyelids with a fingertip of Night Vision.

"I don't want to get his hopes up," Will writes, and pulls my window open. We slip out onto the tree branch, grab shovels and Will's toolbox from the shed, and set off into the darkness.

Eliza and George are already waiting for us at the spot Stefen marked on the first map. It's a field near the border of Corrander, near an abandoned, rotting barn and a stream where a fringe of reeds grows high. George spooks at the sound of us approaching.

"Just us," I call. When we reach them, I add, "No sign of Stefen?"

Eliza gestures to her epee, a kitchen knife, two shovels, and an array of Variant pouches spread at her feet. "I think he's gone and he's never coming back." She picks up her epee and wields it, glittering. "But just in case, we'll be ready." She nods toward a distant tree. "Besides, Beas is up there acting as lookout." Her mouth sours. "And you'll never guess who she brought along to help keep watch."

I glance in the distance. See the vague outline of a boy, who lifts a large hand and waves. "Is that *Thom?* Are they back together?"

"Guess that all depends on what happens tonight, doesn't it?" She sniffs. "Anyway, same deal as the Tempest race. If you hear a kazoo, there's trouble."

"We came prepared," I say, showing her the Stars crowded into my pocket. We roll out the maps to make sure we're looking in the right spot.

Then I jam the spade of my shovel deep into the ground.

We dig and dig, our shovels taking heavy bites of the earth and making a series of small mounds beside us. After a quarter of an hour I am sweating and dirt-streaked, and all we've found is an enormous hole.

"Think he sent us on a wild-goose chase?" I watch Will's mouth curl into a growl. He takes a violent swing at the ground with his shovel and straightens at the sudden sound of a dull clang.

"Whoa," George says, and with one look Eliza and I step back to get out of the way. George and Will begin to dig furiously until Will pauses and bends to pry something out.

He brushes it free of earth: a metal box, the length of my forearm. It's rusted and locked.

He uses a pair of bolt cutters from his toolbox to free the lock. Then he extends the box to me. "Do you want to open it?" he mouths.

My stomach unexpectedly turns, and I shake my head.

George clears his throat. "I'll do it."

He lifts the lid and peers inside. After a moment he nods, then closes the box. "Not sure who they belong to, but those are definitely some old bones."

Will exhales sharply, and a small flame of hope catches light in my chest. Eliza sniffs the air, tilts her face to look up at the starless sky. "So . . . is something supposed to be happening now?"

"I think all the bones have to be reunited," I say. "So he can rest in peace."

"Or maybe we'll just set off more Disappearances and make things worse," Eliza says.

George looks up from the box in his hands, stricken by realization. "That's what Stefen did, then. He dug up some of the bones, but he didn't do it to reunite them. He spread them out even further." He kicks at one of the mounds and sends a spray of dirt into the hole. "Disturbed the grave anew. Set off a new round of Disappearances and made the Curse spread to Charlton. That *rat*."

"You're right," I say, horrified. My blood feels hot and traitorous. "He's — he's —"

"Unhinged," Will says, turning so that I can see his lips. "And yet . . . we couldn't have found this without him."

"We might have found it eventually," George grumbles. "We're sort of brilliant together." He scrunches his nose and hands over the box of bones. "Although for once, I'm glad I can't smell anything."

"Hopefully not for much longer," Eliza says. She opens her hand to ask for a map. "I'll take Charlton. Let's go."

"I'll go with you," George quickly offers.

"We'll meet back at my mother's old house," I say. "Be careful."

Then we divide up the maps and the last pouch of Tempests and split into the night to find the rest.

Thom and Beas take Sheffield, George and Eliza take Charlton, and Will and I head for Corrander.

We have the shortest distance to cover, and I breathe a sigh of relief when we find the second box just where Stefen's map told us it would be — beneath a willow tree a stone's throw from the Corrander cemetery. "Two down." Will gestures when he cuts the lock and looks inside. He closes the box again and tucks it safely under his arm.

"We're going to need something big enough to bury these together again," he says. He touches his face in thought. "I think I have some wood left over from your mother's house." We double back to Sterling, to my mother's monument, the moon sliding in and out of the clouds overhead.

I keep watch while we wait for the others, my Stars at the ready, as Will constructs a small coffin. "This is the last thing I ever thought I'd be making," he says, his cheekbones sharpening as he bites down on a handful of screws. He works them quietly into the soft wood instead of drawing attention to us with a hammer. When he tightens the final screw, he turns the coffin right side up. He stays silent, but his hands keep reaching for the back of his neck.

Eventually I bend to the dirt at our feet and scrape out with the tip of my Star, "Will—can you ever forgive me?"

He swallows, hard. Offers me a hand up. "For what?" he asks, the set of his mouth softening. "You saved us, Aila. What if you hadn't thrown that Star?"

Then he takes the Star and crouches down to the dirt himself.

"What if this doesn't work?" he writes.

I step over the words to stand a breath's distance from him. I look up into his eyes, which are dark and sad and hopeful. "It's going to work," I say softly. I cup my hand around his cheek. "It's going to work."

He leans forward to push my hair back. Runs his fingertip along the curve of my ugly ear, and I stiffen when his fingers reach it. "Why do you hide it?" he asks. "That cute little bump on your ear?"

I nuzzle his chin up with my nose and kiss just where his neck meets the place I love most on his jaw. He flushes and pulls me close to him, tilting his mouth toward mine, when we suddenly hear a dry twig cracking underfoot and jump apart at the sound.

"Aww—" Beas beams at us, drawing Thom's arm tighter around her waist. His other arm is sheltering a small steel box against his rib cage. "Oh, don't stop!" Beas cries, clapping. "I've been waiting for this for *ages*."

"I don't know what you mean," I say, smoothing my hair as my face flames. I step forward to take the box from Thom.

"Mmhmm." Beas grins, picking up a shovel.

Heaviness settles back around us, and the mood dims with the weight of what we're about to do. The four of us turn our attention to digging a grave. We pick a spot right next to the bench, where we can cover the disturbed earth and eventually hide it under a newly planted garden. We dig deep, deeper than any of the other boxes were hidden, deep enough to make sure that what we bury can never be found. Finally, when my arms and legs are aching and the first glimpse of dawn is warming the horizon, a hint of worry begins to creep in.

I straighten. "Shouldn't George and Eliza be back by now?"

"Yes," Thom agrees.

My stomach twists, and I fish out my Star. "Do you think something happened? Should we go after them?"

"Wait." Beas freezes and points to a distant bend in the road. "There's someone coming."

We grab our weapons and fold together into a line, points extended.

"Thanks for the welcoming party," George's voice calls out through the darkness, and I almost collapse from relief. "I know Eliza *looks* frightening, but she's really all bark and no bi—*Oof*," he says, as she clubs him in the stomach with her elbow. He doubles over, and she strides forward with the final box, one that's barely larger than her hand.

I take it from her and align it with the others. When George catches up, he immediately sets to work, arranging the bones inside Will's makeshift coffin with a scientific intensity. We form a protective circle around him, facing outward. When he's finally finished, he stands and brushes off his hands.

"As far as I can tell, they're all here," he says. "I think we're ready."

We turn toward the deep pit we've formed in the earth, and the air grows still.

"So, uh," Thom says. He clasps his hands in front of him. "Should we say something?"

"How about 'Excuse me, Bard,' " Eliza says. " 'We gave you your peace back, now please return ours?' "

Beas steps forward. Puts her hand over her heart and gestures for all of us to do the same. Then she murmurs solemnly, "Mr. Shakespeare: 'May flights of angels sing thee to thy rest.' "

They all look to me, and I unclasp the Stone from where it has become so familiar around my neck. I hesitate. It pools in my hand like water.

I don't think Mother ever knew this Stone was anything more than a pretty trinket. She died without realizing how much damage it had done, how many seeds of resentment it had sown, how much it had protected her all her life.

I wish I could tell Stefen that she tried to send it to him. That she'd wanted to put things right between them and had died before she could. That taking it off when he asked for it might even have been what killed her.

I run my fingers over its smooth glass one more time. This last physical piece of my mother.

Then I return the Helena Stone at last to its rightful owner. I drop it into the coffin and turn away as Will secures the final screws to seal the bones together, never to be separated again.

Will and Thom jump down into the depths of the pit and lower the casket in stages. We help pull them back up out of the grave, and then, with long, shaky breaths, we each take a shovel.

The earliest rays of dawn begin to heat the horizon as my first clump of dirt hits the coffin.

The second shovelful hits.

The third.

And then something knocks into me as strong as a wave.

CHAPTER FIFTY-SEVEN

Birds are adaptable. They fly south and find a way to survive.
Or, they don't.

I've made it as far south as Norwalk.

I stand on the platform and try to ignore the dull ache in my hand. My injury is wrapped in bandages, like that terrible film Phineas and I saw in the cinema a few years ago. The Mummy's Hand.

Me and the mummies. We just keep rising up out of the grave.

I inhale air still dark with morning and try to stop glancing over my shoulder. Wonder if anyone from the underground will come after me for what I did to Larkin. I suppose it doesn't even matter now. I rock on my heels. My hand throbs. And then the breeze changes and my nostrils start to sting.

I take in gulping breaths suddenly tinged with salt.

It fills my nose, my hair, my skin. Dizzying with scents. Soil. Sweat. The breeze itself smells like colors now. Braiding and twining together.

Fruit. The cloying sweetness of perfume. Other things I've never smelled before, and never will again.

Juliet's daughter has actually done it.

She unknotted Phineas's legacy.

I close my eyes.

I picture Matilda. Wonder if it will be enough.

My lungs fill with air that has been set free of the Curse.

Freedom, at last.

I take a step forward.
I imagine sprouting wings.
In the distance, the train horn calls.

CHAPTER FIFTY-EIGHT

The air.

The air around me is coming unmistakably alive again.

It sings with scents, each as different and as layered as harmonies. After months of blankness, it's almost overwhelming — the mix of compost and wet earth and flowers and musk and sweat. Will fills his lungs with it, and he turns to me, his shovel frozen in the air.

"Aila?" I see his mouth move. But I still can't hear him.

We each instinctively look up to the sky, its blank, cloudless expanse still unbroken by stars.

Then Beas takes a deep breath and opens her mouth to sing, but it comes out in a monotone whisper.

She closes her mouth again, confused. "Why isn't it working?" she demands.

"Wait." George picks up his shovel. "Hurry, help me shovel. Scents went first. They must be coming back in the order they were taken."

We rush to fill in the rest of the pit, frantically dumping shovelfuls of earth. We smooth it over, leveling the surface to conceal what we've done.

Then George kneels for a pouch of Variants and dusts them over his head. They fall to coat his eyelashes and the bridges of his cheekbones. He opens his eyes and blinks. "Nothing." He turns his hand to let the wind catch the Variants and carry them into the air. "The Variants aren't working anymore."

"Look!" Beas cries. She points to the sky.

Overhead, it is as though a giant curtain is drawing back. I take a deep breath as the first stars begin to burst through the darkness. I'd almost forgotten how lovely they are.

"Yes," George murmurs, letting the empty Variant pouch fall to the ground, his eyes fixed skyward. "Here they come."

The weight in my chest lifts with each new piercing light.

Three.

Then six more.

Ten.

Constellations knit themselves together in the sky.

Bold stars light with single fires. Then clusters of smaller, distant ones appear in soft wisps. I stop looking after a moment and watch everyone's faces instead.

Joy blooms in my chest.

Beas wears a stunned grin, and Thom is looking only at her. George has dropped to his knees. And Eliza — steely, controlled Eliza — covers her mouth with her hands as tears slip over them. Will is looking at the sky as if he could drink it. As if he's never seen anything more beautiful.

Then he looks at me.

He throws his shovel to the ground.

"Will —" I start to say.

He's to me in three strides.

He takes my face in his hands and kisses me, deep and tender and glowing with joy, in front of everyone. I don't think, I just kiss him back, both of us sweat-streaked and covered in dirt, wrapping my arms around his neck to pull him closer as the stars explode into being above our heads. Thom whoops and yells, "Hot diggity dog!" and dips Beas into a long, low kiss.

Eliza looks dazed, a mixture of shock and disbelief at everything happening in front of her. But when George leans forward, she immediately recovers.

"Nope," she says, stopping him with a manicured hand that is caked with soil. She wipes her damp eyes with her wrist. "Not even once. Not even now."

"But . . . maybe someday?" George grins. His hair is tousled, his face smeared with dirt. He opens his arms to her while also taking a respectful step back.

"Maybe, Mackelroy," she says, eyeing him. She smiles. Looks up again at the sky. "But probably not."

Beas grabs me in an embrace. "You were right, my darling friend!" she whispers. She kisses my temple. "Thank you."

We whoop and holler and scream, jumping and leaping as we scatter our tools in the field behind my mother's house, and then we take off running. Soon I'll come back and plant an entire garden to cover the grave, where no one will ever find it. But for now, the dawn is flooding across the sky and bringing with it the distant sound of horns. "They're starting to realize," George yells over his shoulder, and we run even faster.

We reach the main road just as a honking car comes around the bend and, at the sight of us, hurriedly pulls over.

Mr. Fitzpatrick jumps out, with the engine still running. "Can you smell this?" he demands, thrusting a ripped tuft of long grass under our noses.

"Yes!" Beas cries.

"Yes? Yes!" He laughs wildly. "Why? How?"

We look at one another and smother grins that threaten to burst with pride. No one can ever know what we buried, how much power lies dormant in the ground. It is one final secret that we'll each take to our own graves.

"I have no idea," George says with a perfectly straight face.

"We must celebrate! Spread the word! The Curse is broken!" Mr. Fitzpatrick climbs into his car. "It's a new day for Sterling! Redemption Day! Freedom! The Curse is undone!"

There's a bag overturned in the street up ahead, followed by the strafing of muddy footprints that have taken off into a run. Three, then four, then five more cars pass us, honking and cheering out the window. They pull over at every house along the way to pound on the door and ring the bells. Some of the women even come out in their bathrobes and curlers and climb right into the parade of cars.

One couple is kissing on their front stoop.

A deep blue is steadily seeping back into the door behind them.

"Cliffton, can you believe it? Come on, we're heading to town!" Will's friend Carter yells, slowing the car at the sight of us. "Hop in!"

Eliza and Beas open the back door, and Thom and George jump onto the bumper. But Will doesn't join them. Instead he extends a hand out to George.

"It's over," he says.

"It's over," George repeats, and they shake.

"You coming, Will?" Carter yells.

"I have to get home." Will takes off in a sprint.

I slam the car door and run after him, just like those days when we raced in the snow. With each step and breath I will the Curse to give us back the last thing it took. To let Mrs. Cliffton's Peace seep back into her as vibrantly as the colors spreading across the doors. Garnet reds and deep blues and even a chartreuse come alive against the morning sky as we run past them.

We reach the bridge. Our reflections shimmer back, dancing across the water. My chest is filling with hope and grief and joy and pride and weariness, each one a light and shadow that seem to come hand in hand, just as the atoning and enhancing Variants were unleashed alongside the Disappearances. The way that hope uses darkness to make itself stronger. The way a Virtue was stolen, and we responded by creating so many more: courage, sacrifice, and love. Little lights blooming into the blackest night.

By the time I catch Will, he's at the foot of the driveway, wrenching open the heavy gates. I take his arm, and with one final burst of energy we crest the hill, chests heaving.

The Cliffton's front door has become a forest green.

Miles flings it open and comes running toward us.

"Is —" I gasp. "Mrs. Cliffton . . ."

Miles stops short and looks between Will and me.

"She's upstairs." He frowns, confused. "Same as always."

At his words, my heart falls like a glass shattering.

Will pushes past Miles and runs inside.

"Where were you?" Miles asks. "What's going on?"

I follow him into the foyer. The house smells like leather-bound books, lavender, fresh bread. "Aila, can you smell it?" Miles demands.

"Yes," I say. "Come, Miles," I say softly, and we climb the stairs. I am being pulled toward something else now. Something familiar, but new. " 'Like soft music to attending ears,' " I whisper. The silver sweet sound of Will's voice.

To hear him means the final Disappearance is ended. The Curse has returned everything it took.

Almost.

The scent of the flowers from Mrs. Cliffton's room grows stronger with each step down the hall.

"Mother?" Will asks, his voice cracking, when we've almost reached the bedroom door.

"William?"

I grab Miles and stop, my heart hovering. The voice I hear is hesitant. It is weak and hoarse from screaming.

"Malcolm?" it asks. "What's happened?"

But it is hers. My whole chest takes flight.

Malcolm lets out a strangled cry, and still I hold Miles back. I bring my fingers to my lips. "Let them be," I whisper. Let them revel in getting back what they lost. Their little family, reunited again.

The fear of hope is struggling across Miles's face. "Is the Curse over?" he asks. I nod as Mrs. Cliffton makes a soft sound that is close to laughter, and Miles's face breaks into something so radiant it cracks my heart wide open.

"You did something," Miles whispers. He looks at me with suspicion. "Didn't you?"

I blink, trying to decide if I should tell him that it was our family that started this mess. And now our family has ended it.

"But . . ." His voice wavers before I make a decision. "What about Mother?" He swallows. "She still isn't coming back . . . ?"

"No, Miles." I take his hand in mine and squeeze it. "No, honey. She's gone."

Miles rubs fiercely at his eyes. "I'm not crying."

Tears stream down both our faces. I choke on a laugh. "Me neither."

"Aila? Miles?" Mrs. Cliffton's raw voice rises. "Where are they? I want to see them."

"Go on," I tell Miles, and nudge him forward. He hesitates, raking his hands over his cheeks to dry them. His chin juts out at me. "What's the finishing word?"

I look at his eyes, wide and shining, and realize that we are no longer the wrong things coming together, leaving only tragedy and sorrow in our wake. Instead Stefen, Mother, and I each played our parts in the right combination. Fit each of our flawed pieces together to unlock the Curse's mystery for good.

I already know the answer. Perhaps I always have.

"Miles," I tell him, "we are."

CHAPTER FIFTY-NINE

May 11, 1943

Will is finding every excuse to touch me.

We brush against each other when we pass at school. Steal kisses in the shadows of the hall, in the kitchen. I float through the house, smelling each bursting vase of flowers, taking in the music that plays throughout every waking hour.

Today the scent of cake fills the air, a vanilla confection Genevieve has decorated with cream cheese frosting and strawberries shaped into flowers that bloom right off the edges. Will traces my knuckles hidden under the dining room table. When I blow out the candles, I close my eyes and make a handful of wishes, like seeds scattering from the puff of a dandelion.

My coming-of-age gifts aren't Variant pouches, but normal teenage things. A volume of Elizabeth Barrett Browning from Beas. A *Harry James and His Orchestra* record from George. A wooden box with an intricate lock from Will, which I will wait to open when no one else is around. A new green dress from the Clifftons and a pair of gloves from Miles. Cass sends a pack of Wint O Green Lifesavers and an empty picture frame for a favorite page of a favorite book. I'll fill it with Shakespeare, of course. *Henry IV:*

> Our peace will, like a broken limb united,
> Grow stronger for the breaking.

Finally, Mrs. Cliffton brings out a gift from my father that she's been holding since we arrived: my mother's half-used bottle of Joy, the one that always sat on her vanity. A blur of sadness settles in my chest when I see how much she still had left. But when I open it, the scent of her floods the room, and for one split second it is almost as if she were back again.

I spend the rest of the day just the way I want to, drinking scalding tea with Mrs. Cliffton and talking about books with Dr. Cliffton, who is already inventing a new type of energy-infused glass for greenhouses. In the evening I play cards with Miles until he irritates me and I want him to go away.

In a month we'll return to Gardner. To our old life. To Cass. My father is coming back with an injury to his leg he sustained back in January—the time of his missing letters. He insists he'll be okay, but the injury isn't healing well enough for him to serve. He promises to tell us more when we're together.

That night I write him: "We have some stories for you, too."

Will knocks on my window, and I seal the envelope and climb to join him in the boughs of the tree outside my room. Stars blaze silver and white over our heads as though the sky is scattered with Glimmers. Will can't stop staring at them. He built a swiveling stand to bring the telescope out into the garden on clear nights, and usually I join him. I know what he smells like now, another piece of him I've come to learn. His skin smells like soap and pinewood. His mouth tastes like peppermint.

A mile from here, safely tucked underground, the bones of the past are buried. New life has already started to grow all around them.

Will threads his hand in mine and whispers into my hair, "We could have a future now, because of what you did." His lips faintly graze the tip of my ear. "If you want it."

Maybe someday I will wake my daughter after a thunderstorm. Maybe we will watch the sunrise together from the garden, drinking in air heady with rain and soil, and I will tell her a story I won't have told anyone else—about a world that once withered a little more every seven years, about the knotted branches of our family tree, and the reason I stay to smell the flowers long after everyone else has gone.

It will be a story about colors and music and dreams. About her grandmother. About love.

But for now, I wait until Will's eyes fix on the fading stars. And when the first birds sing with the coming morning, I whisper to him, "*I do.*"

ACKNOWLEDGMENTS

· · ● ● ● ● ● · ·

This book was such a labor of love, and I am so grateful to everyone who read early drafts, brainstormed ideas, offered an encouraging word when I felt like giving up, and helped with childcare so I could make time to write. Thank you.

To Greg, James, and Cecilia: You bring the color, music, and stars to my life. This book is for, and because of, you.

To Sarah and Kevin Bain, Hannah Bain, Andrew and Angela Bain, for dreaming about this with me for so many years, and for your endless support and encouragement. I love and cherish you.

To Mark and Barbara Murphy, and Janlyn Murphy: You were my rock during some tough years. You are each a blessing in my life and I simply could not have done this without you.

Thank you to the Bain, Goldman, Korb, and Shane families. A very special thank-you to Donald Korb for your lifelong generosity and for being my source for all questions about navy life in World War II; and to Doris Bain for your constant encouragement—and for quite possibly praying this book into existence.

To Pete Knapp: Thank you for believing in this book from the beginning and for being its biggest champion. When the right things come together, it is magic. Thank you for making magic with me.

Thank you to Sarah Landis for your editorial eye and for seeing what this book could be, and to my copyeditor, publicist, cover designer, sales team, and the group at HMH Books for Young Readers.

I'm also grateful to the New Leaf Literary and Park Literary and Media teams for all of your behind-the-scenes work to bring this book into existence.

Thank you to early readers and friends who lent support in one way or another over this journey: Chris Iafolla, Jennifer Eastman Carter, Josie Doak, Sarah Dill, Meghan Clemm, Anna Tuttle Delia, Wendy Paine Miller, Alexandra Nesbeda, Caitlin Dalton, Wendy Huang, Jackie Crawley, Meg Bauer, Annmarie Sirotnak, Tessa Kramer, Kirsten Liston, the Friedman, Mantel, and Pink families, my UCONN residency "family," Andy and Bethany Needham, Anna Child, Sarah Hoover Sachs, Henry Clay Conner IV, and Susanne Thannhuber.

I'm so grateful to be part of The Swanky Seventeens. Special thanks to Anna Priemaza, Stephanie Garber, and Kayla Olson, for your incredible enthusiasm for this book and for your friendship.

To the people at Love146 and especially the children you serve, thank you for teaching me to find hope and courage amidst darkness.

To the Evansville, Hong Kong, Tokyo/ASIJ, Indianapolis, Tufts, greater Massachusetts, West Hartford, and San Francisco crews: I wish I could list every one of you. Thank you for your friendship and for making life so beautiful.

To He who can do more than all we ask or imagine: You are the finishing word, and the finishing word is love.

PUSHKIN CHILDREN'S BOOKS

We created Pushkin Children's Books to share tales from different languages and cultures with younger readers, and to open the door to the wide, colourful worlds these stories offer.

From picture books and adventure stories to fairy tales and classics, and from fifty-year-old bestsellers to current huge successes abroad, the books on the Pushkin Children's list reflect the very best stories from around the world, for our most discerning readers of all: children.

THE BEGINNING WOODS

MALCOLM MCNEILL

'I loved every word and was envious of quite a few... A
modern classic. Rich, funny and terrifying'
Eoin Colfer

THE RED ABBEY CHRONICLES

MARIA TURTSCHANINOFF

1 · *Maresi*
2 · *Naondel*

'Embued with myth, wonder, and told with
a dazzling, compelling ferocity'
Kiran Millwood Hargrave, author of *The Girl of Ink and Stars*

THE LETTER FOR THE KING

TONKE DRAGT

'*The Letter for the King* will get pulses racing... Pushkin
Press deserves every praise for publishing this beautifully
translated, well-presented and captivating book'
The Times

THE SECRETS OF THE WILD WOOD

TONKE DRAGT

'Offers intrigue, action and escapism'
Sunday Times

THE SONG OF SEVEN

TONKE DRAGT

'A cracking adventure... so nail-biting you'll need to wear protective gloves'
The Times

THE MURDERER'S APE

JAKOB WEGELIUS

'A thrilling adventure. Prepare to meet the remarkable
Sally Jones; you won't soon forget her'
Publishers Weekly